GIRL, CONFLICTED

To Julie,

Hope you enjoy the book!

Sasha Lane

x

SASHA LANE

First published in Great Britain in 2015 by Sasha Lane
This paperback edition is the first edition

All characters and events in this publication, other than those clearly in the public domain, are fictitious and any resemblance to real persons, living or dead, is purely coincidental.

ISBN 978-0-9934562-0-6

For Grandad,
whose own stories I always loved to hear

Chapter One

'I think tonight might be the night.' I bounce childishly in my chair, nearly knocking over my skinny cappuccino as I barely contain my excitement.

'Okay, talk me through it. What exactly did he say?' My best friend Sophie stares at me, a captive audience, patiently waiting for my response.

'He clarified with me at least three times that I'm free tonight and he's booked us into La Sapiniere.'

'Ooh, nice.' Sophie takes a bite of her lemon muffin.

'I know. It sounds like it, right? I mean we've been discussing how serious it's getting between us, and, you know, I floated the idea past him about moving in together and he didn't even blink. I thought he might try to make a hasty escape but he just took it in his stride.'

'It does sound promising.' Sophie nods. 'And it's been nearly two years of you coaxing him along into an adult relationship.'

'Oh God, Sophie, can you imagine? I'll be Mrs Emma Louise Woodley.' I clap my hands together, forgetting for a moment that I'm in a public place, until I see a few of the other customers glance over in my direction in annoyance.

I really can't believe that this is finally happening to me – at thirty-two, having had a whole host of bad experiences during my dating history, ranging from the weird and bad to just plain crazy. In fact, I think I could fill a whole problem page in a magazine with the long list of relationship and emotional issues that have cropped up – mainly down to the man involved, I hasten to add. Honestly I don't know quite how I've managed to attract only men in severe need of therapy. There actually haven't been that many men in my life, but they have all been odd. Mmm, mustn't dwell too much on that. Anyway, I feel like I've paid my dues, and it's about time I got my happy ever after with the perfect man. And maybe Chris isn't perfect, but the last two years have felt pretty darn close.

'Will you wear a giant meringue?' Sophie is bouncing in her seat now too, her coffee-coloured curls taking on a life of their own, and I can tell that she's almost as excited as I am now that there is the prospect of a wedding to organise. Her neurotic, insanely organised, usually annoying crap might actually come in handy this time.

'Yeah, can you really see me in a big fluffy wedding dress dragging along a frilly puffball skirt that weighs more than me?'

'Maybe.' She studies me, smirking.

Maybe not.

'I'll make you a deal right now. I'll wear a meringue if you, as my chief bridesmaid, will wear something pink and equally frilly.'

'Chief bridesmaid?' Her eyes light up.

'Who else?' I grin.

'Do you think he'll have chosen the ring himself?' She ignores my suggestion of pink and frilly completely. To be fair, she knows me better than anyone, and therefore she is fully aware that a big fluffy wedding gown would be my worst nightmare – much like hers is anything pink.

'How do you think he'll do it?'

'The actual proposal? I don't know. I always imagined that I wanted the "down on one knee" thing, but if we're in the restaurant in front of everyone that might be a bit cheesy.'

'Don't you think it would just be romantic, him declaring his love for you in public like that? Hiding the ring in the champagne or the dessert or something?'

I ponder that for a moment. We all want the fairy tale, don't we? To fall in love with the perfect guy, be proposed to in the most romantic way while being presented with a gorgeous ring the size of a rock, and then plan the dream wedding before living happily ever after. But in reality do we really want that kind of public display of emotion? In a world where romance has morphed into online dating, Skype, and communicating via social media while multitasking, do we still want the sanctity of a marriage proposal carried out in a traditional and somewhat old-fashioned way?

'Maybe it would be romantic,' I concede, unable to help the grin that is pulling fiercely at the corners of my mouth as I sip the last of my cappuccino, feeling like the cat that got the cream. Perhaps some things should stay traditional after all.

'I'm sooo jealous.' Sophie pouts, stirring the dregs of her own coffee.

'What do you have to be jealous about?' I hold my hands up, exasperated. 'Haven't you just started dating your own Prince Charming? I mean, from what you've babbled on about so far, you spent your first date waffling to one another into the early hours of the following morning; so much so that you didn't get the chance for sex.'

'Emma!' Sophie blushes crimson. 'You know I don't sleep with a guy on the first date.'

'I know, I know. I'm just kidding.' I giggle. She's right. Sex on the first date is not necessarily a good move in my opinion. You need to at least let a man try to chase you a bit first; that's what the whole Neanderthal thing is supposed to be about, isn't it? Although I guess it really does depend on how hot the guy is…maybe that instant attraction, 'can't wait to get naked together' impulse can just prove too irresistible on some occasions.

'We did plenty of stuff on the second date, though.' Sophie smirks. She would have sounded coy if she wasn't the colour of a fire engine.

'See, you have a brand new, exciting romance to contend with where everything is fresh and exhilarating and you get that giddy nervousness when you see his name come up on your phone. You get to daydream, wallowing in self-happiness about your gorgeous man.'

'I know, I know. But I'm not even remotely near to getting married at this point in my life.'

'Good job really. Engaged after only two dates would be a bit rushed by most people's standards.'

'Don't be silly.' She rolls her eyes at me. 'I didn't mean I want to marry Connor right now. However, it is our third date tonight.' She taps the edge of her cup, looking thoughtful.

'Engagement on a third date is still a no, Sophie.'

She huffs.

'But a third date is good, and you have nothing to be jealous of. You're still in the immediate, passionate, "can't get past a day without thinking of him naked", "ripping each other's clothes off the minute you're alone" stage.'

'Emma.' Sophie whacks my arm playfully and I giggle.

'Don't give me that. You know I'm right.'

Her little grin gives her away and we both pause for a moment, deep in our own thoughts. Are Chris and I still like that? I can remember the days of not making it out of bed on a Sunday, barely seeing any daylight and only surfacing when sexual exhaustion had morphed into a hunger I could no longer ignore. I swear I was half a stone lighter then. But that intensity doesn't last forever and what we have now is pretty good too. It's comfortable, and loving and... at the point of engagement? I bite my lip.

'So when do I get to meet this amazing guy?' I prompt Sophie. She's been babbling on about him so much over the last two weeks that I feel like I practically know him already, but it would be nice to put a face to a name.

'Not yet.'

'Why ever not? Do I embarrass you?'

She pauses a moment before answering. Sophie is lucky that, due to the length of our friendship, I don't take offense.

'Maybe if we get to date four or five.'

'Hmm. I'll hold you to that. I need to check him out and give him the once over. So where is he taking you tonight?'

'To the cinema, I think.'

'Just a thought: please don't make out on the back row snogging like teenagers while he has half a hand up your top or I might have to disown you.' I shake my head mockingly.

'Don't worry, Connor has behaved like a perfect gentleman so far. Well, at least in public.'

'That's enough detail, thanks. I've changed my mind. You may be my best friend but I don't need to hear about every intimate liaison.' I like to share and I may joke about sex but descriptions of people's actual love life make me very uncomfortable. Some things should just stay between the people involved. Plus when I do finally meet Connor I don't want any images flooding my brain of him in a compromising position.

'Now who's blushing?' Sophie raises her eyebrows at me.

'Can I at least see a picture of Connor? You must have taken some on your mobile phone surely?'

'I might have' Sophie attempts to discreetly slide her phone into her handbag without success.

'Come on Soph. He can't be that bad looking' I joke.

'He isn't!'

'I've been scanning your social media profile but so far this man remains elusive. Usually you plaster the site with pictures detailing your every movement but right now there's just loads of you and me in various states of drunkenness, and a handful of boring work related events'

'Look, just let me have a little bit of time so I'm absolutely sure how I feel about Connor, and then I will show you all the pictures you want'

'And you'll actually introduce us'

'And I'll actually introduce you' she repeats.

A few minutes later we leave the coffee shop and head out onto the High Street.

'Have a great third date.' I hug Sophie goodbye.

'Call me as soon as you can tomorrow to officially give me the news of your engagement.'

'I promise.' I nod.

I head back to my car. During the short drive home, my stomach swirls as I imagine over and over how this evening is going to play out. I feel slightly high from the adrenaline rush and I don't know how I'm going to contain my excitement until Chris actually pops the question.

'Mum? What are you doing? Who is that? Where's my dad?'
'Calm down and shut up. This is just my friend Roger from work.'
'But where's Dad?'

Chapter Two

I'm dressed in all my finery. My little black dress, worn only once for my cousin's engagement party despite it costing nearly a month's wage, pulls in at the waist, giving me curves I don't usually possess. The cut of the neckline shows off my modest cleavage in the best way possible, although I still need my push-up bra to give any impression of boobs hiding beneath my outfit.

Sometimes I envy Sophie with her voluptuous body. She has full boobs and a round bum, yet a stomach so flat that if you didn't know better you would think she did a thousand sit-ups a day to maintain it. I do know better, though: Sophie was just blessed by the good body fairy. She's only been to the gym a handful of times in her whole life, to the best of my knowledge, and that was only because the new spin class teacher was hot. The novelty soon wore off and she realised the gain of ogling him for thirty minutes was not worth the pain of not feeling your bum for the entire time and not being able to walk normally for three days after doing the class. Everyone kept telling her that if she carried on eating anything she wanted her body would catch up with her. So far, despite being in her early thirties, they appear to be wrong and I have yet to see any evidence of this. I, on the other hand, was blessed by the flat-chested boyish figure fairy, so I will be forever grateful to the inventor of the super bra.

Smothered in Chanel perfume, which I save only for very special occasions given that I need a bank loan to buy a decent-sized bottle, I sip my delicious crisp white wine and gaze lovingly at Chris, who is fiddling nervously with his napkin. I don't think I've ever felt happier and so full of anticipation. It's sweet that he's so nervous.

Chris pushes his thick, golden hair back from his face with the palm of his hand and he looks right at me. I smile patiently, wondering whether now we've finished our main course he is going to ask me to marry him. Just as he opens his mouth to speak the waiter interrupts, thrusting dessert menus under our noses. Damn it.

'I can recommend the chef's chocolate soufflé.' He flicks his gaze between us. 'It's lighter than air.'

'That sounds lovely.' I smile through gritted teeth.

'Make that two.' Chris nods at the waiter as he collects the menus and disappears towards the kitchen.

'So.' Chris clears his throat. 'There's something that I want to talk to you about.' He glances down at the table.

Oh. My. God. This. Is. It. My heart thunders in my chest and, with difficulty, I swallow down my excitement. My throat is suddenly as dry as the Sahara desert so I grab my wine glass with a slightly shaky hand and take a grateful sip.

'I've been doing some thinking. You know, we've been talking about some serious things lately.' Chris fumbles the words.

'Yes.' I nod, trying to remain calm. 'Like moving in together.' I prompt.

'That's right.'

He looks…worried? That's normal, though, right? I mean, this is a big thing. I'm sure it's fine. Every man must get a little tongue tied at this moment. Think positive, think positive.

'And…' I fiddle with the stem of my wine glass. He must just be working himself up to ask me.

'And it's just…'

'Yes?'

He stares at me, looking a little awkward, and for a second a flash of disappointment washes over me. My stomach does a little flip like when you go over a hill in the car a little too fast and I suddenly feel like I'm going to hear something that I really don't want to. This isn't how I pictured the conversation going at all and I can feel the sheepish grin that's been plastered on my face all evening beginning to fade.

'You're a lovely girl and everything...'

'What?'

'It's just...I don't think it's going to work out between us.'

Excuse me? I stare at him, completely dumbfounded. Did I actually hear that right? Did he really just say 'You're a lovely girl' after two years of being in a relationship with me? Seriously? And then the sledgehammer hits me with full force – he's breaking up with me. That's what's happening here. There's no marriage proposal. He's breaking up with me.

'You don't think it's going to work out between us?' I repeat back at him a little flippantly and just a little too loudly for such a nice restaurant. I can hear the complete shock in the tone of my voice.

'It's simply run its course, that's all. Don't you think?' Chris looks around nervously before reaching across the table and placing his hand cautiously over mine.

I feel a physical pain coursing through my body before it's laid to rest with a final stab to my heart and my mouth flaps open like a goldfish.

The waiter suddenly reappears, sliding a perfectly formed chocolate soufflé in front of me. I stare aimlessly down at it, realising at this point that I will never get to taste the chef's special 'lighter than air' soufflé. I think I might actually be sick.

'Come on, Emma. This can't be a total surprise.' Chris squeezes my hand a little and I look up, meeting his gaze, trying desperately to see something in his eyes that says this is a mistake. That he's got it all wrong. But his expression is blank as he looks right back at me. His eyes are completely detached from any emotion and that's when the realisation hits me. I'm such an idiot.

'Who is she?' I ask flatly, closing my eyes. I try desperately to contain the bubbling anger that is threatening to spill over, which would cause an embarrassing scene in front of all these other posh diners who actually deserve to be here, enjoying their pleasant, if slightly pretentious, dinner. I hold my breath, sure that I don't actually want to hear the answer to my question.

'Emma, come on.' He shifts uncomfortably in his seat as I snap my eyes open and glare at him accusingly.

'I asked you a question, Chris. Don't you at least owe me the truth after two years of sharing our lives?'

He presses his lips together into a thin line.

'Who. Is. She?' I growl through gritted teeth.

There is a deathly pause during which the background noise of the restaurant seems to be captured and muffled by a bubble. My thudding heartbeat is the only sound that I can hear in the room.

'No one you know.' He swallows noisily like he's just eaten a bug.

There it is, right there. The truth that I knew I didn't want to hear. I roughly snatch my hand back from under his as I blink back tears. So there you go. Two years of building what I thought was an intimate, trusting relationship only to be left stranded on my own desert island of our imaginary life while he sails away into the distance with someone else. The air between us is as sharp as cut glass. How did I not see any of this? How stupid must I be?

'How long has this been going on?' I'm trying to keep my voice low but I can feel a hint of hysteria creeping in.

'It doesn't matter.'

'It matters to me!' I shout a little too loudly and as a result I'm greeted by frowns and stares from the other diners. But I don't care. My whole world is imploding and Chris is sitting across from me as cool as a cucumber, telling me it doesn't matter how long he's been having his leg over with someone else while taking me for a complete fool. It's lies. It has all been lies.

'Emma, you're making a scene.' He glances around, looking embarrassed.

'I'm making a scene?'

'Just calm down.'

That's it. That's the red rag to my bull right there.

'That's why you brought me here, isn't it?' I shout incredulously. 'You thought you could tell me that you've been cheating on me and that you're a total prick, and that I wouldn't make a scene?'

Everyone is staring now, including the waiting staff who flap around, clearly wondering if they should evict us from the restaurant but at the same time realising we haven't paid yet.

'Hey.' Chris has the audacity to look angry with me now.

'Don't "hey" me. All this time I've been thinking that things are going well between us, that we have a future together, and you've been…you've been…' My voice has reached screeching point. 'Argh! You make me sick.'

Chris looks shocked by my outburst and I'm glad I'm embarrassing him. I can't believe he's hurt me like this. I just can't believe he's done this.

I reach forward, grab my wine glass and down the remains of my drink. As I stand up to remove myself from this impossible situation, I knock over the tall white candlestick in the centre of the table. Thankfully it blows itself out before the shocked waiter can reach the table to save it. Everyone is staring at us now, open-mouthed, and a hush has descended over the entire restaurant. Our hideous sideshow is intruding on the rich, posh people enjoying their own romantic evenings.

'I don't ever want to see you again,' I snarl across the table at Chris, before grabbing my shawl from the back of the chair. I turn away from him and hurry across the crowded room. I can hear him call my name as I dash between tables, narrowly avoiding waiters who have resumed carrying steaming plates of food, until I reach the door. But Chris doesn't follow me.

Once out on the street I lean against the cold bricks of the restaurant wall for support, careful to stay out of sight from the large bay windows as I gulp at the chilly night air, focusing all my attention on staying upright and not collapsing in a crying heap on the pavement. My legs no longer feel strong enough to support my body and I shiver in the cool breeze and pull my flimsy shawl more tightly around my shoulders.

What the hell just happened? My life has done a complete one-eighty-degree turn in the time it took for a soufflé to arrive from the kitchen. That's all it took for my relationship with the perfect guy and a dream of a happy ending to disintegrate into nothing. Have the last two years of my life all been a fantasy in my head? Did I imagine everything? Every look, every kiss? No. He's just been playing a game. How many times has he crawled from my bed into hers? Urgh. I don't even want to think about that.

I stand up straight and move away from the wall. Looking around aimlessly, I see that I'm surrounded by groups of friends, laughing and chatting, making their way to bars and restaurants. It's a busy Saturday night, and as I stare at the people around me, I have never felt so alone, scared and alone. I suddenly feel a desperate need for my bed, just to snuggle down in my pyjamas and pull the quilt over my head. To block out this whole stupid evening and the dull ache that is forming around my broken heart.

I wobble unsteadily, flailing between the throngs of people, in search of a taxi. I wrap my arms around myself to try to keep warm but it does nothing to deter the uncontrollable shaking that has taken over my body. As I turn the corner onto the main road I am so grateful to see a black cab heading my way that as I fling my arm out in desperation and it pulls over to the kerb I actually give a little sob.

The few miles home feel like an eternity but I finally make it to my front door. As soon as I have flicked the deadbolt on, to barricade myself in for the night, it's like I've flicked on the emotional switch inside me. A single tear streaks slowly down one cheek like the calm before the storm and then one big, fat tear after another slides down my face, plopping from the edge of my chin onto my 'oh-so-perfect little black dress', and then I begin to cry. Really cry, like I've never cried before. I stagger bleary-eyed into my bedroom and don't even bother to remove my clothes, let alone my makeup, before I starfish, face down onto the bed. I bury my face into my pillows, not giving a damn about the streaking mascara that will no doubt cause a stain. I can hear the strange, gargled sound of heart-wrenching sobs but it's like they're coming from someone else, like I'm having an out-of-body experience and I'm looking down from above, seeing my body heaving on the bed. I watch, mesmerised, until the sobs turn into a whimpering sound like that of an animal in pain and then the claws of sleep dig in deep and welcome me in.

Chapter Three

I wake to the irritating sound of my mobile phone bleating somewhere in my vicinity but my head feels far too heavy to even attempt to lift it from my pillow. For a second I wonder why I'm lying face down on the bed in the first place, and then I remember. The restaurant, Chris's pathetic face as he told me it was over, the realisation that there was someone else, me shouting and then sobbing. My heart sinks and instantly the pain in my chest is back like an ice-cold hand clutching at my heart and squeezing with all its might.

Chris broke up with me. Our relationship is over. He's been cheating on me. He wants to be with someone else. The words flow repeatedly through my head like a solemn mantra.

Ultimately he doesn't want me any more.

I feel physically sick, broken and emotionally shattered.

My heart is willing me to lie here forever, but my body is challenging me to get up. I'm completely dehydrated and my tongue is sticking disgustingly to the roof of my mouth, in desperate need of water. Dragging myself up from my bed, I glimpse my reflection in my dressing-room mirror and I catch my breath; it's not a pretty sight. It's so bad that I have to stop and take a second look. I step closer and stare at the unkempt, almost unrecognisable reflection looking back at me. Last night's mascara has smeared around my eyes and down my cheeks, giving a whole new meaning to the term 'panda eyes'. My face is puffy from all the crying and the sleek, shiny hair that I left the house with last night has morphed into a matted mass that is half plastered to my face from the salty tears and half sticking up on end like I've received an electric shock. In a way I did, and maybe this is my whole body's reaction. It's turned on itself and gone into self-destruct mode.

Maybe caffeine will help.

My mobile phone bleeps again, signalling that a text message has arrived, and I glare at my handbag, the holder of said mobile phone, as it taunts me from the corner of the room. I eye it up warily. I don't even want to look at my phone but it's going to continue to prod me with that beeping sound until I do, and right now that feels like a drill pressing hard against my scull. Similar to pulling off a plaster, I realise I need to do this quickly. I rummage around in my handbag for the phone and glance briefly at the screen before sighing with relief. It's just Sophie. Oh no! She wanted all the details of my wonderful romantic evening. She's going to expect me to be engaged. I rub my temples, trying to dispense the thick fog that is clouding my brain. I'm not ready to regurgitate the events of last night just yet, even to Sophie. I feel too numb to even try to put what happened into words. I switch the phone to silent and toss it onto the bed.

Twisting myself into a knot, I extract myself from my little black dress and pull on my big, fluffy dressing gown, wrapping it around me like a security blanket as I head downstairs to the kitchen.

A few moments later, armed with a steaming mug, I reach the sanctuary of my sofa. As I sit nursing the mug of tea with the television on mute, I realise my mum is wrong – a cup of tea can't fix everything. It doesn't even come close. I'm torn between feeling so angry that I could go round to Chris's place right now and rip his head off and so sad that everything I thought we had we didn't. All the dreams of a future together were mine and not ours.

I quickly come to the conclusion that wallowing alone is only going to lead me to a further depression. Sitting upright and placing my empty mug on the coffee table, I decide that I need to have company or I'll end up drowning my sorrows with the last of the brandy left over from my attempt at a Christmas pudding, and no good will come of that.

I head back upstairs to text Sophie.

Hi. How was the second date with Connor? Last night didn't quite go to plan. Can you come over?

I take a deep breath and press 'send' but I realise, with a feeling of dread in the pit of my stomach, that once I talk about the hideousness of the last supper, it will become a reality. It's not just some horrible dream and there's no going back.

My phone beeps.

Can be at yours in an hour. x

A hot shower does little to improve my puffy face but at least I can now blow-dry my hair back into a more acceptable style. Applying every lotion and potion I can to my skin seems to help, and by the time I hear the doorbell ring I almost resemble my normal self. As I open the door I see Sophie's face, which is initially bright with anticipation but then wavers slightly before she asks the dreaded question.

'What happened?' She frowns at me. 'Is everything alright?'

I step back from the door to let her in but I don't trust myself to speak quite yet. I can feel the emotion building in me again and my bottom lip quivers, causing me to fear that a repeat of last night's sobbing is about to erupt. I walk through to the kitchen and Sophie quickly follows behind me. I switch the kettle on and prepare two coffee cups, and then turn to face her. She hasn't uttered another word but she's staring at me intently with a worried expression, clearly waiting for me to begin to explain why I'm not grinning from ear to ear and shouting that I'm engaged from the top of my lungs.

'He didn't take me to La Sapiniere to ask me to marry him.' I take an awkward gulp of air. 'He took me there to break up with me. '

I lean on the kitchen side for support and watch Sophie's changing expression as she digests what I've just told her. She too seems completely floored by this news: she stands open-mouthed, mirroring my own flapping goldfish response from last night. Then she steps forward and pulls me into a hug. This simple act of friendship is my undoing and the tears begin to flow again.

After a moment or two I regain some of my composure and pull away from her, wiping at my cheeks with the back of my hand as I resume the task of making coffee.

'What happened? Why has he ended things?' Sophie asks softly.

'That's the best part of the story.' I sniff. 'He's been seeing someone else.'

'The bastard,' she snaps, clearly outraged. 'Who is she?'

I see a steely glint in Sophie's eyes.

'I don't know. He wouldn't say. There was a lot of yelling, on my part anyway.' I shrug. 'You know what? It doesn't really matter who she is; it's who he is that matters, and that's someone in a relationship, someone's boyfriend. The truth is, it's him that's the most at fault; he's been playing me. I just, I don't know… I guess I didn't see it coming at all. I thought things were great. I thought we had a future. He was the only long-term relationship I've had. The rest all fizzled out after a few months. I actually thought we had a chance of a happy ending.'

'I know, I know.' Sophie grabs my hand and squeezes it tightly. 'I'm sorry.'

I nod, too choked to speak. Taking a deep breath, I try to put a lid on my turbulent emotions.

'So anyway, how was date number three?' I slide a mug across to her.

A wry smile spreads across Sophie's face but then her expression falters.

'Hey.' I touch her hand gently. 'I'm fine with the fact that you're happy and in love in your new relationship. It's not your fault that Chris ended up being a complete shit.'

'I just feel like it's bad timing, that's all.' Sophie nods slowly as she takes a sip of her coffee. 'It's going really well, though.' She can't help smiling again.

'You really like him, don't you?' I can see the fuzzy glow of lust all around her.

'I do. He's…different.'

'I'm happy for you.'

She looks at me with what I perceive to be a mixture of pity and sympathy.

'Honestly I am,' I reassure her, and I genuinely mean it. 'It's about time you had some decent luck on the relationship front.'

'Are you going to be alright?' she asks tentatively.

'Not right now. But I guess I will be.' I say quietly. What other choice do I have?

Chapter Four

The last week has gone by in a blur of tears and wine, followed by the occasional burst of hysteria. I really have very little recollection of the previous seven days. A week on from the conversation that flipped my life into freefall, I'm still emotionally unstable and unable to come to terms with the premature ending of my vision of wedded bliss. It's Sunday evening and I find myself plodding listlessly around the house, still dressed in my pyjamas and in a state of, well, mourning, it feels like. My mobile phone, lying on the kitchen side, rings incessantly. I wilfully ignore it. I'm in no mood to speak to anyone. But it rings, and rings, and rings.

Oh for God's sake.

I storm into the kitchen and snatch up the phone.

'Hello,' I snap into the receiver.

'Hello, darling. What on earth is that attitude for?'

'Oh, hi, Mum. Erm, sorry. It's been a…' Hideous, life-changing, and depressing eight days and I'm not quite feeling my usual perky self. 'It's been a rough week.' I decide not to add too much drama to the conversation. My mother is quite capable of that all on her own.

'What's happened, darling? You sound sad.'

Damn it. Why can she always sense when things are spectacularly falling apart? It seems that the instant my life turns into a pile of sludge my mum makes an unexpected call.

'I…um…we…'

'Just spit it out, darling. Is it your father?'

'No, Mum. My dad's fine. It's Chris. We broke up.' My voice cracks a little towards the end of the sentence and I cringe inwardly.

'What happened?'

I pause. This is so not the conversation I want to be having right now with my mother.

'He cheated on me,' I say flippantly, although it doesn't make it hurt any less by pretending that I don't care.

'Oh. Right. I see. Well.' She sounds quite angry now.

'It's okay, Mum, you don't have to say all of the usual crap about there being someone better out there and stuff.'

'But there will be, darling,' she says in her motherly tone. 'And I never really liked him anyway.'

I chuckle down the phone. That's just typical.

'See, that feels better, doesn't it? Having a little laugh and a joke? You can't let these things get you down, Emma. Men can be unpredictable and very selfish, I'm afraid.'

'It's not that simple, Mum.' I huff like a petulant teenager.

'You know what I think you need?'

Brad Pitt and a one-way ticket to Barbados? I ponder.

'What's that, Mum?'

'You need to get away from things for a few days. You know, clear your head so you can start to –'

'To?'

'To move on, darling.'

Ouch. That hurts to even think about. I was planning my whole future in my head with Chris and at no time did I imagine having to emotionally detach from him.

'That's a nice thought, Mum, and I would love to go someplace where I could stick my head in the sand and distract myself with other things. But I have a job I need to go to and no money to just, well…'

'Why don't you come and stay with me, darling? Just for two days of fun. I'll pay for your ticket.'

'That's nice of you to offer, Mum, but I can't just drop everything and get on the next flight to New York. Although that does sound very tempting...'

'Why not?'

'Well…'

'I'm sure you can take a few days off work.'

I'm not sure that mum always appreciates that I do have an actual job. Just because I don't work for some giant corporation that does random things with stocks and shares that I'll never understand doesn't mean that my job is futile. Working in a designer boutique doesn't provide the many perks that most people assume, though. I don't spend all day playing dress up with the manikins in between drinking coffee. Most of the clientele I get to serve are rich, middle-aged snobs who like nothing more than to try on every outfit in the shop while the three of us who work there treat them like royalty and they treat us like crap. The clothes are nothing that I could ever imagine myself wearing at any point in my life, though I must admit the shoes and handbags are pretty nice – but they come with an even nicer price tag.

As ours is one of three stores, the owner, Marissa Bamford, is thankfully not based at our location, and she only makes the occasional fleeting visit, usually unexpected (much like my mother, really). Baring a far too canny resemblance to Cruella Deville, and with people skills to match, Madam Bamford spends most of her time at the London store, hobnobbing with the even richer southerners, leaving the running of our store to me and Jenny, with some assistance from Lola. Jenny is a similar age to me and as such we hit it off instantly and are friends as well as work colleagues. Lola is only in her early twenties and still a victim of fashion, so Jenny and I leave most of the displays and manikin dressing to her, while we do the boring paperwork and manage the delicate personalities of our regular customers. All in all, the three of us get on well and make a good team and the shop generally runs like clockwork. In that case, could I take a few days off?

'Um, probably not given that I work for the queen of evil,' I state. Why is it that my mum lives in some fantasy world where she thinks everyone can just do as she wants whenever she says so? She can be so frustrating.

'I'm sure if you explain things it will be perfectly okay, darling.'

Grrr.

'I could ask Jenny tomorrow, I suppose,' I concede, annoyed by the ease with which I crumble under her emotional pressure. I'm pretty sure that Jenny won't mind covering for me but I still feel cheeky asking at such short notice. I'll definitely owe her one.

'Fantastic, darling. Call me tomorrow when you've spoken to her and I'll book the flight for you.'

'Okay, Mum. And thanks,' I add, suddenly feeling all emotional.

'I can't wait to show you some of the wonderful places I've found to shop. And eat.'

'That sounds great, Mum.' I'm convincing myself now that I can just get on a flight to New York with no notice whatsoever. 'I'll call you tomorrow.'

'Bye, darling.'

I put the phone down and stare at it in wonder. My mother of today bears no resemblance to Rosalind Storey, housewife and four times cake-baking champion of the village fete who raised me. That woman is way in the past and long forgotten. It's like overnight my mother morphed from a conservative, middle-aged woman who wore knitted twin-sets into an unrecognisable creature clothed in designer fashion labels and carrying a Birkin handbag. I'm not quite sure whether this transformation was the result of Mum and Dad splitting up or the cause of it, but either way they are both now happy in their polar-opposite worlds.

At the age of sixteen, when they sat me down with only a bowl of ice cream for comfort and told me they were getting divorced, I thought my life had ended. I cried for three days solid, thinking that my life would never be the same again. I veered from blaming myself to hating them both, and I'll be the first to admit that those initial six months were an awkward transition. As a teenager you're usually hung up on figuring out your own life, not trying to work out what the hell's going on with your parents'. They somehow made it work, though, and ever since that bombshell of a conversation in our old living room, Mum and Dad have got on amicably.

By the time Mum announced that she was moving to New York to start a new job I had already moved out into my first flat, so although it was a shock that she was suddenly going to be thousands of miles away in a completely different country, I was used to standing on my own two feet. In fact, her not being around the corner every day may have helped me to grow up just that little bit more quickly.

Over the years I've often wondered what the main reason was for the end of their marriage; as far as I know there was no one else involved on either side. But I guess I've never felt comfortable asking either one of them. Maybe I don't actually want to know.

The following morning I head into work, really hoping that Jenny is in a generous mood. I'm the first one in so I flick on the kettle, and while it boils I go about switching on the lights and the till. I grab a cup and take out of my bag the fresh milk I picked up on the journey. Hmm. I wonder what Chris is doing right now? I wonder if he woke up with her this morning? That horrible thought is my brain's way of forcing the inevitable question to the forefront of my mind: are they are already living together?

'Morning.'

'Oh, hi.' I smile half-heartedly at Jenny as she stares at me curiously. I didn't even hear her come in. I must have been wallowing in emotional hell; that keeps happening recently. She's still looking at me, bemused, and I realise I'm stirring a teaspoon repeatedly around my mug to the point of the liquid sloshing over the edge. I take the spoon out and place it on the work surface, discretely mopping up the spilled coffee with a dishcloth. 'Would you like a drink?'

'Er, sure.'

She hangs her coat up and I busy myself with making another coffee, wondering how I'm going to approach the subject of having a few days off at short notice, like tomorrow. But I might actually be doing her a favour: then she doesn't have to deal with the fallout when my head explodes with all the reoccurring thoughts of Chris and her together.

'So, how are you?' Jenny smiles warmly as I hand her a coffee mug. I swear she sniffs it before taking a sip. How weird.

'Erm, yeah about that.' I clear my throat. 'My mum rang last night and she…well, she thinks it would do me some good to, um, take a few days off, and she offered to pay for my flight, you know, to go out to see her in New York.' I bite my lip and cringe at how needy and selfish I sound, but that's exactly how I feel right now – needy and selfish.

'I think you should go.'

'I mean, I know I would be asking a huge…What?' I look at Jenny.

'I said I think you should go.' She nods.

'But that would mean leaving tomorrow and not being back in work until Friday.'

'Lola and I can cope.'

'But what about –'

'I'll deal with the old dragon. She's out of the country anyway, buying stock from the other side of the world, so she'll never know. We'll just put it down as unplanned necessary holiday due to a family....emergency.'

'That's really very kind of you, but I'm not sure –'

'I'll spell it out for you, Emma. I was trying to spare your feelings, but to be honest I think it would be better for us all if you had a couple of days' break and came back, erm, refreshed.'

I see.

'But I –'

'Emma, you have spent the last week wandering around the shop in a trance, seemingly completely unaware of customers and their demands. You brought Mrs Jones two odd shoes to try on.'

Unfortunately that's right, I did do that. Oops.

'You advised Mrs Luther that an emerald-green handbag matched her eyes.'

Did I? I think for a moment and then an embarrassing realisation pops into my head.

'Mrs Luther is of African Caribbean nationality, Emma.'

'That means she has brown eyes, doesn't it?'

'Exactly. And I was hoping that I wasn't going to have to mention this and you would realise on your own, but...'

I look at her, alarmed.

'But your hair has been getting scarier and scarier by the day.' She exhales noisily, clearly uncomfortable.

Really? I don't...um.

I pat down the sides of my hair, acknowledging that I may have skipped the straightening part of my regime for the last few days. I hadn't realised it was that bad, that I had reached the 'scaring small children and the elderly' stage.

'And finally...'

There's more? I thought the tirade was over.

'You tried to kill me on Friday morning by giving me some revolting concoction of tea mixed with coffee and what tasted like six sugars.' Jenny stands with her hands on her hips, looking a little exhausted from the exertion of detailing my current flaws.

Talk about the truth hurts. I take a moment to process everything that she has said. In all honesty, I have no defence. The last week is just a dark and muddy blur.

'So...' I cringe.

'So, we'll see you on Friday,' Jenny prompts.

'Thanks, Jenny.' I nod in agreement, thinking maybe I need sectioning for a few days rather than a mini break in New York after last week's performance. 'I really do appreciate it.'

'It's okay. Just take a few days, sort your head out. You'll start to feel much better about things.'

I smile, thinking it's going to take more than a few days of distraction therapy to repair my self-esteem, let alone my broken heart.

'You're a big boy now, aren't you?'
'I suppose.'
'And big boys know how to keep secrets, don't they? Don't they?'
'Yes, Mum.'

Chapter Five

Upon landing at Newark airport I can already see a thick frost covering every surface, twinkling like a Christmas card in the weak March sunshine, and I shrink inwardly. I'm so glad Mum reminded me to pack some warm jumpers; apparently it's unusually chilly for the spring season in New York. I make it through the annoying process of Immigration, having practically had to do a full body strip. I'm surprised anyone makes it through unscathed. When faced with a line of men with extremely large guns, it's a wonder that more people don't start behaving nervously and raise suspicion. I felt like I was guilty of something just because I was standing there. Thankfully my bag was one of the first out on the carousel in Baggage Reclaim. It was as if it sensed my urgency and my need to get the hell out of there.

I drag my small roller suitcase through to Arrivals and turn the corner towards the throng of waiting people, pulling my scarf a little tighter around my neck. I instantly see Mum, who is waving frantically at me, dressed in a stunning grey wool coat that sweeps right down to her boots. A bright red scarf is swirled around her shoulders with a matching red beret perched on top of her head. To sum it up, she looks like she should be gracing the cover of a glossy French magazine. I pull at my own trusty, years' old winter coat, doing up the buttons as I shuffle towards her, already feeling the cold despite still being inside the terminal building.

'Hello, darling.' She wraps me into a huge hug and squeezes me until I can't breathe. 'It's so lovely to see you.'

'Yeah, you too, Mum.' I swallow down the lump in my throat while trying to extract myself from her embrace enough to gulp for air.

'Right, let's grab a takeaway latte – that rubbish they serve on the plane is barely drinkable – and then we can get a taxi.'

'A taxi? We're not driving?'

'Driving? Emma, this is New York. Nobody drives.'

'Right.' I nod, wondering what happened to the woman who refused to ever get public transport and insisted on driving everywhere. Every time I see her I'm reminded that the mum I grew up with is around less and less. It's not necessarily a bad thing, it's just weird when you feel like your mum lives a whole life that you have no part of and you only catch snippets of it on random visits.

A few minutes later we collect our coffees and head out to the long line of waiting taxis. Within seconds a driver has taken my bag from me and thrown it into the boot, and we're off. I stare out of the window at the passing sights as we make our way towards Manhattan.

As we hurtle up the expressway I reach into my handbag and pull out my mobile phone. A sliver of hope hovers over me as I stare at the black screen. It's been switched off for ages, since I got on my flight. I should check my messages. Holding down the 'on' button, I hope against hope that there will be a text message flashing in the inbox from Chris. I mean, it's been days – no, scratch that, it's been over a week since that fateful night. Although I know it's crazy and completely irrational under the circumstances, I want him to want me back, to have realised his mistake and to…well, just want me back. I stare patiently at the screen, waiting for the reaffirming bleep that declares your importance in your virtual world. However, I'm met with nothing, silence, a mocking blank screen that might as well scream 'loser' at me in the face of my false hope.

I hate mobile phones as much as I love them. Life in general must have been so much simpler before instant messaging and mobile networks appeared that allow us to be available at every waking, and sometimes sleeping, moment. The mobile phone must be the most contradictory development in technology. While it saves us so much time by allowing us to contact anyone at any given time, it frustrates us immensely as we waste hours, if not weeks and months, staring aimlessly at the damned phone, waiting for a response. Or, like I'm doing right now, willing someone to get in touch. I curse the phone.

Ooh, wait. I have a new text.

I click on the new envelope that has just appeared on the screen, but no sooner are my hopes raised than they are dashed. I feel guilty that my heart sinks when I see that the text is only from Sophie.

Hey. Hope u made it to NY safely. Say hi to your mum from me. x x

I text back quickly: *Just landed. All good thanks. Will be in touch. x x*

Like a moody teenager I throw the phone dismissively back in my handbag and sulk, watching the world whizz by out of the window.

'I thought we could take a stroll in the park later.' Mum clears her throat. 'Stretch your legs after the long flight.'

I glance over at Mum and she's smiling at me but with a slightly worried edge to it.

'That sounds good.' I smile back, placing my handbag in the footwell of the car. I vow to switch my phone off the minute we arrive at Mum's in an attempt to stop next two days becoming an obsessive phone watch that will only result in tears and tantrums when Chris doesn't text or call.

I can't believe he hasn't even texted to see if I'm okay. It's like he's fallen off the face of the earth.

But I haven't tried to call or text him either. Maybe I should?

No. No. I cannot allow myself to be that pathetic. He's the one who's done wrong. He cheated.

So why do I want him to call?

Bastard.

I think I'll give my phone to Mum for safe keeping and to prevent me becoming my own worst enemy.

'It will be okay, darling. I promise.' Mum nods as though she can read every one of my disturbing thoughts.

'I know,' I whisper, and right there and then I decide that this is the last time, at least for the next few days, that I'm going to allow myself to wallow in self-pity and misery over Chris. I'm here in New York and I'm going to damn well enjoy myself.

As we stroll around Central Park later that afternoon, I have to admit that I'm feeling far less distressed, although I'm still in possession of my phone. Despite my better judgement I couldn't bring myself to completely part with it, and I keep sneaking a peek at it every now and then. As I sip my takeaway coffee I realise I haven't thought about Chris for at least an hour…until now, that is. The air feels so much fresher here and the whole atmosphere so open in this vast space, even though it is nestled between four walls of skyscrapers, right in the heart of the city. I think I can actually feel my shoulders dropping a few notches as we make our way across the park to the famous bandstand, surrounded by tall trees sprouting fresh spring leaves.

I'm always in awe of New York. Everything is steeped in so much history and I have no idea how long it would take to see everything of significance in the city. I've only managed the most popular tourist attractions in my three visits over the last two years, but as long as Mum keeps living here I should get to see a few more sights each time I come and stay. New York is like a completely different world; one that feels strangely familiar, given that it's the setting for numerous films and television shows, yet it's alien to me. The streets are so busy with people which I don't understand as there's a constant traffic jam of yellow taxis beeping incessantly. Maybe that's why. I guess if you don't walk, you won't get anywhere very quickly, there's obviously too many people in New York at any one time! I can't tell who is a tourist and who's a local as everyone dashes from one place to another, takeaway coffee in one hand, designer handbag in the other. What I find really amusing about New York, though, is the large number of dogs you find in Central Park that are wearing outfits. I've never seen so many doggy hats, coats and jumpers. It's unreal that dogs have wardrobe collections to choose from depending on the weather, yet it's pretty cool at the same time.

'So what else do you want to see over the next two days?' Mum links her arm through mine as we walk, like she used to when I was a kid, and I smile. I'm lucky to have such fond memories of my childhood despite coming from what some people would view as a broken home. Mum and Dad were happy together for a long time and I always felt loved by them both equally even after they had separated.

I suddenly feel a wave of nostalgia.

'Aren't you ever lonely out here on your own?' I stop walking and look at Mum.

'Who says I'm on my own?' Mum winks rather suggestively at me and I instantly realise how naïve I am.

'Um…'

'Just because I haven't remarried like your father doesn't mean that I don't have gentlemen friends.'

Gentleman friends? What does that even mean? Actually I will sleep much better if I never know.

'Let's just leave that there.' I nod as disturbing images of Mum with some rich, bearded, old man – or worse: someone barely older than me – circle around my mind.

'Really, darling,' Mum chastises me gently while trying to contain her clear amusement at my emotional ineptness. 'I don't know why that makes you uncomfortable. I'm a person as well as your mother.' She smiles.

Hmm.

'I'm not uncomfortable.' I protest meekly before admitting defeat. 'Well, maybe I am. It's just weird talking to you about relationships and your personal life when the only role I every really see you in is that of my mum – although I do get that you're also a person who has her own life.'

'Doesn't Dad talk to you about him and Margaret?'

'Yes, in that they're both well and happy, and that they're going to Spain again this summer. But that's it. They don't talk about, well, anything else.' I cringe inwardly.

My dad and Margaret do not have sex. They do not have sex. I try desperately to remove even more disturbing images from my cruel and tormenting mind.

'Well, there may not be anything more to tell, darling. Margaret isn't the most –'

'Mum!'

'You're right. Sorry.' She does me the courtesy of looking contrite.

'Margaret may not be the most exciting person, but she is nice, and...'

'And?'

'And she makes Dad...'

My mouth is dry. This whole conversation was a big mistake and I don't even know how we got here.

'Happy?' Mum squeezes my arm a little more tightly and I nod gently. I can't help but feel like I have plunged a knife into her back and twisted it with every word.

'It's okay, Emma,' she says reassuringly. 'Your dad and I get on absolutely fine now.'

She's right; that's true. On the very rare occasions that we are all together, such as occasional Christmases, everyone is polite and courteous.

'Well, we never really reached that point of hating each other or anything like that. Throughout everything I have never wished your father any ill. I'm glad he's found someone else and is happy. He and I were both responsible for the breakdown of our marriage.'

I can feel a lump forming in my throat again. 'We never really talk about that, do we?'

'There's not that much to say.' Mum sighs. 'We were happy for a long time. We had you only a year after we were married.' She stops walking and turns to face me. 'And we never wanted another child. We both knew that you were all that we needed.'

'Oh, Mum.' I sniff.

'What can I say, Emma? Life is hard and people change. Financial pressures and the emotional strain of trying to manage your work/life balance constantly provide a challenge, and your relationship will go one of two ways: you'll work harder to overcome these obstacles and it will either bring you closer together or, as in the case of Dad and me, you drift apart. There was nothing sinister for us, no cheating or other people involved, just the sad fact that we had fallen out of love with each other.'

Wow, this is pretty heavy stuff. She has never opened up to me like this before, and I guess I have never wanted to ask about what happened between her and Dad. I just accepted that they were separating. Hell, I was sixteen and plenty of kids at school had come from broken families and they got on with their lives just fine. I was determined to carry on as normal too, but maybe I just hid my feelings. Maybe that's why I always end up in ridiculous relationships, because I am emotionally stunted.

'Anyway, darling.' Mum interrupts my newfound realisation, 'Let's not get all sad and emotional.' She sniffs too. 'This trip is supposed to be for cheering you up. So let's get some takeaway food and an early night. You must be exhausted from the flight and we're five hours behind here so you've had a very long day. Tomorrow we'll head straight down to Fifth Avenue and spend some of my money, okay?'

'Okay.' I nod but my mind is still churning, wondering if all of my relationships have been doomed from the start – and if so, how the hell am I ever going to achieve the emotional wisdom required to get it right when I do find the right person to spend the rest of my life with?

I wake following the best night's sleep that I've had in the last week and a half. It must have been the exhaustion from the flight and the time change; I think I was asleep the instant my head hit the pillow.

Mum takes us for a naughty breakfast of waffles and syrup, and as I swallow my last delicious mouthful I feel ready to take on the magnitude of the fashion capital of the world. We've barely been in Bloomingdale's for five minutes before my arms are struggling to carry all of the clothes that I want to try on. I've found fashion heaven right here in downtown New York and I'm taking full advantage.

'This place is amazing, Mum,' I squeal as my eyes dart around in search of more clothes I can bankrupt Mum with.

'Let's head over to the changing rooms.' Mum nods to my left as she unburdens me of at least six items that were threatening to unbalance me completely.

'I'll wait here, but you must come out and show me each outfit as you try them.' Mum smiles as I hand the slightly bewildered sales assistant my pile of clothes before she escorts me to an empty changing cubicle.

It's pleasantly cool in these changing rooms, which makes a huge difference from the ones back home where you break into a sweat before you've even attempted to get undressed. This causes your previously comfortably sized clothes to turn into cling film, suctioning to every centimetre of your skin and holding on for dear life. You then fight a losing battle trying to clamber into the clothes you want to try on in an undignified manner, as you squeeze, push and pull your body into the fabric, only to decide that you look hideous and the outfit doesn't suit you at all. Then you have to spend the next ten minutes trying to peel the items from your skin without damaging them, all while getting hotter and sweatier by the second. But here in fashion heaven it's cool and spacious, and the lighting doesn't make me hate myself as I glance nervously in the mirror, dressed only in my bra and knickers. Usually the ugly fluorescent glow bounces unflatteringly from every bump of cellulite.

I pull on the first outfit: some black skinny jeans and a cobalt-blue thin-knit jumper with black lace sewn in a semicircle just below the high neckline. I have to admit it looks pretty good and I bite my lip as I look over at the numerous items hanging on hooks on the wall. I may have got slightly carried away in here. Anyway, never mind that. Now for my fashion show.

I edge out of the cubicle and head back onto the shop floor where Mum is waiting for me to present myself. As I stride confidently around the wall of the changing room, ready to show off my new outfit in all its glory, my face suddenly drops. Mum is facing to the side a few metres away, not looking in my direction at all. She's talking to some middle-aged guy with thick chocolate-brown hair who appears to be guffawing at her every word. He's smiling at her and Mum is smiling back and glancing intermittently at the floor. Oh my God, is she flirting with him?

I stand rooted to the spot and just watch them for a second, not sure whether to interrupt or just to skulk back into the changing room and pretend I haven't seen them.

They appear deep in conversation and oblivious to the world around them. He says something that he clearly thinks is amusing, as he's now grinning coyly, and Mum is grinning too. Then she does something totally out of character – she giggles girlishly and plays with a strand of her hair. I have never seen my mum behave like that.

This is surreal.

I don't actually remember instructing my body to move but I suddenly find myself edging closer and closer to them until I'm just near enough to hear their conversation.

'Erm, Mum?' I cough awkwardly.

She turns in my direction, startled as if she's surprised to see me and she's completely forgotten that I was in the changing rooms.

'Oh, sorry, Emma.' She forces a smile, trying to cement her poker face despite the fact her cheeks are burning crimson and her male friend looks like he's just been caught with his hand in the till – and that most definitely isn't a metaphor. 'That looks lovely.' She steps towards me and feels the fabric in a futile attempt to distract me from the fact that I've just interrupted her flirting session with the chocolate-haired stranger and that she now has some explaining to do.

Hang on a minute. When did we do this role reversal where I've now become the disapproving adult and she's the guilty teenager caught out with a boy? I so didn't see this ever happening. Am I getting older or is Mum getting younger?

'Aren't you going to introduce me?' I nod in the direction of the chocolate-haired man and realise up close that he must dye it, as no one has that evenly coloured rich brown hair, and certainly not at his age. A man with dyed hair? I'm not sure that's a good sign.

'Of course.' Mum glances sheepishly at the man and he takes an uncomfortable step towards us. 'This is Parker.'

'Hi, Parker,' I say with a smile, really emphasising his the 'P' sound of his name. Then I reach out my hand. He looks at it sceptically, just for a second, before grabbing it strongly with his own and shaking it with vigour.

'This is my daughter, Emma,' Mum states as she watches the

whole episode with some trepidation. 'Parker is a, um, work colleague.'

Work colleague, my arse. I wasn't born yesterday, Mum.

'It's nice to meet you, Emma.' Parker's voice is rich and chocolaty, just like his hair. He sounds professional and polite, but I'm guessing awkward social situations are not his speciality as he looks decidedly nervous and way out of his depth. I'm sure he wasn't expecting me to spring out from the changing rooms when he spotted Mum and decided to sidle over for a flirty chat.

Parker and I break our handshake, and the three of us just hover, looking uncomfortable.

'So, don't you have, like, a hundred more outfits to try on?' Mum nods at me.

Hmm, yes, I do, I think. But that will mean leaving you two alone again while I disappear out of sight, and who knows what might happen? Who am I kidding? We're in the middle of a shopping store and there are hundreds of other shoppers, and my mum is fifty-five. I'm pretty sure I don't want to witness middle-aged flirting first-hand, especially when my mum is involved; however, I feel compelled to stay.

Mum shoots me a slightly perplexed look, which I interpret to mean 'Get the hell out of here'.

Fair enough. We're all adults I suppose.

'Sure.' I clear my throat. 'It was nice to meet you too, Parker.'

I turn and walk back to the changing rooms, where the assistant is hovering, perhaps making sure I don't make a run for it while wearing the expensive clothes that haven't been paid for yet. I stop halfway and glance over my shoulder. Mum and Parker are still standing in the exact same position, watching me walk away with fixed smiles on their faces, obviously waiting for me to be out of earshot so they can continue their inappropriate behaviour. Is it inappropriate? I wonder as I draw the cubicle curtain and begin changing into my next outfit. My mum is, in fact, a grown woman, and she is single, so I guess she can flirt with whoever she wants. I wonder who he is. He's clearly more than a work colleague. I think some interrogation is required later on. Maybe after I ply her with wine.

As I step out from the changing rooms again in the next outfit, Parker is nowhere to be seen and Mum is waiting patiently for me right outside the changing room door now.

'I really like that colour on you.' She steps towards me and circles me, admiring the clothes.

'Where's Parker?' I try to catch a glimpse of Mum's face but she hides behind me under the pretence of looking at the hem length of the skirt.

'What? Oh he's, um, he's gone, darling.'

'Right.' I nod. 'Back to the office?'

'I don't know.' Mum sounds a little flustered. 'I only spoke to him for a minute or two just to be polite.'

'Of course.' I bite my lip, trying to stifle my smirk.

'I think you're going to test my bank balance today as this outfit looks great on you too. You have such a lovely figure, Emma – clothes just hang exactly how they should on you.'

Hmm. Nice try, but flattery is not going to distract me from Mission Parker.

I try on the rest of the pile of clothes and Mum coos over them all. In the end we decide to take two pairs of jeans, the skirt and three jumpers, which should keep me going for a while until the weather warms up back home.

'Shall we go and get some coffee?' Mum asks as we collect a bag of clothes each from the assistant at the checkout.

'That sounds good to me.'

We head to the nearest Starbucks, which isn't far away. It seems that New York, which used to be renowned for having a Gap on every corner, now has a Starbucks every ten metres – not that I'm complaining. We wait in line as machines hiss and pots are banged and our coffees are prepared. Neither of us speaks and I wonder whether it is best to leave well alone and not to mention Parker again. I guess I just forget that Mum has a whole different life here that I don't know about and rarely get to peek into, so it throws me a bit when I get a snapshot of Mum flirting with a man I don't know.

'Emma...'

'Sorry.' I flick back to reality.

'Your coffee.' Mum points to the large, frothy mug that the poor barista is trying to hand over to me.

'Sorry,' I say again. 'I was miles away.'

As we take a seat in a corner booth I realise how much my legs ache. It feels like we've walked a thousand miles since I stepped off the plane yesterday morning. Mum's right: no one drives in New York, which means they're all used to pounding the streets and striding everywhere at speed…except for the tourists, who shuffle aimlessly while trying to read a map upside down. I'm completely in awe of how easily Mum has adapted to this lifestyle.

'You look deep in thought.' Mum frowns at me as she stirs a powdered sweetener into her coffee.

'Just thinking about things.' I smile.

'Parker is just a friend, darling,' she says awkwardly.

Okay, I wasn't thinking about that particular thing, but if we're going to go down that route then…

'I'm not sure that it's any of my business, Mum,' I say honestly, fidgeting slightly as I tuck a stray stand of hair behind my ear and then wrap it around my finger.

'Emma, my business is always your business, I promise you. It's nothing serious, though. We've been on a couple of dates, that's all.' She says dismissively.

'Are you looking for something serious?' I ask, driven by a strange compulsion, although I'm not sure that I want to dig any deeper into this conversation.

'I don't know if I am.' She shakes her head. 'I mean, I like my life just the way it is. It's uncomplicated. As a retail buyer I earn good money, which allows me to enjoy things like eating out, buying nice clothes and seeing a show with my friends. I like the fact that I don't have to answer to anybody. I can do all of these when and where I please.'

I can see the attraction in that.

'And my work takes me all over looking at new merchandise. I get to fly out to a different country and experience different cultures with just a couple of days' notice. My unattached lifestyle means I have the flexibility to do that, and I go to places I may never have gone to otherwise.'

I bite my lip and shake my head. It sounds like my mum is living out every girl's dream, like some glamorous celebrity, flying all over the world and effectively shopping for a living. I actually feel jealous.

'Oh, darling.' She waves her hand at me. 'I know you think I'm living some enviable luxury life.'

Um, well, yes. Isn't that what you've just told me?

'But there is also a lot to be said for having somebody to share life with. Someone to come home to, to share the bed with – and I don't just mean in a sexual way.'

Oh no, here we go again, diving head first into inappropriate conversations and using that word, sex.

'Sometimes hotel rooms can be lonely, and at the end of the working day it's nice to come home and have someone to share a glass of wine with, to talk about your day with.'

And share a bed with, clearly.

Okay, now I'm seriously depressed. Despite my mum's bravado she really is saying that having it all is pointless unless you have another half to share it with. Maybe she has a point. Fear briefly sweeps over me as a reoccurring picture swirls through my mind: me with greying hair, living alone following failed relationship after failed relationship, wearing flowered-patterned clothes, surrounded by cats, sitting in the dark while they share food from my plate.

'Come on, drink up.' Mum taps my hand. 'I don't know about you but I think we could both do with something a little stronger.'

Now you come to mention it…

'Let's get this shopping back to my apartment and we'll get our glad rags on and go out and enjoy your last night.'

Is it really time to fly home tomorrow already?

'It's gone so quickly,' I pout, not sure I'm ready to revert to my everyday life. I like New York and the promise it holds. Even on the lowest of days it seems to pick you up and give you hope that everything will come good in the end.

We walk back to Mum's apartment, at a very leisurely pace as my shopping bags seem to have mysteriously gained weight, or maybe it's just that my arms are saying enough is enough. I suggest at one point that we take the short ride on the subway instead, but this is dismissed with a look of disapproval. Apparently mum has no desire to experience everything authentic about New York.

Once we have made it home I head for a long soak in the bath and take the liberty of using every one of mum's expensive bath and cleansing products. It really has been nice to take a few days out and recharge. I feel like I'm in a bubble here, protected from the unkind events that have beheld me recently but I know as soon as that plane touches back down tomorrow the bubble will burst as I bounce back in to reality.

Before we leave to go out for food I touch base with Sophie: *Weirdest couple of days ever. Crossed parental discussion boundaries that should never be crossed. Hope you're OK. I've missed you. Can't wait to catch up. x x*

The response is short and sweet: *I hope you remembered something with DKNY on for me...xxxx*

Ah, she didn't forget. I did promise Sophie that the next time I came to New York I would take her back a DKNY purse. Well, I didn't promise exactly but she dropped enough hints that I'd be an idiot if I didn't pick up on the fact that she wanted one; she's spent enough time gushing over mine. I guess I'd better make that purchase at the airport.

My last night in New York is a complete hoot. I don't think I've laughed this hard in a long time. It's just what I need, having felt like I've been on an emotional rollercoaster for the last week. I hadn't realised my mum could be that much fun and I see a side to her that I didn't even know existed.

We go to the most exceptionally pretentious restaurant near Central Park, where we spend the evening people watching, making fun of their behaviour and generally conducting ourselves in a way that perhaps isn't the norm in these types of places. At one point, while we're enjoying a nightcap of very yummy rum and Coke at the bar, the head waiter asks us, in a condescending manner, to 'Keep the noise down, please'. He looks so serious and appalled at our enjoying ourselves a little too much that his request is met with raucous laughter from us both. After that we decide to get the bill and leave, before we upset any more members of the posh clientele and my mother is never allowed back there.

We link arms as we walk, a little merrily, back to Mum's apartment through the park. Even now, in the dark and cold, Central Park has an aura of magic around it, although the wind chill is still less than desirable here; that's one thing for which I don't envy Mum.

'I don't think you'll be welcomed back there in a hurry,' I giggle.

'Oh well. There are plenty of other snobbish establishments for people to look down their noses at me in so don't you worry about that.' Mum smiles. 'Those haughty old buggers should learn to lighten up a little and have a bit of fun instead of always looking like they've sat on a sharp pin.'

'Well, I really had fun tonight.'

'Me too, darling. Don't let it be so long until you visit again this time.'

'I won't. I promise.'

I yawn, feeling exhausted. It's been a whirlwind couple of days but Mum was right: it was just what I needed. Tonight has been the perfect night. For a while I forgot that I was out with my mum. For the most part it felt like we were sisters. She treated me like an adult and not a small child, and I've actually enjoyed the honesty of our conversations about our lives and relationships. It feels like we've grown that little bit closer despite the several thousand miles that usually divide us.

The following morning I throw everything into my suitcase with an underlying feeling of apprehension. I know I need to go home and deal with the fact that I'm newly single again, but I can't disperse the feelings of extreme anger I get at the mere thought of Chris and whoever this woman is. It still feels raw and I'm not really sure how I'm going to achieve closure on this, but I know in my heart I'm not going to be able to move on emotionally until I do. Maybe the seven-hour flight home will provide an opportunity for reflection?

Or maybe I'll just pick up a new book at the airport – distraction therapy has its benefits, I'm sure.

'All done?' Mum asks as I drag my coat and suitcase through to the kitchen, where I'm greeted by the wonderful smells of freshly brewed coffee – not a hint of instant anywhere in the apartment – and warm pastries. Probably a good job I'm going home. Any more days of eating like this and I would be going back a dress size bigger. I have no idea how Mum stays so slim. Come to think of it, it must be the 'no driving' thing here. Breakfast will be burned off by the time you've power walked to work.

'Yep, everything is packed.' I discard my case next to the doorway and ignore it as it topples over.

'I made coffee.' She holds out a steaming mug. 'There are croissants in the oven too. The taxi won't be here for another half an hour.'

'You don't have to come to the airport with me, Mum. I will be fine in the taxi on my own.'

'Don't be silly, darling. I want to wave you off, and I don't have to be in work until this afternoon, so it's fine.'

'Okay, if you're sure.'

'I'm sure.' She nods.

I open the oven and take out two red-hot croissants and my stomach grumbles its approval. By the time I'm drinking the last of my second cup of coffee the intercom buzzes, signalling the arrival of the taxi. Mum carries my case down the stairs and we climb into the car. As we head back towards Newark Airport it feels like only two minutes have passed since I arrived. I stare out of the window as we drive through the suburbs to the interstate, watching people going about their day. Being in New York always feels like you're in a movie set and I forget sometimes that it's real. I always think it would be amazing to live here, but my world back home in England is actually pretty good too, if you exclude the disastrous love life: I earn decent money and have a good circle of friends.

At the airport Mum gets a little emotional as we hug goodbye when they announce my boarding gate at Departures.

'Life might not always turn out just the way we planned it, darling, but I know that you will find someone who loves you and who is worthy of you. He just hasn't found you yet.'

'And how do you know that?' I raise my eyebrows a little sceptically.

'Because I'm your mother, that's how, Emma. Now have a good flight and text me when you arrive home.'

'Okay.' I can't help but smile.

She kisses me on the cheek and I grab my case and wheel it towards the security barrier. I have a small lump in my throat as I turn and wave goodbye before I head through the final grey steel door.

Chapter Six

When I land back in England at what should be late afternoon, the time magically skips forward by five hours to late evening and a time when I should be in bed. I am, after all, back at work tomorrow following my frivolous three days of shopping, eating and drinking far too much coffee. Thankfully I make it through passport control and collect my luggage in a reasonable time and the queue for a taxi moves quickly, so it's not too long before I'm putting the key in my front door and I'm home.

I think the jet lag from the first flight, let alone the return flight, has caught up with me now. My whole body feels groggy and heavy as I wheel my suitcase into the lounge, before abandoning it and heading straight for the comfort of my own bed. I barely manage to take my clothes off before I collapse onto the mattress, pull the covers up and over my head and fall asleep.

I wake in a state of disarray the following morning, unsure of where I am and what time zone I'm in. It takes me a few seconds to realise I'm back in England and that horrible sound ringing in my ears is the alarm clock doing its utmost to get me out of bed. I reach a hand from under the warm quilt and give it a thwack, which thankfully silences it. Begrudgingly I flip back the covers and shuffle towards the bathroom, conscious that I need to take extra care with my beauty regime this morning following Jenny's comments about my wayward hair on my last day at work.

'So how was New York?' Lola bounds up to me as I walk through the back door of the shop an hour later.

'It was great, thanks. I've had a really good few days.'

'I'm so jealous. The shops are meant to be amazing out there,' she gushes.

'They are pretty good, and I did make sure I tried out as many as I could.' I laugh. 'Where's Jenny?'

'She's just updating some stuff on the till. Do you want a cuppa?'

'Yes, please.'

I walk through to the shop floor where Jenny is tapping away on the electronic till.

'Morning.'

'Hey, Emma. How are you?' Jenny studies me.

'I'm much better, thanks, and I just wanted to say thanks again for letting me have the time off at short notice.'

'No problem. I know you'd do the same for me.'

'Well, I promise you I'll be the perfect work colleague from now on.'

Surprisingly the day whizzes by and it's five thirty p.m. before I know it. As we lock up the shop and I wave goodbye to Jenny I contemplate what to do with myself this evening. Sophie isn't coming over until later, but I don't feel like going home alone just yet. While wandering to my car I make the decision to call in on my other best friend, Simon. He's always up for a good gossip and I want to show him all of the pictures on my phone that I took of New York. He usually doesn't go out until late on a Friday night – that's how he manages to still stay up until three a.m. now he's hit thirty. The later he goes out, the best chance he has of not falling asleep in the corner of some bar.

I knock on Simon's apartment door but there's no answer. I'm disappointed. I was hoping to surprise him as I haven't spoken to him since I left for New York on Tuesday morning. He can't have gone far, I muse. It's too early for him to have gone out partying yet. I rummage around in the bottom of my handbag for my keys. He gave me a spare set for emergencies after the third time he managed to lose his own set while drunk and lock himself out at some unearthly hour. As far as I'm concerned this qualifies as an emergency – as well as being in much need of caffeine and gossip, more importantly, I also desperately need the loo.

As I turn the key in the lock and push the door open I am met with a scene that will scar me for life. Nothing in my whole life's experience could have ever prepared me for what my eyes have just been forced to witness.

'Jesus, Emma!' Simon shrieks, standing up abruptly with his manhood on show. Really, I could have made it happily through my life without ever having to see that.

Oh shit. Um. I cover my eyes with my hands.

'Oh God. I'm so sorry. I'll just wait outside. No, don't worry. I'll… I'll just go,' I stutter, backing quickly out of the apartment. 'Ow.' I clatter clumsily into the door frame, giving my elbow a good thump in the process, but even this doesn't prompt me to remove my hands from my eyes until I'm safely back in the corridor and the door to a world I didn't ever wish to see is firmly closed.

Holy crap. I rub at my elbow vigorously, trying to disperse the pain, as my brain attempts to process and then discard forever the scene I have just witnessed. That was...unexpected.

The door behind me creaks open and I cringe as I turn around, knowing my cheeks are burning so hot you could grill bacon on them.

'So you're back then?' Simon smirks at me with raised eyebrows. I can't tell if he's mad or amused.

'I'm so, so sorry.' I hold up my hands in apology. 'I had no idea...'

'What? That I might have company on a Friday afternoon?'

'That you might be entertaining that company, naked, on a Friday at only six o'clock is more the surprise,' I offer, still mortified at my intrusion.

'Don't be such a prude, Em.'

Really? That's being a prude?

'If it's any consolation, you gave James a good fright too. He couldn't get his clothes back on quickly enough. Oh yeah, thanks for that.'

'I...' I close my mouth, realising nothing that I can say will make this situation any less hideous or remove the trauma experienced by all three parties involved.

'It's okay.' Simon sighs dramatically. 'He's just not used to women seeing him naked, that's all. You sure know how to kill the mood, Em.'

I press my lips together hard to try to prevent the giggle inside me escaping. It's not funny and I cannot laugh. I cannot laugh.

It's no good. I feel my bottom lip beginning to quiver and then I can't help it: the laugh bubbles out. Just a little giggle at first, but then it quickly builds until my shoulders are heaving and tears are starting to roll down my face. Simon starts laughing then too and that just makes it worse. I have to lean on the wall for support as I gasp for breath. Simon bends over, holding his stomach.

We're both caught in this weirdly embarrassing but inescapably funny moment when the door opens and a man, who I presume is James – last time I saw him he was naked and facing away from me – appears sheepishly in the doorway. I gulp down my laughter and just stare awkwardly at him for a few seconds before, thankfully, Simon speaks.

'So, shall we hook up again next Friday – minus the buzz kill?' He elbows me none too gently in the ribs while flashing what must be his pulling smile at James.

'Sure.' James smiles shyly, looking at his feet, clearly mortified, although nowhere near as embarrassed as me. 'Catch you on Friday.' He nods at Simon first, then at me. I instinctively nod back. Why? What am I nodding at? I'm certainly not going to be seeing James again, same time, same place, next week.

'I'll call you,' Simon calls after him and James turns around and smiles again.

'Seriously?' I cringe. 'I'll call you? Do people even say things like that any more and mean it? Isn't that code for "You're never going to hear from me ever again"?'

'Tsk. Come on, Miss Pessimistic. Let's get you inside before you do any more damage to my life.'

Simon ushers me into his flat and through to the kitchen. 'I think we both need a drink.' He raises his eyebrows while rooting through the cupboard in search of a tasty numbing agent. He retrieves a bottle of red wine and goes about de-corking it while I grab two wine glasses from the kitchen cupboard.

'How's your elbow?' he giggles, pouring wine into the glasses. 'You didn't half look funny trying to back yourself out of the giant hole you'd just bungee-jumped into.'

'It still really hurts,' I mutter. 'And it will definitely bruise.'

'Hah. I bet it doesn't hurt half as much as my bruised ego.' Simon necks half of his glass of wine. 'I don't think in all my shenanigans I've ever done anything that's made the sexual tension deflate like a burst balloon and my date get the hell out of there thirty seconds after.' He shakes his head at me.

'Knowing you as I do, I find that hard to believe.' I smirk, but Simon shoots me a dagger stare. Maybe I've exceeded the point of making jokes about Simon's sex life today.

'Okay, okay. I'm so sorry.' I take a large gulp of my own wine. 'In fact, I'm so sorry I ever decided to drop over unannounced and let myself into your apartment. Believe me, I've learnt my lesson. Never again.'

'Never again?'

'I don't need to see your white naked ass ever again,' I joke.

'What do you mean? I have an amazing ass.' Simon looks hurt.

'As it is, I might need a course of therapy to deal with the vision of seeing you and, well, another man in the throes of passion.'

'God, you have an elaborate way of saying things. It's just sex, babe. Plain and simple.'

'It didn't look that plain and simple from where I was standing.' I purse my lips.

'Enough, enough! Let's just say that, going forward, that the key I gave you is for actual emergencies, like I'm locked out at five a.m., or there's a sale at Jean Paul Gaultier, or you've found a decent boyfriend for once.'

'Hey!' I punch him in the arm.

'Come on. Chris wasn't all bad, but he was a bit of a wuss.'

'I liked to think of him as romantic.' I sigh.

'Yeah well, never mind all that. It's in the past. Now why don't you tell me how fabulous New York is?'

Chapter Seven

Later that evening Sophie comes over for wine and, well, more wine. It's only been five days since I last saw her, but despite our texts, I realise I've really missed her.

'How are you?' She hugs me tightly as I help her through the front door and offload the large shopping bag that's weighing her down.

'Jesus, Sophie, what's in here?'

'Just some wine and nibbles as promised.' She smiles.

'I'm okay thanks.' I nod. 'I'm fine. In fact, I'm better than fine. A few days' break was just what I needed to get things into perspective.'

'Yeah, and I bet your mum was a good distraction from everything.' She raises her eyebrows comically.

I sometimes forget that Sophie has known my mum for pretty much as long as I have, and she witnessed the transformation of our family life first-hand when Mum and Dad divorced. Mum always treated Sophie like a second daughter; she was round at our house so often. As she only lived two streets away we pretty much spent every spare moment together: playing in the paddling pool, playing dolls, playing nurses, hating boys, daydreaming about boys and, finally, dating boys. At every stage of our lives our friendship has remained strong – except for that one summer when we were fourteen where teenage hormones took over and we both fancied the same boy and our friendship was tested, but we were soon best friends again and said boy was long forgotten.

'Mum does have a good knack of making me realise that I'm normal, for the most part anyway, and that my life isn't completely crazy. But she's also really good at making me rationalise things, mainly through her straight-talking, no-bullshit approach to whatever crisis is brewing. I guess she doesn't do tea and sympathy much any more.'

'Yeah? Well, I guess she's seen a lot, and maybe put up with a lot living in New York.'

'Speaking of New York, I brought you back a little souvenir,' I tease.

'You didn't!' Sophie struggles to hide her excitement.

'Oh, but I did.' I reach into a carrier bag on the kitchen worktop and proudly produce the DKNY purse.

'Oh my God, Emma! I was only kidding. They're so expensive.'

'It's okay. My mum spoiled me loads so I hardly spent any money out there. She wouldn't let me pay for anything and she went halves with me on your purse, so you have her to thank too.'

'Thank you!' Sophie squeals, clutching it like her life depends on it. 'I love it.'

'I'm glad you like it,' I say, genuinely pleased that I have made her so happy. 'You're my best friend and you deserve it for putting up with me and my varying emotional states since Chris and I...'

'You're the best friend a girl could have,' she says, beaming from ear to ear.

'If only men knew how simple it was to make us happy.' I sigh.

'Wouldn't life be much simpler?'

I reach up into a cupboard and grab two wine glasses. Mooching through the shopping bag, I take out two bottles of white wine, a mix of antipasti and some bread that still feels warm, and suddenly I feel starving.

'Has he been in touch?' Sophie asks tentatively.

'Chris? No.' I shake my head.

'Maybe it's for the best.'

'Maybe.'

'I mean, would you really want to take him back after he's cheated, even if he begged?'

A vision of Chris on his hands and knees declaring his love for me and admitting his stupidity passes fleetingly through my mind. I exhale deeply. 'If I'm completely honest then I guess not. I'm just pissed that he's extinguished me from his life so easily and moved on with his new, or not so new, conquest.'

'What did your mum have to say about it?'

'Not much other than things happen for a reason, there's someone else better out there for me, all that kind of shit.'

Sophie nods, taking a sip of wine.

'Oh yes, and that she never really liked Chris anyway.'

Sophie nearly spits her wine out on the kitchen floor. 'I see what you mean about the tea and sympathy.'

'Maybe she's right,' I concede. 'Well, at least I hope she is and there's someone somewhere I might have a chance of finding love with again.'

'I suppose she has experienced first-hand starting her life over when I'm guessing she didn't think she ever would be.'

'I know. I found it hard at first to deal with the fact that she was living a whole different life, seemingly having left me and Dad behind, but I've learnt to accept it. She had separated from Dad long before she went to New York. She's my mum, though, so no matter where she's living – and it just so happens that she's living in the best city in the world – I know she's always there for me. But I'm a big girl and I have you and Simon to lean on as and when required, so it's okay that she's only on the end of a phone most of the time rather than here in person.'

'At least both she and your dad are happy now, even if that is with other people.'

'Speaking of that, I met one of Mum's male friends.'

'Really?' Sophie's eyes widen. 'What's he like?'

'Rich, posh, dressed from head to toe in designer clothes.'

'Sounds like your mum has things pretty sorted.'

'He has dyed brown hair.'

'Oh.' Sophie cringes a little, clearly of the same opinion as me where that's concerned.

'Speaking of "male friends", I have also very recently seen Simon's current love squeeze.' I shake my head quickly to disperse the image.

'How come? He's usually so secretive. He never lets us meet his boyfriends.'

'Meet' might be a little inaccurate. I don't think exchanging awkward glances in the doorway constitutes a meeting.

'Yeah, well, if you walk in on them having sex then he doesn't really have much choice in the matter.'

'What?' Sophie stares at me, her mouth gaping open in a perfect 'O'.

'Yep, and that's not something that any relatively sane human being ever needs to see.'

'Oh my God. What did you do?'

'What do you mean "What did I do"? As soon as I realised what I had stumbled upon I got the hell out of there as fast as I could. I don't know which of the three of us was more embarrassed.'

I top up her glass of wine and slosh a little more into my own glass.

'I bet that was a bit of a mood killer.'

'Apparently so. Simon wasn't very impressed that his Friday afternoon of passion was cut short.' I giggle, covering my eyes at the memory.

'Too much information.' Sophie giggles too.

'Come on, enough of that. I'm trying desperately to forget I ever saw Simon's...'

'No, don't go there! Let's take the food through to the lounge.'

I flick through the music channels on the television and find 'Hits of the Nineties'. It's not long before we are both dancing around the living room, looking completely uncool, with both the old-school tunes and the wine in full flow.

'So how are things going with you and your new bloke?' I ask, munching on a handful of olives while swinging my hips and, unbelievably, not spilling any of the wine from the glass in my hand. For some unexplained reason I excel at multitasking when I'm drunk.

'It's going okay.'

'Just okay?' I look at her sceptically; she's always been a bad liar.

'No. I'm trying to play it down. I think I'm really falling for him.' She glances at her feet, looking apprehensive.

'Really?' I stop dancing for a second and the room wobbles a little.

'Really.'

'Good. It's about time one of us had some luck on the love front.' I gulp down the last of my wine, suddenly feeling slightly sorry for myself and on the fringes of being emotional as well as drunk. The mood in the room saddens a little as the edges get fuzzier, or is that just me?

'I think we're running out of wine. I'll fetch the other bottle.' I blink back tears that have sprung from nowhere and head to the kitchen. As I reach for the wine in the fridge Sophie appears in the doorway.

'Hey, are you alright?' She reaches out and touches my arm.

I lean forward with both hands on the worktop and hang my head.

'I really thought Chris was the one, you know.' I bite my lip.

'I know.' Sophie grabs my hand and squeezes it tightly. 'He had us all fooled.'

'He just…got me, or at least I thought he did. We clicked right from the start. I'm still struggling to understand how we spent so much time together yet he was living a double life and I never saw it. I feel like such an idiot.'

'No one thinks you're an idiot. Anyone who saw the two of you together would have believed that you were the perfect couple.'

'Perfect? It's funny how you don't see things at the time, but when it's all over and you're alone in bed at night, staring at the ceiling, the cracks that had started to appear in your relationship become startlingly clear.'

'What do you mean?'

'Like, it was me every time who started the conversations about us moving in together. He always went along with it but never really engaged with the idea as a reality. It was even me who brought up the subject of marriage. When I think back now his reaction was more "Let's see what the future brings", which I took to mean that it might be what he was thinking our future would hold, when actually he was just shutting me up until he could find the right time to tell me he was sleeping with someone else. I should have known.'

'I'm so angry at him,' Sophie huffs.

'Me too. He was the first guy I really trusted and, you know, actually let in.' I gesture towards my heart. 'He made me feel like I was special. I don't think I realised it at the time, but in my previous relationships I didn't ever think of my future with the guy, or look to plan serious things like houses and marriage. I never even considered it – none of them were going to be the one that I spent the rest of my life with.'

'I know you found it hard to see for yourself that one day you'd find someone who made you want all of those things. I know you've always had misgivings about marriage because of your mum and dad getting divorced.'

'If my mum and dad, who seemed so happy for all those years, couldn't make it work then I've always figured that I don't stand a chance. But with Chris I felt like I'd changed fate.'

'So what made it different with Chris?'

'Intimacy. And I'm not just talking about sex. I'm talking about intimacy in everything we did. We talked about literally everything. Every time we were together we were intimate, whether that was lying together on the sofa watching television or holding hands in the street. It was like that from the very beginning.

'You know, I think the first time that I actually felt like he loved me and that he could be "the one" was when I was really ill last year with tonsillitis.'

'I remember; you were in bed for a week.'

'Yeah, I felt so poorly. But after work Chris would come to my house and make me warm honey and tea to help soothe my throat, and then he would just lie on the bed next to me and cuddle me until I went to sleep. It was at that point I realised that he could be the one I would spend the rest of my life with. If he was prepared to look after me when I resembled Medusa on a bad day and sounded like a drag queen then I thought he was in it for the long haul.'

'I know. I actually used to envy you for that. Most of my previous boyfriends have had serious intimacy issues and even more issues with public displays of affection, never daring to even hold hands let alone kiss me in public. In fact, I remember the last one, Darren, physically pulling his hand away like he'd been burnt with a hot poker when I tried to hold his hand while we were out shopping. What's wrong with men?'

'I could provide you with a very long list,' I offer. 'But you don't need to worry about all of that now. From what you keep saying to me, Connor doesn't fall into the emotionally challenged category.'

'No, Connor's different. He has no issues with being affectionate so far, either in public or behind closed doors.'

'I can remember that new relationship feeling. ' I sigh heavily. 'It feels like a lifetime ago since I met Chris. Do you remember that night?'

'How could I forget? We were at the local music festival thinking we were trendy and down with the kids, and for once the weather was brilliant.'

'Too hot, in fact. We had to keep drinking all that beer to cool us down.' I giggle.

'We were a bit wasted, weren't we?'

'Erm, I like to think of it as merry,' I protest.

'You would.'

'Well, Chris didn't seem to mind.'

'No – he was as drunk as we were when he asked you to dance.'

'God, I daren't imagine how many people were staring at us as he flung me round on the makeshift dance floor to the sounds of Green Day.'

'I think everyone was too drunk to care.'

'Have you noticed that there is a pattern in our lives in that we include alcohol in everything we do?'

'I don't see that as a problem.' Sophie raises her eyebrows skywards before talking a large gulp of her fresh glass of wine.

'No, I can imagine you don't, Miss Pinot Grigio.'

'The subject here isn't me; it's you.'

'Not at the moment, anyway, but there's still time.'

She sticks her tongue out playfully at me. 'Do you remember when you introduced Chris to Simon?'

'I don't know who was more afraid.'

'Si's always been really protective of you, even when we nine years old and playing at the local park at the end of our street. He and I always got on, but he treated you like his little sister.'

'Well, I guess in some ways he was like the brother I never had, us both being only children and living next door to one another.'

'I know he gave Chris a hard time for the first few months.'

'Yeah, he wanted to make sure he was good enough for me. And you know what? After four months Simon sat me down with a large vodka and tonic and told me he didn't think he was.'

'Really? You never told me that.'

'I suppose I didn't take it that seriously. I know Simon means well, but his view on what makes a good prospective partner is very different to mine.'

'Well, of course.' Sophie nods mockingly. 'I mean he's looking for a sultry, sexy man, and you're looking for…?'

'You may have a point.' I shake my head. 'And as fate would have it, I should have listened to him. I was just swept of my feet by Chris. He was quite the romancer at the time. Actually he probably still is now, which is why I'm in this mess. He just went off and romanced someone more desirable.'

'Don't be so hard on yourself.' Sophie tops up our glasses. 'I remember you telling me he told you that he had wanted to ask you out for weeks before he built up the courage to ask you to dance that night.'

'I know. He said he used to see me in town sometimes but he always chickened out. But once we were together he would tell me how special I was, that I was beautiful. He made me feel like I was the only girl in the world.' I bite my lip. 'Do you know what, Soph?'

'What?' She smiles kindly.

'I've just about had enough of being sad and moping around, going over the last two years in my head like some morbid tribute. He's moved on. Admittedly he moved on before actually telling me he had, but still. He's moved on, and I need to. I need to just…get over him.' And to do that I require more wine, or whatever spirit I can find left over from Christmas that I can drink to give me the courage I need, or at least to help me drown my sorrows for good.

'Look, Em, you know I love you, but I don't think it's that simple. I don't think you can just decide to get over someone in an instant and expect it to happen. Not when you –'

'Not when you what, Sophie? Had started planning a wedding in your head that Chris had no intention of even asking you to attend?'

'Well, yes. You saw your future with him.'

'And he clearly didn't see his with me. So that's it. We do not talk about him any more. He is dead to me. I'm not going to waste a moment more of my time whining over that piece of crap. I'm done.' I wave my arms emphatically to make my point.

Sophie just stares at me with what appears to be a mixture of worry and scepticism.

'Now.' I return my attention to drinking. 'I think I have vodka in the kitchen cupboard?'

'So let's keep this as our little secret, eh? Dad doesn't need to know, because there's nothing to tell, okay?'
'Okay.'
'It will just be our little secret.'

Chapter Eight

Okay, so my bravado lasts all of thirty-six hours. That is until I realise it's been two weeks since Chris dropped that bombshell and I left him looking decidedly uncomfortable in the restaurant as I ran for the hills, and I haven't heard a word from him since – not even a text. It's like he's disappeared into a puff of smoke and I'm already a long-distant memory. Maybe it's for the best, I try to convince myself. I mean, what else is there to say to each other? I don't really trust myself to try to speak to him face to face anyway; I'm still too angry. I have been swaying between coping incredibly well and carrying on with my life in a normal fashion and resorting to intermittent crying in the toilet at work. I need to start buying shares in concealer, I've used that much of it on my dark, puffy eyes.

Sophie is doing her best to console me by calling me every night 'for a chat' (really to make sure I haven't slit my wrists or thrown a toaster in the bath with me), but hearing about her loved-up, exciting new relationship is doing little to boost my diminishing morale. She's made me delete Chris's mobile number and email address from my phone so I don't drunk-contact him to tell him how much I miss him and that I might want him back (despite the hideousness of his behaviour) or, alternatively, what a complete wanker he is – neither of which will do much good now or in the long term. Okay, maybe telling him he's a wanker might make me feel a tiny bit better for at least an hour or so. In fact, in anticipation of Sophie making me delete Chris's contact details, I wrote them down on a small piece of paper (although I think I've pretty much memorised them over the last two years) and hid it in my underwear drawer. But Sophie doesn't need to know that.

On the second occasion this week that Jenny, my friend and confidante, finds me snivelling next to the kettle at work, devouring a packet of chocolate digestives, she announces that I am now her 'project' and it's her mission to get me to forget Chris and the last two years of my life. Half of me does agree with her that I need to start to detach – he is, after all, not coming back. He has *her* in his life now, not me. Bastard. But the other half of me is sceptical. It doesn't like change and it wants to wallow in self-pity for a while longer. I'm also deeply concerned as to what her 'project' will entail.

As it turns out I was right to be concerned. It's Friday night and I stupidly agreed yesterday, admittedly under some emotional pressure, to go out into town tonight with Jenny and Lola, the super cool and twenty-something fashionista. I know it's a bad idea from the start as they both drink tequila like its Diet Coke, barely pausing long enough to take a breath between shots. I saw their drinking habits in action at the Christmas party and I'm a little scared; make that very scared. I'm conscious that I've gone through practically a whole vineyard of wine in the last fortnight and the answer might not be at the bottom of a bottle, but hell, I've been thorough in my attempt to test the theory. I know I need to pull myself together and I make a silent promise to start doing that from Monday of next week, if I can just make it through tonight's events alive, whatever they may hold for me. I'd like to take advantage of one last weekend of being unhinged and unbalanced.

At eight o'clock I hover apprehensively in the doorway of Jacob's wine bar on the High Street. I'm suddenly getting cold feet and wondering if this is such a good idea after all. But what's the alternative? Spending another night downing a bottle of Sauvignon Blanc, watching the Cookery Channel while some perfect housewife/model makes recipes I have no intention of even attempting? That's just depressing. With that thought in the forefront of my mind I push the door open and step gingerly into the danger zone, where I'm immediately greeted by a mass of chatter mixed with a vibrant dance tune. It's not hard to spot Jenny and Lola waving at me from across the room and I'm already moving to the beat of the music as I sashay over to them.

Three vodka-and-Cokes later and I'm convinced that Jenny was right to drag me here tonight. It's exactly what I need. A distraction, to let loose, let my hair down after three very, very shitty weeks (my time in New York excluded). I'm still trying to convince her that I don't need setting up with the barman in her local pub, despite her claims that he's very hot, when Lola wobbles back over to our table and giggles naughtily as she places on it a salt shaker, three wedges of lemon and three shot glasses filled with what I can only presume is tequila. My heart sinks. This is bad. Very, very bad. No good has ever, or will ever, come from drinking tequila. I can smell the distinctive fumes already and it almost turns my stomach. I look down at the table hesitantly.

'You're not going to wuss out on us now, are you?' Lola waves one of the shot glasses in my direction, clearly seeing the look of horror on my face.

'Come on. In for a penny, in for a pound.' Jenny nudges me playfully, then reaches for her own shot glass. 'You are a grown woman, though; you can do what you like. No pressure.'

I'm a grown woman who can make her own decisions; I do know that. I might not always very good at making decisions, but still, I'm pretty sure that passing out and waking up in a pool of my own vomit is not what I'd like to do this evening. I glance from Jenny to Lola, and then back to Jenny. They're both staring at me, holding their shot glasses aloft, waiting for me to join them. I'm clearly not going to get a reprieve. No pressure, my arse. Oh what the hell. I pick up the glass and they both giggle in unison. Lola offers the salt shaker and I take it, reluctantly sprinkling a small amount of putrid grit onto the back of my hand.

'Three, two, one!' Jenny shouts like we're in an eighteen-to-thirties' bar in Ibiza and with that I shut my eyes, lick the salt and down my shot. It flips rebelliously in my stomach as I bite into a lemon wedge.

Urgh. That is disgusting. My whole body shudders in agreement.

'Another round?' Jenny jumps up from her seat, gathering up our empty shot glasses.

That wasn't as bad as I thought. I suppose another one won't hurt…

Three shots later I'm relieved that both Jenny and Lola have decided to call it a night. The room has started to take on a fuzzy edge and I'm dancing in a manner I wouldn't dream of when sober. I'm pretty sure my moves resemble those I was shaking down with Sophie in the privacy of my own living room only a few days ago, and that's really where they should have stayed.

'We can all jump in a taxi together,' Lola offers.

'No, don't worry – I live in the total opposite direction of you two.' I shake my head and the whole room wobbles with me. That can't be good. 'I'll get my own taxi.'

'We can't let you go home alone.' Jenny frowns.

'Don't be silly. I am thirty-two years old.' I stand with my hands on my hips defiantly. 'I might be a bit drunk but I'm more than capable of getting myself home in one piece.'

They both stare at me unhappily. Jenny has an overly concerned, motherly look about her. Honestly, I do not understand why she treats me like a baby sister. I'm the same age as her and I'm a mature, independent woman, or something to that effect.

'I insist,' I state, fumbling for my handbag on the seat behind me.

'Excuse me, this is for you.' A bar girl appears out of nowhere behind me and places a drink on the table in front of me. I catch her arm just as she's about to disappear again.

'I didn't order a drink.' I hand the glass back to her but she doesn't move to take it from me.

'Courtesy of the guy at the bar.' She nods over to her right and I see who I think at first glance is Justin Timberlake, leaning casually on a bar stool, smiling sheepishly over at me.

'But…' Now the bar girl has disappeared completely. I glance back over to the bar and see that it's not actually *the* Justin Timberlake smiling at me but he certainly bears a resemblance to him. I turn back round to Jenny and Lola who are gawping at me incredulously.

'You know what?' I say, taking a sniff of the glass and deciding that it smells quite like the vodka and Coke I was enjoying earlier before the nasty tequila. 'I think I might stay for just one more drink.'

'Erm, I don't think so.' Jenny's tone is so disapproving that I laugh out loud.

'Jenny, I will be fine.'

She glares over towards the bar. 'Just because some good-looking guy sends a drink over doesn't mean you have to accept it.'

'That's right.' I nod, lacking some conviction, as I slurp from the glass in my hand. 'Aren't you the one who's been telling me for the last week that I need to have some fun?'

'Well...' Jenny huffs, rather flustered. 'He could be an axe murderer for all you know.'

'That is true,' I agree, glancing over at cute bar guy. 'But unless he intends to brandish his axe and murder me right here in front of a hundred witnesses then I think I'm safe, don't you?'

They both hover, twitching, clearly weighing up whether to stay as my chaperones or admit defeat.

'I promise I will not leave here with the axe murderer. I will only stay for one drink – just one – and then I will get a taxi home, alone,' I try to reassure them. 'Honestly I'm a big girl.'

'You promise?' Lola glances over my shoulder and inspects the guy again, who appears to be watching us intently.

'I promise.' I nod.

They reluctantly leave and walk towards the door, and as I wave them goodbye, I hear a voice behind me.

'Can I join you?'

I turn around and am face to face with the Mr Timberlake Lookalike, who is even more gorgeous up close. His warm blue eyes have a glint of mischief in them, and a soft smile turns up at the corners of his mouth, creating the smallest of dimples. I love dimples. Wavy, thick blond hair is cut short and styled, and I have to fight the urge to reach up and run my fingers through it.

'It would be rude to say no given that you've paid for my drink,' I say, sounding self-assured. The alcohol is fuelling my confidence, which would ordinarily have disintegrated by now, turning me into a mumbling idiot.

He gestures for me to sit down and I shuffle into the vacant booth to my left, taking a further sip of my free drink. He sits down surprisingly close beside me and I can smell the faint scent of his after-shave – crisp and fresh – and that, along with his close proximity, is a heady mixture.

'I'm Johnny.' He smiles, not taking his eyes off me for a second, and I feel my insides somersault with a desire I didn't know was still in me after the last few weeks.

'I'm…' I pause. 'I'm Louise,' I lie, deciding that maybe tonight I can be someone else, somebody totally different, someone carefree, and not a thirty-two-year-old reject, recently dumped out of the one relationship she actually thought was going somewhere. Any-way, Louise…yes, I can be Louise, who works in marketing and is super-sexy and confident.

'So, Louise, tell me something about yourself.'

Hmm. Something about myself? Well, about Louise…Marketing isn't quite exciting enough…

'I'm a lawyer,' I blurt out.

'Wow.' Johnny smiles, seeming more than a little impressed. 'A lawyer. That's pretty serious stuff. Have you tried any cases?'

Shit. I wasn't expecting the third degree. I was hoping just the lawyer thing would be good enough to impress him.

'Erm, I really can't talk about individual cases.' I sip the vodka and Coke. 'Confidentiality issues.' Christ, I don't know how that came to me. I guess I've watched far too many crime programmes on television.

'Of course.' He nods.

'So what do you do?' I ask, keen to divert the subject away from me and my fake career.

'I'm a sports physio.'

That makes sense. He looks pretty toned himself. In fact, he looks incredibly hot; almost too good to be true.

And so the conversation continues. He tells me about his friends, all sporty footballing types, and his family, an older brother and younger sister, and we chat comfortably, like we've know each other for ages. The DJ seems to keep upping the volume so we have to sit closer and closer together to be heard. He's leaning in to hear me as I tell him about my fake life as Louise and he's paying attention to my every word. It's surprising how easily the lies fall from my mouth once I've got going and I'm almost regretting not telling the truth as there's definitely chemistry between us. Mind you, I doubt I will see him ever again after tonight so I guess it doesn't really matter. It's not like I think from one drunken conversation that Johnny could potentially become my boyfriend. This is just Friday night flirting, plain and simple.

'Another drink?' Johnny asks, noticing my empty glass.

I'm tempted, really tempted, but a tiny, sensible voice somewhere deep in the back of my head is shouting through the drunken fog, 'It's late. Go home. You have drunk enough tonight. Leave now before you end up even more drunk and you fall flat on your face.' The voice is right; that really is something that would happen to me.

'That's very kind,' I say, 'but it's getting late and I think I'd better be going home. Do you have some friends you need me to help you find?' For the first time since Johnny joined me it's occurred to me that he's alone.

He glances round the bar. 'I think they must have moved on. Don't worry, I'll text them.'

'Okay.' I pick my bag up from the table and get to my feet a little unsteadily. Shit. How much did I drink tonight?

'I'll walk you to a taxi.' Johnny smiles. 'Just to make sure you're safe.'

Hmm, chivalry? That's quite rare these days...

We slalom through the throngs of revellers still intent on partying long into the night and finally reach the door. As we step out onto the street I feel the rush of fresh air hit me like a sandbag and I wobble.

'Hey, are you alright?' Johnny grabs my elbow and stands me back upright.

'I'm fine, thanks.' I nod, although I don't quite feel fine.

As a taxi pulls up Johnny helps me into the car and then walks round to the other side and climbs in himself.

Hey...what?

'I think you need a cup of coffee or some water, maybe both.' He smiles warmly at me. 'I only live two minutes away. I'll take you back to mine.'

Oh, how convenient. Actually a glass of water does sound nice.

He tells the driver the address. As we pull away from the kerb, I suddenly start to panic. I don't know Johnny that well, or at all really. What if Jenny is right? He could be an axe murderer after all and I'm heading straight into his lair. I promised Lola and Jenny that I wouldn't leave the bar with him. God, I am such an irresponsible idiot. I will probably be subjected to a painful and torturous death and then buried in a shallow grave, left for some dog walker to find, and what for? All for the ego boost of having some hot guy flirt with me? Damn the stupid, poisonous tequila for numbing my sensibilities. Oh, who am I kidding? I'm very rarely sensible. I have dysfunctional written all over me and this is the culmination of my hideous life: a hideous ending.

'Don't worry.' His caramel tones draw me out of my troubled thoughts.

'What?' I glance at him nervously.

'I'm not a psycho or anything. I'll get you some water and a quick coffee so I can make sure you're okay and then I'll get you a taxi home.' He smiles kindly and his dimples reappear.

He doesn't seem like an axe murderer. Having said that I doubt many of them walk around wearing a printed t-shirt which announces their intention to maim and kill. He seems genuine enough, though, and I still feel like I've got some of my wits about me…which is a good job, as the car seems to be slowing down and, yep, Johnny's unclipping his seatbelt and climbing out. He walks around to my side of the car as I fiddle aimlessly with my own seat belt. Finally it releases me. The door opens and he leans in and gently helps me out.

'How are you feeling?' He makes sure I'm upright and standing.

'Actually I feel fine.' And I do. Well, maybe a little drunk and merry but definitely better than I have felt for the last three weeks.

'It's just in here.' Johnny takes my arm and gently steers me towards a smart block of flats which form an enormously tall building in the shape of a large tube with a distinctive cone on top like a party hat. As he buzzes us into the entranceway I notice that everything is clean and shiny and it still has the distinct 'new smell' about it.

'Have you lived here long?' I mutter, taking in the modern art hanging on the walls and the security cameras following our every move.

'No, just moved in a few weeks ago. They're new, just finished.'

'Very nice.' I continue to glance around as we enter the lift.

He presses the button for the top floor and the lift sets off. The unexpected movement disturbs my whole 'I'm not that drunk' notion and I cling to the side for support. It feels like being on the big dipper at the seaside and a slight feeling of nausea creeps in.

Must not be sick. Must not be sick.

We slow to a stop and the doors ping open, revealing yet another clean, shiny corridor. Johnny escorts me out and, with his arm placed at the bottom of my back, he guides me to flat 312.

As we step inside he flicks a switch and soft, warm spotlights light the hallway like an airport runway.

'Go straight down to the kitchen.' He points to a door at the bottom of the hallway and I shuffle carefully towards it.

Physiotherapy must pay pretty well, I muse. This place must cost a fortune. The kitchen looks like something out of a magazine for the rich and famous. White surfaces gleam under more spotlights and every gadget going lines the worktops, but besides that it's very minimalist and clinical. Ooh. I spot an expensive coffee-making machine, one of those where you can make every single drink by just placing a little foil pod into the top of the machine. I wander over to it and start randomly pressing buttons. I've always wanted one of these. I think it would actually be a good investment considering the amount of time and money Sophie and I spend drinking cappuccinos.

'Would you like a demonstration?' Johnny's voice behind me makes me jump and I turn around guiltily, like a child caught with her hand in the sweet jar.

'I'm just jealous,' I blurt out. 'I've always wanted one.'

'Maybe a coffee would do you some good right now.' He smiles and walks over to the sink, takes out a glass from the cupboard above and fills it with water. 'But drink this first.'

I take the glass and sip at the water. See, I tell my conscience, which is still prodding me nervously, he's a gentleman and he's being considerate and has shown me nothing but good manners and kindness. And he's good to talk to. He actually listens, which makes a change. And let's face it, he's pretty hot too.

I watch as Johnny grabs two little foil pods and two mugs and starts pressing buttons on the machine. He clearly presses the 'on' switch first – I missed that one. With a few short whizzes and puffs, two coffees appear and he hands me a mug. I drink the last of the water and place the glass in the sink, clinging on to the steaming hot mug with my other hand.

'Come with me.' He smiles. 'I want to show you something.'

I'm intrigued and a little buzz of adrenaline shoots up my spine as I follow him out of the kitchen and into another room. The lounge is also minimalist with two large cream leather sofas and an obscure creation in the centre of the room which I presume must be a coffee table, although it looks more like a spaceship landing pad.

'Look over here.'

Johnny is standing in front of large glass doors which I hadn't noticed at first, but now I see they frame a view of the whole city. Twinkling lights and illuminations create the most amazing scenery.

'Wow,' I gasp, standing open-mouthed, staring out at the night skyline. It looks like something from a movie. 'I didn't realise this view could exist in real life and look so magical. You must be able to see for miles.'

'Not many people get to see it from this viewpoint. And it is beautiful.'

I realise that he's standing very close to me now as we both gaze out at a mixture of stars and lights. I don't know if it's the water, the coffee or my adrenaline but I'm suddenly feeling a lot sharper and focussed. As I turn to look at Johnny he's already looking at me, and time stops for one tiny instance and we just stand there, caught in a moment. Then, in a second, his lips are on mine; warm and soft, yet demanding. The sensible part of my brain kicks me hard and I know I shouldn't be doing this, but what the hell. It feels good. It feels good to be touched, to be found attractive, for somebody to want me. I kiss him back, feeling the palm of his hand tracing down my spine to the curve in my lower back, which kicks off all sorts of sensations shooting around my body. His hand reaches down to the hem of my dress and pulls it up as he strokes the back of my thigh, and I have to visualise biting my lip to stop myself from screaming out in pleasure.

In a split second of clarity I realise that Chris hadn't made me feel this way for a long time. In fact, it's now glaringly clear that he hadn't touched me this way in a long time. I think that says it all. I should have seen the end of our relationship coming with flashing lights and howling sirens.

As Johnny kisses my neck I can smell his scent, a mixture of the crisp aftershave and a faint hint of soap, and I breathe it in as if my life depends on it.

This is going too fast, way too fast. My conscience screams at me, but I mentally swat it down like a fly and I close my eyes, enjoying the feel of his lips on my skin, enjoying the way my body is responding to him. I feel him gently bite at my earlobe, causing my lower abdomen to do a complete somersault and the room starts to wobble again.

'I want you Louise' he whispers seductively in my ear and I reach my hands up the back of his neck into his thick wavy hair feeling excitement tingling down my spine, knowing I want him too. Before I can say anything Johnny's scooped me up in his arms. Wrapping my legs tightly around his body to hold on I can literally feel the heat between us as he carries me through to the bedroom.

I know I've only just met him but I'm caught up in the moment, swept along by lust. As we reach the bed Johnny lays me down gently and starts to quickly remove my clothes with expert hands.

'Do you have some protection?' I murmur as his mouth finds mine again.

'Of course' he sits up leaning over to the bedside table and pulls a box of condoms from the draw. 'See' he waves a red foil packet at me.

I lay back feeling the comfort of the soft bed beneath me as Johnny removes his jeans and shirt. Closing my eyes I gasp at the feel of his tongue as it traces my inner thigh gently nudging my legs further open. I hear the tear of the foil condom wrapper and I know this is my last chance to stop this before there's no going back.

But I don't want to stop.

I open my eyes as Johnny leans over me and the pull of his blue eyes and dimples is too strong and I reach up tugging his body down towards mine. I can feel him hard against me and I wriggle to adjust myself underneath him. As I feel him push inside me my body succumbs to him and I know right then and there that I'm in serious trouble.

Chapter Nine

Everything hurts. My head hurts, my eyes hurt. In fact my eyes won't even function. They are superglued shut and I can hear my eyeballs scratching on the inside of my eyelids as I attempt, unsuccessfully, to blink. I rub at my temples with both hands, trying to dislodge the pain. What the hell was I drinking last night? Tequila. Damn the tequila. This is all Jenny's fault. I'm going to kill her on Monday. I roll over, squashing my face deeper into the pillow, but the dull ache just slides around to the front of my head and settles over my eyebrows.

A snuffling noise at the side of me nearly stops my heart dead before my whole body freezes and my heart then lurches into my throat. My eyes are open now, stretched to the maximum as they dart around, taking in my surroundings. This is not my bedroom. This is not my own bed.

I almost don't dare to look to the side of me. It's all coming flooding back to me now, gushing around my head like fruit in a blender, and I instantly feel sick. Tequila. Too many shots of tequila. The smooth-talking Justin Timberlake lookalike who charmed the pants off me, literally. Oh God.

Taking a deep breath, I glance down at the bed beside me and, sure enough, there he is, still deep in sleep. He looks just as cute in daylight as he did last night. But that's not the point. That is seriously not the point. What time is it? I lean over slightly towards the alarm clock. Seven thirty a.m. Right. I need a plan. I need to get out of here without waking him up. I need to get home, find painkillers and then erase this whole episode from my memory.

I slither out from under the covers ever so carefully and slowly, until I'm in a crouching position on the floor. This is going to be harder than I thought with a raging hangover. I am completely naked, which potentially means that we had sex last night. In fact, if I were a betting girl then I would say the odds were very high. I vaguely remember him kissing me in front of the amazing skyline but then my memory all goes fuzzy and dark. I close my eyes, trying hard to relive the moments that followed that kiss. Yes, I kind of remember being led to the bed, and I remember the touch of his… naked body.

I scramble around on the floor, looking for my underwear. This is so degrading. My pants and bra are scattered around in a random pattern, along with my dress, which is inside-out and strewn on the floor too, as though I was in a hurry to get my clothes off; well, maybe I was. Oh dear. Holding my head in my hands, I cringe inwardly and reach out to grab my bra.

As I pull on my underwear, still in the crouched position and trying desperately not to wobble over, or throw up, I catch a glimpse of myself in the mirror hanging next to the bedroom door. My hair has taken on its usual morning shape of horror and last night's makeup is smudged around my face like a three-year-old's attempt at painting. This is not good. I cannot believe that I have allowed myself to get into this situation. I'm mortified.

I pull my dress over my head, tiptoe backwards out of the room and pull the door so it's nearly shut. Johnny is still asleep.

Now I just need to locate my shoes and handbag and then I can make my great escape. Fortunately I have left myself a trail, and one shoe in the hallway leads to the other and then on to my handbag on the kitchen worktop. I shove the shoes in my bag – putting them on will only cause unwanted noise as I clip-clop across the wooden floors.

'Don't you want a coffee or something before you leave?'

Oh shit. I've been caught in the act. How disgusting am I that I was just going to sneak out and leave like some…well, I really don't want to use the word prostitute but that is the only one that springs to mind. And how cheap was I? The price of a vodka and Coke.

'Um…' I turn round to find Johnny standing in the kitchen, naked apart from some blue boxer shorts. Oh yes, it's all coming back to me now. His thick blond hair is a little more unruly this morning but he still looks as sexy as hell.

'I have to get home.' I swallow; my throat is so dry. 'I'm meeting a friend for breakfast,' I lie.

'Well, at least let me call you a taxi.'

'No, no. Don't worry about that.' I desperately need some fresh air and to extract myself from this situation. I mean I've only just met him and I've…we've… 'I can walk back towards town. I'll pick one up on the way.' I'm subtly edging backwards towards the hallway as the door to exit this uncomfortable situation pulls at me like a magnet.

'If you're absolutely sure.' He frowns a little at me and I nod. 'See you around then.' He cocks his head to one side.

'Right.' What does that even mean?

I turn round and head to the door. I have no idea if we've even exchanged mobile phone numbers at this point or if there's any intention on either side for us to see each other again, but I'm not about to ask either of those questions right now. I unlock the door and slip out into the new-smelling corridor without daring to look back. I press the button for the lift and wait nervously.

'Come on, come on,' I urge it.

The lift finally arrives and I dive in and descend on the big dipper again to the ground floor. I remember this feeling from last night – of my stomach doing a somersault – and it doesn't feel any better this morning. Alcohol is evil. I'm never drinking again.

The fresh air feels amazing against my hangover, like it's gently slapping at my cheeks to wake me up. Thank God it's still early for a Saturday morning as I make the walk of shame from the block of flats towards town. I'm still dressed for Friday night in my little black dress and heels and am conscious that I could be mistaken for someone you pay for by the hour. My feet hurt from being forced back into high heels but the pain is at least a slight distraction from the complete humiliation that's swirling around me as though declaring my sordid experience to the world.

Once I'm safely out of sight of the building I fish my mobile out from my handbag and ring the first of the four taxi numbers stored in my phone.

'Pete's Taxis,' a gruff voice barks down the phone.

'Hi.' I bite my lip. 'I don't suppose I can get a taxi to Briar's Place?'

'Where are you now?'

'Erm…Grosvenor Keys. Near the river. On the main road near the new block of flats. The really tall one.'

'You're in luck. He'll be with you in five minutes. Name?'

Um. Better stick with reality now.

'Emma.'

'Right.'

'Tha–' The phone goes dead. Charming. 'Customer service at its best,' I mutter.

I hover in the street, feeling more than self-conscious, wrapping my arms around myself to try to shield my bare skin from the cold breeze. It's bloody freezing and my teeth are beginning to chatter, but thankfully, before I've succumbed completely to hypothermia, I see a taxi in the distance. The feeling of relief is immense. As he pulls up to the kerb I see the driver look me up and down with raised eyebrows. I'm really not in the mood for condemnation right now, so as I slide into the back seat I hold my head high, or as high as you can when faced with this situation, and attempt to front it out.

'Briar's Place?' He glances over his shoulder, straining to get a better look at me, and I feel like I'm naked in a large fish bowl.

'That's right,' I say firmly, ignoring the urge to leap back out of the taxi and walk home instead. 'And I'm in a bit of a hurry, if you don't mind.'

'I bet you are.' I hear him chuckle under his breath.

Hmm. Maybe I deserved that.

His badge is hanging from the driver's mirror. Roger Dennis. He's round, so much so that his belly is straining under the steering wheel, and he has a thick grey moustache to match his thick grey bushy hair. All in all, Roger looks like a dirty old man and I will the car to move faster. I bet he likes these early morning calls. I'm sure I'm not the only overdressed young woman in distress that Roger will get to see this morning. I shake my head at the thought but then instantly regret it as my hangover bounces around inside my skull.

A few minutes later we pull up outside my front door and I hurry into the house, hoping Mrs Gardener from next door isn't glued to her window behind twitching curtains as usual or that'll be an interesting conversation next time I have the misfortune to bump into her while putting the rubbish out.

Closing the front door behind me, I let out a huge sigh of relief; I have never been so glad to be inside my own four walls.

'Ow.' Slipping off my shoes one by one, I wince. The balls of my feet feel like actual pins and needles are shooting into them.

Just then my phone buzzes in my bag and I pull it out cautiously. It's a text from Jenny: *Presume you got home okay last night and are safe. x*

Texting at this time on a Saturday morning? Really? Then I remember that she and Lola will be at work by now.

I quickly text back: *Home and safe thanks, enjoy your weekend. x*

Okay, so it isn't a complete lie. I am home, and safe, it just wasn't last night when I arrived here.

Heading into the bathroom, I turn on the shower and notch up the heat by a few degrees before getting undressed and climbing into the steaming cubicle. The hot water pours over my head and I close my eyes, enjoying the feel of it washing away the remnants of last night.

'What the hell were you thinking?' I say out loud. I'm so angry with myself at my behaviour.

I guess I wasn't thinking at all; that's the problem. I wasn't thinking about the fact that Johnny was a complete stranger and that anything could have happened to me. No. All I was thinking about was how nice it was that someone was paying me some attention. It felt good to be wanted, not rejected. Not to be told that you're not good enough, that someone better has come along. I was swept away by his charm and his good looks. And he was very cute, even in just his boxer shorts with a ruffled bed head this morning. But that isn't me. It's not who I am. I don't sleep around. I don't sleep with men I don't know. It felt nice in the moment, but once that initial moment passed the rest is a bit of a blur.

This is the emotional tipping point. Tears run down my face, mixing in with the hot water, and I slide down to the floor with my back to the wall, letting the shower pound my head. I cry, wrapping my arms around myself until I'm huddled in a ball, letting the last few weeks finally get the better of me.

Half an hour later, as I sit curled up on my sofa in my fluffy dressing gown, I feel strangely relieved. Like a dam bursting, I feel like some of the pressure that has been building inside me has now been released. Last night was just the wake-up call I needed. I've been in free fall for the last three weeks and last night I think I hit rock bottom with a thud. I'm mortified by my behaviour – I never thought I would have a one-night stand, that it would be that easy to fall in bed with a guy I had only just met. But trying not to be too hard on myself, I console my guilty conscience by accepting the fact that I succumbed to a set of circumstances that were outside of my control. It wasn't me that decided to crash and burn my relationship, and I was led astray (perhaps I went a little willingly) by Jenny and Lola, and I certainly wouldn't have been drinking that horrible tequila under any other circumstances. So really, if I think about it, none of this is my fault. And that's the line I am sticking to.

Despite his charm and good looks, under no circumstances can I ever see Johnny again: one, it would be a constant reminder of my hideous behaviour; and two, I am so not ready to even think about dating anyone else. Hell, it wasn't that long ago that I was thinking about marriage to Chris.

No one ever has to know about last night; I will take it to my grave. I think denial is the best way to deal with the whole situation. If I don't talk about it then it never happened, and that is the approach I am going to take when I have to face Jenny and Lola on Monday and deal with their barrage of questions.

With that decided, I'm beginning to feel much better. I will never think of last night again. Now if I could just get rid of this damn hangover...

I get up to make another cup of tea and I can't help but think, looking around my own kitchen, how nice one of those coffee pod machines would look. But I must try to disassociate that idea from last night, or I'll never be able to have one, because it would be a constant reminder of my one-night stand. I might as well hang a neon sign stating 'loose woman' above the fridge.

While waiting for the kettle to boil I discretely check my phone. It would appear that even if Johnny did give me his phone number at some point last night I have not saved it, although there is no guarantee that he even did. That thought niggles at me a little: why, I don't know, if I have no intention of ever seeing him again.

As I pour hot water into a mug my mobile phone buzzes again and Sophie's number flashes on the screen.

'Hey.' I grab the phone, trying to balance it between my chin and my shoulder as I scoop the teabag out of my cup.

'How was last night?'

'I'm suffering the consequences now.' I take a slurp of my tea.

'I figured that would be the case. I remember the stories you told me about those two from your work Christmas party.'

'If I say "tequila" then you can kind of picture how the evening went and the extent of my headache today.'

'Oh, Emma. You didn't. Not tequila, especially after the last time.'

'What can I say? I had blocked that evening out so much I had forgotten how bad tequila is.' Two years ago: dreadful evening, violently sick, not good.

'Will you ever learn?' She laughs.

Apparently not, given last night's behaviour.

'So do you fancy meeting for lunch?' Sophie continues, oblivious to my silence.

'Only if we can eat something that's bad for us? I need to feed my hangover.'

'You can. I need to be thin for tonight.'

'Sophie, you're always thin. And what's tonight?'

'Our fifth date. Me and Connor. It's going really, really well.'

'Wow, fifth date, huh? That's good.'

'Shall we meet at Henry's at one o'clock?'

I get the impression that Sophie still feels bad that her relationship is blossoming in the wake of mine disintegrating, but that's not her fault. I really must say something to her at lunch about that.

'I'll drive so I can pick you up. Be ready for ten to one,' I offer.

'Okay, see you then,' she says in a singsong voice.

'Bye.'

I settle back down on the sofa. I have an hour or so to kill so I grab this month's Glamour magazine from the coffee table. Maybe there's a quiz or something in here I can read that will help me deal with my current lifestyle challenges.

Ten minutes later I chuck the magazine back on the coffee table. The only benefit it has given me is advice on what gorgeous clothes, shoes and handbags are 'in' this season, none of which I can afford, and my horoscope which, if it's to be believed, says I am due a nice surprise from a close friend. I shuffle through the pile of magazines. Maybe Cosmo can help me instead?

Having idled the hour away flicking through the advice pages of the many magazines accumulated on my coffee table I realise there actually is no one else – in print at least – that has confessed to being dumped and then having sex with a stranger, so I'm just going to have to figure this mess out on my own. I drag myself to a standing position and go in search of clean clothes. Once dressed in jeans and the only available clean t-shirt I own, I dab on some face powder and blusher and sweep the mascara wand across my eyelashes, careful not to poke myself in the eye with my tequila-shaking hands.

The short drive to Sophie's is actually nowhere near as bad as I thought it would be. Maybe my hangover is diminishing after all. When I pull up at Sophie's she's already halfway out of the door. Despite it being March and warm and sunny, Sophie is dressed for winter, buried under a thick woollen coat.

'You do realise that it's spring, don't you?' I shake my head at her as she climbs into the passenger seat.

'Laugh all you want, but when you catch pneumonia from coming out half-dressed in a small, thin t- shirt' – she raises her eyebrows at me – 'I will remind you of this conversation.' She smiles with satisfaction and I laugh at her motherly tone before I pull back out into the traffic and we make the five minute drive to Henry's restaurant.

'So, things seem to be going well between you and Connor.' I broach the subject as we sip Diet Coke in a window booth. Sophie is studying the menu with intensity and I watch as she bites her lip. 'Sophie, you don't have to stop sharing things with me.'

'I just don't want to rub your nose in it, that's all.'

'And I love you for that, but I'm fine.'

She looks at me sceptically.

'So I might not be totally fine right now, but I will be.' I smile genuinely at her and she nods, looking a little emotional.

'Hey.'

'I'm sorry.' She sniffs. 'I could just kill Chris with my bare hands for what he's done to you. If I ever see him again...'

'I know. He's a shit. But it's done. I need to move on, and you need to let it go too.' I reach over and squeeze her hand. 'So, why don't you tell me what's been going on with you and Connor?'

'Okay.' She smiles sheepishly.

'Okay.' I nod.

'Well, we've been on four dates over the last three weeks and we just get on so well. It's like we've known each other for ages. We like the same things, have the same taste in music and...do you remember that weird sitcom I used to watch?'

'Oh my God, please tell me you didn't subject him to repeats of that on YouTube?'

'I didn't need to. He watched it too.'

I shake my head in mock dismay. 'It sounds like you two were destined to find each other. It must be fate.'

'So, do you want to meet him?'

'Ooh, it must be serious if you're going to let me judge and ridicule him already.'

'You wouldn't.'

'Of course not.'

'Then let's meet for coffee tomorrow morning. Connor and I will already be together.'

She twiddles a thick, dark curl around her fingers and it takes me a second to realise the implication of what she's just said.

'Oh right, so you two...he's...'

'He's staying at my house and...'

'And?' I prompt.

'It will be our first time together.'

'So you haven't slept with him yet?' Oops, that came out wrong. It sounded like an accusation. Fifth date, Emma. Take note for future reference on dating etiquette. Not first date, or first hour...

'I wanted to make sure...you know, before we took that next step.'

'Absolutely.' I nod, blushing. 'And I'd love to meet him tomorrow for coffee.'

'Good. Shall we order? I'm starving.'

'I thought you'd never ask.'

Once home from lunch I spend the late afternoon milling around the house. Feeling much better for clearing my conscience and feeding my hangover I decide, rather virtuously, to go for a jog. I vaguely remember promising myself I would run on a weekly basis when I spent seventy-five pounds on my new trainers in January, which have actually only been out of the box once when I made the mistake of agreeing to go to an army-type gym class with Sophie – a huge mistake that I will not be making again. As I recall, I was yelled at numerous times by some angry, red-faced brute who then made snide comments about my lack of upper-body strength while I slithered on the floor in a sweat-soaked t-shirt, trying to do a press-up. Paying eight pounds for an hour of verbal abuse is not money well spent.

I pull on my comfy jogging pants and a t-shirt that says 'I'm not an alcoholic. Alcoholics go to meetings', which I think is quite funny under the circumstances, and I grab the trainers from their box. But as I close the front door behind me, my enthusiasm is already faltering, and after ten minutes of dragging my body at an intermittent pace around the block, my face is pulsating, I'm sweating profusely and I can barely breathe. This was a ridiculous idea, and I silently promise myself I will never be so stupid as to attempt to run anywhere again, unless I'm being chased. I will wear my trainers around the house instead.

I puff and pant my way back home, stopping every thirty seconds and just walking or leaning on someone's garden wall for support. Once inside I grab my emergency giant Dairy Milk chocolate bar from the fridge, along with a Diet Coke, and resume my position of lounging on my sofa. As I stuff pieces of chocolate into my mouth and watch repeats of crap reality TV, my mind drifts to Sophie and Connor and I grab my phone from the coffee table to text her: *Good luck for everything tonight. x*

She was so excitable at lunch; she must really like this guy. And to be fair, if he's everything that she says he is then it would appear she has found her match. I'm quite nervous about meeting him; it's always a bit awkward as you try to make small talk with your best friend's new bloke. There's so much pressure for everyone to get along. But I'm sure it will be fine. I trust Sophie's judgement. Hell, I trust her judgement a whole lot more than I trust my own at the moment. I'm sure it won't be awkward at all, and if Connor makes Sophie happy then that's all that's important to me.

Chapter Ten

The following morning, at eleven thirty, I make my way towards the coffee shop to meet Sophie and Connor, preparing for an overdose of lovesick couple syndrome. I hope last night went okay; I mean the first time you have sex with a new partner can go either way. Why am I even thinking about this? I do not need to think about Sophie's intimate sex life, especially when I'm on my way to meet said sexual partner. What's wrong with me?

As I reach our usual coffee haunt I pull the heavy glass door open and I'm immediately greeted by the heavenly aroma of fresh coffee and warm pastries and I hear my stomach grumble excitedly. Glancing round, I see Sophie is already here and she's waving me over to the corner table she's acquired, a huge grin plastered on her face. I guess last night went well after all. Connor has his back to me – he seems to be looking at something over Sophie's shoulder – but I can see he is holding her hand. How sweet.

As I walk towards them, feeling a moment of nervous anticipation, Connor turns around to face me and…

Holy fuck.

Ordinarily my language would never be so harsh, but there are just no other words to describe my shock. Sitting next to Sophie, lovingly holding her hand and smiling broadly, just showing his dimples, is my Justin Timberlake lookalike, my one-night stand.

'No, Dad, not the belt. I haven't done anything, honest.'
'Honest? You don't know the meaning of the word, you little shit.'
'It wasn't me.'
'Then who else stole the money from my wallet, eh? Get over here. Now!'

Chapter Eleven

I think I'm actually having a stroke.

A heavy thudding sound floods into my ears, muffling the noise of coffee machines hissing behind me and muting the carefree chatter of the other customers, and I realise it's the pounding of my heart that I can hear as it hurtles towards implosion. I've lost all control of my bodily movements as I stand silently and still like a statue, while my chest constricts so tightly that breathing is now an impossible task. How can this be? I mean, how the fuck can this be happening? Sophie's new boyfriend's name is Connor. I slept with Johnny! I mean…I…I...

Suddenly an unwelcome thought prods at my befuddled brain, wagging its finger in a smug and annoying manner: People aren't always who they say they are. You used an alias that night too: Louise.

Fuck, fuck, fuck.

I told a little lie about my name. Alright a big lie. But I presumed, clearly wrongly, that I'd never see Johnny again, let alone that he would actually turn out to be Connor, Sophie's smart, handsome new boyfriend to whom I'd be introduced over coffee on what should be an ordinary Sunday morning!

Argh. This is too much. This is all far too much.

Maybe I'm actually dreaming. Maybe this is a nightmare and my conscience is just playing me, teaching me a lesson after my recent frivolous behaviour. I reach my hand under my coat sleeve and nip the skin on the underside of my wrist…Ouch! Nope – not a dream.

Now I'm also in pain as well as having a stroke.

Why doesn't Connor look at all surprised to see me? I'm in complete shock at this and he looks completely calm, not even the slightest bit flustered.

I can see Sophie frowning over at me with a slightly worried look on her face, making me aware that since I clocked Connor/Johnny, I've stopped abruptly in my tracks and have made no move to join them. In fact, I'm just standing right in the middle of the coffee shop, probably looking a bit weird.

'Are you okay?' she mouths at me and I nod, forcing the muscles in my face to form some sort of response. But as I glance at Connor, or Johnny, or whatever the hell his name is, I see his expression hasn't changed: he's still grinning at me with a glint in those bright blue eyes that not so long ago I thought were alluring, and that alone is really unnerving.

It's almost like I'm having an out-of-body experience: that I'm watching myself walk over to Sophie. I have no idea what on earth I'm going to say to her. My brain has refused to engage and I feel like a frog has set up camp in my throat and no amount of nervous swallowing is going to dislodge it.

'Hi.' Sophie lets go of Connor's hand and stands up to greet me with a hug like she hasn't seen me in years. 'This is Connor,' she gushes, pulling back from the embrace. Immediately Connor wraps his arm tightly around her shoulders, squeezing her closer to him.

My heart beats to the rhythm of a thousand marching drummers as I glance between the two of them with a jaw-stretching smile on my face that physically hurts. What can I say? I can't simply blurt out "we've already met and I thought his name was Johnny, oh and by the way he might call me Louise". It looks as though Connor/Johnny is going along with the pretence that we're strangers and right now I can't see any other way to deal with this situation. So here goes.

'Hi, Connor,' I manage finally, dispersing the frog and, temporarily, the urge to throw up. 'It's nice to finally meet you. I've heard so much about you.'

I realise that I sound robotic, like I'm reading a script from a book called How to Be Over-Polite in Uncomfortable Social Situations. But I've been thrown so far off my guard that I don't know how to even begin to be myself right now.

The lying bastard. The absolutely deceitful, cheating, smug, hideous piece of crap.

What is wrong with men?

Has some invisible drug been pumped secretly into society that has made men forget any hint of the moral standards that they should possess? Have they all turned into complete freaks overnight? Or is it just me that attracts men with huge behavioural issues?

No, don't answer that, Emma. Now's not the time for that sort of contemplation!

'Shall we sit down?' I suggest, pulling out a chair and practically collapsing into it as my legs give way. I can feel myself sweating and my stomach is doing so many somersaults that it's causing me to become light-headed.

I watch Sophie's mouth move at a thousand miles an hour but I can't hear a word she's saying; the heavy pounding is back, giving the illusion of drowning in a bathtub, swirling closer and closer to the gurgling plug hole. Connor is sitting next to Sophie holding her hand on his knee in what at face value looks to be a loving and caring manner. I can't even bring myself to look at him. I'm so angry and bewildered and I'm desperately struggling with my inner self, which is yelling at me to launch myself across the table and knock that swagger out of him.

Connor has cheated on Sophie and they're only just at the beginning of their relationship. How, and more to the point why, does someone do that? I mean, they've only just…I stop that thought firmly in its track as my brain comprehends the sheer awfulness of the situation. It hits me like a sucker punch in the chest as my conversation with Sophie yesterday morning rings in my ears. A whirlwind of thoughts rumbles through my mind at a hundred miles an hour.

They only actually slept together last night.

It was their first time. Sophie had wanted to take things slowly to make sure…Oh no…That means that I slept with him first. I cheated on my best friend with her boyfriend before they had even...

Urgh! I'm scum, the lowest of the low. There is no worse betrayal in the world than that.

But I had no idea. I mean I would never, ever...But you didn't ask whether he had a girlfriend, did you? my know-it-all conscience prods me. Well...no...I stupidly presumed that he wouldn't have been hitting on me in the first place if he did. And *he* hit on me. *He* sent a drink over for me. *He* initiated everything that night – the drink, the taxi back to his apartment, the kiss that led to –

'Emma?'

I snap back into the moment in a state of panic. Sophie is shaking her head at me.

'Um...sorry,' I mumble, hoping that the guilt I'm feeling isn't plastered all over my face.

'What do you want to drink, silly?' She's beaming. Literally beaming.

'Oh.' Maybe a litre of poison? 'A cappuccino, please.' I force a smile again.

'I'll let you two get to know each other.' She giggles girlishly at both me and Connor, and as I watch her walk away to the counter to order our drinks she looks so happy and so innocent that I actually visualise the knife that I've used to stab her in the back.

I wait until she's definitely out of earshot, then I turn on Connor like a viper, channelling all of my turbulent emotions at him.

'What the fuck are you playing at, Connor?' I growl in as hushed a tone as I can muster under the circumstances,

'I could ask you the same question, Louise,' he shoots back at me, the placid expression still etched on his face, forming the same dimples that only thirty-six hours ago I thought were cute.

'I'm well aware of the fact that I –'

'What? That you told some lies the other night too? A lawyer – really?'

'That's different.' I glare at him.

'I don't see how, Louise.' He leans forward on the table with smugness smeared across his whole demeanour.

'I'm single,' I state indignantly. 'You have a girlfriend – my best friend. I should tell her what a horrible creep you are.'

'Yeah, I wouldn't do that if I were you.' He taps his fingers in a leisurely way on the wooden table that separates us and I can feel a hint of the stroke returning.

'And why not? You don't deserve her. She's lovely and honest and kind.'

'And you slept with her boyfriend.'

Argh!

'I didn't know you were her boyfriend.' I glance nervously over my shoulder and see Sophie chatting to the barista as she prepares our drinks.

'I don't think that's going to make much difference when you tell her you slept with me the night before she did.' Connor cocks his head arrogantly at me.

Shit.

I know that he's right. Sophie would be crushed, as would I be if the roles were reversed. It was a horrible coincidence that I should meet her new boyfriend while I happened to be drunk and vulnerable, having no idea who he was. But I'm pretty sure no good can come from telling her in detail about the sordid experience. What I need is for Connor to disappear so all of this weird, hideous mess can just go away, never to be spoken of again. Then this whole nightmare will over. But how do you make an actual person disappear in a puff of smoke? This isn't a fairy-tale but I need to figure out how to get to the happy ending where Sophie remains happy and none the wiser of mine and Connor's indiscretion but for some reason Connor is not getting the hint. I go over all the possible outcomes of telling Sophie – the fact that I slept with her boyfriend before her is too much to take and she hates me forever – she realises that Connor is a moral less jerk and breaks up with him, but she hates me forever....No. I just can't see me telling her and there being anything other than carnage as a result. There's only one way this can go: I need Connor to break up with Sophie and to get the hell out of her life and mine.

'Right.' I take a deep breath, figuring that I should try to reason with him now; there's no time like the present. 'Friday night was a mistake,' I say calmly. 'It was a freakish chance that you and I ended up in bed together. It would only hurt Sophie if she knew, and that's the last thing I want to do.'

'So?' He shrugs nonchalantly, causing my temper to flare even more.

'So,' I state firmly, 'what needs to happen is that you find some way to break up with her.'

'What?' He looks a little bemused.

'You need to let her down gently, but you need to end this, and soon,' I persist, despite his apparent reluctance to get on board with my simple solution.

'And why would I want to do that?'

I can barely believe what I'm hearing. 'Seriously? You actually think that carrying on seeing Sophie, who just happens to be the best friend of your one-night stand, is just going to...what? Turn out fine? That we can all just be friends? That living with the deceit won't be uncomfortable and unbearable?'

'Well, it seems to me that it's only you who has a problem with this situation.'

'This situation!' Panic is starting to rise from deep within me now. Why isn't he getting the message? 'Look, I'm pretty sure that neither of us wants to be reminded on a regular basis of our night together, particularly given the circumstances,' I hiss.

'Well, you're just going to have to deal with it. I like Sophie, and I'm not going to break up with her just because you're sitting here and asking me to. I'm not going anywhere.'

There's a slight change in the tone of his voice, almost threatening, and he's staring at me with slightly colder eyes now. This can't be happening. It just can't.

'So what have you two been chatting about?' Sophie places a small tray on the table and plonks three large mugs of coffee down in front of us, shattering the tension.

'Oh, nothing much.' Connor looks up at her. 'Emma here's just been telling me she's young, free and single. We'll have to see if we can fix her up with one of my mates.' He looks over and winks at me purposefully.

Did I really just hear that? Is he on another planet?

Oh, right, I get it. This is his idea of a little joke, a chance to mess with my head. He's not only going to blatantly ignore the only decent thing he can do by breaking up with Sophie, but he's going to play me like a sucker while he's at it.

'Oh, that would be great, wouldn't it?' Sophie sits down, practically on Connor's knee, and looks over at me excitedly.

'Um…I'm not...'

Shit. You know what, I'm just going to let that conversation go.

Fortunately for me, Sophie is in complete loved-up mode and, as such, is oblivious to anything else around her, so she hasn't realised that I haven't answered her. Nor has she picked up on the uncomfortable atmosphere that is hanging over us like a cloud of swirling black smoke, choking the very life out of me. She's now babbling on about how she and Connor have done this and that and they're going to the Museum of Modern Art and how crazy it is that Connor has never been. Connor interjects 'um's and ah's' where appropriate as I watch the charade with ever-increasing despair, and I notice that throughout it all he doesn't let go of her hand for a second.

As for me, I attempt to hide behind my huge coffee cup and try to maintain my poker face. It's like watching a scene from a movie where you thought you knew what was going to happen at the end, but suddenly the main character has been killed off and everything has changed, and you know that a happy ending is impossible. I'm still dumbfounded by my conversation with Connor. I can't believe the nerve of that guy. He clearly doesn't feel a crumb of remorse about cheating on Sophie, let alone the fact that he inadvertently cheated on her with her best friend. I mean, you couldn't make this shit up. I want to lean over the table and poke his eyes out with my blunt wooden coffee stirrer. That should wipe the permanent grin off his face. I can feel my anger boiling inside me, threatening to erupt at any second, so I take a deep breath to try to calm myself. This is serious stuff and I need to hold my nerve.

'We should be getting going.' Connor rubs Sophie's knee, clearly picking up on my seething death stares and the anger emanating from my every pore.

'You're right.' She looks over at me. 'Sorry to cut it short.'

No really, it's fine, I think, thankful for the opportunity to extract myself from this madness.

'It's just that Connor needs to drop some stuff back at his place before we have lunch. We have a reservation at Harvey's.'

Wow, Harvey's for lunch? Someone is really pushing the boat out. It costs an arm and a leg for just a starter and a side salad at that place.

'Unless you'd like to join us?' Sophie looks at me excitedly. 'I'm sure they could change it to a table for three.'

Oh dear God, no. I glance at Connor and I'm shocked to see a brief twinkle in his eye at this suggestion.

'Thanks for the offer, Soph, but I have some work to do before tomorrow. A big client thing. Sorry.' I swallow nervously, hoping she doesn't push the point.

'That's okay. Shall I come over tomorrow night and we can have a proper catch up then?'

'Sounds good.' I agree. I'd like to spend some time with Sophie without this creep in tow so I can quiz her about this "relationship". I don't want him anywhere near my home – ever.

'Okay. I'll be at yours around seven.' She kisses me on the cheek and flashes raised eyebrows at me, hinting in Connor's direction, and I squeeze her hand giving her the assurance and approval that I know she's looking to get from me. What else can I do but play along like the dutiful friend?

'Nice to meet you, Emma.' Connor steps forward.

No…really…he's not seriously going to? Oh...yes, he is. He kisses me on the cheek too and I have to hold my breath as the smell of his crisp aftershave forces the images of Friday night, or at least what I can remember of it, to come rushing back forcefully into my mind. I actually have to take a step backwards as he invades my personal space. I look to the floor, avoiding his eyes, praying that he'll spontaneously combust any second now. I should be so lucky.

'See you tomorrow.'

I wave at Sophie and then watch helplessly as she and Connor walk away, out of the coffee shop and down the street, linked arm in arm like any other newly formed couple, full of romance and lust, just happy to be in each other's company.

I sit down heavily on the chair.

A barista appears next to me at the table. 'Is this mug done with?'

'Yes. But can I get another, please, and with an extra shot of coffee? And a muffin?'

I need more caffeine and a sugar hit right now as my mind tries desperately to process the last thirty minutes of my life; in fact, the last forty-eight hours of my life. It's like my world has done a complete one-eighty-degree spin and I'm left hanging upside down by a very thin thread, feeling nauseous and light-headed with no control over the situation and no way to get myself back upright.

What the hell am I going to do? If I tell Sophie that her 'oh-so-lovely new boyfriend' is a disgusting excuse for a human being (with what I can only conclude is a severe personality disorder, given that he appears to be getting off on this whole situation) then I'm going to have to explain why I think that and that I know that he's cheated on her. I'm then going to have to admit it was me who slept with him, and I just can't imagine that conversation with her. Sophie would be devastated, and it would be almost impossible for our friendship to ever recover from something like that. No, scratch that – it would be impossible to ever recover from that.

But I can't just let her carry on going out with him, can I? I mean, I know it'll be awkward for me and hideous every time I have to be in his presence, but that's not really the issue here. Sophie thinks her relationship is something that it isn't. She thinks Connor is someone he's clearly not. In fact, he seems to be a little unhinged and completely lacking morals, and Sophie deserves someone so much better than that. And more to the point, I'm not sure I can live with myself and this awful feeling of guilt that's suffocating me. Nor can I keep up the facade of happiness every time I hear her waxing lyrical about Connor. I also can't guarantee that I won't garrotte him next time I'm forced to be in his presence. If I'm completely honest with myself, Sophie at least deserves the truth, from me as her best friend.

But I can't tell her. I just can't. There has to be another way.

As the barista slides another large mug and a blueberry muffin onto the table in front of me, I mutter my thanks. I'm shoving a large piece of the muffin into my mouth when a thought springs to mind: Isn't gluttony one of the seven deadly sins? Well, I guess that figures. You reap what you sow.

I stare aimlessly out of the window stuffing the sweet soft muffin unceremoniously into my mouth washing it down with large glugs of coffee. What started off as light fluffy sponge now nestles heavily giving me indigestion.

I don't know how long I've been sitting here but the dregs of my third coffee are stone-cold, and the barista has huffed at me four times already: I've clearly outstayed my welcome given that I haven't ordered anything else for a while now. I'm no further forward in finding a solution. If anything, I feel considerably worse now the action replay of the last two days has played over and over in my mind. I need help to figure this out, and in some small way I hope that unburdening my terrible secret on someone else may somehow help. What's that old saying? A problem shared is a problem halved?

I think this particular problem calls for an expert in...well, everything. I take out my phone and call Simon, praying that he has no other plans tonight – and no unexpected guests! I need his words of wisdom, or at least his words of honesty. Simon has never been one to worry about being diplomatic. He doesn't sugar-coat anything.

'Hey, babe. How's things?' Simon answers his phone in the same cheery tone every time I call him.

'Hi. I'm not so good.' I purse my lips. 'You?'

'You know me, Em, I'm always good.'

Annoyingly he's right. Whatever calamity may befall him, he's never one to flounder but merely carries on staunchly without a hint of disruption.

'Do you have plans tonight?'

'Ooh, are you asking me out on a date?' He giggles girlishly.

'Don't be stupid, Si. I need your worldly wisdom not your body.'

'Shame...mind you, you're the wrong sex.'

'So can I come over?'

'Sure, babe. How bad is it? Do we need wine or vodka?'

'Urgh, neither. I'm not drinking alcohol for at least a week.'

'Oh dear. That bad?'

'You have no idea.'

'See you around seven?'

'Make sure the kettle's on. I'll bring the chocolate biscuits.'

I end the call and feel marginally better. Simon is always there for me when I need him.

Chapter Twelve

Simon buzzes me into the building and then opens the door to his flat and welcomes me with a big hug. Instantly I feel tears prick my eyes.

'What's happened, babe?' He ushers me into the flat and through to the kitchen where I dutifully place the chocolate biscuits on the breakfast bar.

'You're not going to believe me when I tell you.' I press my lips together, wondering whether spilling my guts is really the right thing to do after all.

'I'm gay, darling. You'd need to do a lot to shock me.'

'Give over.' I playfully slap his arm.

'So what is it?'

I pause for a second, trying to decide the best way to say this. I decide it's best to just tell him the facts, without emotion and dramatic effect, and then let him sort through them in his own mind before presenting me with his conclusion.

'Okay.' I lean heavily with both arms on the kitchen side for support – both emotional and physical. 'You know Sophie's started seeing that new bloke?' I bite the side of my mouth. Once I say this out loud there's no going back. It's real. It's out there, and I'm hanging myself out to be slaughtered.

'Yeah – Connor, isn't it?' He asks. 'Has she let you meet him yet?'

Um, kind of.

'I slept with him,' I blurt out without any lead-in to the mayhem and before I can engage my brain and say something far less blunt

'Em, I'm not following you.' Simon shakes his head a little. 'You slept with him? I think that's maybe being a little too friendly with your best mate's new boyfriend.' He laughs

'I'm being serious,' I state, my tone changing completely.

'Oh…what?' His whole face frowns in confusion.

'I know, it's bad. It's very, very bad.'

'You slept with him?' Simon's voice is incredulous now as he realises that, unfortunately, I might be telling the truth. 'Like actually had sex with him?'

'Yes, Simon! That's usually what "I slept with him" means. Yes, I had sex with Connor!' I run my hands roughly through my hair.

'Whoa!' he gulps.

'Whoa? Is that it?' I throw my hands up in the air.

'Okay, okay, hush, hush. Calm down, Emma.' Simon pulls me into his arms. 'You've just landed this thing on me like an exploding bomb and I need a moment to –'

'I came to you, Si, because I thought I could talk to you. I thought you were my friend and you could help me figure this out,' I mumble almost incoherently into his chest, rubbing my forehead on his sweater.

'Look, Em, you're not making any sense at the moment.' He kisses my hair. 'Let's get a cuppa and you can start from the beginning so I can try to get my head around this whole thing. I need to hear the full story though, no details left out, right?'

'Yes.' I take a deep breath, a little calmer now. 'I'll tell you everything.'

Simon lets out a deep sigh. 'Bloody hell, Emma. You don't half get yourself into some tricky situations,' he states in an ever-so-slightly condescending manner, which isn't becoming and really isn't helping my mood.

I huff petulantly before slouching off to the lounge and slumping on the sofa.

Five minutes later, sitting side by side, armed with tea and chocolate biscuits, I begin to tell my disastrous tale.

'He came on to me when I was drunk in a bar. In a million years it would never have occurred to me that he was Sophie's boyfriend. Why would it? Plus I'd never met him before. You know what Sophie's like: everything's always so cloak and dagger until she's analysed all there is to know about the bloke, and only then do you get to meet him. She wouldn't even show me a picture of him. There was nothing about him on her social media profile. She has been keeping him under wraps. He told me his name was Johnny anyway, and at that point there was no reason to suspect that it wasn't.'

'Ooh, that's clever.'

'Simon!'

'No, well, it's not good for you, but you know I'm fond of using an alias myself. That way if I wake up on the wrong side of a drunken regret then I can scarper and there's no permanent damage done.'

No permanent damage done? I shake my head at him. 'I don't understand your lifestyle, Simon. Don't you want to find someone long term who you actually like and want to wake up next to?'

'Honey, I'm a free spirit, a butterfly if you like. I'm not ready to be captured by the big net of monogamy just yet. But the issue here isn't me and who I do or don't sleep with.'

'Fair enough. We can dissect your intimacy and commitment issues another time.'

'Em, I'm committed to living my life to the full and I don't have problems with being intimate. In fact –'

'Enough, please.' I hold up my hand to silence him. I witnessed enough of his intimacy first-hand the other week, thank you very much. 'The issue here is me. I'm in an emotionally fragile state and don't want to be further scarred by details of your latest conquest.'

'I'm just kidding. You know I don't kiss and tell.' He chucks me another biscuit. 'All I'll say is that the tall, dark and handsome stranger from the train journey to work is no longer a stranger.'

'Oh, Simon.' I can't help but giggle at him and he joins in too. 'I wish my love life was as simplistic as yours.' I sigh emphatically.

Simon shrugs. 'Life is as simple as you want it to be, babe.'

'Yeah? Well, I guess I need to not sleep with the same guy as my best friend if I want simple.'

'Sorry, we're getting off track. Talk me through it.' Simon looks serious now and he remains quiet, apart from intermittently slurping his tea, until I've finished explaining everything to him. Then he says, 'Well, he sounds like a complete bastard to me, and he's clearly taken advantage of you when you were very obviously drunk.'

'That may be the case but I'm a grown-up, Si. I have to accept responsibility for my own actions.' I pause. 'And I used a fake name too.'

'Oh.' His expression changes to surprised. 'It's all coming out now. Why did you do that, hun?'

I swallow down the lump of emotion that's forming in my throat.

'I guess I just wanted to be someone else for a night. Not sad, pathetic, dumped Emma, recently cheated on and replaced with a new, younger model at the grand old age of thirty-two.'

'Oh, honey.' Simon cocks his head to one side.

'I know. It was stupid and pathetic.'

'No, Chris is stupid and pathetic, but that's a whole other story and don't get me started on that.'

'Thank you.' I smile. 'I know he is, but he wasn't always that way. Do you remember how head-over-heels in love I felt when I first set eyes on him?'

'Do I? I remember having to physically restrain you from throwing yourself at him on a number of occasions.'

'Yeah well, he was cool and handsome, and loads of girls were trying to chat him up. But at the end of the night he came to talk to me and to ask me to dance. I thought he was even cooler once I realised he was the lead singer in a band.'

'Yeah, I was so jealous. He's very cute, even if it pains me to say so now. Although it was pretty obvious from the first time I spoke to him that he wasn't gay. I can see what the attraction was there, though.'

'I often wondered what would've happened if his band had actually had a break, you know, and got a music contract before they decided to call it a day and get ordinary jobs. I could've toured the world with them, staying in a different country every night.'

'Yeah, I doubt it. If they'd got a big break then he'd have been sleeping with a different woman in a different country every night!'

'Anyway.' I cast Simon a scolding look.

'Sorry. Is it too soon to joke about his infidelity?'

'Too soon.' I purse my lips, and then after a pause I say, 'Speaking of infidelity, do I tell Sophie about Connor?'

'That's a tricky one, Em, and in all honesty I think only you can know the answer to that question.'

'What do you mean? You always know the right answer to solve my problems.'

'This is out of my league, hun.'

How did I ever reach that level of calamity?

'Anyway, how's your mum doing? Any news on her mysterious love life to take your mind off your own crazy shit?'

'I haven't really spoken to her since I got back from New York. You know what she's like. Communication with her is always intermittent and usually when you're least expecting it.'

'I know. She does seem to live in her own little world. She spent most of her time while we were kids growing up trying to persuade me to be your boyfriend.'

'Give her a break.' I giggle. 'Back then she wasn't…well…'

'Observant?'

'That's not fair, Simon. If you didn't know you were gay then how would she know?' I raise my eyebrows skywards.

'A fair point, although even after everyone found out, I still think she thought you could "turn" me.'

'Well, I am an amazing Goddess,' I joke.

'You are, hun. But you don't have the right wobbly bits for me.'

'Always one to keep the conversation highbrow.'

'You're in no position to judge me, lady.' Simon puts on a posh, condescending voice. 'For the first time since I can remember in the history of our friendship, I'm not the one in the huge pile of emotional pooh.'

'I know, I know.' I hold up my hands in surrender. 'I'm the devil, not a Goddess, and I really am buried up to my neck in it.'

'It'll all work out, Emma.' Simon pulls me into a hug. 'You'll see.'

I hug him back but I can't help but wonder how on earth this is going to sort itself out. My earlier idea of getting good advice from Simon has fallen flat on its face. Maybe that's because there is no good advice for those who find that they've accidentally slept with their best friend's boyfriend. But there must be some solution. I mean, this must happen more often than you think? No, really, it must...mustn't it? Okay, I guess – thankfully – it doesn't.

Chapter Thirteen

After a turbulent night's sleep following my unproductive talk with Simon, I drag myself to work the following morning, naughtily applying my makeup in the car, trying to avoid the disapproving stares from other drivers as I crawl through the morning commute. Honestly it's only a bit of blusher and mascara; I'm decent enough to apply my foundation before I left the house.

As I walk through the rear door of the boutique Jenny is already there waiting for me, coffee cup in hand and curious expression on her face.

'So, what happened with that cute guy after we left on Friday night?' She taps her impossibly long nails on her cup.

'Can I at least take my coat off before we start the Spanish Inquisition, please?' I protest at her.

'That means something happened,' she raises her eyebrows, taking a gulp of coffee.

'Why? What would make you think that?' God, I hate this woman – her intuition is on a par with a bloodhound following the scent of a fox. She can smell the truth a mile off.

'Because you're stalling. If nothing had happened, you'd have just said so.' She looks at me with an annoying 'See, I know everything' look.

Damn it.

I could try to front it out but I'm crap at lying and I fear my guilt-ridden conscience will 'out' me immediately.

'Okay, you got me,' I concede. 'Something did happen.' I decide to go for small white lie rather than giant whopping lie.

'I knew it!' Jenny looks overly pleased with herself and I feel the need to dowse her excitement. This really needs minimising and nipping in the bud so it can all be forgotten about by the time the shop closes today.

'Hold your horses. All we did was have a drink, a chat and a small kiss on the cheek as I left to get a taxi.' I really can't go into the intimate details and the disastrous consequences of Friday night. Not with Jenny. Not with anybody ever again. It was bad enough confessing all to Simon, and a fat lot of use he was.

She raises her eyebrows at me sceptically now and I turn my back on her to hang up my coat, hide my blush and buy myself a couple of seconds. I really am crap at lying.

'Now, can I get my caffeine fix in peace, please, before we start work? It's Monday and you know I won't function without it.' I try to brazenly brush past the subject, and for some reason unbeknown to me, Jenny just lets it go with a short, swift nod.

'We've got that order of new handbags arriving today,' I remind Jenny as I spoon coffee into a cup, add hot water and milk, and stir it hurriedly.

'Yeah, I know, and I guess I'll have to change the window displays as Lola isn't back in again until tomorrow.'

'Right, let's get to work then.'

I take a mouthful of coffee and head out from the staff area onto the shop floor, keen to get on with the day and out of the confines of the interrogation booth before Jenny decides to take a pitch at round two.

This is the time of day that I like best: when everything is quiet, there are no customers yet and it's just nice and calm, so you can simply take some time to wander around the store making sure everything looks as it should. With half an hour until opening time I get on with doing a stock check, leaving Jenny to fight with the very unhelpful and flexibly challenged mannequins. I hate changing them. It's like fighting with a dead body (Or at least how I presume a dead body would behave. I haven't quite added murder to my list of mistakes yet, although Connor has some potential to fall victim of that if he doesn't get the hint and shove off soon.) They're heavy and unwilling to bend and move in the direction you need them to, almost as though they weren't designed to actually wear clothes at all, and by the time you've finished changing three outfits you're sweating like you've done an hour-long gym class. (Or how I imagine I'd feel after a gym class; it's not like I ever go to the gym.)

Thankfully the day passes without much incident and shortly after lunch the delivery arrives. I'm momentarily in heaven as I'm surrounded by gorgeous handbag after gorgeous handbag.

'What do you think of this one?' I ask Jenny as I strut up and down the shop like a model on a catwalk, swinging a quilted, oversized taupe bag around and pouting in an exaggerated fashion.

'It's perfect for you,' she gushes, clutching a cobalt-blue evening bag. 'I think blue is more my colour, though.'

'It is perfect for me. I just need to find two hundred and fifty pounds, after my measly staff discount, to be able to pay for it,' I huff. 'I'm seriously in the wrong job. What do women do for a living who can afford to spend three hundred pounds on a handbag?'

'They sell their souls to corporate gold-diggers.'

'Hmm, I wonder how much my soul is worth?'

'Or they sleep with really rich old men?' she adds.

Urgh! I stare down at the pretty handbag. On second thoughts, how old?

'But you wouldn't get to play dress-up for a living if you didn't do this job.' Jenny notes sarcastically.

'That's true…pros and cons, I guess.'

I put the taupe bag in the window display alongside the new clothes Jenny has forced the mannequins into and continue unpacking the stock. I'm not quite ready yet to go down the road of getting a decrepit sugar daddy to buy me gorgeous handbags and fund a lavish lifestyle.

As I leave work at six o'clock to make my way home I can feel the nerves beginning to bubble at the bottom of my stomach. I know Sophie is going to be waxing lyrical about Connor tonight, and she's going to ask me what I think. It's one thing avoiding answering a direct question and another totally lying to your best friend's face. Feeling emotionally shredded at the moment, I don't think I can do either.

As seven o'clock approaches I wait with trepidation for the doorbell to ring, wearing out the carpet as I pace the living room floor. I stare down at my hands and realise that they're actually sweating.

And here she is. Right on cue, as the clock ticks over to seven, the doorbell chimes. I answer the door and Sophie comes bustling in carrying a striped cupcake box.

'For dessert,' she declares, waving the box in the air. 'I presume you've eaten.'

'Yes,' I lie. I don't think biting my nails for the last hour counts as actual food, though.

'Great. Do you want to put the kettle on? They're strawberry and cream, your favourite.'

'Sure.'

I take the box from her as she wanders through to the lounge and flops down on the armchair. I don't deserve a cupcake. I'm going to hell. Straight to hell.

I busy myself making us tea, going over in my mind the possible responses I can provide to what will undoubtedly be Sophie's first question: what do I think of Connor? 'He seems to really like you' – not a lie, and possibly the safest option. Yes, I'll go with that; that should work. I take a deep breath, exhale heavily and carry the mugs of tea and the cupcakes through to the lounge and place them on the coffee table.

'So.' Sophie looks at me expectantly as I faff around taking a cupcake from the box, trying to buy myself some time. 'Do you like Connor? Isn't he perfect for me?'

Okay, here goes.

'He seems to really like you.'

'I know, and we have so much in common. We can just talk for hours and hours like we've know each other for years.'

'It's only been a few weeks, Sophie.' I take a bite of my cupcake, realising that the sound I hear rattling through my ears is the metaphorical pin I've just stuck in her balloon, and it's slowly deflating.

'What do you mean?' She looks at me a little taken aback. Whoosh, pop – there goes the balloon.

I swallow my mouthful and pause. I need to be careful how I play this.

'I just mean, don't get too carried away, that's all. Its early days.' I shrug, trying to lighten my inference.

'Right. I know. But I've finally met someone who actually gets me. Aren't you happy for me?'

Shit, she already looks hurt by that one comment.

'Absolutely.' A wave of guilt washes over me. 'I just don't want to see you get hurt again'

'I'm not going to get hurt. Connor is really nice, honestly. I'm sure you'll see that once you get to know him a bit better.'

Yeah, I think I've already been there, done that – no pun intended – and I'm definitely finding I like Connor less the more I get to know his twisted, screwed-up personality.

'You're right.' I chew the last mouthful of my cupcake and pick up my mug. 'I guess you know what you're doing.' I take a drink and there's a moment's pause.

'I know what Chris did to you was…horrible,' Sophie says quietly.

That's so not it! I bite my lip. I actually wish that was the reason for my inability to gush over Connor.

'And it must be hard for you to…you know…think of meeting someone else. But you will.'

'I know that, Sophie,' I say flatly, trying not to feel angry at the hint of accusation that I'm simply jealous or something. 'But I'm not ready for that now. You know what? Maybe I do just need to get to know Connor a bit better. Why don't we all go out again?' I suggest and Sophie relaxes, looking happier, and I appear to have restored the balance of harmony between us once more.

Clearly my warning fell on deaf ears yesterday. Well, I think Connor Matthews and I need to have a more in-depth conversation so I can make sure he realises that I'm not messing around, and I'm not going to take any more of his arrogant, cocky shit. This is not a game. It's real life with real people's feelings, and he needs to disappear from our lives as quickly as he appeared in them before somebody gets hurt.

'Nobody wants you around, boy. You're the reason your mother left. She didn't want you and I don't want you now.'

Chapter Fourteen

'Hi, Connor.' I smile politely as he and Sophie approach me at the bar the following Friday night. 'It's nice to see you again.'

It's not nice to see him again. In fact, I feel even more maddened than last time by the soft smile smeared across his face, masquerading as a friendly expression.

'Hi.' Sophie gives me a quick hug.

'Hey, do you want to find us a table? It's getting busy.' I look at Sophie. 'Connor can help me with the drinks.'

'Sure.'

She heads off into the crowd and I turn to face Connor, the previous niceties now wiped instantly from my face.

'Maybe I didn't make myself clear the last time that we met,' I snap, hearing the disdain in my own voice.

'About what?' The full, arrogance is back on his face.

'You know damn well what about,' I hiss.

'Come on, Emma. Sophie's happy.' He turns to look in the direction she went, then snaps his glare right back to me. 'Don't you want her to be happy?' His eyes stare questioningly into mine without blinking at all.

'Of course I want her to be happy,' I retaliate. 'Just not with a creep like you.'

'Now, now,' he taunts.

'Can I help you?'

I hear the barmaid behind me and I swivel around. 'Hi, sorry, can I get two vodka tonics please, and…' I turn and raise my eyebrows at Connor.

'A pint of lager.' He says flirtatiously to the pretty barmaid, which just angers me even more.

'You need to end things with her,' I say sharply as I turn back round to face him.

'Or what? You sound like a broken record, Emma, and it's starting to get really boring.'

'Don't push me.' I point my finger at him as I feel my temper bubbling at the surface, threatening to boil over. 'Or I'll tell her what happened myself and then she'll see you for what you really are: a liar and a cheat.'

'Tsk…One really shouldn't cast aspersions, especially when one hasn't behaved very nicely either,' he says in a mocking tone.

'I mean it.'

'No, you don't.' He looks all superior. 'Because if you tell her, that'll be the end of your friendship and you know that. Once she finds out that you've had a roll in the sack with her lover then there's no going back.'

'You're wrong,' But in my mind I'm not wholly convinced. 'She may react badly at first, but we've been friends for too long to not be able to get over this.'

'Are you sure?'

'Oh, fuck off!' I snap, knowing that my reaction is giving him just what he wants. He's getting a rise out of me and getting off on the fact, but I can't help it. I want to claw his eyes out every time I see his face. 'Just do it. Put her out of her misery and let her get on with her life while you slither back under the dark, slimy stone that you crawled out from so neither of us has the misfortune of being in your company ever again.'

'That'll be eight pounds ten, please,' the barmaid calls.

I turn around and hand over nine pounds before grabbing mine and Sophie's drinks and pushing right past Connor, leaving him chuckling to himself at the bar.

We spend the rest of the evening chatting amiably with no hint of the heated exchange that occurred at the start of the evening. I'm on my best behaviour, laughing in all the right places, engaging Connor in conversation. All the while he sits across from me watching my every move like a hawk observing his prey and I can't help but feel a little unnerved. Connor regales us with stories of his travelling across Europe a few years ago and I feign interest, but as I watch Sophie hanging off his every word, completely smitten, I can't help but wonder whether one word of it is true. I suspect it's bullshit, just like everything else about him.

As the evening draws to a close and we hug goodbye, I purposefully pull Connor towards me tightly under the pretence of a friendly exchange and, with a happy expression etched firmly in place, I remind him one last time: 'Do it this weekend. End it with her.'

Over the next two days I don't let my phone out of my sight as I wait impatiently for the call that I'm equally wanting but dreading. The call where Sophie is heartbroken over Connor breaking up with her, which leads me to give fake consolation as I try to pretend that I'm sorry about the outcome. Well, I am sorry that Sophie will be hurt and upset, but all the while I'll have to deal with the fact that I'm the instigator of her pain as I offer her words of comfort and a shoulder to cry on.

But by seven o'clock on the Sunday evening I haven't heard a peep from Sophie and my curiosity gets the better of me. I call her from my mobile and I hear far more rings than usual before she answers.

'Hi.' I put on my most cheerful voice. 'I've not heard from you all weekend so I just thought I'd check in with you. Is everything okay?' I bite my lip as I wait for her response.

'I'm sorry, Emma.' Her voice is all girly and fun. This is not the sound of a distraught and dumped girlfriend. 'It's just that I've been otherwise engaged. Connor's been here all weekend and…well…we haven't made it out of my flat.'

What?

'Connor, stop it,' she giggles. 'I'm trying to talk to Emma.'

I can't believe him!

Chapter Fifteen

I've reached depths that I thought were way beyond me. It's five p.m. on a Tuesday evening, almost two weeks since that frightful phone conversation with Sophie, and clearly Connor has ignored my every attempt to get him to disappear. More worryingly, Sophie has become distant and uncommunicative, with only the occasional text to me despite my barrage of phone calls and messages, which is most unlike her. I haven't physically seen her since that night at the bar with Connor, which feels very wrong; we usually meet up at least once a week. She cancelled our arranged drinks last Thursday by text, claiming she was really tired from a big project at work. I've tried to remain open-minded and have just put it down to complete emotional and loved-up blindness: she's caught up in the exciting initial phase of a new relationship where you want to spend every second together and all other relationships come second to this. I'm pretty sure Connor will have been doing his best to encourage this too, and to keep me out of the picture. Simon hasn't heard a peep out of Sophie either and he's taken even greater offence than I have to this.

So here I am, loitering outside of Blackley's Bank, where Connor supposedly works (although this could be a complete lie too), waiting for him to appear through the revolving glass door so I can...well, I don't know, but I can at least challenge him on what the hell is going on. I've lied to Jenny to get out of work early under the pretence of a dentist appointment. (In reality I haven't been to the dentist in years; it's unnatural for anyone to want to stare into another human's mouth and poke about, plus everything a dentist does causes severe pain, which in itself makes me question a person's desire and motivation to qualify as a dentist when it's clearly an excuse to perform legal torture.) Anyway, it's now three minutes past five. Where is he? Connor doesn't appear to me to be the world's most conscientious person, so I expected him to fly out of the door at five on the dot.

Aha...there he is.

I see him striding out of the revolving door with a petite blonde who's looking up at him. He's clearly saying something either so funny or so interesting that she can't bear to even take her gaze from him and look where she's going. He guides her out of the door and she giggles at him as they part company and...Oh my God...did he actually just wink at her as she waved goodbye?

That's just further fuel to my already burning fire, and I march over to him as he walks away from the building.

'Connor!' I shout after him. As he turns around I get a smidgen of satisfaction as I see a look of hesitation and wariness flutter fleetingly across his face before the smug mask slips back into place. 'You haven't done it, have you?' I snap accusingly once I've caught up with him, completely ignoring any niceties or greetings such as 'hello' first.

He just raises his eyebrows in an 'I'm so bored of this already' manner.

'You need to break it off with her.' I point my finger accusingly in his face. 'Or I'll tell her the truth, I swear.'

'See, I don't think you will. I think you're bluffing.'

'Really?' God, he makes me angry. 'Just try me.'

'Yeah.' An annoying, sneer spreads across his face. 'See, I'm not sure she holds your opinion in such high regard these days.'

I take a deep breath. He's just trying to wind you up, Emma. Don't let him.

'And why would that be?'

'Well, you haven't been very supportive to Sophie recently, have you? Those messages via instant messaging could have been a bit friendlier.'

'I don't know what you're talking about, Connor. I don't have an instant messaging account. I haven't been sending Sophie any messages other than a few' – okay, many – 'texts from my mobile.'

'Really?' He frowns at me in an exaggerated cartoon character kind of way. 'How strange. It sure looks like you have an instant messaging account given all those messages she's received from you on her phone, full of jealousy about her new relationship and being...well…generally not very friendly at all really, Emma.' He shakes his head mockingly at me.

I feel the cold hand of fear slither around my heart, gripping it tightly, causing my breath to catch in my throat as a horrible realisation hits me: he's even more devious than I could have imagined. My stomach sinks with the knowledge that maybe I'm finding this out far too late and the damage is already done.

'I mean, your new messaging account is under your nickname.' He taunts. 'Your nickname is Emmie, isn't it? Isn't that what Daddy calls you?'

Holy fuck. How does he know that?

'What did you do? What have you said to Sophie?' I can hear the hysteria creeping into my voice. . 'Are you now impersonating me, you fucking lunatic?'

'It's not what I've said to her, Emmie, it's what you've said to her. You've not been very encouraging recently, have you? You are the one she's starting to doubt now. Sophie doesn't need you any more. You're no longer required. All she needs is me in her life. Just me. She isn't going to leave me.'

Oh, holy Christ.

It's all slotting into place now. Sophie being distant on the phone, her cancelling drinks last week. She's not just tired and busy with work, she's avoiding me because she thinks I'm being a crap friend. Before I can stop myself I lunge angrily at him like a wild animal, clawing at his coat. I don't feel completely in control of my actions any more. I've never been so angry or scared, bloody terrified actually, of someone and what they might be capable of.

'Why are you doing this to me?' I hiss, my face only inches from his. Adrenaline is taking over now and I can feel my temper boiling over past the point of normality and into the unknown. 'Ouch!' Pain shoots up my arms.

'Take your nasty little hands off me.' He grabs at my wrists and squeezes until it feels like every bone in them might snap in two. His voice is gravelly and low. 'Don't even think about touching me again. I remember you that night. Drunk and cheap. You were so eager to get into bed with me it was embarrassing.' He looks at me with utter disgust and I feel every ounce of colour drain from my skin as I take a step back from him.

'What do you imagine Sophie would really think of you if I told her how her best friend, poor dumped, downtrodden Emmie, couldn't wait to get her knickers off the minute someone showed her the slightest bit of attention?'

No! It wasn't like that.

'Stop it,' I spit back at him, trying to be strong as I drown in my own humiliation.

'How grateful little Emmie was that I took pity on her. How cheap you were. One drink, wasn't it? For a drunken fumble between the sheets.'

'You…' I grit my teeth.

'What, Emmie? What?'

I'm dumbfounded. I want the ground to open up and swallow him whole right now in front of my very eyes so this whole horrible nightmare stops.

'Then I could tell Sophie how you tried to creep out of my flat like some common whore.'

That's enough. This is more than I can take.

I turn on my heel and run. I run as fast as I can to get away from him, still hearing his laughter as I ricochet off a wall and nearly fall as I stumble blindly in my urgent need to put distance between me and what can only be described as the devil himself. I don't know what I walked into that night in the bar but its got its claws well and truly into me and Sophie. The sliver of daylight that I'd been clinging on to with the hope that I could get Connor to get out of our lives has now disappeared. He's a psychopath. A complete and utter psychopath.

I don't stop running until I reach my car. Breathless and shaking, it takes me three attempts to unlock the car door and I climb in and frantically lock myself in. I gulp air as my whole body heaves. It takes me a moment or two to realise that I'm crying. Tears are streaming down my face and pooling under my chin. It's hopeless. It's all so hopeless. I don't know what to do any more. I don't understand why Connor is doing this to either one of us, but I know in my heart he isn't going to go away easily. I don't want to lose Sophie forever. I can't lose her, but just letting things lie, leaving her with Connor thinking god knows what about me just isn't an option. Our friendship means too much to me. I couldn't do that even if I tried. Whether I like it or not I've no choice but to tell Sophie. I'll just have to deal with the consequences.

I'm so ashamed of that night. Maybe Connor is right, maybe he found it easy to get me into bed. But I had my reasons: feelings vulnerable and hurt. At the time I couldn't imagine ever feeling as bad as that again, but I was wrong. This is worse. This is much worse.

I fold my arms across the top of the steering wheel and lean forward, resting my head on the top of my hands, and I sit there and sob. Then, in a momentary flash of realisation amidst the clouds of despair, it suddenly hits me: if Connor has only just left work then he isn't with Sophie. I need to see her. I need to see her now and put an end to the lies that she's being fed.

Looking in the driver's mirror, I wipe the last of the tears from my eyes. Then I start the engine and nearly wheel-spin the car out of the car park in my haste to get to Sophie's house. I've no idea whether she'll even be home, but I have to do this right now.

Chapter Sixteen

Good, there are lights on in Sophie's house, which means she must be in.

Once at the door I hover reluctantly. Now I'm here I'm really not sure what I'm going to say. It feels like there's some distance between us, but there shouldn't be.

'Hi,' I call as I knock on the door while letting myself in to Sophie's house like I would at any other time. 'Hey, there you are.' I see her in the corner as I walk through to the lounge, but then I stop dead in my tracks.

'Oh, hi, Connor.' I almost choke. 'I didn't know you were going to be here.'

He just stares at me blankly while leaning casually on the fireplace. Suddenly I feel uncomfortable and a shiver runs down my spine. This is wrong. This whole situation is wrong. I feel like I've inadvertently walked into a minefield and my next move could set off an explosion.

A hint of conceit hides at the corners of Connor's mouth. As I turn to face Sophie I notice she has tears in her eyes and she just looks...well...completely wrong.

'Sophie, are you okay?' I take a step towards her but she instinctively takes a step back. 'Soph, what's going on? You're scaring me now!'

I hear the fear in my own voice. I'm too late. I knew it the moment I saw him here before me. I'm too late.

'I just need to ask you something and I need you to tell me the truth, okay? Just be honest, Emma.'

This isn't good. Nothing is right about this situation. The whole atmosphere is wrong. Sophie is looking at me in a weird, angry, staring way and I feel like the bottom is about to fall out of my world for the second time this year. He's told her, God damn it. He's only gone and told her.

'Is it true?' she whispers.

My stomach flips like I'm on the big wheel at the fairground.

'Is what true?' I ask, flicking my gaze across to Connor, who is now standing right behind Sophie, his hands placed on her shoulders in a protective manner. His posture tells me exactly what Sophie means.

'Have you been flirting with Connor?'

What?

'What? No! Why would I?'

'So you didn't come on to him in the pub the other week when we were all together, asking him to…to...'

'To what, Sophie? Me? Come on to him? Is that what crap he's been filling your head with?' I glare at Connor but he just raises his eyebrows at me and purses his lips. 'And when exactly is this supposed to have happened that night?'

'Look, I know you've been going through a rough time with how Chris treated you and everything –'

'That doesn't mean I'd come on to your boyfriend, Sophie,' I interject. 'You know me, Sophie; you're my best friend. We've know each other for nearly all of our lives. Listen to what you're saying. You know I'd never do that. He's saying this to turn you against me. It's lies, Sophie, all lies.'

'So you haven't been turning up unannounced at his work? Weren't you there just this evening before racing over here to see me unannounced because he threatened to tell me?'

I glance at Connor, whose self-satisfied veil is straining his whole face. I want to kill him, but not before I've pulled his fingernails out one by one and listened to him scream in agony.

'Emma?'

Fuck. Fuck. Fuck.

'Yes, okay, I waited for him outside his work today, but only today, to try to get him to…'

'To what exactly?'

'To break up with you, alright? You deserve so much better, Sophie.' I exhale deeply as all the fight leaves my body. I thought I could win, but it looks completely out of my reach now. I'm going to lose this fight and God knows what the fallout will be.

'To what?' Sophie looks a mixture of hurt and confused and I feel like the worst person in the whole world. 'Who's suddenly put you in charge of my life, Emma? You don't even know Connor, so why do you believe he's not good enough for me? Why would you be telling him to break up with me?'

'Look, Sophie, we've been friends for...well...forever, and you know how much you mean to me. I'd never, ever say or do anything on purpose to hurt you.'

'Come on, Emma, are you sure you're not just trying to get back at Sophie?' Connor finally interjects.

I glare at him. 'What the hell are you talking about?'

'You know, because you've never quite forgiven Sophie for encouraging you to break if off with Mark.'

What the...

'You told him about me and Mark?'

The fight within me is back with a vengeance at the mention of this, and it's my turn to get angry now. Sophie at least has the decency to look contrite for having divulged personal information about me to this snake.

Mark was the love of my life, or at least I thought he was. But when the time came for us to both go to university, Sophie thought it would be too hard for us to have a long-distance relationship. Our universities were two hundred miles apart, and in hindsight she was right, but at the time I felt like she should have been more supportive and I accused her of being a bit jealous of our undying love. As it happens he got over me pretty quickly once the first term of university had started, and when I turned up to visit him unexpectedly, thinking it would be romantic to surprise him, I found him in bed with a fellow psychology student. I just can't believe Sophie told Connor about that.

'How the hell did that even come up in a conversation?' I snap challengingly at Sophie.

'It wasn't even really about you,' she mumbles, looking uncomfortable.

'I bet it wasn't.' Connor must have been pulling dirt about me from her since day one of this escapade.

'Connor was just talking about his sister being in a long-distance relationship and how these things can be hard, that's all.'

'His sister?' I cock my head and raise my eyebrows. 'Are you sure he even has a sister?' I realise my tone is getting harsher by the second but this is unbelievable.

'Emma, why are you being like this? If you care about me so much, why can't you just be happy for me?' Sophie stands tall with her hands placed firmly on her hips in a defiant pose. 'Why do you have it in for Connor so much when he's been nothing but nice to you?'

Nice to me? Huh!

I pause, feeling the pounding of my heart as it reverberates all the way through my body. I can't believe he's turned this whole thing around on me. Even worse, Sophie is falling for his shit. I know I've no other choice: I'm going to have to reveal him to her as the nasty, two-timing cheat that he really is. But the only way I can do that is to tell her everything – to tell her about that night, about Connor's games. In my head this seems like the only solution, but in my heart I feel the heavy dread of fear as I'm about to put my friendship in serious danger.

'He's only being nice to me in front of you, Sophie. In secret he wishes I'd just disappear, don't you?' I glare at Connor now, trying to goad him into the conversation, instead of him watching from the side-lines as my world implodes.

'That's just not true.' Connor sounds almost convincing.

'And why wouldn't Connor like you, Emma? Apart from the fact that you keep hanging around his work trying to get him to break up with me?'

'Because he knows that I know what he's really like.'

'And what's that, Emma?' Connor chips in again. I don't even bother to look at him.

'He knows that I was going to warn you that he's…'

I look at Sophie. Her face is angry and creased into a frown as she waits for me to finish my sentence. She's holding her breath and every muscle of her body appears taut.

'That he's a cheat,' I accuse, standing tall and defiant, my hands placed firmly on my hips now too – mirroring Sophie's pose.

There, I've said it. I've said it out loud.

'What do you mean he's a cheat?' Sophie looks warily at Connor and then back at me.

'She's lying, babe. Don't even bother listening to her.' Connor is immediately by Sophie's side, his expression unreadable.

Sophie presses her lips together as if thinking carefully about what to say next.

'Why would you say that, Emma? Why would you think that Connor has cheated on me?'

Oh God. Here goes. I need to open my mouth and say the actual words. This is harder than I thought it would be, and as I look into Sophie's wide eyes, filled with fear and despair, I swallow nervously feeling the prick of tears.

'Okay, you have to realise that I couldn't have known. I didn't know who he was. I mean, he used a different name. Hell, I used a different name.' I wave my arms around, floundering. 'It was a mistake. I wish I could take it back but I can't.' I realise that I'm rambling now, but as I glance up and meet Connor's eyes I see a flicker of fear wash over his face. He shouldn't have called my bluff. He should have just left us alone.

'Emma, you're not making any sense. What do you mean you didn't know who he was and you used a different name? What mistake?' I can hear the panic in Sophie's voice now and her eyes are wide and questioning.

'It was me that he cheated with,' I whisper as a silent tear rolls slowly down my cheek. 'That's how I know – because it was with me.'

I stare at Sophie, not daring to move, my eyes pleading with her to let me explain.

Her face crumples. 'Are…are you saying what I think you're saying?' Her voice breaks.

'Sophie, you're not going to believe that I actually slept with Emma, are you?' Connor interjects loudly. 'I mean, this is crazy.' He pulls her around to face him. 'She's just jealous, babe, of what we have, because she's alone and sad. She wants you to be as miserable as she is. What kind of friend does that make her?'

'Sophie!' I grab her arm but she flinches away from me and I pull back in shock. It feels like I've been stabbed in the heart, the physical pain is so acute. 'Sophie,' I whisper softly, but she doesn't move a muscle.

Connor glares at me over Sophie's shoulder. Tears flow freely now down my face, soaking into my t-shirt. I can't let him do this. I can't let him win. I need to make her listen. It can't be too late. He can't have turned her against me.

'Let me explain what happened,' I beg. 'It was before I'd even met Connor,' I continue and Sophie at least turns around to face me, but with Connor's arm still draped around her shoulders in a protective – controlling – gesture.

'Emma, just stop this,' he snarls at me like a caged animal.

'No!' I shout. He needs to shut up and let me tell her so she can understand, so she can forgive me.

'It's okay.' Sophie sniffs as she touches Connor's hand. 'Let her speak.'

I exhale loudly. 'Okay…okay…it was the Friday night – you know, when I went out with Jenny and Lola, just after Chris and I… Anyway, it was late and we'd been drinking – a lot. He, Connor – sent over a drink for me. And we started talking. And one thing led to another and we ended up back at his flat.'

'This is a joke.' Connor shakes his head. 'Are you going to let her continue with this charade?'

'So what are you saying? You didn't know it was Connor? You didn't know it was my boyfriend?' Sophie's voice is flat – emotionless.

'Exactly. He said his name was Johnny, and I said mine was Louise. I'm so sorry, Sophie.' I start to really cry now. 'We…had a…a… one-night stand.'

It's out there now in the open, bouncing around the room like an out-of-control firework with no way of knowing what damage will be done by the flying sparks.

A heavy silence stifles the room as the enormity of my revelation shocks all three of us. Like a true player, Connor is the first to recover and he moves quickly, so quickly that I don't expect it, and grabs me roughly by the shoulders.

'What the fucking hell are you trying to do?' he spits, angry eyes bulging at me as he shakes me hard. He looks like a maniac and I'm stunned. He's really frightening me now. I can feel his hands digging into my skin as he squeezes me in his grasp. There's pure hatred in his eyes and they look almost completely black instead of their usual vibrant blue.

'Connor, get off her, let her go!' Sophie jumps into action and pulls at his arms, forcing him to release me.

I pull away from him, gasping for breath, wiping the tears from my face with the back of my hand. A burning sensation shoots through my shoulders.

'But she's fucking lying, Sophie. She's trying to split us up. I just don't know why she'd want to hurt you like that.'

Oh he's good, he's very good. In fact, I think an Oscar nomination might be due for this performance.

'Sophie, I just…I can prove it!' A light bulb flicks on inside my head. 'I can describe his flat to you. I can prove that I saw it that night.'

This outburst seems to silence even Connor: he must realise now that I've got him, good and proper. He knows I've seen it. With him. I wrack my brain and try to remember what I saw as I walked through the rooms. Shit, I wish I hadn't been so drunk. I close my eyes for a second, placing myself momentarily back in that night.

'You have beige walls and beige carpet,' I state, staring straight into Connor's eyes,

'Sophie's shown you pictures of me and her. You've seen pictures of Sophie in my apartment on social media. That's how you know what it looks like.'

'No. No. That's not it. And your bedroom is…is…'

'Is what, Emma? Black and white? Yeah, I know.'

Damn him!

'This is bullshit.'

'You knew that I'd say that your bedroom is black and white so you blurted it out first to make it look like –'

'Enough!' Sophie holds up her hands and I close my mouth.

Connor is fidgeting like a predator waiting to pounce, his dark eyes darting between me and Sophie. Sophie looks to be near breaking point and I can feel my own colour, and sanity, fading rapidly.

'Emma, you're my closest friend.' She swallows back tears. 'So I owe it to you to listen to what you have to say.'

'Sophie, no!' Connor snaps.

'How come you've never mentioned this supposed one-night stand to me until now?' She stares at me, her lips pressed together in a thin line, and waits for me to speak.

I take a moment to try to compose myself and to get right in my head what I want to say.

'I didn't know who he was, I swear to you, or I'd never, ever have…' I trail off.

'So you're adamant that this actually happened?' Sophie whispers and I can't help but feel angry that she's doubting me.

'It happened!' My voice gets a little higher. 'I wouldn't be going through all of this if it hadn't. I wouldn't make up something so awful. I'd never intentionally hurt you, you know that. It just happened. We met. I was already a bit drunk, and I should never have accepted a drink from him, let alone gone back to his flat.'

'See, she's just admitted she was drunk and was behaving like a slut. Going back to a guy's flat for sex when you're drunk and you've only just met him? Nice behaviour.' Connor looks down his nose at me before facing Sophie. 'She probably can't remember who it was she slept with, and it certainly wasn't me. But that's a convenient story.'

It's harsh, but he's right. I'm totally ashamed of my behaviour that night, which is why I got the hell out of there the following morning as quickly as I could. But right now I must resist punching him in the face, at least until this whole mess is over.

'It really doesn't sound like you, Emma. You've never, to my knowledge, had a one-night stand before.'

'I know, I know, and I haven't. But I was a complete wreck. Chris had just dumped me for that other girl. I was feeling incredibly low, and I guess I was flattered by the attention. I felt attractive again.'

'You're pathetic,' Connor growls. 'Pathetic and bitter. And you're trying to drag Sophie down to your level. You're disgusting!'

I bite my tongue and hold back tears of anger and frustration.

'I think I've heard enough,' Sophie says calmly – far too calmly for this situation really.

'Sophie, you're not actually going to believe what he's saying, are you? I'm telling you now so you can see his true colours, so you can see that you deserve better than him, better than this.'

Her bottom lip quivers for a moment and I want to pull her into a hug. I've hurt her, I know that, and I don't know how to make it all better, but I need to know that she believes me, that –

'I don't know what to believe.' She stares at the floor and I feel my heart sink all the way down to the pit of my stomach. 'It's like Daryl Jones all over again.'

'What? We were kids, Sophie. Just kids. How can you still be mad about that? We were fourteen years old with raging, confusing hormones and we both liked the same boy. We both just had a stupid crush.'

'You were jealous of me then and you are now too.'

'Sophie...' I take a step towards her.

She looks up, shaking her head. A single tear trickles slowly down her cheek. 'I think you should go, Emma.' She swallows noisily. 'I think you should just go.'

'No, no, I'm not leaving it like this. I can't leave things this way, Sophie.'

'I need to think, Emma. I need to sort this all out in my own head. This is just too much. It's all too much to take in. I don't know what to think or who to believe.'

'Sophie,' I state flatly, 'if I leave, all that's going to happen is that he's going to work on you, chipping away at you until you believe every word he says.'

'I think you should go,' she repeats.

I stand there for a moment as the enormity of what's happening here really takes hold. I feel sick. It can't be over like this. This can't be the end of years of friendship. But as I look up and glance between a distraught Sophie and a now remarkably complacent Connor, I realise it is. This is the end.

'I'm afraid we have some concerns about your son's behaviour. He seems to be overly aggressive towards the girls in the class and it's reached a point of being unacceptable. We have no choice; we're going to have to suspend him.'

Chapter Seventeen

It's been nearly two weeks since Sophie and I last spoke. Normally it's unheard of for us not to at least text every twenty-four hours. It feels strange, but everything in my world is at odds, like it's tipped on its axis and I'm hanging by a very thin thread. I have spent most evenings over the last two weeks pouring over Sophie's social media profile watching as each day more photo's of her and Connor appear seemingly replacing the catalogue of our friendship with a portrayal of their love life as with each new photo of Sophie looking longingly at Connor appears, one of Sophie and I having fun disappears. It's like our friendship is being deleted one photo at a time and Connor is winning the battle of cutting me permanently out of Sophie's life. I've picked up my mobile phone a thousand times and put it back down again. Sending a text saying I'm sorry seems futile, but I've still sent five texts saying just that but all have been met with no response.

It's Saturday and the shop has been busy as hell. Both Lola and Jenny are working too, and we've barely had the chance to have a lunch break between us. At four thirty I hear the door open and I glance up from the new stock I'm pricing to see Mrs Winklebarrow-Smith – a snide old bat who comes in here just to make our lives miserable. She's awkward, rude and overly demanding of our time, but she spends a small fortune on a regular basis so we have no choice but to grit our teeth and get on with it. I'm in no mood for her antics this afternoon, though, so I keep my head down, avoiding eye contact and hoping she'll target Lola or Jenny to assist her with her sharp demands.

'Am I invisible today?' she bellows.

Oh crap.

I look up and there she is, standing right in front of me. I glance around. Jenny and Lola are nowhere to be seen. Damn them.

'Sorry, Mrs Winklebarrow-Smith, I was just busy with this new stock. I didn't hear you come in.'

'Well, as a customer surely I'm more important than putting stickers on bags.' She purses her blood-red lips.

God, she's intolerable.

I put down the stock pricelists feeling my patience already reaching capacity. 'What can I help you with today?'

'That red dress you had in the window last week?'

'Yes.'

'I want one in a size twelve.'

Size twelve? Who's she kidding? We have this argument every time. She refuses to admit that she's a size sixteen and we have to endure a load of abuse about our 'unnaturally small sizes' until we finally get her into the correct dress size. But thankfully today that's not going to be a problem.

'I'm sorry, that dress has been very popular. We only have two left and they're both size ten.'

'But I need one for the tennis club dinner tomorrow evening.' She pouts unattractively.

'I'm sorry. We don't have any more coming in until next Thursday,' I state calmly.

She glares at me but I stand my ground and meet her stare. After a few seconds she huffs nonchalantly.

'I'll try one on then.'

What? Did I not say that in English?

'But they're both size ten,' I repeat.

'And I said I'll try one on!' she raises her voice.

'But you're not a size ten, Mrs Winklebarrow-Smith.' I put down my pen and lean both hands on the counter, waiting for her next comment.

'How dare you? Get me that dress to try on this instant.'

I'm not going to allow her to attempt to squeeze herself into a dress that's three sizes too small. She's done this before and the dress split halfway through her trying to climb into it. Not only was the dress ruined (she didn't bother to pay for it), but after ignoring her shouts for a number of minutes I eventually had to extract her from it, which left mental images I've tried very hard to forget.

'Okay, I'm sorry, but I'm not going to do that.' She's really testing me now and I'm getting tired of her shit. 'The dress is a size ten. You're a size sixteen.'

'I'm a size twelve,' she retorts, her hands now placed accusingly on her hips.

Jenny has reappeared across the other side of the shop and she's watching the exchange between us with a slightly concerned expression. But I don't care. I've reached boiling point and everything suddenly seems far too much to take. The burden is too heavy, and my usual coping mechanism is about to fail dramatically.

'Unless you've lost two stone since you were here last week then you're still a size sixteen,' I continue.

'I've never been so insulted,' she growls.

Really? I find that hard to believe.

'Get me the manager. I want to complain.'

'Why don't you just –'

'Emma!' Jenny appears at my side. 'What appears to be the problem?' she asks calmly, smiling widely at the shrivelled-up prune opposite me.

'I want to buy the red dress that was in your window last week,' Mrs Winklebarrow-Smith croaks, looking hard-done-by, 'but she won't let me try the dress on because she says I'm too fat.'

'That's not what I said,' I mutter, looking down at the counter, my earlier fight dissolved.

'You know what' – Jenny turns to face Mrs Winklebarrow-Smith – 'the cut of that dress is very sharp and the size ten is really like a size eight.' She states convincingly. Geez, she should have been a politician, the way she can defuse tension. 'So why don't we get you a glass of wine and then we can go through some of these really exciting new designs that have just arrived today? I'm sure we can find something that will look fabulous on you and will certainly turn heads at your tennis dinner tomorrow.'

Mrs Winklebarrow-Smith glares at me for a second, like I'm something unpleasant that she's had the misfortune to tread in, then she looks at Jenny and smiles with satisfaction. 'I like my wine dry and very chilled.'

'I'm sure we have one you'll like.' Jenny agrees confidently now the danger has passed. 'Lola?'

Lola appears out of thin air at my other side, her eyes wide. Clearly she's heard the whole fiasco.

'Could you get Mrs Winklebarrow-Smith a glass of dry white wine, please?' She asks and Lola nods silently before disappearing into the kitchen area.

'Emma.' Jenny looks right at me now. 'Why don't you finish pricing that new stock in the back room where you'll have more...space?'

I grab the clothes and shuffle towards the stock room. I can't believe how I've just behaved. I'm so embarrassed. I've never been that unprofessional at work. If Marissa Bamford finds out, I'll be sacked in an instant, maybe justifiably so.

As I lay the clothes down on the large wooden table in the centre of the room, Jenny pops her head around the door.

'What the hell was that?' she hisses.

'I know, I know.' I hold up my hands in submission. I can feel the emotions of the last few weeks brimming close to the surface and I just want to be left alone.

'You stay in here until she's gone.' She glances behind her. 'I'll smooth things over and ply her with wine.'

I press my lips together, trying to plug the dam that's at bursting point, and I shake my head up and down vigorously.

'And then we'll talk.' She turns to head back out to the shop and I catch the door before it closes.

'Jenny?'

She turns back.

'Thank you,' I whisper.

An hour later, once we've closed the shop for the day, I'm dragged in silence to the wine bar three doors down the street. Lola ushers me into a booth in the far corner while Jenny collects a bottle of wine and three glasses from the bar. She quickly pours wine into all three and then pushes one right under my nose.

'Okay, talk.' She raises her eyebrows at me and takes a sip of wine.

I glance awkwardly between her and Lola. They're both staring at me and I wonder exactly what I should start talking about – there is so much crap to potentially discuss. Maybe I should start with my earlier outburst.

'I'm sorry about today,' I mutter. 'It was extremely unprofessional and I'm mortified at my behaviour. I promise that won't ever happen again.'

'Yep, I already figured out that bit,' Jenny carries on, staring straight at me. 'And to be fair, Mrs Winklebarrow-Smith could do with taking down a peg or two. But...'

'I guess I'm just a bit tired, that's all. I've not been sleeping well lately.' I take a large mouthful of my wine and look down at the table. I feel completely at odds with myself at the moment, like an alien has taken over my body and mind and I'm no longer in control of them.

'Emma, we're worried about you.' Lola touches my arm gently. 'Please tell us what's wrong. This is more than just sleep deprivation.'

'You haven't been yourself for the last two weeks,' Jenny adds. 'Worse than the initial few days after you and Chris broke up.'

I consider telling them everything. Carrying around the weight of the situation is almost unbearable and I have no one to talk to about it. I've already burdened Simon with my story, to no avail. Sophie won't return my texts. She obviously can't stand the sight of me and she still believes that creep over me, which hurts. Really hurts. But I've seen him in action; I know how he works. If I do tell Jenny and Lola then they may hate me too. They may not understand how easily this happened, or how sorry I am. But in reality they can't make me feel any worse about myself than I already do.

Right, here goes.

I pick up my glass and down the remaining wine in one. Lola opens her mouth to speak but Jenny holds up a hand to shush her and refills my glass.

'That guy I met' – I cough to clear my throat – 'when we went out a few weeks ago…' I look up at Jenny and I see her bite her lip. 'Well…I lied. I didn't just talk to him and then go home.' I let out a deep sigh.

Jenny looks at me with a 'I knew it' look. Any other time I'd take great satisfaction in wiping that expression off her face, but not today.

'It's really not what you think.'

'Okay.' Jenny's self-congratulatory expression falters a fraction and her voice sounds wary, as though she's now anticipating that I'm about to drop some sort of bomb which is going to negate this.

'I stayed for another drink…I'd had far too much to drink…and I…I went back to his place.'

'I see.' Jenny drinks the last of her wine and tops it up with the remainder of the bottle. 'Did you sleep with him?' She leans closer to me, although the bar is still pretty empty and I'm quite sure that no one can hear us – it's Saturday teatime, after all, so most people aren't ready to start chugging alcohol for another couple of hours yet.

'Oh God.' I put my head in my hands.

'I see,' she repeats annoyingly. She waves her hands dismissively. 'So you slept with him. It happens, I mean…oh my God, Emma!' she exclaims suddenly grasping my arm, nearly frightening me to death. 'Are you pregnant?'

'I'm not pregnant!' I state a little too loudly, causing the barmaid to glance over in our direction and frown before her gaze turns to the empty wine bottle on our table.

'Um, can we grab another bottle, please?' Jenny calls over to her.

She collects a fresh bottle from a glass fridge and brings it over to us. We sit in silence with the cloud of suspension hanging over the three of us until the barmaid places the bottle on the table and Jenny thanks her and she disappears back out of ear shot.

'So, if you're not pregnant then what's the crisis? Having a one-night stand is…' Jenny struggles to find the right word.

'Irresponsible? Horrible? So unlike me?'

'It's not necessarily horrible' Lola chips in but as I look at her she hurriedly picks up her wine and avoids my gaze.

'Well I'm not exactly proud of it, meeting a guy and sleeping with him and –'

'It happens, that's all I'm saying' Lola's voice is unusually a little louder now 'you don't have to make out it to be so seedy.'

I just stare at the usually mild mannered Lola and she blushes crimson and then I realise, she's had a one night stand before. Oh no, she's going to hate me too. Here I am practically calling it –'

'I just think that if you're adults then you can make decisions yourself about what you want to do in your own sex life. You shouldn't have to feel…judged' she continues before taking a large gulp of wine.

'I'm sorry. I didn't mean to judge anybody, Lola.' I need damage control here before I alienate everybody around me. And Lola's right, one night stands aren't bad for everyone, just when you sleep with your best friend's boyfriend. 'It's just that my situation isn't as black and white as that, and if two adults both want to have sex because it feels right in the moment then you're right, it's up to each and every one of us how we conduct our lives, sex lives included'.

Silence hangs over us again and I see Jenny glance at me and then at Lola.

'It wasn't planned' Lola says softly 'but I don't regret it either.'

'I understand' I top up her wine 'it's just that I did regret it and -'

'And it can just be…well…uncomfortable – you know, the following morning. I mean, what did you do? What happened? Are you going to see him again?' Jenny carries along the conversation avoiding further discomfort for Lola by firing far too many questions at me at once.

Okay, there are very different answers to all of those questions.

'Well, the really short version is that I got completely shit-faced downing tequila.' Both Jenny and Lola look guiltily towards the floor. 'And then I got charmed by some Justin Timberlake lookalike who honed in on my desperate, miserable, recently dumped car wreckage of an emotional state and I fell for his charms hook, line and sinker, feeling flattered by his obvious interest in me. We went back to his flat under the premise that he was going to make me coffee and we…well…you know.' I'm not one to ever share those type of details. 'And the following morning I got the hell out of there as quickly as I could.'

'You sneaked out of there?' Jenny looks at me wide-eyed.

'No,' I sulk, sounding suitably offended.

'Oh, sorry.'

'Don't be,' I concede, biting my lip. 'It wasn't through lack of trying. If he hadn't woken up and caught me trying to scoop up my belongings and head for the door then I'd have crawled out of there on my hands and knees rather than face him the following morning.' I take another gulp of my wine as I realise it physically pains me to speak about the whole episode.

'He was kind of cute if I remember, though,' Jenny muses. 'Did you agree to see each other again then?'

Oh, the irony of it!

'Not exactly.'

'What does that mean?' Lola asks quietly.

'It means I haven't reached the punch line yet.'

'It gets worse?' Jenny tries to remain expressionless but I can see her face morphing into a cringe.

'He already has a girlfriend,' I state flatly.

'Shit…does she know? Did you know?'

'No, of course not. You know that's not who I am, and it's not like he walked up to me, bought me a drink and talked about his gorgeous girlfriend all night before asking me to climb in the sack with him.' My heartbeat thunders in my chest and I can hear my voice getting higher and higher, on the border of hysterical. Said out loud it does all sounds seedy and dirty, and I feel shame smothering me, causing me to become defensive.

'I'm sorry. I know you wouldn't do something like that and I understand how you must feel really bad for his girlfriend. But he's the complete asshole who hit on you when he already had a girlfriend and you shouldn't feel like it's your fault.'

'Jenny's right.' Lola agrees. 'He's the complete jerk here.'

'Wait a minute.' Jenny frowns. 'How did you figure out that he has a girlfriend?'

And there it is – the uncomfortable truth.

'You know my best friend, Sophie?'

They both nod in unison and I try to get the words out but they're stuck in my throat. I pull my hands nervously through my hair and they both stare at me, waiting for me to say something. But as I sit there in a silent fight with myself, the penny appears to drop and Jenny's eyes widen even further.

'Oh no...your best friend, Sophie? She's the girlfriend? Holy shit, Emma...' Jenny sits open-mouthed, seemingly shocking herself with the mere suggestion.

I bite my lip.

'No, surely not. I mean, you're kidding, right? This is a joke?' Lola asks a little nervously. 'I mean, how could this possibly happen?'

This is definitely not a joke.

'She introduced me to him over coffee the following Sunday morning.' I hang my head in shame.

'Holy fuck…' Jenny puts her hand to her mouth, looking visibly traumatised.

I think that was my exact response too.

We all sit there in uncomfortable silence as Jenny and Lola, obviously dumbfounded, battle to make some sort of sense, any sense, of what I've just told them. It would seem that spilling my guts and sharing my problems hasn't made me feel better in the slightest. Now I just feel like I've disappointed even more people.

For some unexplainable reason I feel the need to divulge even more disturbing facts about that evening, and I go on to explain about the fake names and that I hadn't actually met Sophie's amazing new boyfriend at that point so it was an honest mistake (even if the whole one-night stand thing was something that I should never have done), and that if I'd have had any inkling of who he was I would totally not have gone there.

'Does she know?' Jenny whispers. 'Sophie? Does she know?'

And here's where it gets a whole lot worse...

'Pour more wine and prepare yourselves,' I state, and Jenny grabs the bottle. 'I told her. There was no other option. He's playing us off against each other like it's all some big game to him. He's been goading me since that Sunday morning when the three of us came face to face.'

'What did he do when you walked in the coffee shop?' Lola asks.

'He smirked, and for some reason unbeknown to me he didn't even look shocked to see me.' I shake my head. 'I've tried to reason with him, to get him to break up with her, but he refuses.'

'What? How exactly does he think this is going to play out?' Jenny seems angered now the initial shock has worn off.

'That he'll remove me from the equation.'

'Like that's going to happen. Sophie is your best friend.' Jenny shrugs seemingly dismissing the idea.

'It's already happened. Sophie and I are done; I'm done,' I hear the defeat in my own voice. 'I'm currently about one text away from a restraining order.'

'What? She's actually swallowed his crap and won't speak to you?'

'How did he turn her against you?' Lola looks at me, astonished.

'I told her what happened, that we had a one-night stand. I even described his flat to her. But he'd pre-empted everything I said with a whole other explanation before I'd even got there. He's convinced Sophie that I'm just jealous of them because I'm alone and have just been dumped by my long-term boyfriend.'

'And she believes that?' Jenny shakes her head.

'It's a long story, but there have been one or two occasions in the past when we've crossed swords over boys during our friendship. But they were years and years ago – you know, when we were young and stupid.'

'But the point is,' Jenny suggests 'he's a complete nutcase. Sophie clearly needs to get rid of him, and quickly.'

'I know.' I put my head in my hands, rubbing my temples. 'But how do I get her to see that if she won't even speak to me? He's probably been poisoning her against me at every available opportunity, like a cyanide drip, until she can't see past this.'

'So you're going to have to make her see,' Lola states with a lot more confidence than I have right at this moment.

'And how do I do that exactly?'

'You could try to engage him in conversation – you know, get him to confess to everything, while all the time recording him. Then you can play it back to her and she'll see!' Jenny seems excited by this ridiculous suggestion.

I shake my head at her. 'I think you've been watching too many crime movies, Jenny. One – he'll probably be suspicious if I try to talk to him again, given the last experience we had after I waited for him outside of his work. And two – even if I could engage him into a conversation that didn't just involve us both tearing strips off each other, it's unlikely that he'd confess all to me. In fact, I'm probably the last person he'd ever confess anything to. It would be like a murderer walking around with a smoking gun and wearing a t-shirt emblazoned with the slogan "I did it". It just wouldn't happen. And in any case, I don't have a tape recorder.'

'God, you're such a defeatist!' Lola exclaims. 'If you provoke him enough, he might let something slip that will incriminate him. It doesn't have to be a full and frank confession, and you might not have a tape recorder but you do have a mobile phone with a recording device on it.'

'Oh. Right.' Mmm, this might not be the craziest idea after all. 'But how do I get him to talk to me? I can't get caught loitering outside his work place again.'

'You know where his flat is.' Jenny shrugs, as if she's stating the obvious. 'You're going to have to follow him to find an appropriate place.'

'Follow him? As in wait outside his flat under the cover of a bush and then sneak after him like a stalker?'

'Yes.'

'Well, that's just great. I've always wanted to pursue an alternative career as a sleuth from a teenage novel.'

'Don't mock.' Jenny purses her lips. 'Have you got a better idea?'

I'm silent for a moment as I ponder. Actually I don't.

'No.'

'Then…'

'Then I guess I'll give it some thought,' I concede.

As I loll in the bathtub later that evening, trying to soak my worries away, I mull over Jenny and Lola's suggestion. It almost seems farcical to stalk Connor into submission, but I'm not sure I've been left with any other option. Sophie won't return my calls or texts, so

I need some cold, hard evidence to prove to her what a shark he really is.

Chapter Eighteen

It's Sunday morning and I'm taking refuge in the comforting aroma of freshly brewed coffee, but as I hover undecidedly at the coffee shop counter, glancing between a double-chocolate-chip muffin and the Victoria sponge to complement my latte, a blurry vision catches my attention. A slight movement of something familiar. As I glance over my shoulder, my heart lurches into my mouth. My ex-boyfriend, Chris, and a pretty blond girl who looks...about twenty two, I gulp, are snuggled cosily in the corner of the coffee shop on a leather sofa. I stare, mesmerised, as his hand strokes the back of her hair and they giggle together, oblivious to the world around them. Then I feel the knife plunge into my back and twist in between my rib cage as he kisses her softly on the lips. It's intimate and romantic and I'm drawn to watching it with all the morbid fascination of motorists passing a car accident: you know you should just look away from the ghastly scene but you can't help but stare. I swallow down the contents of my stomach, feeling my hands beginning to sweat profusely.

'Hello are you going to order something or not?' the woman behind the counter snaps at me and I turn back round to face her. I must look as bad as I suddenly feel as her face immediately softens. 'Are you feeling alright? You've gone awfully pale.'

My heart is urging me to flee the scene. I may have gotten over Chris but I don't need to observe his new found happiness with some young girl over my morning coffee. But my head it telling me to stay. He lives in the city so this won't be the first, or the last time I will bump into them so I might as well deal with it now.

Hmm. Well, maybe half deal with it.

'I'm fine,' I whisper, barely audible over the hissing coffee machines. 'I'll have both.'

'I'm sorry?'

'Both!' I snap back. 'A slice of cake and the muffin, and make the latte extra-large.'

The woman opens her mouth in protest at my rudeness but thinks better of it.

'That'll be six pounds forty-five.' She snaps with a hint of attitude as the other woman behind the counter starts grinding beans and banging and slamming things. I rub at my forehead as a dull ache throbs painfully. I mean really, does it need that much force to make a cup of coffee?

I move my eyes to my right without turning my whole head. Chris and the mystery woman – sorry, girl – are still completely engrossed in each other and clearly haven't seen me. I grab a newspaper from the pile and collect my food and coffee from the end counter before scooting across to the far left-hand side of the coffee shop. I squeeze into a chair at a small table for two and fling the newspaper open, holding it up and hiding behind it like some spy, and then glancing around the side and over the top to make sure they're still in my line of sight.

I guess that's the 'other woman'. Now that I've seen her in the flesh, and not just in the depths of my cruel imagination, I feel really strange. I thought that if I set eyes on her I'd be really angry and that I'd want to kill her; that I'd storm right over to them and tell them what I thought of the two of them playing around behind my back. But now, now I'm here in that moment, all I feel is sadness. Emptiness and sadness. I'm sad that I was more committed to our relationship than Chris. I'm sad that I thought that our connection was strong and that we had a future together. I'm sad that he appears to have been cheating on me with someone who has barely finished puberty. But most of all, I'm sad because if I think back over the two years that we were together, if I'm honest, I can't ever remember him looking at me the way he's looking at her right now. That's what hurts the most.

I break off a large piece of chocolate muffin and stuff it into my mouth. Whoever said you shouldn't use food as an emotional crutch had clearly never tasted these muffins. As I chew I don't know quite what comes over me, but before I can stop myself I reach for my mobile phone from my handbag and click on the camera button. I know it's wrong, and at some point in the near future I'll regret it, but I can't fight it. It's like a compulsion. I need to take photographic evidence. Why? The sensible part of my brain prods me harshly. To continually torture myself? I don't know, but I slide the phone just to the edge of the newspaper so as not to look conspicuous, and as Chris nuzzles the neck of the 'other woman' I click the button to capture the moment.

Instantly I feel sick and I lower the phone in shame and shove it roughly back into my bag. I can't quite believe that I've just done that. I glance over the top of the newspaper. Shit, they're standing up…and heading this way. I crouch down further for a few seconds before daring to look again, but when I do all I can see is the back of Chris's jacket as the door closes behind them and they walk off down the street and out of my sight. I sit there for a moment, watching the door, before lowering the paper. Staring down at the half-eaten muffin and slice of sponge cake on the table in front of me, I take a moment to sip my latte. Then I proceed to devour every last crumb.

I don't know how long I sit there, wallowing in gluttony and self-pity, staring over and over at the photo on my phone, but as I drink the last of my latte it's stone-cold and I baulk at the taste. I can't shake the heavy fog that's shrouding me. My whole body feels sluggish and slow, like I'm in a dream, not really here, and as I stare out of the window I realise it's starting to get dark. How long have I been sitting here?

What's happening to me? I was getting over him, coming to accept that we weren't meant to be and that he loves someone else. But it was a lot easier to deal with without the intimate reality of it being slapped around my face, shoved down my throat and then squeezed tightly around my heart. I still have feelings for him. It's natural I still have feelings for him. I can't switch my emotions off in an instant just because I'm angry.

Damn it, this is doing me no good. I push myself up from the chair and lurch towards the door. I gulp at the fresh air as I make my way home, trying desperately to push the images of my skinny, blond, younger replacement from my mind.

Chapter Nineteen

Later that evening I forcibly drag myself from the sofa. I've been lolling here for the last hour, reminiscing about the love I lost, or the love that technically ran off with a young blond girl but nevertheless. I need to clear my head of all thoughts so I head for the shower to wash off the glum veil that has swamped and suffocated me since I saw Chris and his new girlfriend sharing cake and kisses in their world of loved-up happiness. Wallowing in self-pity really is becoming too frequent an activity, and an annoying one, and I'm pleased to have the distraction of dinner with Dad and Margaret at their house this evening.

After a quick shower I pull on clean clothes and feel instantly refreshed. A sweep of blusher and mascara and a quick spray of perfume and I'm nearly ready to go. I collect my handbag and keys, swirling on a slick of pink lip gloss with my spare hand as I head for the door. It's surprisingly cold and I shudder as I climb into the car, quickly switching the engine on and turning the heat up to full blast. An old Madonna song plays on the radio and I find myself singing along to the words as I rub my hands together until I can feel warm air coming through the front vents. The numb, sick feeling that took hold of me earlier starts to lift as I drive, and my stomach grumbles loudly, reminding me that I've survived on only coffee and cake today, and even if they have both been in large quantities, it's not enough. It's dusk and a grey haze appears to be hovering just below the skyline causing an eerie gloominess but the street lights haven't switched on yet so I press on the break and take it slow as my mind begins to wonder to what Margaret will have made for tea. Her home cooking is fantastic. Dad has put on a good stone of weight since they've been together, but he's happy and that's all that really matters. I guess at their age a few extra pounds is expected and irrelevant. Why can't the rest of us live in a world without –?

Shit!

I slam the brakes on as a loud bang comes from the front of the car and a streak of fluorescent yellow flashes across my bonnet. I think my heart has actually stopped beating.

What the hell was that? My hands are still gripping the steering wheel with white knuckles, despite the car being stationary, and I daren't make a move to get out. My eyes are staring into the grey night so fiercely that they feel like they're going to pop right out of my head, but it's so dark on this lane that I can't see anything.

Then I hear a groan, like an animal that's in pain. Oh God, what if I've maimed and injured a poor animal? Oh no, I can't possibly look at that.

It takes my brain a second or two to realise that very few animals, if any, are fluorescent yellow. I open the door and take a deep breath before sliding cautiously out of the car. I can still feel my whole body, particularly my legs, shaking like a jelly from the shock.

Oh my God! I've killed someone. I've actually killed someone!

A man clad completely in black and yellow Lycra is sprawled in front of my car.

Hang on...hang on, I think I see movement.

'Are you alright?' I bend down next to him.

'I think I'm okay.' He sits up gingerly and I take in the black cycling helmet. 'Just a bit stunned.'

'I'm so sorry, I'm so sorry,' I ramble, seriously panicked now. 'I just didn't see you at all. You came out of nowhere.'

My heart is thumping heavily in my chest. I could have killed this guy. I shouldn't have been so busy singing along to the eighties' Madonna track, trying to forget my stupid excuse for a love life, and simply not concentrating. A shiver shoots up my spine at the thought of the potential consequences. I really could have killed him.

'It's okay, it's okay.' He's on his hands and knees now, trying to stand up. 'It was my fault.'

'No, no, I wasn't paying attention.' I reach out my hand but then pull it back. 'Maybe you should just rest for a minute.'

'Neither was I – paying attention.' He points to his ears as he sits back down and I see small black wires protruding from under his helmet. 'I have a terrible habit of listening to Iron Maiden on full blast while cycling,' he laughs.

I crouch down further until I'm at the same height as him, and I see that he's only about my age. He unclips the strap on his helmet and gently pulls it off his head, and I just watch him helplessly, thinking what a surreal situation this is.

'I think I should call an ambulance.' Slightly delayed reaction by me – how useless am I in an emergency? 'You've obviously had a bump to the head,' I continue while standing up to go and get my mobile phone from the car, 'and, well, pretty much everywhere else too.'

'No, please. I don't need an ambulance. It's just a few bruises, I think, particularly to my ego, but no blood, see?' He points to his knee where the Lycra is torn.

'Still, I think you should be checked out by someone. At least let me get you, and your slightly crumpled bike' – I cringe inwardly as I look at the front tyre, which is no longer in line with the rest of the bike – 'to the hospital.'

'Really, there's no need,' he protests again.

Headlights suddenly appear, lighting up the road and nearly blinding me, and I shield my eyes as another car pulls up. A middle-aged man with thick grey hair and a larger than average beer belly climbs out of his car with some difficulty and ambles over to us.

'Are you both okay?' he asks, a little out of breath from the minute amount of exertion he's just used.

'I'm fine, thanks.' Bicycle Man looks up at him. 'It looks worse than it is, honestly.'

'You don't need any help?' The grey haired man looks at me and I flounder for a minute.

I'm not sure whether we need help or not. I'm not sure exactly what to do in this type of situation, and I'm not sure whether I should accept help from a total stranger, Good Samaritan or not. I've seen too many horror movies where the Good Samaritan turns out to be the serial killer, and although the guy in front of me may not fulfil that role, he has all the attributes of a middle-aged flasher; he just needs a beige waterproof mac.

'We're fine, thanks, and thank you for stopping and enquiring,' Bicycle Man responds very politely.

'Well, if you're sure.' The man shrugs his shoulders and wanders back to his car.

'So…hospital?' I prompt once Flasher Man is safely out of earshot.

'No need,' Bicycle Man reiterates again.

'Yeah, well, I say there is. I mean, from a personal, selfish point of view I'll not be satisfied until a medical professional says you're not going to drop dead from internal bleeding or something a few hours from now.'

'That wouldn't be good.' He smiles and I notice cute little dimples forming. I like dimples. Wait...no...um...déjà vu…

'No, it wouldn't be good.' I shake my head. 'My life is already pretty disastrous at the moment without adding manslaughter into the equation.'

He looks at me a little suspiciously before raising his eyebrows. 'Alright, if you're sure it isn't too much trouble then I guess it can't hurt to get checked out.'

'Right.' I nod. 'Let me help you up. It's freezing and you're only wearing Lycra. Don't you have a coat?' Oh God, now I sound like Sophie.

'Um, no. It makes riding the bike a bit more difficult if I'm wearing my three-quarter-length wool blend.'

Hmm, is that a hint of sarcasm or humour?

'Never mind, I have a blanket in the boot of my car.'

He leans slightly on my shoulder, for my benefit more than his, I think, and I push upwards until we're both upright. He's taller than me and his physique is clearly impressive even through the thick layer of Lycra.

'We'd better inspect the damage to your car.' He glances towards the bonnet.

'My car?' I'd forgotten all about the fact that the bike hit the front driver's side of my car and that his body then bounced across my bonnet like a giant ping-pong ball.

'Oh dear, there's a bit of a dent.'

He leans over, touching the car, and I just stare at him for a second. He could be half-dead with a ruptured spleen or something and all he's bothered about is a dent in my five-year-old car. Mmm... He's quite cute really, though. Totally opposite from what I usually go for in a guy – he's got really dark brown hair for a start and I like blond guys – but his warm brown eyes have a seductive pull to them and yep, I have to admit he's attractive.

He glances at me and I'm almost positive he caught me checking him out. Way to play it cool, Emma! 'Yes, well, never mind that. I have insurance,' I say, flustered, feeling my cheeks starting to burn up. 'Right. Well, we can sort all that out. I'll give you my details and stuff so they can claim off my bike insurance. It was my fault. I wasn't looking at the road ahead and I couldn't hear your car coming because of the heavy metal music turned up so loud in my earphones.'

'We can sort out the technicalities of who did what once we know you aren't going to drop dead on me, okay?' I usher him closer to the car door.

'Okay, okay.' He holds up his hands. 'Let's get my bike into your car.'

I need to put the back seats down to have any hope of getting the bent bike frame in the car, but together we manage to squeeze it in. He wanders around to the passenger door and climbs awkwardly into the car while I rummage around in the boot for the blanket. Then I remember that Sophie spilled red wine on it last Bonfire Night while we huddled under it watching fireworks and it's still loitering at the bottom of my laundry basket. Shit.

I climb into the driver's seat.

'Here, you must be freezing.' I grab my scarf from the back seat and hand it to him. 'Put this around you; you might be going into shock or something. Sorry, my friend...borrowed my blanket and she hasn't returned it.'

He looks at the scarf with blatant amusement. 'I think the only shock will be if I turn up at hospital encased in leopard print,' he chuckles.

I glare at him with my 'Just do as I say' face and he seems to take the hint. He pulls the scarf begrudgingly from me and wraps it around his shoulders.

'There...better?'

'Much.' He replies with a hint of humour. 'Where were you on your way to anyway? I hope all this isn't keeping you from anything?'

Oh...tea with Dad and Margaret. Damn it!

'Give me two seconds.' I rummage around in my bag for my phone again. 'Then we'll be on our way, I promise.'

'No problem.'

I dial Dad's number and shake my head, thinking about how this conversation is going to go. Most of the time I try to hide the crazy stuff I get into from him.

'Hello?' Dad's gruff voice answers.

'Hi, Dad, it's me.'

'Hey, Emmie.' He always calls me my childhood nickname, which used to make me feel warm and comforted, but now my breath catches in my throat as I think of Connor sneering as he mockingly called me Emmie. 'Are you on your way?'

'Um, not exactly. I've had a little...' I glance at my injured passenger. '...a little incident.'

'Emmie, is everything okay?'

'Yes, fine. I'm fine. I'm just not going to make dinner tonight. I'm sorry.'

'Oh.' I can hear the disappointment in his voice. 'Margaret made Hotpot, your favourite.'

'I'm sorry, Dad. I'll make it up to you.'

'No worries, Emmie. I know it must be important for you to cancel at such short notice. How about the same time tomorrow evening instead?'

'Absolutely.'

'See you then, honey, and take care of yourself.'

'Thanks, Dad. Bye.' I hang up the phone and start the engine. 'Right, let's go.'

We arrive at the hospital within ten minutes, and once I've finally found somewhere to park – I mean, how many people are actually in this hospital at any one time? – I manage to half help, half hinder getting him from the car to the reception area of the A&E department as despite being knocked off his bike he seems reluctant to accept my offer assist him.

'Hello. How can I help you?' mutters an incredibly large black woman sitting behind a Perspex shield without even lifting her head.

'Um, we need to see a doctor,' I state, rather agitated by her somewhat blasé approach.

'Name?' She shoves a form and clipboard under the sliver between the Perspex window and the desk.

Ah...well...a name? I glance sideways and realise that, rather embarrassingly, I don't know his name. In the panic from running him over, scraping him off the road and into my car, and then driving erratically to the hospital I forgot the formalities of introductions.

'Joseph. Joe Stark,' he offers.

Right. Joe. That's a nice name.

'And what appears to be the problem, Joe?' The receptionist just sounds bored now, which is hovering on downright rude.

'Well, this young lady here knocked me off my bike,' he says flatly.

'Oh, no...I didn't...well, that might have actually happened but...'

My head feels like it's going to explode as the receptionist looks at me with a look of utter disgust, raising her eyebrows so high you can barely see them any more under her fringe. I look nervously at Joe and see just a hint of his dimples again.

'I'm just kidding,' he laughs. 'I happened to not be paying attention and I fell off my bike. This nice young lady...' He gestures at me but I've no idea what he wants. 'If she'd just tell me her name too...'

Oh, right. Of course.

'Emma.'

'Thank you. This nice young lady, Emma, picked me up off the ground and was kind enough to bring me here.'

'I see.' The receptionist is still looking at me like I'm a monster with three heads.

'I think it's just bruising.'

'You're in luck, Mr Stark. We have a nurse on duty who can see you shortly, if it's just as a precaution and we're not that busy yet. The rush usually starts at kicking-out time on a Sunday night.'

I glance around the waiting room and see a variety of people with bumps and cuts and the odd sling. For an A&E department it does feel unusually quiet. But if the receptionist is right then this is the calm before the almighty storm.

'She'll call you in a minute. If you want to just take a seat?'

'Thanks.'

Joe points to the right and we head towards the nearest Formica chairs. Well, I walk; Joe hobbles, still refusing my offer of help.

'You don't have to hang around, you know. I'm sure you have better things to do on an evening than sit in a hospital waiting room.'

'Actually my plans got kind of side-tracked,' I say jokingly, hoping it's not too soon to make light of the whole incident.

'How inconsiderate are some people?'

He looks at me with a cheeky expression and I decide that I quite like Joe. He seems like an ordinary guy with no stupid agenda and no hidden demonic personality. Okay, so I don't actually know that for sure, but his name is definitely Joe as he's put it on an important medical form – no need for an alias here.

'And I also have, on the back seat of my car, what remains of your bike, which I'm guessing you might actually want to keep,' I state.

'Ah, yes, I'd kind of like that back.'

'So, I guess I'll stay here and give you and your bike a lift home once the nurse has given you the all clear.'

As if on cue a nurse suddenly appears. 'Mr Stark?'

'Well, I guess that's me.'

Joe struggles to a standing position and shuffles off down the corridor with the nurse. At the door he turns around and smiles at me, just for a second, and I find myself smiling broadly back at him before the door closes and he disappears from sight.

I look at my watch. Eight o'clock on a Saturday night, and what an eventful night it's been. I can't quite believe that I've knocked a cyclist clean off their bike. My fault or not, it could have been so much worse. I think I need caffeine. Glancing around the waiting room, I see a vending machine which looks like it serves hot drinks.

A few minutes later, as I flick through a three-year-old copy of Good Housekeeping, I realise my mistake and instantly regret it.

This is not coffee. It's not even palatable. In fact, the dark brown, sloshy liquid which has cleverly disguised itself as a warm, caffeinated drink tastes more like engine oil mixed with windscreen wash. I discard it on the small table beside me and continue to flick through scone recipes and the most fashionable tablecloth patterns.

I don't know how long I sit there, but it feels like the land that time forgot. People come in and go out, more come in, and are all greeted with the same cheery reception. In the middle of my trying, and failing, to complete the Good Housekeeping crossword I look up to see Joe hobbling, if slightly easier than before, back down the corridor towards me and I feel a weird sensation of…guilt? Excitement? Fear? I don't have time to decide before he's standing right in front of me.

'So, are you still in one piece or am I really in trouble?' I stand up nervously.

'Calm down. It's just as I thought, some bruising and swelling but nothing's broken and my head is fine thanks to my shockingly expensive helmet. I guess I owe the sales guy on that one – it was worth every penny.'

'Good.' I exhale, relieved. 'I'm so glad you're okay.'

We stand there in weird, awkward silence.

'I think I've taken up too much of your evening already.' He cocks his head to one side and grins sheepishly. 'Shall we get me, my dented pride and my bike home?'

'Sure.'

'Here's a copy of the hospital form with my contact details on.'

I just stare at the piece of paper.

'Just in case. For insurance purposes.'

'Right, right; of course.' I fold it up and slid it into my bag.

Once back in the car I attempt to make small talk for the short journey to Joe's house in between him giving me directions. It's just across the other side of town, only ten minutes or so from the hospital.

'So how long have you been cycling?' I ask. 'I'm guessing you take it pretty seriously given you have all the kit and stuff.' I glance discreetly at his Lycra-clad body again. I always thought that men wearing tight, stretchy clothes was a bad idea, but I might have to reconsider.

'I've been cycling for a few years now.' He sounds animated now. 'I just love getting out in the fresh air and having that...freedom.'

'I know what you mean.'

'Oh, do you cycle too?'

What? Hell no.

'No…um…no, but I do run.' Okay, so I've been jogging once in the last thirty-two years, but it was in the last few weeks so it's not a total lie, and it does count, surely?

'That's great. So you know what I mean? It feels good to get outside and stretch your legs.'

'Mmm...great, yes, stretching legs, fresh air. Is this your house here?' I pull up to the kerb alongside a small row of stone built terrace houses displaying neatly cut grass and a variety of colourful hanging baskets. They look cosy and quaint.

'Ah, yes, it is. Thank you for getting me home.'

'It's the least I could do under the circumstances.'

There's a slight pause as we sit in the car and Joe looks at me with an expression that I can't read.

'Right.' He unclips his seatbelt. 'I guess we'd better get the remains of my bike out of the car.'

'Um…yes.'

This is easier said than done. It went in with a lot less effort than it's taking to get it back out. After a careful amount of nudging it this way and that, we finally manage to extract it from my back seat. As Joe stands on the pavement at the side of the car, clutching his bike frame like his dearest possession (maybe it is?), I suddenly remember.

'Here.' I reach into my handbag and pull out an envelope and a pen. I scrawl my contact details and car registration across the envelope before handing it to Joe. 'These are my details; you know, to give to your insurance company.'

'Oh. Thanks.' He looks down, seemingly scrutinising the information.

'So...'

It's not getting any warmer out here and I really want to get back into my car now and go home and drown myself in a large glass – no, wait...maybe the whole bottle of wine – and try to erase yet another hideous evening in the life of Emma Storey. There seems to be a recurring pattern here – not with running people over, thankfully, but with me getting myself into trouble and drowning my sorrows. What is wrong with me?

'So...I've got your number.' Joe fiddles with the envelope, still limping slightly as he readjusts his bike frame that's threatening to topple over.

'Yeah, I'm pretty sure you have everything for the insurance claim, but just get them to call me if they need anything else.'

'Right...and you have my details.'

'Yep. I'll pass them on to my insurance company too.'

I'm still feeling guilty as I take in the bump on his head and the torn Lycra hanging off his leg. He's clutching the bent remains of his bike like a child with his teddy bear. I still can't believe that I hit someone with my car tonight.

'Right.' He's still doesn't make a move towards his house.

Okay, this is getting a bit awkward now.

'Would you like me to help you inside?' I offer, wondering whether that's what he's waiting for.

'Er...no.' He laughs, looking down at the pavement, clearly embarrassed to be offered help again by a girl.

'Then maybe I should get going.'

'Absolutely. I've taken up your entire evening and ruined your dinner plans.'

'Really, it's fine. I'm just glad you aren't seriously hurt. I can do without adding aggravated manslaughter to my list of hideous issues to deal with.'

'I promise I'll take more care in future.'

'Good.' I look at him one last time. 'So will I.' I smile and turn to walk away.

'So, um, can I use this phone number?' he calls after me.

I turn back around, confused. 'Yes, if you need anything else then just give me a ring.'

'Okay...so how about a date?'

What? I just nocked this guy off his bike resulting in a hospital visit and now he wants to take me out for dinner? Is there a whole new dating etiquette that I'm not aware of?

'You're asking me out on a date?' I stand rooted to the spot and eye him suspiciously.

'Sure…well, just dinner or something. To make up for your cancelled dinner plans tonight,' he offers.

'Did you bump your head harder than we thought? The nurse did say you were definitely okay to come home, didn't she?'

'Definitely.' He takes a step forward with some difficulty, clearly still in pain and naturally still clutching his bike. 'What's so hard to believe? You seem like a nice girl, Emma – driving awareness issues aside.' The corners of his mouth twitch.

Cheeky!

'I like you.' He shrugs.

'You don't even know me. Just about all you do know about me is that I nearly flattened you tonight.'

'So it's not the most conventional way of meeting someone new, but still…'

I bite my lip. He is kind of cute. But this is the last thing I could have expected from the events of this evening.

'Oh.' He looks slightly embarrassed. 'You have a boyfriend.'

'No, no I don't.'

'In that case, why not? It's just dinner, no pressure. We'll simply celebrate that I'm still alive, and if you have a good time, I'll let you take me out again.' He grins now, showing his dimples in all their glory again. I'm a sucker for dimples, but that's what got me into a whole heap of trouble last time.

Hmm. He's quite nice, though, and has a sexy mouth and…oh, what the hell. What have I got to lose? Actually…let's not go there again.

'How's Friday night?' I cock my head to one side, trying to give the impression of being aloof.

'Friday is good. I'll text you on Thursday with where to meet.'

'Okay.' I agree a little too quickly to play it cool.

'Okay.' He holds my gaze for a second. 'I'm going to go inside now because it's freezing and I think I need to lie down.'

'Oh God, certainly, go inside.' I turn around and walk to the driver's door of the car.

'Goodnight, Emma.'

'Goodnight, Joe.'

I jump in the car and turn the heating up to full blast. He wasn't kidding about it being freezing; I'm struggling to feel my feet. I watch as he shuffles away into the house. He gives a little wave before the door closes behind him and I sit there for a minute staring at it, dumbfounded. What a crazy evening it's been. I really didn't see that coming. I sometimes get the feeling that my life is being filmed for some amusing documentary on how not to behave that at some point will be aired on national television for everyone to revel in my stupidity.

As I make my way home extremely cautiously I go over the evening's events in my head. I mowed down a cyclist (even if he was somewhat to blame) who turned out to be very attractive and quite charming and now we're going out on a date. I mean, it doesn't get much weirder than that. Sophie would laugh her head off. It still feels really strange that I can't just ring her up and tell her about all of this. In fact, it feels like a lifetime since we spoke. It's been the hardest few weeks of my life. We've never gone three days let alone three weeks without speaking and it feels like my right arm has been cut off. We used to share everything, and right now I'd love to tell her about meeting Joe.

As I pull up to my house I feel exhausted, both physically and mentally. I need to try to prevent this crazy shit from happening to me. If only I knew how, though. It's not like I go looking for it. Having walked through the door, I hang up my coat and kick off my shoes before heading to the bedroom, where I collapse on the bed, not even bothering to take off my clothes let alone my makeup. I pull the quilt up tightly around me and fall instantly into a deep untroubled sleep.

'Don't you even think of raising your belt to me again, Dad, or you'll regret it.'
'Who d'you think you're speaking to, son!?'
'I mean it, Dad. You've raised your hand to me for the last time; I promise you.'

Chapter Twenty

As the alarm clock starts ringing I'm being chased by an assassin. The ringing has given away my hiding place and I'm holding my breath, waiting for the single death shot to be fired. As the gun goes off I sit up in bed with a jolt.

What on earth did that mean? I doubt I'd find that in any dream book analogy.

I shake the last few images of the weird fantasy world from my mind and then instantly remember the events of last night and hang my head in shame.

Right. Deep breath, Emma; let's put things into perspective. I can focus on the negative points of the previous evening – chiefly, that I hit a cyclist with my car. Or I can focus on the fact that I'm going out on a date on Friday night with an attractive man who doesn't seem to be a complete psychopath or have a hidden agenda, given that it was me who bumped into him. Literally.

Or was it? Did he know I'd be driving that way to my dad's house last night? Did he cycle into my path on purpose? Now I'm being ridiculous! What person in their right mind would risk his life steering into the path of a car?

Okay, Emma, the sensible side of my brain shouts – that's enough hideous speculation for today. You need to get up, get dressed and get to work.

As I arrive at the shop forty minutes later Jenny is making the teas and Lola is standing chatting to her, still wearing her coat having presumably just arrived herself.

'Morning.' I call to her cheerfully, pulling off my coat and hanging it on the stand next to Jenny.

'What's with you?' Jenny stops stirring the tea and looks at me inquisitively.

'What do you mean?' I frown 'All I've done is say "morning".'

'For the last month or so you've dragged yourself into work with barely a half-smile plastered on your face and you've drowned in self-pity over your ex-boyfriend and the freak your friend is dating…'

A bit harsh…no?

'And now this morning you breeze in here all happy go lucky, seemingly without a care in the world.'

Well, I don't think it's quite like that. I glance at Lola, who's nodding with pursed lips, and then back at Jenny, who's still staring at me, looking smug.

'Okay, spill it.' Jenny taps the teaspoon on the worktop.

'I'm sorry?'

'Did you get some last night?'

Did I what?

'No! Why would you think that?'

'Because after all that crap I figure that's the only thing that would put a smile back on your face so quickly. Unless your friend has come to her senses and dumped that creep...'

'Not that I'm aware of.' I bite my lip.

'So you've not tried to challenge him yet in an attempt to record him?'

'No. But I have given it some further thought and it might actually be feasible to try.'

'Right then. Who is he?' Jenny raises her eyebrows, waiting for me to divulge.

God, she's annoying. How does she do that? How does she see through me in a millisecond?

'So what if I did kind of meet someone last night?'

'I knew it!' Jenny hands me a mug of tea.

'Ooh, how exciting.' Lola also takes a mug from Jenny and then hovers, looking at me all bright-eyed.

'Well, the thing is…I knocked him off his bike while driving to my dad's house for dinner.'

I watch their faces freeze mid-smile, their mouths open slightly in shock. Now it's my turn to look smug…until I replay in my head what I actually just said.

'It's not as bad as it sounds…' I protest. They both continue to stare at me, saying nothing. 'Okay, so maybe it is, but he's absolutely fine apart from some bruising to his head and knee.'

I cringe. This sounds horrendous when I actually say it out loud.

'Let me get this straight.' Jenny rubs at the side of her temples with her free hand. 'The reason you've skipped in here so cheerily this morning is because you maimed a cyclist last night.'

'Well, when you put it like that I sound like a complete maniac.'

'Er…that kind of is how you put it.'

'Shall I try again?'

'Please…before I really start to think you've lost the plot.'

'I was driving to my dad's house for tea.'

They both nod in unison.

'When a cyclist came out of nowhere and crashed into the side of my car and sort of skidded over my bonnet.'

Jenny's eyes widen.

'Honestly, he's fine,' I insist. 'In fact he's so fine that he's asked me out on a date on Friday night.'

'Hang on! Let me make sure I've understood you correctly. You knocked this poor sucker off his bike and he dragged himself back up off the road and asked you out on a date.' Jenny looks incredulous.

'If you squeeze in a trip to Accident and Emergency then yes, that was pretty much my evening.'

'Damn.' Lola shakes her head at me. 'What am I doing wrong? I go to bars, to clubs, dance with men, and still don't get a date.'

As Jenny and I burst out laughing at Lola's complete awe of my situation I hear the front door jingle – the first customer of the day.

'I'll go.' I put my cup down on top of the filing cabinet and open the door to the shop floor.

'Good morning, Mrs Ronan.' I see a familiar tall, middle-aged woman striding towards me.

'Do you have this in a size twelve?' She hands me a dark-green evening dress with her usual lack of grace.

'Of course. Let me get that for you.'

The minute the shop is empty again and I enter storeroom, Lola and Jenny pounce on me like vultures on roadkill.

'So are you going to go out with him?' Jenny looks a mixture of surprised and indignant.

'You're damn right I am.' I shrug. 'I mean, how often does a really cute guy fall at your feet…literally?'

'But you don't know anything about him, do you?'

'That's exactly the point, isn't it? We go out, eat food and talk. Isn't that normally what a date entails?' Minus drunken sex this time… no, that last time was different. That wasn't a date, that was –

'I know that's what usually happens on a date, Emma, but your recent track record makes me…'

I cringe.

'…cautious.'

Oh.

'Believe me, Jenny; it makes me cautious too. But I actually think this guy isn't emotionally stunted or a psychotic creep, so unless he proves otherwise I'm going to give him the benefit of the doubt.'

She frowns at me sceptically.

'I have to.' I wave my hands around emphatically. 'Or I'll never date another man again and I'll end up cold and alone forever, living the life of a spinster, having children avoid my house or throw eggs at the windows as they run past in fear.'

I hear Lola giggling in the corner while pretending to hang up some stock.

'Is that what you want for me, Jenny?'

'Don't be stupid,' she scoffs. 'I just worry about you, that's all.'

'Thank you. That's very kind of you. But really, you don't need to worry. You just need to be there for me holding a bottle of wine if it all goes wrong and it turns out I actually can only attract the world's worst rejects. Deal?'

'Deal.' She concedes.

Later that evening I repeat the same journey as last night to my dad's house, but this time at about twenty miles an hour all the while scanning the road for moving objects that have the potential to fling themselves into my path. I finally pull slowly and carefully onto Dad's driveway breathing a sigh of relief having made it unscathed.

'Hey, Dad,' I call a few moments later, pushing the front door open.

He appears from the lounge and wraps his arms around me until I'm ensconced in a bear hug. 'Hey, Emmie. Is everything okay? We were worried about you after you cancelled dinner last night.'

'I'm sorry, Dad. Um, something just came up…'

'Hi, Emma.' Margaret comes in from the kitchen with her usual warm greeting. We don't hug or kiss hello – she's just not one of those types of people; but she always makes me feel welcome. 'Sorry you missed my hotpot last night.'

'I'm sorry too.' Her hotpot is legendary in these parts; well, in most of the street anyway as she sends Tupperwares full of it round to all the elderly folk.

'It's lasagne tonight.'

'That sounds great.' I'm starving, and as if on cue my stomach growls approvingly.

'It won't be long.' Margaret heads back into the kitchen and Dad ushers me through to the lounge.

'Sit down, Emmie, don't hover.' Dad points to the sofa and he sits down next to me. 'Are you sure that you're alright?' He takes hold of my hand and waits for me to answer, his eyebrows creasing deeply.

A lump forms in my throat as I look back at him; he looks older these days and that scares me. I forget that he's nearly double my age. Now the once-thick head of hair is thinning slightly and there are more than a few speckles of grey.

'I'm absolutely fine, Dad.' I state as convincingly as I can. 'I just had a minor bump in my car on the journey here last night.'

'Oh no, Emmie. You crashed your car? What happened?' He looks more concerned than ever now.

'It wasn't really a crash, Dad.'

'Are you alright? Is there much damage? How have you driven here tonight?'

'Dad, calm down. My car is still in one piece. There's not much damage, just a small dent, and I'm fine.'

'Was anyone else hurt?'

'No, Dad, the other guy is okay too.'

'What's wrong, Michael?' Margaret appears in the doorway.

'Emma's been in an accident. She crashed her car last night' Dad waves his hands dramatically.

Not helping, Dad.

'Oh no! How did that happen? Are you hurt?' Margaret interjects 'I bet the other driver was speeding-'

'I didn't say there was another driver' I protest but it falls on deaf ears.

'They're always going too fast, aren't they Michael-'

Who's they?

'I'm always saying that'

'I know Margaret, and you're right. Nobody has any time for anything these days. Always in a rush; no time to wait'

Bloody hell, this is turning into a pantomime.

'Look you two' I sound a little harsher than intended 'It wasn't a crash; just a little bump' I soften my voice trying to defuse the situation.

'But-'

I hold up my hand to silence Dad.

'A cyclist rode into the side of my car and fell off his bike' I explain calmly. I figure under the circumstances of their over-reaction it's morally acceptable to blame the other party.

'Oh dear. Are they okay? Are you alright? What's the damage?' Margaret fires more questions at me.

A cute guy and a date on Friday night?

'Um, not much damage; it was only a minor bump, and I'm not hurt in the slightest,' I insist. 'It was just a bit of a shock at the time. Now, shall I get washed up for dinner?' I ask, desperate to move the conversation on and not to go into further details.

Dad just looks at me warily for a moment.

'I'll go and check on the food' Margaret states still looking flustered.

As we sit around the dining room table a few minutes later the room is filled with the most wonderful aromas and my plate is piled high with lasagne and salad and these yummy little roast potatoes that Margaret makes.

'How's work?' I ask Dad in between mouthfuls of food.

'On the countdown to retirement, Emmie. Only six months to go. Then we're off around the world, aren't we, Margaret?'

'Oh yes. I can't wait. Just sun, sea and cocktails for three whole months.'

'Three whole months? Wow, I'd forgotten the cruise was for that long. It sounds amazing.' I'm officially jealous. Not that I want to spend three months on a boat with Dad and Margaret, but three months of sunbathing and cocktails? Definitely count me in.

'Have you seen your mother lately?' Dad asks – out of politeness, I think.

'Yes, I went out to New York for a couple of days last month. She's fine.'

'Good.'

'How's Sophie?'

'Oh, um, she's…really busy at work at the moment, Dad.' I'm not getting into that whole scenario tonight. 'I haven't seen that much of her recently.'

'I don't know – you career girls.' Margaret shakes her head at me – although I'm not really sure how she's including me in that category; 'career girl' isn't quite how I'd describe my current employment situation. 'You don't want to miss out on things in life by being too busy.'

'If you mean marriage and babies, Margaret, then I think the first thing on the agenda would be to find a boyfriend, don't you? And that's easier said than done, believe me.'

'Margaret, there's more to life than having a boyfriend,' Dad pipes up.

Thank you, Dad.

'So, there's no one on the horizon?' Margaret continues regardless.

Well, maybe the guy I hit with my car last night? No…

'She's only just got out of a relationship, Margaret. Leave the girl alone,' Dad butts in before I can answer myself.

I continue eating my food without making comment. I know Dad was pretty upset with how things ended between me and Chris. He really liked him and I think he was quite hurt when I told him that Chris had been cheating on me. Dad's always been overprotective of me. No wonder I try to shield him from the realities of my disastrous life.

'I'm just saying, that's all' Margaret continues undeterred 'I was reading an article in a magazine, I can't remember which one – they all have similar names'

I hope this is going somewhere but I'm not optimistic that it's going somewhere good.

'When I was at the hairdresser last week getting my colour done - when was it Michael? Tuesday or Wednesday?'

Does the day matter?

'Tuesday I think Margaret' Dad says between mouthfuls of food.

'Oh yes, Wednesday was the church coffee morning wasn't it?'

I hope she gets to her point before the end of the meal; and my patience.

'Anyway' Margaret shakes her head 'the article was talking about how advances in science mean that…' she pauses.

'Mean that?' I prompt.

'Um, that women, of a certain age' she clears her throat.

Did she really just say that? Women of a certain age? I'm pretty sure that's a full blown national offense to use that terminology.

'I'm just saying you have options nowadays, if you don't find someone until…well, you can freeze things now'.

Oh no, no, no.

Are we really having a conversation over dinner about how if I don't find someone to love, and who loves me back, in the immediate future then I can freeze my eggs and have a baby at some old, decrepit and unacceptable age?

I glance at Dad who's stopped eating and, although looking decidedly uncomfortable, is actually nodding along with Margaret. So that's it? I presumed "over the hill" at thirty two. That's just great.

Honestly, it's no wonder I struggle with emotional issues.

Chapter Twenty-One

Friday night: date night has arrived.

It's three minutes until my taxi is due and I'm feeling strangely calm for a first date. Maybe it's the unconventional way we met that makes me surprisingly optimistic: surely whatever tonight brings it can't be as bad as that. I'm meeting Joe at the cinema and after the film we're going for an Italian, which sounds perfectly normal and not pretentious at all. I like Joe even more for the fact that he isn't trying too hard to impress me. He texted me on Thursday night just like he promised and his texts were chirpy and cheeky but with no kisses on the end, which is fine – he's clearly not presumptuous either.

A car horn beeps outside and I peer through the curtains and see the taxi waiting. I'm already standing in my coat with my shoes on and my handbag in hand. This is very strange indeed. I was ready with time to spare and I'm now leaving the house in a calm manner, which is almost unheard of, and as I head into a potentially nerve-wracking situation, I've never felt so good. I lock the front door behind me and hurry to the taxi.

'The retail park in town, please,' I instruct the driver and he sets off turning up the radio and we begin our short journey to the cinema accompanied by unexpected random reggae beats.

As we pull up to the side of the cinema building I immediately see Joe standing casually against the wall, looking even more attractive than the last time I saw him. To be fair, the last time he was probably ten shades whiter having been unceremoniously detached from his bicycle and he was wearing weird Lycra stuff. This time he's dressed in jeans and a navy-blue shirt with his dark-brown hair swept up in a trendy flick that looks like he just ran his hands through it and it formed the perfect style. How nice would it be if my hair behaved like that without the need for time-consuming grooming with a multitude of products and appliances? Men don't realise how lucky they are.

'Excuse me?'

'Sorry?' I was completely lost in my own world for a moment then and hadn't realised that we've come to a complete stop and the driver is waiting for me to pay him and get the hell out of his car so he can move on to his next fare. Whoops.

'That'll be five pounds, please.'

'Right.' I pull a five-pound note from my purse and hand it through the gap in the clear screen that separates me from the driver.

As I step out of the taxi the nerves that were previously nowhere to be seen now descend on me in a frenzy. As Joe sees me he gives me a little wave, causing my stomach to flip like I'm on the big wheel at the fairground and my palms to sweat.

'Hey.' He smiles as I get closer to him.

'Hey.' I repeat back, dumbly fiddling with my hands.

'It's good to see you again,' he says with a confidence I can't even pretend to muster under these circumstances and I blush furiously.

'You look much better,' I say with more conviction than I feel.

'Yeah, just a bit of a limp now, that's all.'

'I hope you're not permanently damaged.'

'I saw the doctor again today and he thinks I'll be just fine.'

'Thank God for that.'

'Yeah, my bike is a write-off though…'

Oh dear. I get the feeling that his bike is a very precious commodity, or maybe just a really expensive one that will need replacing. And I broke it…

I decide to quickly change the subject. 'So what film do you fancy watching?'

'No, no. I chose Italian food so you get to choose the film.'

'Alright. Something with a bit of action and gun fights; no romantic comedies.'

'Phew.' Joe fakes relief. 'I thought you were going to make me sit through two hours of mushy rubbish.'

'And would you if I'd asked?' Now's the test.

'Of course.' He dutifully agrees.

Okay. He passed.

As we queue up in the ticket line I feel like I'm fifteen years old again and I'm on my first ever date with Jack Derrange – but this time his friends aren't hiding behind the drinks counter waiting to sneak into the row behind us to throw popcorn at my head and make immature comments while I try to decide whether Jack has placed his hand so close to mine because he wants me to grab it or just because it's comfortable there. I learned at that very early stage of the dating game that being brave doesn't always pay off. At the exact moment I made my move and went to grab Jack's hand he reached for his drink, therefore moving his hand, and I ended up grabbing his crotch. Absolutely the worst ever day of my life. Well, up until the whole Johnny/Connor debacle anyway. It took the remaining three terms of school for the rest of the class to stop laughing at me and for the lads to stop covering their manhood with their hands anytime I walked near them. Honestly, kids can be really cruel. Actually, so can adults come to that...

But I'm not fifteen years old now. This isn't school. And I'm hopefully in the presence of someone a lot more mature than a teenage boy.

'Emma, Emma?'

'Um, yes' while I've been daydreaming we've made it to the front of the ticket queue.

'What film?' the girl behind the ticket desk asks sounding bored.

We choose to see the latest action film. Joe thinks I'm cool because I like fast car chases and lots of gun fire. In reality all of that's good, but the lead male role in this film is mega hot so I'd have watched it regardless.

Throughout the film I sneak a few glances in Joe's direction. He seems engrossed in the movie and he makes no move to hold my hand. I'm certainly not going to risk trying to reach for his hand after the Jack Derrange embarrassment.

As the final credits roll and the lights flick back on, nearly blinding us all, Joe turns to me.

'Good choice.'

'Yes, I thought so. Plenty of action with a good storyline.' And a fit bloke half-naked at the end...

'Are you ready to grab some food?'

'Yes, I'm starving.'

'Great.'

Joe stands up, then steps to one side to let me out into the aisle. As I take a step downwards I feel the palm of his hand briefly in the small of my back and it makes me all hot and wobbly inside. I glance back at him over my shoulder and he's just smiling, oblivious to the fact he's made me squirm with just one touch. Or is he?

I focus my mind on my feet, careful not to fall flat on my face as we continue down the steps and out of the cinema door into the lobby. It's busy, and we have to swerve between stumbling children carrying popcorn tubs so immense that they can't see around them. Finally we reach the exit. Joe holds the door open for me and we slip outside into the night where the fresh air is cool and calming. The Italian is only a two-minute stroll down the street and we begin walking at a leisurely pace.

'Are you warm enough?' Joe asks.

'Yes, I'm fine, thanks.'

He starts talking about a scene in the film as we walk.

Still no hand holding. Maybe I'm going to have to be brave and make the first move…maybe he's just shy. No, wait, he wasn't too shy to ask me out – even in the weird circumstances of that night. Maybe he's not the hand-holding type. Some men have issues with public displays of affection, although if that's the case then it's not a good sign…

'Emma, are you okay?'

I stop walking and look around me, realising we've reached the restaurant and I haven't been listening to a word Joe has said.

'Sorry.' I feel myself blushing. 'I was just…'

'Come on.' He leans forward opening the door for me, and I scoot inside into the warmth, grateful for the distraction from that potentially awkward moment.

A waiter heads over to us.

'Table for two?' he asks with a hint of an Italian accent.

'Yes please' Joe answers and we're whisked away to a seat at the window. The waiter hands us both a menu in super-quick time before whipping out his notepad and pen. 'What can I get you to drink?' He asks curtly, looking more sinister, though, than friendly.

Joe orders an Italian beer and I ask for a glass of Chianti. The waiter snaps his notepad closed noisily and disappears in an instant.

'So…' Joe leans forward, putting his forearms on the table, 'it occurred to me that I don't know much about you, Emma. Other than your passion for action movies and your knowledge of where the Accident and Emergency department is.'

Hmm, only knowing the bare minimum about me might not necessarily a bad thing…

'I guess I don't know much about you either.' I shrug.

I press my lips together. I worry that I don't have the right controls in my brain to separate what he needs to know from what he should never know about me. I don't want to end up spilling my guts and telling this guy exactly who I am and what's going on in my life at the moment. That would no doubt frighten him to death and end up with his making a lame excuse and leaving, never to be seen again.

'So let's start with the basics.' Joe leans back in his chair now looking relaxed.

The basics? Okay...what are the basics?

'Such as?' I prompt, hoping the first question will be an easy one.

'Where did you grow up?'

Oh, that's okay.

'I grew up not far from here, in a very small village, a sleepy little place where everyone knows everyone and everybody knows everybody's business. I don't think it's ever changed or ever will. I couldn't wait to move into the city.'

'I can understand that.' Joe looks at me warmly and his cute dimples appear making him look even more attractive.

'I had a happy childhood, although my parents separated when I was a teenager.'

See? Too much, Emma. You didn't need to divulge that!

'Oh. I'm sorry to hear that. It must have been hard.' His face becomes serious.

'It's okay.' I assure him. 'It was a long time ago and they've remained…civil. Dad has remarried. I was on my way to see him and Margaret the other night, um...well, the night we met.'

'Of course.' Joe's eyes glint and the dimples are back. 'What about your mum?'

'My mum…lives in New York.'

'Wow, that's cool.'

'Yeah, it's great. I love New York. It's my favourite city. I fell in love with it the first time I visited Mum there.'

'Any siblings?'

'Nope. Just me, an only child. What about you?'

'Ah, well, I don't really like to talk about my family.' Joe's face takes on a mask of seriousness and he sucks in a sharp intake of breath. 'You see, since the' – he lowers his voice – 'murder trial. When people recognise the name and make the connection…'

Oh my God. My insides do a flip. He actually is a psychopath. I've done it again.

'Really…?' I hear the cringe in my own voice. I knew it was all too good to be true. Of course there's something wrong with him...

'No.' He shakes his head. 'But you should see your face!' He's clearly very amused.

'You're playing me,' I say flatly.

'Yes.' He holds up his hands. 'I am. I grew up on the outskirts of London with two brothers, one older, David, one younger, Matt, and my mum and dad. Dad is an engineer and Mum works in Accounts at a decorating firm. Just normal, hard-working people.'

'With no family secret.'

'With no family secret,' he repeats, still grinning, and I laugh then too.

'That would have been a pretty interesting reveal for a first date,' I raise my eyebrows at him.

'Hang on.' He stops laughing. 'Are we on a date?'

For a split-second I hesitate, but then I see the glint in his eyes again and I know he's still just messing with me. Before I can say anything the waiter appears out of nowhere with our drinks and interrupts the moment. He places our drinks down with exquisite precision before dashing off again at an unnatural speed.

'You're quite the joker, aren't you?' I take a delicate sip of my wine.

'Sorry.' Joe picks up his beer. 'I tend to do that when I'm nervous.'

'And why would you be nervous?' I ask, genuinely intrigued. I can't remember Chris ever being nervous on a date, and Connor certainly wasn't lacking in confidence sending a drink over to me that night. Maybe Joe's different. Maybe he cares more. I think I like the fact that he's not completely self-assured.

'Because I really like you, Emma,' he says, looking straight at me, making me feel naked, like he can see my innermost thoughts.

I wasn't expecting him to say that, and to be so…honest.

'Are you ready to order?' a voice booms.

What is with this waiter? Does he listen into people's conversations so he can pick the most inappropriate moment to demand their attention? He fiddles with his moustache which I've only just noticed bears an uncanny resemblance to Hitler's. I'm sure that's not a good sign and I'm finding it difficult to force myself not to laugh.

I stare down at the menu, having not even given it a glance before. Joe orders some bread and olives to start, and I choose a vegetable and pasta dish for main course while Joe orders a steak. Once the waiter has retreated again in an imaginary puff of smoke I bite my lip, wondering how to take the conversation forward.

'So what do you do for a living?' Joe asks now we're alone again.

'That's a matter of opinion.'

He frowns at me inquisitively.

'Well, on face value I work in an upmarket ladies' boutique playing with clothes, shoes and handbags all day, which should be every girl's dream. But in reality I spend my days being talked down to by snooty rich women who make forty look young and who think that "below the knee" is the only hemline ever created. I basically help them choose their glamorous outfits for various social events, and in some unfortunate cases I also help to, um, assemble them in their attire.'

'Oh, that can't be pretty.'

'Sometimes it can be downright scary.' I giggle. 'But I work with two great girls and we muddle along together.'

'Sounds like you don't scare easily, which is why you weren't fazed when helping me after I'd bounced off your car.'

'I can honestly say that I've never been so scared in my life.' I fiddle with my hands on the table and then take a large gulp of wine. 'I thought I'd killed you,' I murmur.

'I'm sorry. I promise to pay more attention in future when cycling with my headphones in, okay?'

'Deal,' I bite my lip. 'Is your bike definitely not recoverable?'

'No, I'm afraid not. It's gone to bicycle heaven. But my new bike is on order and should be with me any day now.'

'Do you cycle everywhere?'

'No - It's purely a for fitness, and I kind of like the rush of adrenaline when going fast although I'm learning to slow down these days' he cocks his head a little at me 'I own a car as well.'

'Oh, right.' I don't know what made me think he would go everywhere on his bike like a child. That was a really silly question to ask him.

The food arrives and it both looks and smells amazing. As we dig in the conversation takes a lighter note. Joe tells me that after spending several years as a gym instructor (that explains the super-fit body under the Lycra) he's now retraining as an architect, which is very impressive but I'm a little scared by this. He sounds far too intelligent, far more intelligent than I am anyway. He enjoys, or did enjoy biking in the evening and at the weekends to keep fit, until I came along the other night anyway, as having spent so long working in a gym he has very little desire to work out in one. I can completely empathise with that: I possess no desire to ever go in to a gym either – for very different reasons, though. I'll never clad myself in tight-fitting clothes and sweat profusely while some super-skinny bitch yells at me to 'feel the burn.'

As the waiter collects our empty plates and we order coffee I realise I'm having an even better time that I thought I could on a first date. Once he got over his nervous joke-making Joe, it turns out, is pretty good company. And he likes me. Really likes me. I realise that we skipped right past that moment but perhaps I should tell him that I like him too. I don't want him to take my non-response as an indication that I don't.

'Emma, I can see the cogs turning inside your head again. You've got that glazed look about you that you had at the door when we first arrived here.'

'I'm sorry. It's not you; it's me.'

'Well, that's never a good line to hear on a first date.' He looks worried. 'That's usually the start of a lame conversation to end things when what you really want to say is, "It's totally you."'

'No, that's not it. God, I'm just making things worse now.' I put my head in my hands.

Why when I open my mouth does hideous stuff flow out like lava spewing from a volcano? Why can I not, just for once in my life, have a normal conversation without my mouth making decisions all on its own instead of communicating with my brain first?

'No, the thing is…' I look straight across the table at Joe and then lean in a little closer, just to make sure we're not overheard by any nosy diner or the annoying waiter. 'I really like you too.'

'Oh!' A look of relief creeps slowly onto Joe's face.

'I should have said so earlier, but I'm just hopeless when it comes to…well, relationships as a whole. I never say the right thing at the right time and usually, like now for example, I just make a right old mess of things.' I exhale, deflated by my honesty.

'You know what, Emma?' Joe reaches over and takes my hand in his. 'I think you say just the right thing at the right time.'

I can feel myself grinning, not playing it cool at all; but there's something extremely attractive about Joe's chivalry: the opening doors, the sweet things that he says. He's still clutching my hand and gazing softly at me from across the table as the waiter reappears with our coffees. He clears his throat and Joe releases my hand before the waiter places the drinks on the table then makes a hasty retreat.

'So where were we?' Joe raises his eyebrows at me in what I take to be a seductive manner.

'I think I was really starting to enjoy our first date,' I say coyly back.

'On that basis I feel confident to ask, are we going to do this again?' He looks a little serious now.

'I'd really like that,' I respond without a moment of hesitation.

'Good!' He relaxes. 'Me too.'

We finish our coffee and get the bill, which Joe insists on paying despite my very vocal protest. I like chivalry but I also like being an independent woman who can pay my own way; but I realise it can be a difficult balance to achieve and therefore in the end I accept his generosity with grace.

As we leave the restaurant it's turned noticeably colder and I shudder, wrapping my coat tightly around me.

'Let's get you a taxi.' Joe glances around. 'It's freezing out here.'

'I'm alright,' I chirp up. I'm not quite ready for this night to end.

'If we head towards the main road, I'm sure we'll be able to flag one down there.' Joe grabs my hand and we start walking at a pretty quick pace.

Mmm, I like a strong, confident man…

On the main road a few other couples are also looking to get a taxi but several empty taxis are heading towards us so it shouldn't be a long wait. We stand just back from the kerb and Joe turns to face me.

'When am I going to see you again?'

Ooh…as soon as possible, please.

'How about Tuesday night? We could go for a drink in town,' I suggest. 'The wine bar on George Street usually has a good atmosphere.'

'Tuesday it is then.' He reaches up and cups my face gently with his hands. The feel of his touch is electric and every nerve ending in my body stands to attention.

'What is it about you, Emma, that I find so enchanting?'

Um…I've been called many things in my time but enchanting has never been one of them. Is he drunk? He can't be; he only had two beers?

'I haven't been able to get you out of my head since I first set eyes on you as you appeared hovering over your car bonnet, looking down at me, stricken, as I lay in a heap on the road.'

Well, you had just collided none-too-gently with my car…

And then:

Oh my God, he's kissing me and…wow, it feels good. Kiss him back, Emma!

My brain kicks me into action and I press my lips firmly against his. They're warm and full and sensual and, yep, I'm actually a bit wobbly on my feet as he gently pulls away from our embrace.

They say you can tell a lot about a man from the way he kisses you. If that's the case then that one kiss right there tells me everything I need to know about Joe Stark.

As he waves me off in a taxi a few minutes later I feel light-headed and giddy and it occurs to me that I've never felt this excited about a guy before; not even Chris. No-one has ever made me feel so wanted; so attractive. I realise that I've been moping around over the last few weeks, going over and over every little detail in my head, crucifying myself repeatedly for the situation between Sophie and me, but it has done me no good. Tonight I feel like a new person and that can only be a good thing. I reach up and touch my lips, reliving the kiss. Maybe it's the wine at dinner, maybe it's the rush of happy hormones, maybe it's just that I feel like I've had fun for the first time in ages, but as the taxi turns down my street I'm hit with an overwhelming feeling that everything will work itself out and come good, and not a minute too soon.

Chapter Twenty-Two

The following morning as I prepare the first coffee of the day I make Jenny and Lola envious as I swoon over Joe and regale them, in between the occasional yawn – I really shouldn't have stayed for that last drink – with snippets of our first date. My chatter is met with giddy faces and Jenny even swears she's going to aim her car at the next male cyclist she sees.

'He sounds too good to be true' Jenny states 'and usually I would say that that's exactly what he is but' she shrugs 'Joe sounds genuine, and if I were you Emma, I'd hang on to him'

'I'm definitely going to' I can't help the huge grim that's been a permanent fixture on my face since last night 'I just can't quite believe my luck.'

'He actually said that he really likes you? Just like that, without you having to prise it out of him?'

'Yep'

'It's not fair' Lola shakes her head 'all I ever meet are guys who are more interested in themselves and getting drunk rather than having a romantic meal.'

'That's because most of the men you meet are already drunk and in a nightclub' Jenny -chides.

'Hmm' Lola looks thoughtful.

'I guess this is just the weirdest situation of being in the right place at the right time. If I hadn't been going to Dad's for dinner then I wouldn't have bumped into Joe on his bike and I wouldn't be standing here telling you about how gorgeous he is.'

'Okay, don't rub it in' Jenny chides humorously 'Are you going to be this annoying all day?'

'Did I tell you how amazing it was when he kissed me?'

'Um, I think you mentioned that'.

'If you were my friend you'd be happy for me. Why can't you do that?'
'Because he's lying to you; it's all lies'

Chapter Twenty-Three

The start of the week goes by in a whirl and it's soon Tuesday night. I'm greeted in the wine bar by Joe, whose opening line is, 'You look amazing.' It doesn't matter what the rest of the evening holds, I'm hooked from those words onward.

We sip a few beers and Joe tells me all about his little brother, Matt, who is a genius, apparently, and is working on some kind of design that will save the world – or something to that effect. I wasn't really listening, just gazing into Joe's brown eyes and staring at his full lips. All I can think about is our kiss on Friday night and those soft lips. I want them to kiss me again, and maybe more. I want to feel his lips all over me, while we're all hot and naked and –

'Emma? Are you listening to me?'

'Of course!' I answer confidently. 'That sounds really impressive,' I say, hoping that I sound convincing and I haven't just said something totally inappropriate.

It seems to work as he pauses for just a second before continuing his story while I fall right back into daydreaming about his smoking-hot body being pressed tightly against mine. This really is turning out to be a nice evening…

'Do you have time for one more drink?' Joe asks and I realise that the time has flown and the wine bar is starting to empty.

I glance so my watch – it's quarter past ten. I need to be in work for eight thirty tomorrow so I should really be getting home...

'Just one more then.' I barely hesitate.

Joe jumps up from his seat and heads to the bar. As I watch him walk away I can't help but find myself beaming. If this time last week, as I set off to Dad's house for dinner, you'd told me that I'd be sitting here now with a hot new guy I'd have been very sceptical, but here I am.

'What are you smiling at?' Joe sits down next to me and places another beer on the table. I know I'm going to regret this in the morning when I can't lift my head from the pillow and my grooming regime takes another hit. I'll just have to take the hair straighteners to work.

'Nothing...I'm just happy, that's all.' I fiddle awkwardly with the neck of the beer bottle.

'Good.'

I glance at him and notice that he's moved a little closer to me.

'I'm sorry, Emma, but there's something that I've been wanting to do all evening.'

Oh no, this doesn't sound good.

'Don't look so worried,' his dimples form at the corners of his mouth as he lifts my chin with his hand, pulling my face gently towards him. 'I've just been wanting to kiss you all night.'

He leans in and brushes his lips on mine and I instantly melt. I feel his tongue probe my lips, parting them gently, and I instantly respond, caressing his tongue with mine, enjoying the butterflies flapping wildly in my ribcage and the longing in my lower stomach. I reach up and touch his face, pulling him deeper and deeper into me. I don't care that we're in a public place and people might be watching. I'm caught up in the moment, behaving like a lust-crazed teenager for once, and it feels amazing.

As I pull away, gasping for breath, I think I might actually have died and gone to heaven. I'm making out in public with a fit guy who's been wanting to kiss me all night. How hot does that make me? Okay, so that might be a little self-indulgent and ever so slightly narcissistic, but I think this is the one and only time I can get away with thinking that.

'I think we'd better get you home,' Joe whispers as the bar begins to empty.

'I guess so,' I reply in a breathy voice, still tingling all over from our passionate kiss.

He grabs my hand and leads me outside while dialling his mobile to call for a cab.

'So...' My eyes meet his as we stand cuddled together on the street, keeping warm while we wait for the taxi.

'So?' He pulls me just a little bit closer.

'Are we, like, um actually...going out?' I stutter stupidly.

'Going out?' He laughs softly. 'You're so funny, Emma.'

'I am?' That's a good thing, right – as in funny ha-ha not downright weird?

'Well, do you kiss people like that when you're not going out with them?' He cocks his head to one side with his eyebrows raised.

Well, not on a regular basis, I admit; however, there have been drunken...oh, right, I see what he means.

'So I'm officially your....girlfriend now?'

'If you'd like that role going forward,' he says in a faux-serious voice.

'I'd like that very much.' I'm suddenly very serious myself.

And in that instant the god of romance deserts us as a car pulls up alongside the curb and the driver leans out the window and barks 'Taxi for Stark?' at us.

We huddle in the back seat of the car, both in silence following our 'we're now in a relationship' revelation. I'm feeling quite embarrassed now, but I've no idea why. Maybe it's because this is all moving along rather quickly. I mean, we've only been out on two dates. But what is the timescale that we should be following? Whose rules say that this is going too fast, and how many dates should you go on before agreeing that you're actually somebody's girlfriend? It's a potential minefield, but in reality the only people whose opinions count are the two people involved, and Joe seems pretty okay with being my boyfriend, and me being his girlfriend.

'So, do you want to meet for coffee on Saturday?' I ask tentatively.

'That sounds good to me.' Joe kisses my forehead and strokes my hair.

Mmm, I could get very used to his touch.

As the taxi pulls up outside my house there's only time for a quick kiss goodbye on the lips before the taxi driver clears his throat in an attempt to eject me from his car. I stand on the pavement watching the taxi pull away and feel sad that Saturday is four days away and I won't see Joe again until then. It sounds silly and pathetic but I feel it nonetheless. I've been catapulted onto a new emotional roller-coaster that I didn't see coming and didn't think I even wanted right at this moment, but now I'm on it I want to cling on and enjoy the ride.

Chapter Twenty-Four

On Wednesday night it's my turn to do the stock check of handbags once the shop has closed for the day, which means staying behind for a good few hours. I wave goodnight to Jenny and Lola as they head out of the back door at five thirty and I switch on the kettle to prepare some caffeine to get me through the task ahead. Thankfully this month it shouldn't be too laborious. The new system Jenny put in place on the computer has really made a difference – thank God she's conscientious; I'd never have taken the time to create it.

As I put the last few handbags back into the draws in the store cupboard I glance at my watch and am pleased it's only seven thirty. I think I'll treat myself to a Chinese takeaway and a bottle of wine from the off-licence on my way home. There are two nights of soaps to catch up with on TV, so a lazy evening in my pyjamas is just what's required.

I step out of the back of the shop and close the door behind me and lock up already thinking about my choice of Chinese meal. Stopping at the shop at the end of the street I collect a bottle of white wine and call my food order through to the takeaway near my flat for collection once I'm situated in my car. As I make the short journey home, via the Chinese takeaway, I find myself daydreaming about Joe. I can already feel the excited butterflies starting to flap in my stomach at the thought of seeing him again on Saturday.

I park on the road outside my house and climb wearily out of the car carefully placing the bottle of wine under my left arm as I grab the bag of hot food in one hand and my handbag in the other. As I approach the main door I feel somebody close by and the hairs on the back of my neck stand up instantly. I'm still too far from the safety of the door so I straighten my spine to my tallest capacity and grip the bunch of keys that that are still in my hand tightly (a distant memory of a self-defence class Sophie and I once took springs to mind) and I await the inevitable attack.

'Emma.'

I turn around sharply to see Chris hovering about two metres away from me, looking sheepish and a little sickly.

'Jesus Christ, Chris! You scared the crap out of me,' I hiss.

'Sorry.' He shrugs pathetically and I feel anger rising within me.

'What are you doing hanging around in the dark out here?'

'I was waiting earlier when the shop closed, I thought you'd be home but then I figured out maybe you were doing a stock check as it's Wednesday – you used to do them on Wednesday's didn't you?'

'Yes, yes, but…so, what? You've just been waiting out here for the last two hours for me to appear at my door?'

'Pretty much.' He shrugs.

God, he's annoying!

'But why?'

'I need to speak to you, Emma.'

'Have you not heard of a telephone, Chris? Or maybe you've forgotten how to use it since you haven't bothered to even drop me a text since that night.'

He has the decency to look contrite.

'Anyway, I've nothing to say to you,' I state, trying to sound as dignified as I can. He looks like hell. His thick golden hair that I used to love running my fingers through now looks a little dull and flat. His face even looks different, like it's sagging a little around the corners of his mouth. Did he always look that way or was it that I just didn't see it? Rose tinted glasses can disguise a lot, I guess. But a little part of me wonders whether all's not well with my blond replacement and whether this is him crawling back to ask me to take him back. Well, I know what he can do with that thought –

'I'm getting engaged.'

I stand there for a moment, wondering whether I've heard him correctly or my mind is playing horrible games with me. Did he really just say that he's getting engaged?

'Um…what?' I grab the drainpipe to my left for support as my knees suddenly feel like they're going to buckle beneath me.

'I said…' He clears his throat. 'I said I'm getting engaged.' He looks at me apprehensively and I've no idea what expression is plastered on my face. 'I thought that you should know, that's all.' He shrugs again.

'You thought that I should know?' I repeat in a monotone.

'In case you read it in the paper.'

I take a moment to digest this last bit of information.

In the fucking paper? Are you kidding me?

I press my lips together to hold in the retort I so desperately want to blurt out and I take a moment to regain my composure. I'm not in love with Chris any more. I'm happy in a new relationship. I don't really care any more about her it's just simply the shock of them getting married so soon. I mean they've not even been together for that long…I hear the words and then I really hear them.

'Emma…' Chris glances around nervously.

'I hope you're very happy together' my voice sounds a lot more even that it feels.

'So you're not…'

'Bothered? No Chris. We broke up. We've both moved on. That's what happens in life'

He looks at me a little bewildered.

'So you're not angry?' I swear he looks annoyed by this fact.

'Of course not. Thank you for telling me though' I swallow.

'Um, right'

'Was that it?' I ask brightly.

'Well…yes' Chris frowns.

'Then I'd better be getting in' I point to the carrier bag in my hand 'My food's getting cold'

'So you've moved on?'

'Look' I avoid that question 'I appreciate the heads up but I don't think we really need to stand around discussing our relationships do we?'

He just looks at me uncomfortably.

'Like I said, I wish you both well. Goodnight Chris' I say in a cheerful tone as I put the key on the lock and nearly snap it in two as I yank it to the left and fling the door open before heading into the house waiting for his response.

I storm through to the lounge while trying to balance a bottle of wine in the crevice of my arm and not to drop the Chinese food all over the floor, although it would be irrelevant as my appetite has completely disappeared. Dropping the bag of food and my handbag to the floor I allow the bottle of wine to slide out of its carrying position and roll along the carpet. I lean on the wall and take a deep breath, exhaling slowly to try to stem my trembling body.

I flounder making my way to the kitchen, stopping to collect the rolling bottle of wine on my way. I open the bottle removing the cork roughly and slosh the wine into the first glass I can lay my hands on which happens to be a tumbler.

I drink the glass pretty much in full and refill it without thinking as I lurch back into the hallway to retrieve my handbag. Maybe I had a lucky escape after all. I spent so long thinking he was the one that I became blinded by his excuses to his complete spinelessness. He made up so many reasons not to commit to me over the last year of our relationship, and as it turns out he probably did me a favour – or I'd still be pushing for us to move in together and still trying to ignore that nagging feeling that it was never going to happen.

Finding my mobile phone, I hit Sophie's number on speed dial. It's instinctive and I don't even think about it for a second until my brain catches up, kicking me as I remember: I can't call Sophie. I sigh heavily as the burden of our tattered relationship nestles heavily in my heart. I stare at the phone for a moment before dialling Simon's number instead

'Hiya babe.' Simon's usual cheery tone greets me and I don't even bother with the niceties of "hello".

'He's only getting engaged'

'Who's…What?'

'Chris…Chris is getting engaged'

'To…her'

I pause for a moment. He didn't actually say it was but…

'Of course to her. You'll see their announcement in the local paper' I say incredulously.

'Oh…um...how did you find that out?'

I take a deep breath and exhale feeling some of the fight leaving my body 'He came by my house just now to tell me'

'Okay. Well that's good at least'

'What exactly is good Simon?'

'That he didn't just let you see it, honey. That would have been… harsh.'

I bite my lip. Maybe Simon's right. Maybe it was the decent thing for Chris to come and tell me. I don't know why I feel so angry; it's not like I still have feelings for him. Well, not those kind of feelings anyway.

'Are you really upset?' Simon's tone is serious for once.

'Yes. No…I guess it was just a bit of a shock. I couldn't even get him to commit to moving in together with me after two years and now he's getting married.'

'So what did you say?'

'I told him that I hope they'll be very happy together and I wished them well.'

'And do you?'

'No! I wish them a lifetime of misery and depression and I hope that his penis stops working on their wedding night just for good measure.'

'Emma!'

'He seemed to be annoyed by my lack of reaction as though he expected me to burst in to floods of tears or something.'

'So what? He treated you like shit. It will do him good to know that there are consequences to actions, and to realise a few home truths no doubt, like you're over him and not waiting for him to come crawling back.'

'Well said by the man who's dodged every consequence of his own actions for as long as I can remember.'

'Hey, cheap shot! Although to be fair I've usually done a complete runner and never returned to the crime scene. He could learn a thing or two from me.'

'Oh Si, he was probably shagging her for months before he had the decency to end things with me – and I use the word "decency" lightly as there's nothing remotely decent about him or his pathetic, needy, emotionally deranged existence.'

'So you're clearly not bothered. I can see that now.'

'I'm sorry. Alright, I'm done with the childish remarks.'

'Are you really okay?'

'Yeah, I'm fine. He just took me by surprise. When I looked at him I didn't feel love or attraction, just…annoyance that he's appeared in my life unannounced. I'm really happy with Joe and nothing's going to spoil that. Chris getting married provides some closure on our relationship that I probably didn't have before given how he ended it.'

'He's in the past sweetie.'

'I know' I take a mouthful of wine, my earlier anger now completely dispersed 'and I can't wait to see Joe again on Saturday.'

'What are your plans?'

'Nothing really. We're just meeting for coffee at Café Crespo and seeing where the day takes us.'

'That sounds nice.'

'Thanks for listening Simon.'

'Any time, hun.'

'Goodnight.'

'Love you, Ems.'

'Love you too.'

I put down the phone and swirl the dregs of wine around in the bottom of my glass. This is the last time I'll allow myself to feel self-pity over Chris. I actually feel weirdly at ease with the situation now. He's in my past now, well and truly, and Joe Stark is my immediate future.

I down the last mouthful of wine and head to the bathroom to fill the bath with bubbles and bath oil. Ten minutes later I'm fully submerged in the aroma of ylang ylang essential oil, feeling the tension of tonight slowly ebb away and the evil thoughts of Chris dispersing.

Chapter Twenty-Five

'I'm telling you, that is the case. Did you not see Columbo as a teenager?' Joe asks incredulously.

'Who? No, honestly I can say I never watched that.'

'Well the bad guy is always the one that is overly helpful in the police investigation. Honestly, you watch any television crime show and you'll see what I mean.'

I'm glad I've found someone on my conversation level. I was a little worried that Joe was far too intelligent for me and he would find my mindless waffling silly but it seems like he too shares a love of a non-too serious debate.

'So I need to be suspicious of those who are too nice. Is this what you're telling me?'

'Exactly.'

'Then maybe I should avoid you.' I joke.

'No way Emma. There's no getting rid of me now I'm afraid' he leans in and kisses me.

It's Saturday morning; the time I used to spend gossiping over skinny lattes with Sophie. Instead, as my turbulent existence determines, I'm snuggled next to Joe on a squashy leather sofa in a coffee shop across the other side of town from my usual Saturday haunt. For starters, I don't want to bump into Connor and Sophie: no matter how much I want her to speak to me, that will never happen while her Rottweiler is hovering next to her. And secondly, the last time I frequented my usual coffee shop I had the misfortune of seeing Chris and my blond replacement, now his fiancée – urgh! – slurping coffee, and each other, completely oblivious to other human beings around them.

'Shall I get us another coffee or are you ready to go?' I ask hoping that Joe wants to stay a bit longer. I'm enjoying just relaxing in his company and feeling like we're in our own little bubble just sitting here chatting.

'Yeah, we're in no rush. I'll have another latte.'

'Great.' I swivel around trying to get out of the sofa and up to an upright position when -

Oh God. From the corner of my eye I catch a swiftly moving object and realise with instant horror that it's Simon, sashaying across the coffee shop towards us. What the hell is he doing here? Do I have a homing device that activates the minute I step near a skinny latte that calls all unwanted people to my presence?

'Hi, gorgeous!' Simon arrives at our table with his usual happy expression, completely ignoring the death stare I'm giving him.

'Simon. What are you doing here?' I smile falsely through gritted teeth. This coffee shop is nowhere near his flat, so why is he here, disrupting my otherwise very pleasant Saturday morning?

'So is this the guy you've been telling me about, hun?'

Ah, it all becomes clear now. He's here to ruin my life further.

Simon turns his attention to Joe, who's looking a bit bewildered as I sink down into the crevices of the brown leather cushions.

Apparently not remotely bothered that he's performing a death-by-embarrassment execution, Simon pulls a spare chair over from the table next to us.

'No, please sit down, Simon, and join us.' I glare at him, hoping he'll take the hint, which would be a miracle in itself. I should know better than to expect that from him after all these years!

'Don't get your knickers in a twist, Em. I'm just being friendly.' He winks at me.

I've experienced Simon being 'friendly' before and it usually results in him revealing embarrassing secrets about me, or telling his own shocking stories, neither of which give a great impression to a new boyfriend…and Joe is my boyfriend. We definitely established that the other night.

'It's more likely that you want to interrogate us both until you've embarrassed me even more than you have already.' I raise my eyebrows at him.

He raises his eyebrows back at me in mock offence. 'So cynical for someone so young.' He turns to face Joe again. 'Let me introduce myself, seeing as grumpy over here is too busy looking like she's chewing a wasp.'

I kick him none-too-gently under the table.

'I'm Simon, the other best friend.'

Other best friend? What will Joe think? I haven't actually talked about Sophie with Joe yet. I mean, where would I begin to explain the situation between Sophie and I?

'Pleased to meet you.' Simon holds out his hand and Joe, who's been watching our exchange with some amusement, shakes his hand firmly.

'I'm Joe.' He states politely.

'Oh, don't worry, honey, I know who you are.' Simon winks at me appearing to be twice as camp as usual this morning. 'You're the one she nearly squished like a pancake while daydreaming at the wheel.'

Dear God...why? Why? What on earth will Joe think? He's so... well, not camp in the slightest. What if he's uncomfortable with gay men? Chris and Simon didn't exactly hit it off and Chris always behaved weirdly around him like he was scared Simon was going to come on to him. Despite me reassuring him several times to the contrary Chris always had that stupid notion that a gay man obviously fancied all other men. What if Joe feels like that too?

'Nice strong handshake; that's good.' Simon states looking over at me and I struggle to refrain from leaping over the lattes and strangling him, but then Joe starts laughing, really laughing hard, and I can't help but laugh too, half from Simon's behaviour and half from relief that Joe doesn't seem to have taken any offense or look uncomfortable at all.

'You're impossible.' I slap Simon on the arm between giggles. 'Honestly, do you make it your life's mission to embarrass me constantly?'

'What?' he protests, all innocent like he hasn't just arrived at our table and turned the morning on its head.

'And quit making snipes about my driving – you haven't even got a licence.'

'Okay, okay, I surrender. I'll play nice.'

'See, was that so hard?'

'Right, let's start again. So what are you two love birds doing with your Saturday?'

'Well, once we've finished our nice, quiet, peaceful cup of coffee' – I see Simon roll his eyes at me – 'we're off for some retail therapy and a late lunch at, well, wherever takes our fancy.'

'Retail therapy?' Simon shakes his head at Joe. 'It's a little early in this relationship to be under the thumb, isn't it?'

'Actually it was my idea,' Joe states with a completely straight face, which silences Simon. I stare at him with a 'Isn't my boyfriend so handsome and wonderful?' look, which causes Simon to roll his eyes at me yet again.

'Shall I get us some more drinks if we're staying here a bit longer?' Joe stands up.

'Mine's a black coffee, please.' Simon grins at Joe.

Once Joe's out of earshot I turn to Simon.

'What the hell are you doing?' I hiss while trying to keep the pretence of a smile firmly fixed on my face.

'Look, I was worried about you, you know after that whole Chris thing the other night –'

'I appreciate that, but how did you know I was here and what are you doing here too?'

'You told me on the phone when you rang up the other night in a tizzy about Chris–'

Damn it!

'so I thought I'd better come down here and make sure that this one wasn't going to do the dirty on you and treat you like pooh.'

I scowl at him sceptically.

'And you're a great judge of character I suppose?'

'Slightly better than you sometimes, sweetie.'

'Thanks for the vote of confidence.'

'I'm just trying to look out for you, honey.' He protests 'I want to see you happy, and you do have a tendency to be your own worst enemy sometimes.'

I glance over towards the counter where Joe is just collecting our drinks.

'I know you're just trying to be a good friend.' I hold up my hands in submission. 'But can you please tone it down a bit? You'll scare him to death.'

'Tone it down a bit?'

'Yes, please.'

'That's rich coming from the person who frightened off my Friday lover after –'

'Let's not get into that again, please, Simon. Believe me, I wish I'd never done that! But come on, give me a break. I really like Joe.'

'Okay, Princess Emmie. Your wish is my command.'

I shoot him a disapproving glance.

'Honestly a guy could take offence from your evil stares.' He pretends to sulk. 'Anyway I don't know what you're worried about. I'm not the most eccentric person he'll have to meet. Wait until he has to meet your mother.'

That's a fair point…

After another coffee Simon and Joe are chatting away so much that I struggle to get a word in and they look perfectly at ease in each other's company, and yet again I'm shown what a really nice guy Joe is.

Half an hour later Joe and I leave the coffee shop, and Simon, behind and I agree to meet Simon for lunch tomorrow. As we head towards the shops Joe takes hold of my hand as we walk alongside the edge of the park. It's a beautiful sunny morning and the grass is littered with families and children kicking balls around and eating ice creams. It feels like summer might actually be just around the corner.

'He's a character and a half,' Joe squeezes my hand gently. I love the fact that he now takes hold of my hand the instant we're in each other's company.

'You have no idea,' I laugh. 'I know Simon can be a little…different, and sometimes ever so slightly too much, but he's a good guy and a good friend. I've known him practically all of my life.'

'Really?'

'Yeah. He lived next door to me when we were kids growing up. He went to a different comprehensive school but we always stayed close. He's kind of like the brother I never had.'

'Have you always known he was gay?'

'I think he's always known, and for the most part I knew too. You know, once we got to an age of…Well, anyway, he never pretended to be into girls or anything to fit in with everyone else. I think most people figured it out and just got on with it. There was no big announcement or anything. It was always: "This is who I am, so accept me or don't." He wasn't going to change for anyone.'

'That's brave.'

We cross the road heading up towards the pedestrian area and the start of the shops as a mixture of food smells from grilling bacon to sweet pastry waft towards us in the warm breeze.

'Yeah, it hasn't always been easy for him. His dad was pretty cool about him being gay – I think he'd suspected it for a long time – but his mum found it hard to deal with. My mum, on the other hand, spent most of our teenage years trying to encourage us to be boyfriend and girlfriend because Simon was "such a nice young man".'

'She didn't realise he was gay?'

'You haven't met my mother.' I shake my head, remembering her innocently saying, 'I'm sure it's just a phase, darling,' when I explained for the hundredth time that Simon wasn't into girls. I think being in New York has at least widened her understanding of different people.

'What's your mum like?' Joe squeezes my hand.

'That's a whole different conversation on its own, and one probably better had while there's alcohol around.'

'You're funny.' Joe shakes his head.

No, actually I'm being very serious....

We reach the shopping centre and spend the next few hours in a complete role reversal, wandering from shop to shop while Joe muses, undecided, over three different styles of trainers – really, I didn't think it was that difficult a choice, but who am I to question the fashion decisions of the male species? It makes a change from Sophie trying on a thousand different items in a hundred different shops only to then go right back to the start and purchase the first item that she set eyes on. I miss Sophie...

Over lunch, which consists of tapas and wine, Joe startles me with an unexpected question.

'So if Simon is your other best friend, then who's the best friend I'm yet to meet and impress?'

I pause, holding a forkful of Spanish omelette, as my stomach drops. I'd forgotten Simon's comment. How do I go about explaining why Sophie and I are currently not friends without fully telling him everything, which could open up a whole can of worms about the outcome of that fateful evening?

'Um, I...'

Joe's face drops. 'Have I said something wrong?'

'No, absolutely not.' I shake my head. 'You haven't.'

'It's just that I want to show you off to my mates, but before I subject you to a night of beer, football and appalling attempts at humour – and, potentially, the occasional sexist joke that I'll have to apologise for – I thought I'd better pass the best friend test first.'

He really is too good to be true.

'I'd love for you to meet Sophie,' I state, putting my full fork back down on my plate without eating the food. 'I know she'd really like you...'

'But?' He looks at me questioningly.

'But...' I take a large gulp of my wine. 'We had a big falling-out last month, before I met you...and we haven't spoken since.'

'Oh. Right. That's...'

'Horrible. Truly horrible.' I swallow hard.

'You miss her?'

'Terribly. Prior to this we've been inseparable since we were kids.'

'Surely if that's the case then you can sort whatever it is out?' He says softly but I shake my head. 'There's no way back?' He reaches over and strokes my hand with his thumb.

I pause, pressing my lips together before answering.

'Not right now.'

'What happened?'

I knew that question was coming.

'I'm really not ready to talk it. Is that...alright?'

Joe looks at me seriously for a moment. 'Okay.'

I reach for my fork and continue eating, although my appetite has all but gone. Joe reaches his hand across the table and grabs mine, giving it a little squeeze.

'Hey, I'm sorry for asking. I'm an idiot.'

'No, you're not at all,' I say genuinely. 'Please don't feel bad. I want to work things out with Sophie, I really do. I just need to figure it out in my own head first, that's all. I need to figure out the way back.'

'I understand.' He raises my hand to his lips and kisses it gently. 'If you want to talk it through then I'm here for you.'

As the afternoon goes on I start to forget about the awkward conversation over lunch and I relax in Joe's company once again. I feel a little fuzzy around the edges from drinking wine in the early afternoon – will I ever learn?

We make our way back to Joe's house around six o'clock. When he suggested we go back to his house earlier I agreed as it felt like the right thing to do but now where on our way I'm feeling a little pressurised. I mean, what is he going to expect of me when we get there? Just a cup of tea and a chat? The last time I went back to a guy's house it was Connor's and I certainly don't want a repeat of that. I know Joe is different but maybe he will expect sex too and I'm just not ready for that yet. We've only been on a couple of dates…

'Emma? Are you okay?' Joe interrupts my swirling thoughts.

'I'm fine; just thinking about Simon.' I lie.

What if he expects sex and I say no? How will he take that? Oh god, why is the dating game such an emotional minefield?

It's too late to question things any further as we soon arrive at Joe's house. It's close to town, just on the other side of the park, and as he unlocks the door I don't really know what to expect – I only saw it from the outside when I dropped him off after the hospital that night. A complete mess with cycling gear strewn all over the place maybe? Or completely immaculate and like a show home à la Connor/Johnny?

Stepping inside, I realise it's somewhere in between. It's a fairly small terrace house but it instantly has a cosy rather than cramped feel about it. Thankfully there are no weird Lycra items lying around the place, but the remains of his crumpled bike are tucked away in a corner next to the door and I bite my lip, still amazed at the fact that that is how we met.

'Come through.' Joe heads down the hallway and I follow him into the kitchen.

'Beer?'

'Yes, please.'

Joe pulls open the door to a huge American fridge that takes up half of the kitchen and reaches in for two bottles of beer. He opens them and passes one to me and I take a swig.

'Let's go through to the lounge.' He cocks his head over his shoulder towards the next room.

The lounge is simple but homely. A two-seater sofa is joined by a matching armchair that sits next to the window. The television is mounted on the wall and Joe busies himself scrolling through some music channels until he settles for some old R&B tunes.

I stroll around the room, tapping my foot to the beat of a song I used to dance to in bars a lifetime ago while I look at photos of Joe: on his bike, muddy but laughing naturally into the camera lens; looking smart in a suit at what I presume is his younger brother's graduation, given he's standing next to a young man in a cap and gown; and then with a woman of whom he's the spitting image – she must be his mother. He looks genuinely happy in every picture.

I pick up a picture of Joe sitting next to an elderly woman, holding a large bunch of flowers and smiling a crooked smile.

'My gran.'

I turn around, still holding the picture. I hadn't realised that he was behind me.

'On her last birthday before she passed away.' He swallows and it's clear that the emotion is still raw.

'I'm sorry.' I don't know what else to say.

'It's okay.' He takes the photo frame and places it back on the shelf. 'She had an amazing life. She was a big part of our lives growing up and I admired her.'

'That's …lovely.' No wonder he's such a gentleman. He's clearly had plenty of good female influence in his life.

'You know what's weird?' he says softly, reaching up to stroke my hair with his hand.

I hold my breath, hoping this is a 'good weird' and not a 'bad weird'.

'I feel like I've known you forever, but really we've only just met.

There's still so much that I want to find out about you, Emma, and I can't stop thinking about you. I want to know everything about you, everything.'

It feels a little intense and overwhelming. I'm not used to such full-on openness about emotions from a guy. But it seems like honesty is most certainly the best policy with Joe, and minus the last few weeks of my life there are no, no skeletons in the closet and nothing to hide. So I take Joe's hand and we sit down on the sofa.

'Ask away.' I offer, and so does he.

Before I know it I'm rambling on about things I haven't thought about in years. Just life in general, things I've done, places I've been to. I learn more about Joe too, which all seems genuine; he seems genuine, and the more I get to know him, the more I trust every word that he says.

'It's getting late.' I glance at my watch, noticing that we have been talking non-stop to each other for hours, only taking a pause to collect a further beer or two. 'I should be making a move to go home.'

But before I can attempt to get up from the sofa Joe pulls me in close and kisses me deeply, his tongue pushing my lips apart gently, teasing and probing mine.

'Stay the night,' he whispers between kisses. 'Stay here with me.'

I pull back for a second as self-doubt bursts my happy bubble.

I thought that I was ready to move on emotionally; I thought this is what I wanted, needed. But I'm just not ready to take that leap of faith and move into a physical relationship yet. It's not Joe, it really isn't: I'm still scarred from my last battle with Chris, let alone Connor. I'm not sure I'm ready to allow myself to fall again. To be vulnerable. What if I get it so wrong again? I'm not sure I can put myself in that position so soon.

I can feel the weight of my emotion crushing me as I look into the open, kind, honest face of Joe, who's leaning back and is now looking at me with a hint of apprehension and defeat.

See. This is what I do to guys. I mess it up every time. Just when things are going great, I ruin things with all my crap. Tears prick the corners of my eyes and it takes all my inner strength not to just collapse in a heap on the floor and wallow. How can I expect him to understand the emotional turmoil that I carry around with me when even I can't figure it out?

'Hey.' Joe leans forward and brushes a stray tear from my cheek. 'What's wrong? I mean…if you don't want to…I just…shit.' He runs his hands through his thick hair. 'Have I got all of this completely wrong?' He looks at me as though he's desperately trying to understand why our moment of romance and passion has deflated like a three-day-old balloon.

'No, it's not you; it's me.'

'Right.' Joe drops his hands into his lap. 'I think I've heard this before, and I know where this is going.'

I stand up, running my hand through my hair. He stands up too, and suddenly it's like there's a void between us. I like Joe, a lot, and I need to fix this now or he'll walk away from this relationship and all my emotional baggage. I don't want this to be over. Am I going to let Chris and his lack of moral decency and his aversion to monogamy thwart every relationship in my future? Will I always fear that the next guy I meet is some lunatic like Connor? Does every man on this planet only have a dark, evil agenda?

'No…wait.' I grab Joe's arm as he goes to turn away from me, his shoulders drooped. 'You don't understand.'

'No, I guess I don't.' He looks defeated. 'I read the signals wrong.'

'No…no, you didn't.' I twist my hair nervously around my fingers like I used to do as a small child. 'I like you…I do…it's just…'

Joe looks right at me, his eyes imploring me to tell him, to let him in to my thoughts, but and after a second he just nods, gently taking a step closer until our bodies are nearly touching once more.

'You don't have to explain.' He kisses me gently on the lips and a defiant tear slips down my cheek.

He brushes away the tear, then covers my cheek in soft little kisses.

'I'm sorry.' I shake my head.

'What are you sorry for exactly?'

'For this? For….' I take a deep breath. 'Look, I've made some pretty huge mistakes recently, some of which admittedly have been my own doing.' Drunken night out with Conner/Johnny could have been avoided. 'Some of which haven't.' I can't be completely to blame for Chris cheating on me, can I? 'Anyway, I guess I've had a few bad experiences.' I press my lips together.

He cocks his head to one side and looks at me for a moment. 'I kind of figured that out.'

Really? How?

'I know what you're thinking. How can a man possibly figure all of that out when men are usually so emotionally challenged?' He looks at me expectantly.

Well...

'Because I'm that good.' His dimples crease in the corners of his mouth and I can't help but relax a little despite my tears. 'Look, I understand that you've been hurt, yes?'

'Yes.'

'Is it anything that you want to talk about?'

'Not right now.'

'Okay. Do you still have any feelings for the guy?'

Hell no! Except complete contempt – and I'm pretty sure that's not the kind of feeling Joe has in mind.

'No, no feelings.'

'Then you take as much time as you need. I'm not going anywhere.' He pulls me into a gentle hug.

Can I accept that amid all the frogs leaping around, blighting my every move, I've found a prince just waiting for me to become his princess?

'I'll stay,' I murmur into his chest. 'I want to.'

'I'll never do anything to hurt you, Emma. I promise.' He brushes his thumb across my lips and my body defies my instinctive fear by sending a tingling sensation all the way down my stomach until it reaches my lower abdomen. 'Let's take things nice and slow.'

I'm unable to utter even a single word as he wraps his arms around me, pulling me so close to him that I can feel his heart beating a rhythm in his chest and it's a deafening sound filling my ears.

As we snuggle together under the covers, me in one of Joe's t-shirts, him still wearing a t-shirt too and his boxer shorts, I can smell the faint scent of his aftershave mixed with soap powder, and as I hold the t-shirt I'm wearing to my face, breathing it in, I feel a sense of calm. Although I still can't quite dispel the slight fear of him seeing me with no makeup on for the first time in the morning, and the likelihood that my hair will have morphed into a frenzied state during the night.

Joe is true to his word, though, and he really does just want me to stay the night; no pressure, no trying it on under the covers. Just the two of us cuddled together with no agenda. His arm is draped protectively over me, and as I press myself closer to his body I feel warm and safe and complete. Listening to the soft, gentle sound of his breathing, I close my eyes and succumb to sleep.

'You don't need her. She's trying to come between us. We only need each other'

Chapter Twenty-Six

'Morning, beautiful.'

I open one eye to see Joe standing at the side of the bed as a wonderful smell of coffee and toast suddenly fills the bedroom.

'Hey.' Joe leans down and kisses my forehead. 'There's coffee and breakfast when you're ready.'

I didn't even hear him get out of bed, but he's dressed in some jogging bottoms and a fresh t-shirt and he appears to be wide awake.

I open both eyes now and smile. Waking up to coffee and toast – I could get used to this. I've spent too much time living on my own.

'I'll be through in minute.' I pull the covers up slightly, suddenly feeling a little self-conscious.

'Okay.'

As Joe leaves the room I jump out of bed and lunge towards the mirror hanging on the wall. Thank God the hair fairy has been kind to me: for once my hair isn't stuck up on end or plastered to my face; there's just the odd strand out of place. I pull my fingers roughly though it, wincing as I catch a knot or two, before pushing it behind my ears.

I rub my forefinger across my teeth and swish my tongue around my mouth before pinching both of my cheeks a little until a flush of colour fills them. Well, under the circumstances, that's about as good as it's going to get. I didn't exactly come prepared for a sleepover – no overnight bag with toiletries and makeup to hand.

As I pull open the bedroom door and follow the welcoming smell of breakfast I'm conscious that the t-shirt I'm wearing barely covers my modesty and I pull the hem further down over my knickers as I make my way into the kitchen.

'Hi,' I mumble sheepishly and Joe turns around to face me.

'Coffee?'

'Please.'

He hands me a steaming mug and he leans in, kissing me softly on the cheek. 'You look amazing.'

I can feel the heat shoot into my cheeks. I've never felt so vulnerable, standing here half-naked and makeup free, and yet so…well, desired.

'Please, go through to the lounge and sit down. I'll bring the food.' He waves me away.

I can't help thinking how surreal this whole situation is. He's a guy living on his own. I expected day-old pizza and a can of Coke for breakfast at best!

I wander through to the lounge and sit down in the corner of the sofa. As I look around the room feels lived in and the atmosphere's relaxed; in fact, I'm relaxed. It feels like this is exactly where I should be.

We eat toast and drink coffee while curled up together on the sofa, idly watching a Sunday morning cookery programme.

'What are your plans for the day?' Joe ask as he finishes off the last slice.

'I'm meeting Simon for lunch later, remember?'

'I'm not going anywhere yet but I have football practice in –'

The front door opens and closes with a bang, but before either of us have time to react a tracksuit-clad figure appears in the lounge doorway.

'Morning, Joe....Hey, who's this then?' Tracksuit Man glances amused, in my direction as I scrabble to pull Joe's t-shirt down to cover my bare legs and any potential flash of my pants.

'Ben, what are you doing here?' Joe scowls at him, standing up.

'Just thought I'd give you a lift to football practice. I didn't know you had…company.' Ben grins, taking another glance at me.

I feel like one of those animals at the zoo on display in a glass box.

'Yes, well, thanks for that.' Joe sounds all flustered. 'Why don't you wait in the kitchen and grab yourself a coffee.' He tries to ushers Ben out of the doorway.

'Don't I get an introduction first?' Ben protests, standing firm.

Joe huffs loudly before turning to look at me and then back to Ben.

'Ben, this is Emma. Emma is my new girlfriend, or at least I hope she still will be after you're through with embarrassing us all.'

Ben rolls his eyes.

'Emma, this idiot here is my mate Ben, or at least he was up until about thirty seconds ago.'

'Nice to meet you, Emma.' Ben says chirpily in my direction.

'Nice to meet you too.' I squeak.

'Ignore Mr Sarcastic here. He's not usually so tetchy – he must really like you.'

'Kitchen!' Joe points towards the door as I blush crimson.

'Okay, okay!' Ben holds up his hands. 'I'm going.'

'I'm so sorry.' Joe turns to me as soon as Ben is out of earshot.

'Don't worry,' I puff out the air I've been holding in for the last thirty seconds. 'I guess I had to meet him sometime. Although admittedly I'd have preferred it if I was fully dressed and it wasn't quite so obvious that I'd just spent the night here.' I bite my lip.

Joe looks mortified. 'He's a good guy, really. Just a bit forward sometimes. I'm sorry.'

'Stop apologising.' I stand up and give him a kiss. 'I should be getting ready anyway. Is it alright to jump in the shower?'

'Of course. There are clean towels in the cupboard at the top of the stairs.'

'Thanks.'

'Last night was...great.' Joe smiles coyly placing his hands on my shoulders giving them a gentle rub 'I could get used to waking up with you.'

'I'm glad I stayed.'

He leans in and kisses me on the lips. 'Me too.'

As I head towards the bathroom Joe goes into the kitchen and I hover for a second in the hallway, straining to hear the conversation.

Ben: 'She seems nice.'

Joe: 'She is nice; very nice.'

Ben: 'Too nice for you, mate.'

Joe: 'Sorry, I don't think I've met your girlfriend.'

Ben: 'Fair play. I'm just messing with you. You're obviously keen or you would've told me about her. Where did you two meet?'

Oh dear God....

There's a pause.

Joe: 'We just bumped into each other one night, that's all.'

Phew!

Joe: 'I really like her, Ben, so behave, will you? I don't want you scaring her off with any more unscheduled visits like this morning.'

I head to the bathroom feeling giddy like a teenager. Joe thinks I'm nice; very nice!

I leave Joe's house half an hour later on cloud nine, and by the time I'm heading down the high street to meet Simon for lunch I'm practically skipping, feeling like a teenager all over again.

'Uh oh – looks like somebody is in lurve.' Simon giggles as I bound into the pub and over to the table. It's already busy with diners enjoying a traditional Sunday lunch and I can smell the delicious aromas of roast beef and Yorkshire pudding.

'Shut up.' I glare at him, feeling my blushing cheeks giving me completely away.

'Mmm, slightly crumpled clothes and slightly messy day-old hair? Me thinks somebody didn't make it to their own bed last night from the shopping expedition and they stayed over at their new man's house for the first time. Am I right?'

'Can I get you something to drink?'

I nearly die as the waiter appears at my side, quite obviously having heard Simon's last comment as he tries – unsuccessfully – to remain professional and to hide his smirk.

'A white wine, please,' I snap curtly to hide my embarrassment.

'Make that two.' Simon grins and gives the waiter a wink.

I shake my head at Simon in utter despair.

'Were you at the back of the line when they were giving out manners, morals and any awareness of boundaries or other human beings?'

'Oh chill, Emma; I'm only having a bit of fun with you. You're so serious these days.'

I choose to ignore Simon and stare at the menu instead.

'If truth be told, I'm a little...envious of you,' Simon states, catching me completely off guard.

'Envious?'

'Yeah.'

'I don't understand how that could possibly be.' I look at him, bewildered, and he cocks his head to one side and just looks at me. 'Okay, Simon; talk me through it.'

'You've your heart broken by some jerk.'

'I hope you're going somewhere with this,' I scowl.

'And here you are: ready to trust someone again, ready to fall in love.' Simon shrugs his shoulders.

'And I want to...'

'What? Have a serious, monogamous relationship?'

'Maybe.'

Oh my God, Simon actually looks like he's being serious for once.

I'm stunned by this revelation. 'I thought you loved your carefree, wham-bam-thank-you-ma'am love life.'

'Are you mocking me?' Simon huffs.

'Never. It's just that this is totally out of the blue from you.'

'Well, maybe it's time that I grew up and tried to find the perfect guy. You know, like you have.'

'Ah, well, that should be easy then,' I say with a hint of authority. 'All you need to do is experience emotionally crippling humiliation as your heart and self-respect are passed through a blender, before going on to meet a psychopath who tricks you into bed, destroying your relationship with your best friend in the process. Then, when you finally spot the man of your dreams, you must run into him with a car, bruising him as you do so.' I watch Simon trying not to laugh.

'When you put it like that, maybe my current love life isn't so bad after all. I may have to think this through a bit more.'

'That would be my advice.' I state. 'Best make sure you're really ready for everything that comes with trying to find "The One" before you set off down that path.'

'Agreed. Now, are you having the roast beef?'

As I sit on the sofa at home later that evening with a cup of tea I can't help but chuckle at the situation this morning. At least Ben walking in to find me half-naked on Joe's sofa was nowhere near as bad as me walking in on Simon and his 'friend'. Damn it – I'd tried so hard to get that image out of my head and now it's right back in there! God, Sophie would laugh her head off if I told her, especially as she goes on about me being a prude. I instinctively reach for my phone, but then stop.

It's been weeks since we last spoke, and that night was so horrible. Things were said that should never have been said. Crap from years ago dredged back up. It became a mud-slinging match with seemingly all the brown stuff hitting me. But surely our friendship is stronger than that? We've never gone so long without speaking. I'm going to call her right now and sort this out, whether Connor is there or not!

My hand hovers over the keypad but my heart slowly sinks. I can't do this over the phone. I need to figure out how to make this alright face to face, and soon. I miss sharing everything with Sophie. I miss her no-nonsense advice. I miss my best friend. Instead I click onto the social media site curious to see if there are further updates about her and Connor.

That's weird.

I scroll down my list of contacts but Sophie's no longer there. As a knife twists between my ribs I realise she's defriended me from her social profile which is the final severance of our friendship.

Chapter Twenty-Seven

'Keep this weekend free.'

Joe announces as I tidy up the Chinese takeaway cartons the following Wednesday evening at my house. I stupidly suggested he come over and that I would cook something nice, but then I remembered I haven't cooked anything since, well…never.

'I'm whisking you away for two days,' he states looking quite pleased with himself.

Ooh, that sounds interesting. 'Where are we going?' I ask excitedly.

'Never you mind. You'll see when we get there.'

'Spoilsport.'

'It is your Saturday off this weekend, isn't it?'

'Yep.'

'Great. Then be ready nice and early.'

'Nice and early? What time do you call that?'

'How does eight thirty sound?'

'On a Saturday morning? Not particularly good.' I cringe jokingly.

'Well, it'll be worth it, I promise.'

'Okay.' I shake my head. 'But only because it's you.'

'Cheeky.' He grabs my bum and plants a kiss on the tip on my nose.

'I'm going to the pub with Jenny on Friday night so I'll be on my best behaviour and will be in bed for eleven thirty at the latest.'

'Good.' He kisses me full on the lips, causing me to tingle all over. 'I'll see you then.'

'Bye.'

I feel myself lusting after him as he grabs his coat and heads for the door. My heart sinks a little as I watch him wave and then the door closes behind him.

It feels like forever before Friday night finally arrives. Jenny's local pub is busy; I didn't expect to be queuing at the bar to buy my first drink of the evening. Not only is it Friday night but she neglected to tell me that it's music quiz night too – hurrah! Not – which means there are groups of people huddling at the bar and at tables of varying ages, all looking overly excited at the prospect of a quiz. I hate music quizzes – if a song was released prior to the Madonna era then I neither have a clue nor any interest in it.

'I hope you know your stuff,' I state as we squeeze into a small table in the corner of the pub.

'Don't be silly,' Jenny chides. 'I don't come here for the quiz, you're so naive. I just come for the totty!' She waves flirtatiously at a group of young men who've just sauntered towards the bar. They resemble a boy band, they all look so fresh. A dark-haired guy who looks in his mid-twenties, dressed in a checked shirt with stylish hair waves back at her.

'Seriously?' I look around me and realise that the majority of the crowd are either ten years older than me or ten years younger. 'You're impossible.' I shake my head at her in both amusement and envy. I've never being anywhere near as confident as she is with men.

'It's alright for you: you're all loved up with Joe, aren't you. Me? I'm young, free and single, and definitely on the lookout.'

'Well, when you put it like that...'

'Exactly. I'm not the one being whisked away on some secret romantic weekend tomorrow.'

'Maybe not, but it looks like the fifth member of the boy band is as keen on you as you are on him.' I tip my head in the direction of the trendy youth, who's now propping up the bar and trying to discreetly eye up Jenny from his prominent position. 'That reminds me, don't let me drink too much tonight. I don't want to be hungover and feeling rubbish for my romantic weekend. For some reason Joe's picking me up at half-eight, so I need plenty of beauty sleep before then.'

'I might just go and get us another drink before the quiz starts,' Jenny states and I realise my "I'll be on my best behaviour" comment to Joe is potentially going to be disrupted by Jenny as she slides out of the confinements of our small table and sidles up to the funky boy band youth at the bar.

I stayed over at Joe's house again last night and he didn't make a move on me at all, apart from cuddling. He's also never once even hinted at staying over at my house. But now I think I want him to. I don't know whether it's him trying so hard not to sleep with me that kind of makes me really want to now. But how do I make a move after I made such a big deal of not wanting to rush into sleeping together? It's ironic really, but ever since that first night of sleeping in his arms I can't get the thought of sex off my brain. It's all I can think about; I feel like a hormonal teenager. I want to feel the warmth of his body next to mine as I go to sleep. I want to feel him touch me. I want to feel his body all hot and sweaty and naked.

God, I need a cold shower!

I take a gulp from my large glass of wine. Mmm…I wonder where he's taking me this weekend. A whole weekend away, just the two of us, sounds amazing, and maybe the time will be right to take things to the next level then. Surely sex must be on the agenda for him too? If not I must work on my powers of seduction. Who am I kidding? I've never seduced anyone in my life! Maybe I'll have to settle for pure and simple honesty. I'll confidently tell him that I've changed my mind and I'm ready to be, well, physical. Oh God, I can't possibly say that. I'll sound like an idiot...

I fish my phone out from the depths of my handbag and send Joe a text while Jenny is otherwise disposed, so I don't look all soppy and needy and 'can't be out with my friends for five minutes without texting my boyfriend' in front of her.

Don't know what to pack? What do I need to be dressed for? X

I've strewn the best part of my wardrobe across my bed and have stared at it for the best part of an hour before coming out tonight and I still haven't packed even a pair of pants. My phone buzzes and I glance down at the screen.

Pack warm, comfy clothes. See you tomorrow, bright and early. x

Mmm. Warm and comfy? That doesn't suggest a sexy, romantic weekend...

'Hey, put your phone away. The quiz is starting.' Jenny elbows me none-too-gently as she sits back down beside me, placing another glass of wine in front of me.

'I thought you weren't bothered about the quiz?' Honestly sometimes Jenny is exasperating.

'I wasn't, but Todd is.'

'Todd?'

'Yeah.' She smiles girlishly towards the bar and I swear she flutters her eyelashes. 'Todd is a budding musician. He plays the guitar.'

Wow, I wasn't that far off with the boy band label.

'The guitar – that's pretty cool.'

'I know. Can you imagine how much fun it would be to date someone from a band?'

'Hold on there, groupie. Has he actually even played a gig?'

'I don't know. We haven't got that deep into conversation.'

'Right.'

'But I'll find out more when he takes me out tomorrow night, thank you very much, Miss Pessimist.'

'A date?'

'Yep.'

'I'm proud of you, Jenny. Here you were complaining about being single not five minutes ago.'

'See? It might not just be you who gets to have a romantic weekend after all.'

Yes, in my warm comfy clothes….hmm.

There's no further time to mull over what lies ahead for my weekend as we're shushed by the table of middle-aged men whose attire clearly screams 'geography teacher' at the side of us as the quiz master takes his place on the podium.

Chapter Twenty-Eight

The doorbell rings at exactly eight thirty. That's one thing I've noticed about Joe: he's punctual to the second – so unlike me. But this morning I'm almost ready, just rechecking my bag for the hundredth time, following a turbulent night's sleep imagining all sorts of weird activities from pot-holing to skydiving being thrust upon me this weekend. Surely he would need my permission, and maybe to make sure I have a will (not that my worldly goods amount to much) before I could be pushed out of an aeroplane? Dressed in skinny jeans and a thin cable-knit sweater, which I hope are appropriate, I open the door with a grin already plastered on my face. Despite my apprehension, I'm really excited about this weekend.

'Morning!' He kisses me hello then hands me a takeaway coffee. 'Thought you might need this.'

'Thank you.' I take the cup gratefully. I think I may need a few more of these this morning to get me up to full speed.

'Medium skinny latte.'

'Exactly how I like it.' I take a sip. 'I'll be two minutes. I need to grab my overnight bag.'

'How was last night?' Joe asks a few moments later as I clamber unceremoniously into his car while trying not to spill my latte down myself.

'Well, I was forced to participate in a music quiz in which I knew very few answers – nineties' pop and dance being my only specialism.'

'I see.' Joe is clearly trying, and failing, not to look amused at this.

'And Jenny snagged herself a date with a budding musician.'

'Musician, huh?'

'Well, he plays the guitar in a band – that's about all she managed to get out of him last night. As to what band, who knows? But it was enough to convince Jenny that he was worth spending tonight with.'

We set off travelling away from the city but I'm still none-the-wiser in regards to our destination. Admittedly my severe lack of direction and any sort of geographical knowledge are a hindrance – how ironic that I spent last night giggling at geography teachers in corduroy trousers. Who's the joke on now?

An hour or so later as we drive down a secluded coastal road. I strain my neck trying to see the sea like I did as a kid when we took trips to the beach. I couldn't wait to strip off down to my swimwear and run like hell into the surf regardless of the temperature outside. I'm a little more reserved nowadays, but I still love the feeling of the first time I catch a glimpse of the rolling waves.

'Where are we going?' I glance around, seeing cliff tops and not much else.

'You'll see.' Joe winks at me as he leans over and gently strokes my knee.

'I'm drawn to a horrible fear we're driving to a cliff edge where I'll be expected to camp in a tent or something...' I glance at him nervously, hoping against all hope that camping isn't what's in store for me. Apart from the ridiculousness of sleeping outside on the floor, surrounded by huge spiders when there's absolutely no need, if there are no plug sockets at our destination then I can't promise that my hair won't scare people by tomorrow with all this sea air and no straightening appliance to hand.

He laughs at my camping suggestion, which I take to be a positive sign.

'Either that or our accommodation is a beach hut?' I offer. At least they have electricity, which is a plus and offsets the fact they're only the size of a human coffin. Mind you, that would mean that we'd have to be very close to one another this evening...

He simply raises his eyebrows at me so I take this as my signal to shut up and be patient.

I don't have to wait long as a few minutes later we pull up at a quaint little white cottage. I climb out of the car – with difficulty, as my legs have seized up on the journey – and take note of the views from the cliffs, which are fantastic. Every direction I look in I'm met with panoramic coastal scenery.

'Joe, this is amazing.'

He looks at me. 'Worth the drive?'

'Definitely worth the drive.' I nod before kissing him.

'Mmm...I think we'd better get you inside.' He gives me a long, lingering kiss back.

'It's my mum's friend's cottage. We used to come here as kids but there wasn't much room for us all so we used to let David have the single bedroom and Mat and I used to camp outside in a tent.'

'It's lovely.' I'm extremely grateful there will be no camping in store for me.

The cottage doesn't disappoint on the inside either. A small hallway leads to the kitchen and lounge with a real open log fire – very romantic – and upstairs there are two bedrooms, one double, one single, and a small bathroom with just enough room for a roll-top bath positioned next to the window overlooking the sea.

Joe comes up the stairs behind me with our bags and places them in the double room.

'So, what do you want to do now?' He nuzzles my neck from behind as I stand gazing out of the window, already feeling completely relaxed. 'A stroll along the beach maybe?'

'That sounds...perfect.' I turn around and kiss his full, warm lips. He pulls me close, folding his arms around me as his tongue finds mine, and my lower stomach does a somersault, prompting me to try to take things further.

'Right then, we'd better wrap up warm.' Joe breaks away and my stomach sinks, deflated.

I rummage through my bag for a thicker jumper before pulling on my boots and coat as we head out into the very fresh air. Blimey, you can definitely feel a chill when the sun hides behind a cloud. Joe puts his arm around my waist and I snuggle into him as we walk along the sand with the waves rolling and crashing a few feet away.

Once we reach the small coastal town of Whitby we're surrounded by a mixture of wonderful food smells: fish and chips on sale in a number of cafés along the seafront along with the sweet smell of candyfloss and hand-made fudge. Childhood memories flood back of me begging Mum and Dad to let me eat candyfloss as big as my head, and when they finally gave in, stuffing my face until I felt sick.

After a lunch of fish and chips I resist the urge for candyfloss and settle for some mint fudge instead. Then we walk and chat going from gift shop to gift shop, enjoying the sea air. The afternoon soon runs away from us – it's surprising how easily you can lose track of time wandering around with no agenda. We grab a bottle of red wine from the off-licence for later and begin our stroll, hand in hand, back along the sand to the cottage. I'm amazed at the number of children still playing half-naked in the surf, watched by parents wrapped up in numerous layers of clothing. I don't think I felt the cold either at their age. I guess kids don't care about being warm where sea and sandcastles are involved.

As we finally approach the front door of the cottage Joe hands me the keys.

'You open up while I grab some logs from the store around the back for the fire.'

I push the heavy wooden door open and head towards the kitchen. It's half past five – that's an acceptable time for a glass of wine on a Saturday, I think. In fact, by my recent standards it's about four hours too late.

I carry two full glasses through to the living room where Joe's lighting the fire and within seconds a warm orange glow fills the room and the logs begin to crackle, making me feel instantly cosy.

'I was being presumptuous,' I say, handing him a glass of wine. 'Cheers.' I tap my glass against his.

'To us.' He says.

'To us.' I take a sip.

We sit down on the squashy beige sofa and I can already feel the warmth of the fire from the open flames.

'I had a really nice time today.' I glance at Joe and take another, larger sip of my wine.

'I've always loved the beach. The sea air and the feeling of standing on the edge of the country; it inspires me and makes me think that anything's possible.' Joe takes a drink of his own wine.

I don't know if it's the alcohol or the crackling open fire but suddenly I feel hot, in more ways than one. I look longingly at Joe and thankfully he gets the hint. He takes the glass of wine from my hand and places it on the coffee table, and then pulls me close, kissing me hard on the lips, his hands running through my hair. Adrenaline kicks in, sending electricity shooting around my body until I feel like I'm going to explode.

I lie back on the large sofa cushions and pull Joe down on top of me, wriggling to get comfy. I'm already panting with the anticipation of his touch. As Joe leans on his forearms over me, our lips still locked in a passionate kiss, I tug his jumper up and slide my hands down his jeans and underneath his boxer shorts, feeling his smooth skin beneath my fingers. I grab playfully at his bum and hear him groan gently, which wafts my flame of desire, and I grab him again, pushing him harder against my hips, feeling the swirl of excitement and sexual craving tingle through my every nerve ending until I'm drowning in my own need, my own want, for Joe to take me right here and now in front of the roaring fire, like in the movies.

'I want you to make love to me,' I whisper, barely able to contain the erotic sensation coursing through my whole body.

'Are you sure you're ready?' Joe's eyes meet mine as he strokes a strand of hair from my face.

'I'm sure.' I've never wanted someone so much. It's not the physical attraction alone – that's been there from the start; it's everything else. I feel loved and safe, and I'm as certain as anyone can be that Joe would never hurt me.

His lips find mine and I immediately respond, kissing him hungrily, wrapping my arms around him. As I pull away for air he takes my hand and I stand up with jelly legs and allow him to lead me gently upstairs to the bedroom.

We stop next to the bed and Joe starts to undress me ever so slowly, stroking my belly with his fingertips as he nudges my jumper up inch by inch, making me want to scream with pleasure. In between planting small kisses on my cheeks and working his way up to...oh my! As he nibbles my earlobe my whole body clenches and I struggle to refrain from destroying his whole seduction by ripping my clothes right off. As he pulls my jumper above my head his thumbs graze both nipples on the outside of my bra and my knees buckle. Jesus Christ! I feel incredibly vulnerable but unbelievably turned on.

Next it's my jeans, and as Joe reaches for my top button his thumb strokes the sensitive bit of my lower stomach and I instinctively take a sharp intake of breath. Wow, I never thought someone undressing me could be so erotic, but it's heightening the anticipation, and my arousal.

His fingers brush my inner thighs as he pulls down my jeans and I step out of them, leaving me standing in my bra and pants. I'm so grateful that I'm wearing the hideously expensive set that Mum bought for me the last time I was in New York. Usually it's pure luck if my bra and pants even match.

'Okay.' Joe gives me a long, lingering kiss and my whole body stands to his attention. 'Your turn.' He steps back a little and I look at him, suddenly feeling incredibly shy. Now he wants me to take his clothes off…?

I step forward cautiously and slide my hands gently underneath his t-shirt, feeling his toned stomach. He tenses slightly as I trace his belly button with my forefinger before running it up to his chest. I brush my fingertip over his right nipple and he groans softly, and I can feel my own pulse quickening at the realisation that I'm turning him on. I pull his t-shirt up gently and he raises his arms, helping me to take it off. I discard it on the floor as I gaze at his bare chest. Placing my hands on his shoulders, I trace his breast bone with kisses until my mouth reaches a nipple and I clasp it gently between my lips, licking it with my tongue as it hardens under my touch.

I'm spurred on by his reaction: I look up into his face and his eyes are closed and his lips are parted slightly. I release the button and zip on his jeans and slide my hands around over the top of his boxer shorts and grasp his bum cheeks as I pull him closer to me until our nearly bare bodies are touching and it feels electric. I can feel him harden against my thigh, causing my breath to come in short, sharp gasps as my adrenaline shoots into overdrive.

'Okay.' Joe opens his eyes wide. 'Enough is enough.' He sweeps me up, reminding me how strong he is, and places me down on the centre of the bed.

I pull his face towards mine and kiss him hard on the mouth. His tongue searches for mine and finds it wanting. He pulls me to a seated position and unhooks my bra, releasing my small, pert breasts, and he cups them roughly in both hands and licks each nipple. They stand to attention instantly at the feel of his tongue.

Oh my God…

He slides his hands down my body and within seconds my pants are removed and he's buried his face between my legs.

Whoa…hang on a…whoa…My whole body melts as he teases a finger gently inside me and I cry out, wanting more, as my whole body clenches excitedly at his touch.

He slides off his boxer shorts and…wow…

He reaches into his jeans pocket and pulls out a foil condom packet.

As he lies back down on top of me I can feel the heat between us, the sexual desire that has been building for the last few days now overflowing, and I want to feel him touch every part of me. His seduction has worked and I want him now.

He leans a hand either side of my body and gently slides himself into me. I open my legs wider, encouraging him deeper and deeper, and he responds, pushing himself against me. I grab at his buttocks and throw my head back as he starts to move rhythmically, like he can read my body and my mind.

I groan as he tongue finds its way up my neck and to my ear and –

'Ah!' I gasp as his teeth graze my earlobe. His fingers find my nipples and they tingle beneath his expert touch.

We pick up the rhythm slightly and Joe slides a hand underneath me to grasp my bottom. I can feel my orgasm building as he pulsates faster and faster. Then, as he slides a finger underneath my buttocks and caresses me from behind, I succumb, releasing a shudder of adrenaline through my whole body. As my mind swirls he grabs me tighter and pushes deeper into me, until I feel his own release.

He nuzzles my neck with his eyes still closed and I wrap my arms around him, feeling his hot, sweaty body suctioned to mine as his heartbeat thunders against his ribcage. I take a few deep breaths to try to steady my raucous breathing.

We lie there, wrapped in each other's arms, emotionally drunk and dazed. The silence is comforting, and right there, for these few seconds, everything feels perfect. The troubles of the last few months have melted away and I'm consumed only by Joe and how I feel when I'm with him; how he makes my body feel with his every touch; and how I want to lie here in his arms forever.

My eyes open with a jolt. I don't even remember falling asleep. But then I feel Joe's arm still wrapped around me as we lie together, and I relax and snuggle back into the sanctuary of his warm body.

'Are you awake?'

I jump.

'Erm...yes.'

'Good.' Joe leans up on his forearm and kisses my cheek. 'Because I'm about ready for round two.'

Round two? I was thinking –

He reaches his hand up and cups my breast, giving it a gentle squeeze, and my body tingles all over as my brain flicks from groggy to fully engaged.

But I haven't brushed my teeth. My hair must be hideous. My make-up must have worn off. I'd probably scare small children if I came face to face with them, and he wants to make love to me now, like this?

Joe doesn't appear to be deterred by any of my reservations as he rolls on top of me and buries his face in my neck, tracing the line from my collarbone up to my ear with his tongue as I squirm beneath him. He makes his way back down, planting kisses across my shoulder and chest, before glancing up at me with a cheeky smile, and then he continues his mission, kissing the line of my breastbone down to my belly button and then...!

My body wakes up now with an electric shock, nearly causing me to jump right off the bed as Joe's tongue teases between my legs, gently licking and probing, and I can feel myself getting moist.

This is surreal. I've never felt so wanted; so desired. Usually my inhibitions curb my libido, but like an instant addict I crave Joe's touch. I feel like I'm on another level; another planet. Even with Chris it never felt like this. Why am I thinking about him? Now, when I'm in bed with my new boyfriend? What's wrong with me?

I'm flipped right back into the moment, kicking Chris into a distant memory, as I feel Joe slide a finger inside me, then out, and then slowly, ever so slowly, back in.

Oh God, please do that again.

I arch my back in response. Being incredibly brave and ignoring all my usual apprehension and complete self-consciousness, I reach my hand down until I find Joe's penis; already hard and awaiting my touch. Joe groans gently as I take my hand and run my fingers up and down, feeling him harden further. He reaches over producing another foil packet and I lie back.

Then Joe's mouth is on mine, and he's kissing me deeply, pushing his tongue inside. I kiss him back hungrily as he nudges my thighs wider with his knees and slides his body between them. I feel him enter me and we climb right back on the rollercoaster. It's hot and frantic as desire takes over and Joe grabs at my buttocks, pushing himself deeper inside me. I wrap my arms around him and press my body tightly against his, feeling my emotional-drug high surging. Joe makes me feel so sexy, like my whole body is so far out of my control that I'm on a knife's edge, torn between self-control and ultimate submission.

I can feel the adrenaline and ecstasy building inside me as Joe's rhythm takes my arousal to a whole new level and I groan, gasping his name. I feel his body stiffen against me and I lie back and succumb to the moment. Drunk on adrenaline and high on sexual euphoria.

It's still dark as I feel myself being nudged gently awake.

'Morning,' Joe whispers into my hair, before kissing my forehead.

Is it? I'm quite sure it's still night-time. In my world the morning doesn't start until daylight has honoured us with its presence.

'I made coffee...'

Oh alright then. I sit up groggily in the bed and pull the covers up tightly around me.

'Thank you.' I take the steaming mug from Joe and gratefully take a sip. 'And I don't mean to be rude, but isn't it Sunday?'

'It is.' Joe nods, his expression blank but with slight dimples tugging at the corners of his mouth.

'So why are you up when it's still dark outside? And more importantly why am I awake if it's still dark?'

'I'm going to show you something amazing,' Joe nudges me.

I thought you already did that last night...

'Come on. Get dressed.'

'Get dressed?'

'We're going to watch the sunrise from the cliff tops.'

Oh, I see. We're not getting all hot and sweaty again. Shame... Hang on a minute – did he say that we're going to sit on a cliff in the dark?

Torn between protesting against leaving the nice warm bed and remembering that this is the beginning of a relationship, which means we're still supposed to feign enthusiasm for everything, I begrudgingly get out of bed. Then I see Joe's grin and I can't help but smile too.

'It's a good job you're hot,' I say in a flirtatious manner as I slide past him, naked, towards the bathroom.

'You're pretty hot yourself.' He gently pinches my bum. 'And if you don't get into that shower quickly then we may not make it out until after sunrise.' He cocks his head to one side as if studying me, and I resist the urge to try to cover my body with my arms and scuttle a little more quickly into the bathroom.

'Okay. I admit at first I wasn't completely convinced,' I confess ten minutes later. We're cuddled together on a blanket overlooking the most amazing skyline: oranges and pinks swirl over the shimmering sea below us as it laps against the cliff side.

'Really? I'd never have guessed from the fact that I had to practically drag you physically from the cottage,' Joe laughs.

'Okay, so I'm not always one for the great outdoors in the middle of the night, but...'

'But?'

'But I've never seen a sunrise like this. Ever. You were right: it's amazing.' I stare out at the vibrant colours as they sweep across the twinkling blue sea. 'It feels almost magical.'

'See? I knew you'd like it.'

'Thank you, for this whole weekend.' I turn to Joe and kiss him. 'It's been...perfect.'

'I've loved spending this weekend with you. I love waking up next to you. In fact, I love...you.'

I'm so caught up in the moment of feeling loved and wanted that it doesn't occur to me that I don't say anything back.

'What do you mean you've met him before? Where? How?'
'I really wish I didn't have to tell you'

Chapter Twenty-Nine

I'm still love drunk from the 'I love you' moment as Joe drops me off at home later that afternoon. I almost can't believe my luck. I've found the most kind and thoughtful boyfriend in the most unusual – no, unbelievable – circumstances, and I think I love him too.

I wave goodbye as his car pulls away from the kerb. I know that I'll be seeing him again tomorrow night, but the niggling ache in my heart confirms that I miss him already.

A little deflated, I let myself into the house and plod heavily through to the kitchen, dumping my overnight bag in the hallway as I pass. I find the remains of a bottle of wine in the fridge door and pour a glass, but before I can enjoy the first sip my mobile phone comes to life. I glance at the phone but I don't recognise the number. I consider flicking it straight to voicemail but curiosity gets the better of me.

'Hello?'

The line is quite crackly and I can hear muffled sounds but nothing else.

'Hello?' I call again.

'Emma? Sorry about the noise – I'm collecting my luggage.'

'Mum?' Oh my God. 'Collecting your luggage from where?' I ask cautiously.

'From the airport, silly.'

'Yeah, Mum, I figured that bit out. Which airport are you at?'

'Leeds-Bradford"

Shit! What's wrong with this woman? Why didn't she tell me she was coming? Why is my mum like an international genie who appears in an instant without warning? I know she's been spending most of her time flying between Sydney and New York, doing something very complicated in the finance world that I wish I understood, but how has she ended up detouring to here? Given that I stayed at her apartment last month I'm guessing she won't have booked herself into a hotel and instead will be looking to invite herself over to my house for the duration of her stay, however long that may be. Which means I'll be forced to hand over my comfy bed. Which she'll moan about continuously, while I slum it on my sofa with a sleeping bag I've had since school.

'So can you come and collect me? I'll grab a cappuccino while I wait.'

Just like that. As though I have nothing more pressing to do. Okay, so maybe I don't have plans this evening, but that's not the point. I could be doing something really important.

'Um, I thought we agreed that you were going to call before you visit? You know, so I could make plans?'

'Make plans? Am I interrupting something? Aren't you pleased to see your mother?'

And the guilt trip starts now.

'Of course I'll be pleased to see you, Mum.'

'Well, what's wrong then? Do you have a boy staying with you or something?'

Shit! Joe! Oh my God. He confessed his love for me yesterday and now instantly I'm going to have to ban him from my life until the genie disappears back into her bottle.

Fuck, fuck, fuck.

Could she have picked a more inconvenient time to descend on my world? There's no way on earth that I'm letting her meet Joe. Not a chance!

'No.' I scowl automatically even though I know she can't see me. 'I do not have a boy staying with me.' More's the pity.

'Great, then it will be us two girls, drinking wine and letting our hair down.'

'How long are you here for, Mum?'

'Only a few days. I fly back out on Wednesday.'

'Great,' I reply hesitantly through gritted teeth. 'I'll set off to the airport now.'

As I drive to the airport I'm torn between feeling guilty that I'm not overjoyed by my mum's unannounced arrival and feeling unsure of what to say to Joe. He can't come over tomorrow night now. I'm not ready to introduce him to my family; it's too soon.

As I pull into the arrivals pickup area I spot Mum instantly. She seems to be coercing some poor young man into pulling along her luggage trolley, which is loaded with a disturbingly large number of matching cases. My stomach sinks. That looks like a month's worth of clothes, not a couple of days'.

I pull up to the kerb and climb out of the car. Mum waves over at me and then points her young hostage in my direction. By the time they arrive at my car the boy, who I now see looks only about sixteen – the shame of it – is blushing deeply and sweating profusely. I offer him an apologetic shrug and grab the trolley from his grasp.

'Thank you so much. I'll take it from here.'

He wipes his brow before making good his escape.

'Mum, you can't collar some stranger to carry your bags for you.'

'Don't be silly, darling. He didn't mind. It's good for these young people to learn some manners.'

'His manners seemed fine, Mum, but I think you may have crossed a number of moral boundaries.'

'Tsk.' She waves at me like she's swatting a fly. 'That's what's wrong with the youth of today. Far too sensitive. It's always some political this, some moral that. It's not like in my day. We didn't have it easy.'

Yes, I muse, it must have been a hard life growing up in middle-class suburbia with my well-to-do grandma and grandpa. I usher her into the car before she can offend anyone else.

I struggle lifting the first of the suitcases into the boot, wondering what the hell she's packed and how the hell she's got this through baggage control without someone suspecting there's a dead body or something in here. I fit the second case in the boot with some difficulty but then run out of room and have to unceremoniously shove the third case onto the back seat.

'Mum, are you sure you're only staying for a few days? That's a lot of luggage for a short trip.'

'I'm on my way back from Hong Kong.'

Of course.

'Hong Kong?'

'Amazing place, really interesting culture.'

Yeah, I bet they thought you were pretty interesting too.

We drive back to my house, making small talk about how my job's going, and how my mum is taking on the male-dominated world of finance – which scares me to death. I can never imagine her in a serious business meeting talking about the Dow Jones or the FTSE or whatever. And it's one thing her doing that in the Big Apple, but how on earth does she cope in Hong Kong? She doesn't speak Cantonese, Mandarin or whatever the hell language they speak over there; well, not to the best of my knowledge anyway. But maybe I'm wrong and my mum is fluent in the language of Hong Kong. I shouldn't really be surprised at anything where she's concerned by now.

Thankfully for the entire journey we manage to avoid any conversation that relates to Parker of the dyed hair, or any other male interest that my mum may have. I silently pray that we can continue to bypass this topic altogether over the upcoming days – and my love life too for that matter!

By the time we arrive at my house it's already starting to get dark.

'I might have a shower to freshen up,' Mum says as I try single-handedly to drag her luggage from the car.

'Of course. You know where the bathroom is. There are clean towels on the shelf above the bath. I'll make some food for us for when you're done,' I offer optimistically as my mind rapidly thinks over the lacking contents of my fridge. Somehow I don't think leftover cream cheese and crackers will quite suffice.

As Mum heads off to the bathroom I go through to the kitchen, where I grab the dregs of the wine I poured into my glass two hours earlier but didn't get to drink and down them in one. I fling the cupboard doors open, scanning the shelves, grateful to see that there's a bag of pasta and some sauce and a jar of olives. That will do nicely, thank you. In the fridge I find a fresh bottle of wine – that's something I'm very rarely out of – loitering on the bottom shelf like an oasis in the desert. Something tells me I'm going to need a large glass of this. I'm pleased to see that there is more food than I thought in the fridge. A low-fat yoghurt is sitting proudly on the shelf next to some leftover cottage pie that I'd originally planned on warming up for my dinner this evening – I really do need to stop living like a student now I'm in my thirties. I take a wine glass from the drainer and pour a glass for Mum before refilling my own with a large measure and busying myself with the pasta.

Ten minutes later, as I'm getting ready to serve, Mum appears in the doorway still with her hair and makeup perfectly in place but wearing grey jogging bottoms and a t-shirt that matches, which is so out of character and in contrast to her usual glamour that I'm forced to hide a wry smile.

'Any of that going spare?' She points to my wine glass.

'Of course, over there,' I point to her glass before tipping the pasta through a sieve and sloshing it into bowls. I pour on the sauce and olives and we grab a bowl each and shuffle to the stools at the little breakfast bar in the corner of my kitchen.

'Sorry I don't have a dining table,' I offer as Mum wriggles on the stool, nearly sliding straight back off again.

She steadies herself before taking an elegant sip of her wine.

'My home is nothing really compared to your apartment in New York.' I suddenly feel house shy rather than house proud.

'Oh, your home is lovely.' She looks around the room. 'Although I do agree that my current apartment is quite nice – much better than the first place I rented. Do you remember that God-awful place I was staying in? There was barely enough room to swing a tiny cat,' she laughs.

Actually it was a pretty good-sized apartment; it simply didn't have the right zip code, as they say over there. Mum wanted to live by Central Park and the first apartment was at least a ten-minute walk away. Clearly not impressive enough for her co-workers.

'You must come over and stay again soon. We had so much fun the other month, didn't we?'

'We did.' I take a mouthful of pasta while remembering the mammoth shopping trip. Credit where it's due: Mum does know how to shop, and she knows all the best places.

'Is work going okay?' Mum asks.

'It's fine.'

'And Simon?'

'Um...he's fine.'

'How's Sophie?' Mum raises her eyebrows a little at me as she scoops pasta onto her fork.

'Jesus mum, what's with the third degree?' I snap.

'Emma, you've answered 'fine' to every question I've asked you since you picked me up, and the last few times we've spoken on the phone you've made up some excuse to get off the phone before I've barely said 'hello.'

I hold my initial protest for a moment as I realise that it's true. I haven't wanted to talk much because I've not wanted to tell mum about Connor and Sophie, or to curse things with Joe by telling her so soon that I've met someone so I've avoided saying anything at all really.

'Sophie's fine,' I reply, hoping this line of questioning will come to a halt if I act nonchalant.

'What's happened, Emma?'

'What do you mean?' I protest without much conviction. 'Why should something have happened?'

'Come on. I can tell that something's bothering you and I think it's more than your breakup with Chris.'

Mum never was a huge fan of Chris, and as always she's straight to the point, clearly seeing through my attempt to dismiss the subject of Sophie.

'I'm your mother, after all, and I know when something's wrong.'

I put down my fork and fiddle uncomfortably with my hands. This isn't a conversation I want to have at this moment in time, especially not with my mother.

'I'm over Chris,' I state. 'I've accepted that I'm better off without him. But it hurt that he could do that to me after two years together. I felt like an idiot that I didn't see it coming.' I bite my lip as I remember that night in the restaurant. It does still hurt, but nowhere near as badly as it did since I gained some closure that night outside my house when he announced his engagement to me.

'Come on, Emma. You can tell me what's really bothering you.'

'I don't get on with Sophie's new boyfriend,' I say dismissively. That's not a complete lie, is it?

'It's more than that. I know you Emma. When you clamp up like this, it's usually something to do with the opposite sex.' Mum reaches over and squeezes my hand. 'I won't judge, I promise. Is it a problem with a man?'

I try to keep my expression neutral. A problem with a man? Well…

'I've made mistakes with men too, you know. More than you –'

'Okay!' I hold up my hand in submission. 'If I tell you, will you promise not to share details of your past encounters with stock brokers or whoever? My ears can't take it – you're my mother and that's too much information.'

'Honestly!' Mum shakes her head at me, grinning. 'I'm a grown woman as well as your mother, you know. I'm allowed my own life.'

'I know that. And I'm more than happy for you to enjoy living it. But I can't quite deal with the knowledge of your sex life, so no intimate details. Promise?'

'I promise.' She nods. 'So what's really gone down with Sophie?'

I take a deep breath. I feel majorly weird about having this conversation with my mother, but we're both adults, as she's clearly pointed out, so I'm prepared to give having a grown-up conversation a go. I begin by explaining how I ended up at the bar in the first place on that Friday night. Before I know it I've blurted out the whole tale to mum (minus some of the less appropriate details, like how drunk I was, and how I was scrambling around on the floor searching for my underwear once I realised I wasn't snuggled up in my own bed the following morning, and the really bad part where I was going to sneak out. Okay, so maybe that wasn't the worst part, but it wasn't good).

I watch her face throughout and I'm surprised to see that her expression doesn't falter as she listens intently, taking the occasional sip of her wine.

'So then I showed up on the Sunday morning to meet Sophie and her new boyfriend, Connor, for coffee and there he was, "Johnny", sitting right in front of me, holding her hand and staring straight at me.'

There's a poignant pause.

'I think we need more wine.' Mum slides off her stool and walks over to the fridge, placing her empty pasta bowl in the sink as she passes. She returns to the table and tops up both of our glasses.

I hold my breath, waiting for the chastising comment, but Mum takes me completely by surprise.

'One-night stands happen, darling,' she shrugs.

What? Mum isn't going to judge me?

'As long as you're careful, you know –'

Oh please, don't let's get onto the subject of contraception…

'So this guy cheated on Sophie with you, but you didn't know who he was at the time.' She twirls the stem of her wine glass around between her fingers.

'Yes,' I confirm. 'But that's not the worst of it.'

She raises her eyebrows. 'Did you tell Sophie?'

'Yes. But not at first. I collared Connor a couple of times and told him in no uncertain terms to break up with her and to leave Sophie alone, but he wouldn't. I had no choice, you see. I told her for her own good, so she could see what he was really like.'

'And I'm guessing that she didn't take it very well?'

'No.' I remember the night in her house, the horrible fight. 'We haven't spoken since.' I pick up my wine glass and take a large gulp.

'Well, I can understand that.' Mum sips her own wine. 'What I don't understand is this Connor guy. What's his game?'

Right to the point again, Mum.

'He denied all of it,' I say, hearing the defeat in my voice. 'Said I was making it up because I was jealous of their relationship given….' I pause, still angry at the accusation. 'Given that I'd been dumped.'

'Ouch!'

Exactly.

'He deserved a fucking Oscar for his performance.'

Mum frowns. 'Language, Emma.'

Whoops. That's the effect of my earlier wine on an empty stomach. 'Sorry.'

'Anyway…' I move swiftly on. 'Sophie believed him and, well, now she won't even return my texts.'

'I see.' Mum exhales deeply. 'It's all a bit of a mess really, isn't it?'

I laugh then, really laugh, and Mum looks over at me, confused.

'Talk about stating the obvious, Mum,' I say, still giggling, and she starts laughing too.

'Well, I need a moment or two to digest all of this before I can try to come up with a solution. It's a bit unexpected.'

'Like you flying in from Hong Kong.' I down the last dregs of my wine and Mum stops laughing. 'Oh, Mum.' I'm suddenly sorry for my sarcasm. 'I didn't mean that. I'm glad you've come to stay.'

'Are you sure? I can always book into a hotel for the next few days.'

'Don't be silly.' I stand up and give her an awkward hug.

She hugs me back tightly. 'We'll figure it out, darling. We'll get you and Sophie back to being friends.'

'I hope so, Mum; I really hope so.'

'Look.' She pulls away from me and pushes a loose, wavy strand of hair behind my ear like I'm five years old again. 'I'm only here for a three days and I'd like to be able to spend some time with you. Can you get some time off work?'

'Ah, I don't think I can, Mum; not at such short notice. Not again.'

'Not even for your own mother? I barely get to see you these days.'

Yes, but you did move to New York.

I mull it over for a moment.

'I'll call Jenny. It can't hurt to ask,' I say, reaching for the phone.

'Great. I'll make us both a coffee.'

I leave Mum in the kitchen and walk through to the living room to make the call. Jenny picks up after two rings.

'Hey, Emma. How's things? Have you had a good weekend?'

'Hi, Jenny. Sorry to ring you on a Sunday night.'

'That's okay. How was your romantic weekend?'

'Oh, yes, it was lovely, thanks. Really lovely.'

'Good.' She pauses. 'Is everything alright?'

'Well, yes and no.'

'Oh dear.' There's panic in her voice now.

'No. Don't worry. I've not had another hideous encounter with my ex-best friend's boyfriend.'

'I'm glad to hear it. So what's up?'

'My mum has flown in unannounced for a couple of days.'

'Flown in?'

'Yeah, she's heading back to New York from Hong Kong.'

'Oh, wow. That's cool.'

'Yeah, it is. But the thing is, she's landed on me unannounced. I didn't know she was coming or I'd have asked sooner but…'

'You want some time off.'

'Um, yes. A couple days if possible. I know it's really short notice, and if it's too much to put on you and Lola then I completely understand, especially after you covered for me the last time.'

'Emma, chill out. It's fine. You can do my next two Saturdays to make up for it.'

'Deal.'

'You can take the next two days if that's any good, but I need you back in on Wednesday as neither Lola or I are working that day so you're on your own.'

'Absolutely. That would be perfect.'

'Okay then. Enjoy your time with your mum. I'll catch up with you when I'm back in on Thursday, when I'll expect a full moment-by-moment account of your two days with Joe. Don't think I didn't notice that you brushed right past that.'

'Of course.' Although I might have to be brief about some of the details of our time at the cottage. 'And Jenny?'

'Yeah?'

'I really appreciate it – and I'll make it up to you and Lola, I promise.'

'I know you'll do the same for me one day when I need it.'

'Oh, and one last thing…'

'Sure.'

'How was the guitarist from the boy band?'

'We'll talk next week,' she chuckles.

'Okay. Thanks again. Bye.'

I hang up the phone as Mum walks in carrying two mugs.

'It's sorted. You have me for the next two days.'

'Perfect. I'll drink this then get off to bed, if you don't mind? I've lost track of what time zone I'm in and I can feel the jet lag setting in.'

Half an hour later, as I lie on the sofa wrapped in my old sleeping bag, I stare at the ceiling not feeling even slightly tired as I relive every moment of the last forty-eight hours. Joe said he loves me! He said he loves me, and I love him too. But I'm not ready to have him meet Mum right now, especially given she doesn't even know that I'm seeing someone. Let's face it, my life is like a soap opera at the moment – it's hard to keep up. I feel kind of unsettled that I revealed so much to her tonight but it felt like...I don't know, that maybe our relationship has moved to a different level or something. She was pretty honest with me about her life when we were in New York.

But for now I want to keep everything about Joe to myself.

Mmm...I close my eyes and remember his touch. The way my body reacted to his. The connection, both physically and emotionally. I can feel myself getting hotter and hotter as a tingle of adrenaline ricochets up my spine and my lower stomach flips. Then, like a water balloon bursting and dowsing my flames of lust, I remember that my mother is sleeping in the room above me and I roll over and switch off the table lamp and force myself to sleep.

Chapter Thirty

'Morning, Emma.'

'Argh!'

Bright light floods into the room, burning my corneas as my eyes open – then I immediately snap them closed in defiance. What is it with everyone waking me up? Why can't I be left alone to sleep?

'Wakey, wakey.'

I smell coffee, which is good, but why is Mum so chirpy? And why do I hurt all over? Oh yes, that's right, I'm squashed into the corners of my sofa in a sleeping bag.

I open one eye gingerly and see her hovering next to the sofa holding a steaming mug.

'What time is it?' I cringe.

'It's already eight, darling. Come on, get up. I've planned a really good day for us.'

I shuffle my body onto one side and prop myself up on my elbow.

'Did you really say eight?'

Mum raises her eyebrows at me and pushes the cup of coffee in front of my nose. I grasp the mug and take a sip. Mmm, that's better; I can already feel the caffeine starting to work through the fog towards my brain.

'So what are we doing today?' I ask a little nervously. Seriously, she only arrived last night so how can she have planned a full day already?

'Well...' Mum sits down on the edge of the sofa. 'I thought we could get some retail therapy this afternoon, maybe have lunch at Carlito's – if it's still as good as I remember from last time.'

'It is, and that all sounds great, but I'm...' 'Officially skint' is probably the appropriate terminology.

'Oh, don't worry about money; this is my treat. You've allowed me to crash here at short notice so I'm going to spoil you, okay?'

'Okay!' I surrender very quickly. I could get used to this.

'But first we can go for a facial at the spa.'

'That all sounds great, Mum, but are you sure?'

'Absolutely. It'll be some bonding time for us to reconnect properly; and we can take your mind off your worries with Sophie.'

'But if you're paying for all that then we're going to the coffee shop for pastries and proper coffee for breakfast – my treat.'

'Lovely.' Mum smiles. 'Now get moving.'

'How the hell are you this energetic after a long-haul flight?' I whinge as I clamber off the sofa with great difficulty and head upstairs to the bathroom.

'Vitamins, darling. I found this amazing new plant extract,' Mum calls up to me.

I shake my head as I close the bathroom door and turn on the shower. My mum has a lotion or potion for everything and her vitamin cupboard looks like a dispensary chemist.

I'm smiling to myself as the heat from the shower penetrates my skin, warming my body back to life, but -

Joe!

I'm going to have to put him off. But what can I say? I don't want you to meet my Mum sounds a bit "off" but I like the little bubble that we're in; just the two of us - without any added complications. If I say I'm ill then he won't want to come over. That's it, I'll have to say I'm ill, that I need to rest in bed. Alone.

I rub at my temples. Here I am planning to lie to the one decent guy in my life who's told me that he loves me. I grab the shampoo and squeeze a dollop into my hand before massaging it onto my head. I'm definitely going to hell on a first-class ticket.

Half an hour later and Mum and I are in the car heading into town.

'So did you sleep well?' I ask out of politeness, but then instantly regret prompting this conversation.

'I don't know how you sleep in that bed, Emma. You really need a new mattress.'

'The mattress is only two years old, Mum; it's fine.' I stare forward and concentrate on driving, thinking next time she turns up unannounced I might make her sleep on the sofa instead. It's hard to stop myself from smiling at the thought.

We enter the coffee shop a few minutes later, and as Mum goes off to get us a table I order two large cappuccinos and a selection of pastries. There's something European about eating chocolate croissants for breakfast and somehow for that reason alone it doesn't feel so guilt-ridden.

I've not taken two bites from my croissant before I nearly choke as it sticks in my throat.

'You have got to be kidding me,' I mumble, staring across the coffee shop. It's deja vu. I should have known better than to return to the same coffee shop that I saw Chris and her in last time, but I didn't think lightning struck the same place twice.

'What?' Mum turns around in her chair. 'Oh God, is that –?'

'Yes,' I hiss. 'That's Chris with his new girlfriend. No wait – fiancée.'

'Fiancée?' Mum sounds shocked. I guess I forgot to mention that little gem last night.

What are the odds of seeing them here again? Am I stuck in the Bermuda triangle destined to bump into Chris or is this God's way of punishing me by rubbing my nose in the fact that...

'Do you want me to say something?'

'Jesus, Mum, no! He hasn't seen us. Let's quietly sit over there out of sight and hopefully they'll leave soon.'

'Well, it's not right, the way he treated you.'

'And how would that conversation go then, Mum? Are you going to walk over there and tell him that it's not on that he clearly doesn't find me attractive any more and he prefers someone half my age – well, not quite half, but considerably younger. I mean, that would be humiliating.' I stare at my half-eaten pastry, realising my appetite has instantly evaporated.

'No, of course I'm not going to say that, but...' She stands up.

'Mum, sit down,' I hiss.

'It's okay, Emma, I've got this.' She glances back at me over her shoulder in a cool fashion.

I hang my head in shame and wonder if I've time to make a hasty retreat towards the door without being seen. I can't believe that my mother is walking over to my ex-boyfriend, ready to tell him off like a naughty child. I stare up at the heavens. If the ground could open up right now and swallow me whole, I would be eternally grateful.

'Hello, Christopher.'

I hear Mum's voice loud and clear, and ever so slightly patronising, and I look up to see that she's standing right in front of them. The blond girl is staring at Mum warily, like you would at a tiger that's wandered out of its zoo enclosure, and I feel a little wave of happiness as I note that Chris has gone white and looks like he's swallowed a great big fly.

Mum now has her back to me, and despite teetering on the edge of my seat and straining with all my might, I can no longer hear her over the hissing and banging of coffee production and the general chitchat of the other customers. A few seconds later I see Chris glance over at me with a sheepish look that's tinged with what I can only presume is annoyance and/or embarrassment, before he and his new fiancée stand up and scarper like rabbits hearing a gunshot. I watch them leaving the coffee shop without so much as a backward glance as Mum saunters back to the table with a satisfied expression planted firmly on her face.

'What did you say?' I ask dreading the response.

'Nothing really, Emma.' Mum sits back down and has a drink of her coffee.

'Nothing really? That's why did they run out of here like the place was on fire?' I raise my eyebrows questioningly.

'Okay, so I might have said something that made them feel a little...uncomfortable.'

'Mum...'

'I only mentioned that the candle of illicit love can soon burn out and that the burden of guilt from cheating can, you know, have an effect on the trouser department.'

'You did not say that?!'

'The truth hurts sometimes, Emma.'

Oh my God!

I sit there, momentarily stunned, before the giggles set in, and then I'm laughing so hard that I'm holding my stomach and tears are streaming down my face. Mum's staring at me like she doesn't see why what she's said is so funny, but to me it is; it's the funniest thing in the world. No wonder they got the hell out of here so quickly. Talking about drooping sexual performance is enough to put anyone off their morning coffee!

'Calm yourself down, Emma. People are looking.'

I take a few gulps of air to try to steady myself. 'I'm sorry.' I wipe my eyes and take a slurp of coffee until the heaving in my shoulders finally subsides.

'So what shall we do for dinner tonight? Shall I cook us something?' Mum suggests.

Tonight. Must text Joe now.

'No, don't worry about cooking. I'll pop out and get us a takeaway – my treat, to say thanks for the facial.'

'Fair enough; that sounds nice.'

'If you'll excuse me, Mum' – I reach into my handbag for my mobile phone – 'I forgot to text Jenny something about work.'

'Shall I grab us another coffee? One for the road?'

'Sure. Thanks, Mum.'

Once Mum's left the table and headed back over to the counter I press the text button on my phone and begin typing.

Hi. Not feeling too well today. I have a cold and cough that have come out of nowhere. Think I should cancel plans tonight. Really sorry. Feel like I need to rest in bed. Will call you tomorrow x

I press the send button, feeling like a complete fraud. It's a lie, but it's only a little one.

'All sorted?' Mum plonks down a mug on the table in front of me.

'Um, yes,' I slip my phone back into my bag.

We arrive at the spa a short time later and I'm presented with a menu of options for facials I've never heard of with ingredients I don't understand. Mum is clearly on board, though, and completely in her comfort zone as she interrogates the beauty therapist about the anti-ageing benefits of one facial compared to another. It all sounds far too complicated, so I leave the choice up to Mum. Unfortunately for me, I realise all too late that this is a mistake.

'Should it really smell this bad?' I ask from the depths of my white towelling robe a short while later as I lie on a treatment bed wrapped in white sheets like an Egyptian mummy. The sounds from a rainforest are playing in the background, which is causing a war between two instincts: one telling me to relax and the other to pee.

'It's seaweed, darling. It has fantastic benefits for your skin.'

'I don't think that's the question I asked, Mum. I asked whether it should smell like death?'

'Honestly, Emma, you'll thank me when you look in the mirror tomorrow and you look five years younger.'

I'm only thirty-two, and I don't think that I look particularly old. Hang on a minute – is that an insult? Is she implying that I look old? Move on, Emma; move on. If I've learned anything about my mother over the last few years it's not to pursue such lines of enquiry, as no matter what she says in return I'll still end up feeling like I've been underhandedly insulted, whether that was the intention or not.

The rest of the spa experience is much more enjoyable as we sit in a lovely conservatory, still in our fluffy towelling gowns, and pass the time drinking fruit tea and perusing fashion magazines. By the time our session has finished I feel completely relaxed and it's a struggle to get showered and dressed. As I look in the mirror while blasting my hair with the hairdryer I'm pleasantly surprised to notice that my skin does appear a bit plumper and I do in fact look a little younger. Damn my mother. I hate it when that woman is right?

Before we leave I check my phone to see whether Joe has responded to my earlier text. Sure enough, there's a flashing envelope on the screen. I click it.

No worries. Hope you feel better soon. Will call you later to see how you are. x

A phone call – that's fine. That doesn't involve Joe and my mother being in the same room.

Chapter Thirty-One

It's nearly six in the evening by the time we get home, having taken a detour to include every boutique in town – which I'm not complaining about! We dump our shopping bags in the hallway and I leave Mum with the task of preparing plates and wine as I head out to collect Chinese food. Thankfully I'm only gone twenty minutes or so as I'm starving. I think that seaweed stuff might have given my metabolism a kick earlier too.

'Hey, I'm back,' I call through to the kitchen as I try to remove my shoes without losing any items from the large brown paper bag that holds the takeaway food.

I'm met by silence, which is strange.

'Mum...'

Now free from my shoes I pad down the hallway and into the kitchen, where Mum is standing, clutching a wine glass with a weird look on her face.

'Didn't you hear me calling you?'

Oh holy crap!

Standing next to Mum is Joe, looking decidedly uncomfortable.

I open my mouth to speak, but realise pretty quickly that my brain can't think of any viable words to send to my mouth at this current moment, so I close it, pressing my lips together.

How has this happened? I cancelled plans with Joe specifically so this very event wouldn't occur.

'I think you two need to talk,' Mum says, nodding at me with a knowing look on her face.

'What about the –'

'It'll heat up later,' she calls over her shoulder as she heads out of the kitchen, closing the door gently behind her.

I turn to face Joe with a mixture of thoughts churning through my mind. He said he loves me. What the hell is he doing here? I lied to him and he now knows it. I love him. Please don't let him be angry with me.

'I know you said not to come over...' Joe shoves his hands in his jeans pockets.

'I said I was ill,' I say sheepishly placing the brown paper bag onto the small table. 'I'm not ill.'

He points to his left. 'I brought soup.'

I notice the container from the noodle and soup bar in town on the kitchen side next to the kettle and my heart flutters then sinks. He brought soup to make me feel better. But I lied.

'I know I said I wasn't well and that was a lie, but –'

'But?'

I can't read his expression now.

'But my mother just landed on me with no warning. She was already at the airport when she called me and I wasn't ready for you to meet her, or maybe for her to meet you, I don't know.' I realise I'm rambling, the words are falling out of my mouth with very little thought process, but I can't stop. 'She's only here for a couple of days and I thought...' I flap my arms aimlessly.

'So you didn't want me to come over because your mother is here?'

'Well, yes. It's complicated. My mother is...It's complicated.'

'And you didn't want her to meet me yet?'

'Look, it's early days in our relationship and she arrived unexpectedly and –'

'And that's the only reason?'

'Of course that's the only reason. What do you mean?' I realise Joe has stopped looking all scrunched up and uncomfortable and now he looks relaxed and is smiling. I frown. 'You look relieved.'

'I am relieved! Yesterday I tell you I love you, and this morning you're cancelling plans to see me.'

It takes a second for my brain to click into gear.

'Oh.'

He thought I was cancelling because I had cold feet or something.

'I thought maybe I'd scared you off. That I'd come on too strong.'

Wow. I thought it was only women who had emotional flip-outs. It never occurred to me that Joe would think I was avoiding him because he said that he loved me. If anything, I think that makes me love him even more, and then I remember: in my excitement at his declaration of love, I didn't say it back to him yesterday. No wonder he thinks he's said something wrong.

'Absolutely not; you didn't come on too strong.' I step forward and take hold of his hand, giving it a little squeeze. 'I love you too. I know I didn't say it back yesterday, but I do. And this – today: I panicked about my mum turning up and did what I always do, which is, well, something stupid. I lied, and I'm sorry.'

'It's okay. Meeting your other half's mother can be a delicate scenario.' He brushes my cheek gently with his thumb.

'Thank you for bringing me soup.'

'This soup can fix any ailment, I swear. If you were ill, that is.' He cocks his head.

'Given you're here now, would you like to stay for dinner? We have plenty of Chinese food.' I figure it's safe, seeing as he's already come face to face with Mum.

'Thanks for the offer, I appreciate it, but you wanted it to be you and your mum, so I'm going to go home and leave you to spend some quality time with her.'

'Are you sure?'

'I'm sure.' He leans in and gives me a lingering kiss. He gives my bum a little squeeze before pulling away.

'I'll be all alone again by Wednesday night if you're available for food and possibly wine?' I raise my eyebrows.

'It's a date. Come to mine for seven.'

'Okay.'

'And bring your overnight bag.' Joe winks. 'I'd better be going.'

'Right.' My thoughts returning to our hot, frantic sex…

'Interesting lady, your mother.' He turns and pauses for a second as he reaches the kitchen door.

Oh no.

'How long were you alone with her?' I dread to think what conversation they had prior to my arrival.

Joe grins and heads out of the door.

'Ms. Storey…' I hear him call.

Wait! Wait! I hurry into the hallway to find my mother standing opposite Joe talking animatedly at him.

'Are you sure you won't stay?'

'No, really, I have some stuff to do. But it was nice meeting you.'

'It was lovely to meet you too.' Mum gives me a sideways glance.

'I'll see you on Wednesday.' I roll my eyes at Joe.

'See you then. Goodnight, Ms. Storey.'

'Please, call me Rosalind.'

The second Joe has left the house and the door has clicked shut behind him Mum swirls around to face me, her expression one of amusement.

'Something you forgot to mention?'

I don't take the bait. 'The Chinese food is going cold.' I turn and head back into the kitchen.

'Alright, alright. So you don't want to talk about it.' Mum follows me into the kitchen.

Clearly that means: 'I don't understand why you hid your boyfriend from me.' I decide that if I'm going to get any peace over the next two days then I need to play the whole thing down.

'We've not been together very long and we're taking things nice and slowly, that's all.' I hope I sound convincing.

'If that's the story you're sticking to then fine, but I wasn't born yesterday, you know.'

'What does that mean?'

'It means that I saw the way you two were looking at each other and I'd say that this is pretty serious.'

I shrug nonchalantly.

'And why you felt the need to hide this lovely young man from me I don't know.'

Maybe now isn't the time to go into that.

'We'll see how things go. But for the moment do you want to pour me a glass of wine while I share out the food?'

There's a short pause, but then Mum takes the hint and she collects the wine from the fridge and starts pours me a glass as I scoop chicken chow mien onto our plates.

As we tuck into our food the conversation moves away from Joe but heads into another area that I'd rather avoid.

'So what are we going to do to get you and Sophie back on track?' Mum asks between mouthfuls of egg foo young.

'I really don't know, Mum.' I shake my head. 'The situation is pretty bad. I've tried to contact her by text and email as she won't answer the phone to me but so far she's ignored my every attempt to get her into a conversation of some sort with me.' It still hurts that she's deleted me from her social media profile.

'You two have been friends for so long.'

'I know. I really miss her. She doesn't even know anything about Joe.'

'Oh, so I'm not alone on that.' Mum feigns offence but I shake my head at her. 'So what are you going to do about the situation?'

'I could hire a hit man to make Connor disappear once and for all.'

'Let's call that Plan B, shall we? Any other thoughts?'

I take a sip of wine, remembering my conversation with Jenny and Lola that night in the wine bar after I'd flipped out at Mrs Winklebarrow-Smith.

'Lola at work suggested that I approach Connor and try to goad him into saying something incriminating while all the time recording the conversation on my mobile phone.'

Mum considers the idea. 'That could work.'

'Are you kidding me? Doesn't that sound like some plot from a television drama? I mean, surely people don't do things like that in the real world. Do they?'

'What have you got to lose?'

'Well, it could backfire on me like the last time and then I'd look like the bad guy again.'

'Again? What was your mistake last time?'

'That I underestimated the slippery fucker.'

'Emma!' Mum frowns. 'Language, please.'

'Sorry. He gets me that mad and brings out the worst in me.'

'What did you do actually do, though?'

'I waited for him outside his place of work. I figured that would be my best chance of catching him without Sophie being there too.'

'I see. So could you do that again?'

'I guess so.' I shrug, drinking the last of my wine.

'Then it sounds to me like you have no choice but to try again if you want your friendship with Sophie back.'

'I suppose you're right. Maybe I'll have to give it a try.'

'Sometimes we have to take risks, Emma. Yes, it could go wrong, but if Sophie means as much to you as I think she does then the risk is worth taking.'

Mmm. Wise words from my mother. Damn it, it appears that she's right again.

Wednesday morning arrives before I know it, and at the airport as I hug Mum goodbye in the drop-off bay, amid clouds of exhaust smoke and beeping taxi horns, I get that familiar twist of emotion. But I know she's only ever a plane journey away, and the weird thing is that we've become closer since she's lived halfway around the world, away from me.

'Take care, darling, and don't be a stranger, okay? Call me if you need to talk things through.'

'I will, I promise.'

'Good luck with Sophie. Let me know how things turn out. You know I'll only worry about you if you don't.'

'I'll call you over the weekend, Mum. Hopefully it will all be sorted out by then.'

'Are you going to try to see Connor tonight?'

'No, I'm staying at Joe's tonight.'

'Of course.' Mum gives me an exaggerated wink.

Did she really just do that?

'Anyway, I must get moving or I'll be late for work,' I say to hide my blush. 'Have a safe flight.'

'Speak soon.' Mum gives me a little wave and then she heads into the departures terminal with her mountain of luggage.

My journey to work is taken up with thoughts of Connor. Am I really going to entrap him? How easily would he going to admit that he's been lying to Sophie? He's already wary of me. How much do I need him to say to incriminate himself? And more to the point, how long a recording can I make on my phone? I make a mental note to dig out the instruction manual for it, which I've never bothered to read and, if my memory serves correctly, is sitting in the kitchen drawer collecting dust with all of the other stuff that I keep 'in case' but never really do anything with.

I'm alone in the shop today so I'm busier than usual, but thankfully this makes the day pass quickly. I scoot home and throw some essential items into my overnight bag and then take a speedy shower to freshen up.

Before leaving the house to head to Joe's for the night I root around in the kitchen drawer, and lo and behold the mobile phone manual is exactly where I thought it was. I flick through the pages but there must be hundreds of them, many of which are written in languages that I don't even recognise. After some considerable time, which I didn't have to spare, I find the section that I'm looking for. Five minutes. That's all I'll have. Five minutes to record Connor. And this is going to be a one-chance-only event, so I'd better get it right in my head and ensure I don't cock it up by letting him bully me again. I must ignore any attempt by him to provoke me. I need to be strong.

Damn it; this time I will be strong.

'Stop it, Rhys; you're scaring me.'
'Tell me the truth. Did you lie to me? Did you sneak out of here last night to meet her? To listen to her poison?'
'Rhys, please! Please don't hurt me.'

Chapter Thirty-Two

'I've missed you,' I mumble into Joe's chest as he plants kisses down my neck.

I've been in his house literally thirty seconds and I'm already turned on. Joe's touch has instantly awakened my sexual appetite and I can feel my whole body tingling with desire, craving more.

'I've missed you too.'

Joe slides his hand up my jumper and teases my nipple through my bra, sending shoots of electricity reverberating around my body. I can feel my heartbeat quickening as his lips find mine, kissing them hungrily. I push my tongue gently into his mouth in search of his as he reaches a hand down the back of my jeans, caressing the bare skin on my bottom. As he tugs suggestively at my thong that's my undoing.

The heat between us goes up about a hundred notches and in an instant we turn into animals, frantically pulling at each other's clothes. I undo his shirt with lightning speed and rip it from his shoulders, unveiling his bare chest. Two seconds later my jumper is lifted above my head and discarded on the floor. Joe unzips my jeans and I step out of them, standing my bra and pants in his kitchen. He quickly removes his own jeans and boxer shorts in one fell swoop and I'm satisfied to see that every part of him is pleased to see me.

He lifts me up and places me on the kitchen worktop.

Jeez, that's cold!

Whoa!

His fingers caress my thighs as he slowly removes my knickers, which heightens my carnal need. As they drop to the floor Joe unclasps my bra, cupping my breasts, kneading them gently as his mouth finds a nipple and...oh, I feel like I'm going to explode. My breath is coming in short, sharp pants and I'm starting to feel light-headed. I can take this no longer. I grab at his naked bum cheeks, pulling him closer to me, and he lifts me onto him.

I wrap my legs around his body, pushing him deeper inside me. The pace is frantic as we move together, his mouth on mine, then nibbling my earlobe, which is…wow!

As his hips grind against mine I lean back onto the work surface, propping myself up on my hands, arching my back. He tongue traces the line from my stomach to my chest and I can feel my orgasm rising to the surface. As he licks one nipple lustfully, then the other, I groan in response, pushing my hips forward to meet his.

Leaning towards him, sliding my hand up the back of his neck, I tug none-too-gently at his hair and he closes his eyes. Taking hold of my buttocks, he takes it up a gear. It's fast and furious and I gasp loudly as my orgasm takes over, my heart thundering in my chest, adrenaline swirling deliciously around my body. A moment later I feel Joe climax too and I collapse against his hot, sweaty body as he wraps his arms around me, nuzzling my neck.

I try to steady my breathing. If this is going to be the regular pace of our love-making then I really need to start working. Maybe this counts as a workout?

'I don't know what's happened here,' I whisper into Joe's ear. 'I mean, you invite me around for food and beer, and so far I've been presented with neither. In fact, you've taken advantage of me before I could even make it out of the kitchen.'

'I'm sorry.' He leans back a little so we're eye to eye and he stares straight at me. 'I couldn't help myself. It's been three days since I last saw you naked and I had an urge to get you out of those clothes.'

'I see.'

'It's your own fault. You shouldn't be so damn sexy.'

Did he really say that? How corny! Hang on – me, damn sexy? Surely not.

'Speaking of your clothes, we'd better get you back into them before I can't resist you again and we go for round two.'

'I might need to refuel before that.'

'Okay, that's fair.' He lifts me down from the worktop and I untangle myself from him. 'Let's start with a beer.'

He opens the fridge, takes out two beer bottles, flips off the tops with a bottle opener and hands me one. I take a gulp; we really did work up a thirst. I've never had sex in a kitchen before. That was... exciting. We stand there for a moment, naked, drinking our beer, and I start to giggle.

'What's so funny?' Joe cocks his head at me.

'This. Being naked in your kitchen, like it's the most normal thing in the world.'

'What? I'm naked all the time in my kitchen. Aren't you in your own home?'

No, I realise. I'm always clothed, even if it's only a dressing gown. Maybe I have some sort of naked intimacy issue? Anyway…

'If that's the case then you may want to double-check that the front door is locked or the next time Ben drops in unannounced he may get more than he bargained for.'

I know I did when I let myself into Simon's flat! Argh – I'd buried those images in a hidden corner of my mind; now I'm back to square one!

'I guess you're right,' Joe chuckles. 'So what do you fancy to eat? I'm ravenous.'

'Me too. Are you going to cook?' I ask a little too optimistically.

'To cook?'

'So you're going to order takeaway?' I ask.

'That almost cooking.' He smiles widely at me.

'It's not even close,' I tease, but that's exactly the type of cooking I love.

'I'll let you choose what kind of food and I'll pay.'

I mull it over for a second. 'That'll work.'

Chapter Thirty-Three

The following day is the day I've been waiting for and dreading with equal emotion. The weather is cold and damp and I huddle under my coat, looking up at grey skies that threaten rainfall at any second. I turn my gaze back to the bank across the street, holding my breath, feeling a toxic mixture of adrenaline and fear as I wait for Connor to appear. And right on cue, as the big hand on my watch signals the turn of the hour to five o'clock, he appears in the revolving glass door, alone this time.

He sets off down the high street in the opposite direction to me at an alarming pace, forcing me to scuttle out of my hiding place between a second-hand clothes shop and Harry's Hardware and hurry after him. Other workers are spilling out onto the streets, all anxious to get home before the imminent rainstorm descends. Connor is only a few metres ahead of me now and I check my mobile phone, but it's too early to turn on the recording application.

Suddenly I'm knocked off my feet and the world is spinning and the concrete is riding up to meet me.

Ouch! I lie sprawled on the cold, wet ground surrounded by a sea of feet.

'I'm so sorry, I didn't see you,' a voice above me booms.

I roll over onto my back and look up to see a large old man towering over me. He leans down, holding out his hand. 'Are you hurt?'

'Um, no.' I shake my head despite feeling a burning sensation on both of my knees. 'I'm fine.'

'Let me help you up.' He wiggles his hand, gesturing for me to take hold.

'No, really, I'm okay.' I push myself up onto my knees and then straighten up to a standing position and brush myself down.

'Are you sure you're alright?'

'Yes, yes.' I wave him away.

The old man hesitates for a moment before moving on.

Where is he? Where's Connor? Damn it, I've lost him now in the crowd. Stupid old man. I turn my head frantically but I don't see him.

'Why are you following me?'

I nearly jump out of my skin as Connor appears out of nowhere right in front of me. His face is only inches away from mine and I can smell the same crisp aftershave that haunts me from that night. My whole body begins to tremble as ice creeps through my veins. I swallow nervously, wondering whether he can hear the nervous thudding of my heart and smell the fear that I can taste in my own mouth.

'I…I...don't know what you mean,' I stutter defiantly.

'Yes, you do,' he sneers. 'You've been following me since I left work. I saw you hiding across the street before you'd even made your move.'

Shit.

'Huh, do you think I'm stupid or something?'

I press my lips together, trying to compose myself. I can't believe I've been caught out so easily.

'Now, I'll ask you again. Why are you following me?'

I realise with a sinking heart that this situation is about to blow up in my face. I don't want to provoke Connor into saying anything yet. He took me by surprise and I haven't turned on the recording device. Anything he says to me now he can deny. I need to front this out. I'm only going to get one chance to goad him into saying something incriminating and this isn't the right time. I'm thrown and the moment has gone. I take a step closer to him, defying every urge in my body to run like hell, and I stand as tall as I can.

'Just know that I'm watching you.' I glare at him. 'And when you slip up, I'll be waiting.'

And with that I turn on my heel and walk away with trembling legs.

'Haven't you had enough yet, Emma?' I can hear the laughter in his voice. 'Okay, if you're ready for more then bring it on.'

I feel physically sick as I push past people, staring down at the ground, stepping between the colourful footfalls. I daren't look back but I can still hear Connor's mocking tone ringing through my ears.

The bastard. The rotten bastard. It's all a game to him; it has been from the start.

Then it hits me; I have an epiphany right there in the street. I stop dead in my tracks, ignoring the annoyed curses of the people around me. This is too much. My brain goes into overdrive.

Glancing up, I realise I've stopped outside a coffee shop, so I push the door open and walk to the counter.

'A skinny latte with an extra shot, please.'

As I hold out my hand to pay with my debit card I can see that it's shaking noticeably from the adrenaline that's kicked in, but it's not with the fear that I felt only moments ago.

Two minutes later I'm seated in a corner booth frantically stirring my coffee and watching it swirl around and around the mug. Connor's words from our confrontation at Sophie's house, when I was trying to prove I had been in his flat, play over and over in my head: 'Sophie's shown you pictures of me and her. You've seen pictures of Sophie in my apartment on social media. That's how you know what it looks like.' I didn't see it then, but it's all making sense now. He was right: I had seen pictures of him and Sophie together in his apartment after I'd been introduced to him that day we all met for coffee. But what if he had seen pictures of me and Sophie too, before that fateful Friday night? There were dozens of pictures of me and Sophie on her social media profile from nights out before she systematically deleted them one by one. I can't believe I haven't clicked onto this before. He knew who I was that night in the bar. He knew I was Sophie's best friend when he sent over that drink. He orchestrated this whole thing.

Holy shit.

But why? What would he have to gain? Why would he want to do that to his girlfriend? I can't think of any sane reason that any normal human being would have, but Connor doesn't appear normal and there's no getting away from it:

In my heart of hearts I know he must have done something like this before – you don't wake up one morning and decide to coolly cheat on your girlfriend, and certainly not with her best friend – and if he's done this before, he'll do it again. Once a cheater, always a cheater; or in this case, once a complete psychopath, always a psychopath.

He set me and Sophie up good and proper. Both of us.

Chapter Thirty-Four

'Simon?'

'Emma? What are you doing here? I wasn't expecting you hun.'

'Are you alone? Can you let me up?'

'Sure.'

I hear the door buzz and I push it open then take the flight of stairs two at a time. Simon is already stood with the door open to his flat as I arrive breathless.

'Emma, you're scaring me. What's wrong?'

'I figured it our Si' I push past him into the flat feeling jittery, not that the three latte's I've consumed in quick succession has helped.

He closes the door behind us.

'Figured what out?'

'Connor. Sophie. Everything.'

'Emma - you're not making any sense'

'Do you have wine?' I scuttle through to the kitchen 'I need a drink.'

'In the fridge' Simon calls after me 'and pour me one. I'm guessing I'm going to need it'.

'Connor new who I was when he sent that drink over to me in the bar that night' I thrust a glass of white wine at Simon a few moments later.

'But…how? How could he know who you were?'

'Social media. Pictures all over Sophie's profile of me and her. He recognised me Si, he knew I was Sophie's friend. He knew what he was doing.'

'Shit.' Simon takes a large drink of wine. 'Are you sure?'

'He instigated us going back to his flat. I was going to get a taxi home.'

'So, he slept with you knowing he was cheating on his girlfriend with her friend and he's been…what? Getting off on it since?'

'I know' I gulp at my own wine hoping it will relax me enough to stop my chest from feeling like it's imploding 'It's sick isn't it?'

'You need to tell Sophie, Emma, and soon. If not, then I will. I'm not going to let her keep seeing that psycho when he's been playing her all along.'

'No Simon. I need to tell her. But before I do I need to get him to admit what he's done.'

'And how exactly are you going to get him to do that?'

I tell him about Jenny and Lola's plan of recording him.

'Seriously honey, you need to be careful. If he's that much of a nutter he could do anything to you if you provoke him.'

'If I'm honest, I'm terrified. But if I don't do this then Sophie won't listen to me, or you for that matter. He's been drip feeding her his poison and she's well and truly under his spell.'

'When are you going to do it?'

'Tomorrow night, when he finishes work. I need to end this Si, and now.'

'Be careful, Emma.'

'Of course.' I reassure him 'I'll call you when it's over and I've made Sophie see the truth, I promise.'

Later that even evening as I sit in bed with a cup of tea finally feeling like my heart rhythm is returning to normal my thoughts turn to Joe. I stare down at his text from earlier:

'Are you free tomorrow night? How does dinner sound? My place at 7. Don't forget your overnight bag (no pyjamas needed!) xx'

I contemplate calling him and telling him everything. I feel like I want his support on this. I'm really scared of confronting Connor and how he's going to react especially after last night. I can still hear his stinging comments and the sound of his laughter as I fled. But all Joe knows is that Sophie and I fell out, he knows nothing of Connor and the reason why we aren't speaking. I instinctively went to Simon earlier as I needed to vent and to share my realisation with someone already in the know about Connor.

I want to tell Joe, I really do, but telling him means starting the story from the beginning and I don't want to have to confess all to him over the phone about going back to Connor's flat in a drunken state and sleeping with him. I don't want it to cause Joe to look at me differently. He loves me, I know that, but what if finding out I've had a one night stand makes him think less of me, and maybe love me less. I don't want to put that out there because I'm not ready to accept the fact that revealing this could change things between Joe. I've finally found some happiness and I'm not going to let my indiscretion with Connor destroy anything else in my life.

I press the reply button and type:

'Sorry – have last minute plans with Jenny but would love the same offer for Saturday night xxx'

Two seconds later the phone beeps with his reply:

'It's a date. Goodnight. Love you x'

I smile down at the phone and type back:

'Love you too xx'

'It's over Rhys. You're the liar, not her...Ouch!'
'It's not over until I say it is'

Chapter Thirty-Five

The following day I'm a jittery mess at work, which earns me concerned glances from both Jenny and Lola.

'What's going on with you?' Jenny pulls me to one side, removing the large pair of scissors from my hand. What was I even doing with them?

'What do you mean?' I say, trying to sound dismissive.

'I mean, why are you like an over-caffeinated chimp at a tea party today? You've dropped about a million things already and I've been watching you carrying those scissors around for no purpose for the last hour and I'm scared that you're going to accidentally impale yourself on them.'

Oh.

'I'm sorry. It's just...' I press my lips together.

'Just?'

'I've got him, Jenny.'

'Got who?'

'Connor. It's all a setup, everything.'

She frowns. 'I'm not following you.'

I glance around, making sure that the shop is still empty.

'Connor knew who I was that night at the bar. He sent that drink over to me knowing I was Sophie's best friend.'

'What?'

'I didn't figure it out at first but then it hit me. When I was trying to describe his apartment he made a comment about me knowing what it looked like because I must have seen pictures of him and Sophie in his apartment on social media. It took me a while to realise but if he was making out that I'd seen picture of him on her profile page then he must have seen all the pictures of me and Sophie on there.'

'Oh God! So he knew all along.'

'Yep.'

'Why would he deliberately cheat on his new girlfriend with her best friend?'

'That's the question I can't answer. But I'm damn well going to find out.'

'You're going to confront him?'

'You and Lola were right that evening in the pub. I need to confront him and get him to say something incriminating while I'm recording him.'

'You're really going to do that?' Jenny looks at me wide-eyed.

'Tonight. Tonight is when he has to answer to me.'

At five o'clock I'm right back where I was only twenty four hours ago, across the street from the bank where Connor works and it's not long before he appears in the revolving door and is on the street. I step out boldly from my hiding place and notice with satisfaction that he's seen me too, and there's a look of confusion beginning to spread across his face as I march purposefully towards him. I'm not scared this time; I'm angry, angry and looking for the truth; ready to demand the truth. The recording app is active on my mobile and I've placed it under my clothing on my chest, facing outwards so that it has the best possible chance of picking up our conversation given the background noise. I can feel the black tape that I've used to secure the phone in place pulling at my skin a little, prompting me to get this over and done with quickly. The five-minute countdown is ticking.

I stop about a metre in front of Connor and he watches me with an expression that I can't quite read.

'Okay.' I hold up my hands in submission. 'You've got me. I've been following you again. But I'm done. It's over; no more.'

He raises his eyebrows at me quizzically. 'And why is that, Emmie? Why are you giving up so easily? You don't come across as the quitting type.'

So he wants me to keep harassing him? This is what he wants?

'I'm not a quitter,' I snap. 'But I've tried and tried to get Sophie to see sense and she won't. She won't even speak to me, as I'm sure you well know. So you win.' I shrug my shoulders emphatically.

'I win?' He doesn't look convinced by my little speech.

'I'll go away.' I lick my lips nervously. 'I'll leave you and Sophie alone.'

'And why would you do that after all…this?' He gestures at us standing here, antagonists, in the street.

I let out a deep breath and look him straight in the eye. 'Because of all this. Because I care about Sophie and I want her to be happy, and me continually texting and emailing her…well, it's not making her happy. So I'll back off.'

I watch as his look of confusion turn to conceit, then I turn to walk away. 'One thing, though.' I turn back around to face him, resisting the urge to rip his annoying face right off.

He raises his eyebrows again, looking almost amused now.

'You knew exactly who I was that night in the bar, didn't you? You'd seen my picture before.'

The arrogant masks slips, only for a nanosecond, and I glimpse a hint of panic. Then quickly he's back to his nonchalant self.

'You're crazy!' He shakes his head.

'You'd seen all of the pictures of me and Sophie on her social media profile and you recognised me in that bar that Friday night.'

He's looking decidedly edgy now and I try to hide my own feeling of superiority. It feels good to have caught him off-guard and to let him know that he's not quite a clever as he thinks he is.

'You can't prove that.' He stares at me sternly, his eyes emotionless and cold, and that's all I needed to hear. That one response tells me that I'm right.

'I guess not.' I cock my head to the side. 'But humour me for a second.'

He looks at me warily now; a tiger facing a lion.

'You weren't surprised when I walked into that coffee shop the following Sunday morning while you sat there hand in hand with Sophie. Why?'

'Why?'

'Why would you come on to me, knowing that I was your new girlfriend's best friend?'

His expression doesn't change.

'Why would you entice me into your apartment; into your bed?'

The smirk's back now as he steps closer until he's standing right in front of me and I swear I can hear his heartbeat. I can hear my own erratic thumping heart and can feel fear emanating from my every pore. A film of sweat begins to bead on my forehead as he leans in closer to my ear and his crisp aftershave immediately pricks the senses in my nose.

'Why?' he whispers and a shiver of ice trickles down my spine. 'Because I could.'

'Because you could!?' My anger overshadows the realisation that I've got him to admit it on record.

'Because it amused me to watch your face as you realised you'd made the most catastrophic error of judgement.'

God, he's a complete sicko.

'I enjoyed watching you scramble around, fighting with your conscience. I must admit you threw me that night at Sophie's house; I didn't think you had the balls to tell her.' He laughs now and I realise he doesn't have any normal human feelings; he has no conscience. He's pure evil, plain and simple.

'So it was all a game to you, to amuse you for a while, despite the fact that you completely destroyed two people in the process?'

'You know what, Emma? I'm bored of this conversation now. Why don't you stop playing your silly little game of stalking me?' He leans in close again. 'Or I might start stalking you,' he whispers.

Okay, we're done here.

I need to get away from him now before this goes any further. I take a step back safely into my own personal space and look one last time into his eyes. There really is nothing. No guilt; no remorse; no emotion whatsoever.

I shake my head and quickly stride away from him, glancing behind me intermittently to make sure he's not following me. But he doesn't; he stands there and watches me walk away. I wait until he can no longer see me, and then I run. I run as fast as I can, and don't stop until I reach my car.

I fumble for the keys in the bottom of my handbag, gasping for breath as I press the key fob to unlock the door. It takes me three attempts to get the key in the ignition as my hands are shaking uncontrollably. I slam the car into reverse and shoot out of the car park, causing another driver to beep his horn and make a hand gesture at me through the windscreen, but I don't care. I need to get away from Connor and get home, so I can check the recording on the phone, which thankfully is still strapped to my chest.

I reach my house in record time and lock the front door behind me before pulling my top up and gently peeling away the black tape that's holding the phone in place. I almost daren't listen. The recording will have ended automatically when the time expired and I've no idea at what point in our conversation this happened. I click the play button on the screen to listen to the recording and instinctively hold my breath.

There's Connor's voice; it's slightly muffled but there's no mistaking that it's him. I listen intently as the conversation repeats itself. He sounds so smug, so sure of himself. And then I hear it. It's faint because he was whispering it in my ear, but you can make out what we're saying just clearly enough as he admits that all of this was a game for his own amusement. I've got him! I can't believe Lola and Jenny's stupid plan worked.

Now I need Sophie to listen to this, which might be easier said than done. Connor isn't with Sophie now, though; he's in town. But maybe he's going to hers.

I um and ah for a second, but I know I need to do this as soon as possible and now seems like as good a time as any. I grab my handbag and throw my phone back in it before jogging back out to the car. As I climb into the seat adrenaline is coursing through my whole body like I'm on a drug-fuelled high and I don't feel myself at all. I start the engine and head to Sophie's house.

On the five-minute drive I go over and over in my head how I can get her to listen to me, but the only solution I can come up with is brute force. I'm going to have to force my way in and make her listen to the recording so there's no way that she can deny the truth – or Connor for that matter.

Chapter Thirty-Six

As I pull up outside Sophie's I scan the area. Connor's car is nowhere to be seen, which is about as much confirmation as I'm going to get that Sophie is alone. I feel incredibly nervous now I'm here and I climb out of the car slowly, taking deep breaths to steady myself.

It all seemed so clean-cut in my mind, but now I'm here I'm unsure how this is going to turn out. Sophie may be even madder at me than last time for following Connor again, but I've got to try. Even if our relationship only worsens, she needs to understand what a creep Connor is and she needs to get rid of him for her own good.

I march up to the front door, pooling my inner strength, and ring the bell before I can debate this whole thing in my mind any further and make myself even crazier than I already have been over the last few months.

As the door opens I see Sophie's face drop.

'I've told you that I don't want to see you, Emma.' She goes to close the door but I block it half with my foot and half with my shoulder.

'Hey!' she shouts.

'Sophie, I know you're angry with me but I've got something that you need to listen to.'

'No. I've heard more than enough from you, Emma. I don't want to hear anything else you have to say.'

'No, you haven't, and yes, you do,' I protest. 'And this isn't what I have to say, it's what Connor has to say.'

'Emma –'

'No, Sophie. I'm sorry, but I'm not leaving until you hear this. If our friendship ever meant anything to you then you'll give me two minutes. That's all I want: two minutes of your time. I promise.'

She pauses, and I don't know if it's the tone of my voice or the tug on her former loyalty that changes her mind, but she relents and slowly holds open the door.

'Two minutes.' She says sternly and I nod silently as I step inside and follow her through to the kitchen.

I glance around nervously.

'Connor isn't here.' She sighs, folding her arms in what I perceive to be a defensive position. 'We're alone.'

'Right.' I clear my throat. 'I can't explain to you right now how I got this – there's no time – but I need you to listen.' I pull my phone out of my bag and press the play button on the recording before placing it on the kitchen table. Sophie looks down at it sceptically, then she hears my voice on the recording.

The hairs on the back of my neck stand on end as I watch her face, knowing Connor's voice will follow in a second.

'You've got me. I've been following you again. But I'm done. It's over; no more.'

Sophie shoots me an angry stare, her mouth open. 'You've been following Connor again? Christ, Emma!'

I hold up my hand to silence her. 'Keep listening,' I urge, sounding sharper than I intended, but it does the trick and she closes her mouth and huffs.

'And why is that, Emmie? Why are you giving up so easily? You don't come across as the quitting type.' Connor's voice can be heard fairly clearly and I see her eyes widen, but she remains silent and the recorded conversation continues.

'I'm not a quitter. But I've tried and tried to get Sophie to see sense and she won't. She won't even speak to me, as I'm sure you well know. So you win.'

Sophie drops her gaze and her shoulders sag.

'I win?'

Sophie stares back at the mobile phone like it's a nasty insect that's crawled onto her hand.

'I'll go away.' My voice sounds timid, defeated. 'I'll leave you and Sophie alone.'

She looks up at me now, tears filling her eyes, but her mouth is pressed into a firm line as conflicting emotions flash across her face.

'And why would you do that after all…this?' You can hear the smugness in his voice now and it's making my toes curl. I hate doing this to Sophie, but she needs to hear every last word of this, no matter how painful it is.

'Because of all this. Because I care about Sophie and I want her to be happy, and me continually texting and emailing her…well, it's not making her happy. So I'll back off.'

I glance at Sophie. A single tear trickles slowly down her cheek and I swallow down the lump that's rising in my own throat.

'One thing, though.'

This is the bit where I turned back around. We're getting close to the part where it's going to hurt Sophie the most.

'You knew exactly who I was that night in the bar, didn't you? You'd seen my picture before.'

Sophie head jolts down and she glares at the phone, then back up at me, then back down at the phone. She reaches for it.

'I've heard enough,' she snaps, grabbing the phone and pressing the pause button on the screen. 'Why won't you let this go, Emma?'

'He knew, Sophie, he knew. Listen!'

I prise the phone from her hand and press play again, biting my lip as my heart thunders like a brass band is marching fiercely around in my chest. My hands are trembling now as I hold on to the phone.

'You're crazy!' Conner's voice continues.

'You'd seen pictures of me and Sophie on social media before we met that day in the coffee shop, and you recognised me in that bar that Friday night.'

I see Sophie's eyebrows raise slightly.

'You can't prove that.' Connor sounds angry now.

'I guess not.' Pause. 'But humour me for a second. You weren't surprised when I walked into that coffee shop the following Sunday morning while you sat there hand in hand with Sophie. Why?'

'Why?'

'Why would you come on to me, knowing that I was your new girlfriend's best friend?

Sophie catches her breath and clenches her fists and her whole body stiffens.

'I'm sorry,' I say, looking straight into her eyes, because I know what's coming next.

'Why would you entice me into your apartment; into your bed?'

I can see the hurt written all over Sophie's face and I'm sorry that I ever went out that Friday evening. If I could go back in time and change it, I would, but I can't. I can't take it back. It will always be there.

'Why?' Connor's voice is a whisper but you can just hear it. 'Because I could.'

Tears flow freely now down Sophie's whole face, but she makes no move to wipe them away. I want to step forward and hug her, but I'm rooted to the spot; I daren't move.

'Because you could!?' You can hear the anger and disbelief in my voice.

'Because it amused me to watch your face as you realised you'd made the most catastrophic error of judgement.'

I think Sophie's heard enough and I press the pause button on the phone.

'No!' She grabs the phone. 'I want to listen.'

'Okay.' I swallow and she presses play.

'I enjoyed watching you scramble around, fighting with your conscience. I must admit you threw me that night at Sophie's house; I didn't think you had the balls to tell her.'

Sophie's whole body is trembling violently now as Connor's laughter echoes from the phone.

'So it was all a game to you, to amuse you for a while, despite the fact that you completely destroyed two people in the process?

'You know what, Emma? I'm bored of this conversation now. Why don't you stop playing your silly little game of stalking me…or I might start stalking you.'

There are a few muffled sounds – I had started to walk away from Connor – and then the recording stops. Silence bounces off every corner of the room and you can taste the tension.

'Sophie…' I whisper softly.

'The fucking liar!' she screams and I watch helplessly as she hurls my phone at the wall and it crashes to the floor, breaking into several pieces. Well, I guess I deserved that at least.

Sophie's emotions appear to have reached boiling point and they're bubbling close to the edge. I cautiously take a step forward and reach out slowly, gently touching her arm. This time she doesn't flinch or pull away.

'I'm so sorry…about everything. I never meant to hurt you. I was trying to protect you by telling you. I always knew that it could backfire. I guess I didn't realise how badly.'

I watch as Sophie fights back more tears and fiddles awkwardly with her hair. It feels like there's a huge void between us that's getting wider and wider. I want to start to put the last few months behind us. I desperately want my friend back.

'I miss you,' I say earnestly, and I've never said a truer word. I'm lost without Sophie to share my life with. .

'I miss you too,' she whispers. 'Oh Emma…I'm sorry I didn't…'

'It's alright,' I grab her hand as the hugest wave of relief washes over me. 'It's going to be okay.' I put my arms fully around her and pull her into a tight hug.

'But all those awful things I said. I didn't believe you. I pushed you away.'

I pull away and hold her at arm's length, looking her straight in the eye. 'I can't even begin to imagine how it must have felt when I told you that I'd slept with Connor.'

She winces.

'So I understand how you must have been totally freaked out.'

'But still…you were…you are my best friend.'

'And that's why it was a million times worse for you to have to get your head around the situation. Believe me, I know – my head was totally screwed too.'

She bushes away a stray tear. 'I know that now; but I should have seen it then too.'

'Sophie, neither of us are to blame for this whole thing. It's all Connor; it's always been Connor. He played us both from the start. What I don't understand is how he became so emotionally damaged that this is how he gets his kicks.'

'I know it must have been hard for you, to come here today after everything that's happened, after everything I've said. But thank you – thank you for not giving up on me, on our friendship.'

The door bursts open, causing us both to physically jump.

Chapter Thirty-Seven

Connor suddenly appears, filling the room, his eyes staring wildly around. He's practically foaming at the mouth like a rabid dog. He looks completely out of control. I've never seen him like this before – he's always been so calm and collected – and I'm immediately thrown off-guard.

He slams a bottle of wine down on the bookshelf next to the door. He must have stopped to pick it up on the way to Sophie's clearly not expecting me to have come here following our exchange.

'What the hell are you doing here?' he spits, glaring at me across the room as I stand protectively in front of Sophie. He sounds really angry and a little unhinged, in fact a lot unhinged. I can feel Sophie's fear as Connor turns his attention to her.

'Has she told you, eh? That she's been snooping around, following me like some nosey fucking bitch?'

'It's over, Connor!' I shout sternly at him. 'It's over.'

'It's only over when I say it is; not you,' he snarls at me, then he shoots an angry stare at Sophie. 'What crap has she been filling your head with now?'

'You lied, Connor.' Sophie's voice is quiet in the exploding atmosphere. 'Everything about you is a lie.'

'That's not true.' Connor shakes his head vigorously.

'I heard it all, Connor.' Sophie's tone is mockingly. 'You think you're so smart, yet you didn't consider for one minute why Emma was so persistent in following you and provoking you into talking about us.'

A look of confusion crosses Connor's face and he frowns, as if trying to figure it all out, but the pieces don't make any sense to him.

'Emma recorded you, you fucking idiot. I heard it all, everything you said. "Because you could". I heard it clear as day, straight from your mouth.'

The colour drains from Connor's face now and his cocksure stance is drooping rapidly.

'You never loved me.' Sophie steps in front of me so she's standing face to face with Connor. 'You probably never even liked me in the first place.' I see a tear trickle down her cheek and she swipes it away defiantly.

'She's poison, Sophie.' Connor's voice takes on a guttural growl.

'No!' Sophie shouts. 'It's you who's poison, Connor, and I want you to leave right now. Get out of my house and don't even think about ever contacting me again. It's over!'

There's silence as a stand-off forms in the centre of the room. Connor looks from Sophie to me and then back to Sophie. I stare at her too. The relatively composed Sophie from five minutes ago now looks like a completely different person. Her face has a hard expression and her chin is jutting out, like she's daring Connor to refuse her order to leave. There are no more tears, just anger.

'I said now!' Sophie yells.

It happens so fast that I don't even see Connor move, I only feel his vice-like grip as his hand squeezes tightly around my throat.

'You fucking bitch,' Connor spits at me venomously, his face only millimetres from mine.

I don't know how or why, it must be an instant reflex and that whole survival instinct, but I bring my right knee up sharply and jab it forward into his groin as I reach my hands forward and claw at his face with my nails. I can hear screaming and I've no idea who it's coming from, but the grip on my throat barely loosens at all. I'm struggling to breathe, which seems to spur on the fight within me, and I launch my knee forward again, harder this time.

Then, suddenly, Connor pulls away from me, clutching his head. He wobbles, falling groggily into the wall, before collapsing into a heap on the floor. I stand still, like a polaroid picture, with my arms raised and my leg poised to make a third attempt at kneeing him, and then I see Sophie standing to my left, clutching the bottle of wine from the bookcase in her right hand, and I realise that she saved me. I double over gasping for breath. The pain in my throat is intense and I can feel a burning sensation deep within my lungs. It takes me a second or two to regain my equilibrium.

Sophie's staring at Connor's slumped body with an expression of fear and panic, and I know that she may have momentarily stunned Connor but that man is like a cat with nine lives.

'We need to get out of here and call the police.' My voice is raspy like I've smoked a thousand cigarettes. I grab my handbag from the floor and look frantically through it for my keys.

'But I might have killed him,' Sophie stutters, still clutching the bottle of wine by her side. 'I hit him really hard.'

'Good,' I can still feeling the adrenaline pulsating around my body. 'He'll be fine.' I croak glancing down at Connor crumpled on the floor, but the truth is I've no idea whether he will be and I don't really care. 'He's still breathing, it looks like he's got a concussion. And it was self-defence, for God's sake; he had me by the throat!'

'I know, I know.' Sophie stares down at Connor. 'What do we do with him?'

'Let's lock him in the house and get the hell out of here,' I reason.

'He has a spare key!'

'Well, does he have it on him?' I'm starting to panic now.

'I don't know!' Sophie's voice has risen to a whole new octave.

'Let's get out of here. My car is outside. We'll go to the police and tell them everything…' She doesn't move. 'Sophie, come on,' I prompt.

'Right. Yep. Let's do that.'

She grabs her keys from the hook next to the door and we rush outside. I take one last look at Connor, who's still not moving, and then we lock the front door behind us.

'We'll go in my car instead. It's over there.' Sophie points to the left and we run. The doors bleep as Sophie presses the key fob and we jump in, locking them instantly behind us.

'Where's the nearest police station?' Sophie asks as she frantically clips in her seatbelt and turns the key so hard in the ignition that the car makes an awful screeching sound before the engine bursts into life.

Erm. I don't –

'Aarrgghh!' Sophie screams.

My head bolts upright and my breath sticks in my throat. Connor's face is pressed against the driver's side window, and now he's banging his fists on the car roof. The sound is so loud that I think the roof could cave in.

'Oh my God! Oh my God!' Sophie's hysteria is rising 'He must have had the spare key with him after all.'

'Drive, Sophie, fucking drive!' I shout wracking my brain as to where the police station could be. 'The corner of St James Street' Thank god I remembered 'Head for the city library – it's across the road from that'.

She rams her foot down on the accelerator and the car lurches forward and swerves across the road. I pull myself around to look over my seat and through the back windscreen. Connor is scrambling to get into his own car. His headlights glare and his car starts to move forward.

'Shit! He's following us.'

'What?!' Sophie looks behind her too.

'Keep driving…and keep looking forward,' I urge

'Emma, I'm scared. I've got a really bad feeling about this.'

'It's going to be alright, Sophie. Try to stay calm,' I try to keep my voice as neutral as possible. Glancing behind, I see Connor is making up some ground and closing in on us. 'I'm going to call the police right now' I search my bag for my mobile phone but then remember it's futile. Sophie smashed my phone and the remains of it are still strewn all over her living room floor. Shit.

'Stay calm?!' Sophie looks over at me and then back to the road ahead. 'I've found out that my boyfriend has been lying to me for the last two months, he's turned up at my house and attacked you forcing me to hit him over the head with a bottle of wine and now he's chasing us in his car!' She's gone past the line from hysterical now into full-blown crazy. 'Does any of that sound like it's calming to you?!'

Well, when you put it like that...

'Sophie, I get it. I know it's a lot to take in.' I hold on to the car door handle for dear life as we race down the ring road, darting between traffic.

'A lot to take in?' She shrieks. 'I don't know what to think any more. This is all crazy. It's not normal.'

I look over my shoulder again and my heart jumps into my mouth. Connor is right behind us now and I can see his eyes glaring, fixated on us as he edges closer to the rear of Sophie's car.

'Er...Soph. Can we go any faster?' I bite my lip as I turn back around.

'Oh my God, is that him right behind us? Are those his headlights?'

'Yes, it's him.'

'Shit, what's he doing? Why is he chasing us?'

'Just drive, Sophie. Drive faster.'

The car jumps forward at speed and it temporarily puts some distance between us, but Connor soon catches up.

'I'm scared, Emma.' Tears are trickling down Sophie's cheeks now as she clutches the steering wheel with white knuckles.

'I'm scared too.' I swallow down my heart, which is still in my mouth, refusing to let me breathe. 'But we're nearly there. The police station is only at the end of the road. What the...?!'

Connor's car pulls alongside us; he's driving on the wrong side of the road only inches from the side of our car. I hear Sophie scream, a blood-curdling scream, and then the world starts spinning.

Slow motion.

Bright lights ricochet around, blinding me from every angle.

A mixture of noises, all mangled together: a sharp, scraping noise, a loud horn, screaming again; someone is screaming.

Then the world flips upside down and there's silence: loud, thundering silence pounding in my ears. My head hurts, really hurts. I can see Sophie's face, eyes wide, shouting something to me, but I can't hear a thing. I can see her lips moving frantically, her face white. The bright lights dazzle me one more time before someone flicks a switch and it all goes dark.

Chapter Thirty-Eight

I'm dreaming, I know I'm dreaming, but it feels so real. I can hear voices all around me, shouting instructions, calling random names that I don't recognise. I'm being poked and prodded and I try to resist, try to push them away, but it's no use. My arms are too tired and too heavy to lift. Every muscle in my body feels weighed down, so I'm unable to move. I must be in a really deep sleep. It's dark and the blinding lights that were hurting my eyes have disappeared. It's calm and peaceful; the voices seem to be fading so I can barely hear them any more. They fade and fade until it all becomes quiet and still once more.

'Emma…Emma.'

'Mum? Is that you, Mum?' I sit up on the warm grass and see Mum running towards me, her rich brown hair blowing freely in the breeze.

'Emma – you scared me. You mustn't hide from Mummy, okay?'

'Okay,' I nod. 'Can I have ice-cream now?'

'Of course. Let's go and find Daddy and see whether he wants one too.'

She reaches out her hand and I place my small hand in hers.

I can see Dad in the distance but I can't get to him. He's waving and smiling, but suddenly cold fog is rising from under my feet. No – wait Daddy, wait for me. Panic erupts within me as I try to move but I can't. The fog is getting higher, covering the warm, green grass, getting thicker and thicker, swallowing me up whole until I can't see anything. I'm surrounded by clouds like thick cotton wool.

But then it clears, like a bubble bursting.

'Off you go to school, Emma. You're going to be late. It's your last day so enjoy it. Whatever happens, whatever grades you get, you know that Mum and I are proud of you; and we love you.'

'I love you too, Dad.' I hug him.

I'm feeling horribly nervous about today. I don't want to disappoint them. Mum and Dad are both so smart. As their only child I feel a huge responsibility to be smart too. I know they love me, but something doesn't feel right; and it hasn't for a while now but I can't put my finger on it.

'Bye, Dad.' I kiss him on the cheek.

'Come straight back home. You know Mum and I will be waiting to hear how you've done.'

'I will, Dad; I promise.'

I close my eyes briefly and when I open them again I'm pacing the floor of the lounge in the house I grew up in, with its beige carpet and dark-green sofas.

'Darling, sit down, please.'

I glance from Mum to Dad and then back at Mum. Mum looks worried and Dad is fidgeting nervously in his armchair, not quite able to meet my eye. This is it. Suddenly it feels like a huge weight is pressing down on my chest. Whatever has been bubbling along in the background for the last six months or so is about to surface, and from the look of them both it isn't going to be good news.

Mum starts to speak first. I can hear every word that she's saying but my brain has gone into resistance mode. It's only accepting the odd word here and there.

'Love you…not working…still care…not together…future happiness…so sorry…be okay….love you…separating…moving out…'

It's like I'm underwater, trying to listen to her. I can see her lips moving and Dad looking pained, and then my brain lets it all flood back in like a waterfall and the words swish around and finally fall into the right order. My parents are getting divorced and my whole world, at the age of sixteen, is imploding.

Then the waterfall comes gushing in behind me, sweeping me away over the edge of the rocks and sloshing me down into the fast-flowing river below. I try to gulp for air, but my mouth fills with the frothing water. The current pulls me faster downstream and I try to grab on to a low-hanging tree branch but I can't quite reach.

Sophie is running along the riverbank, shouting to me to hold on, hold on. I stretch my arm out but there's no way she can reach me.

'Sophie,' I gurgle, swallowing a huge mouthful of water as my head goes under the surface. 'Sophie, please don't let me die. Please don't let me die,' I call out to her, but I'm drifting further and further away.

Please don't let me die…

Chapter Thirty-Nine

'She opened her eyes. I know she did.'

Is that Sophie's voice that I can hear?

'Please step aside so I can get to her.'

That sounds pretty stern, I giggle. Sophie's getting told off. But by whom?

'Emma? Emma, can you hear me?' The stern voice again.

Yes, loud and clear, I answer. But why is it pitch-black? Where are we? Who is this? Sophie?

'She not responding. You must have been mistaken.'

'I wasn't! I know she opened her eyes.'

Is Sophie crying?

I'm right here. I can hear you, I call loudly.

'I know you really want her to wake up, and that's understandable, but you have to be patient.' The stern voice has taken on a softer edge.

Hang on a minute. Wake up?

'It's early days. These things can take a while. There's no set timescale.'

Set timescale for what? What things?

Why can't you hear me? I shout louder.

I can feel the panic rising in my chest now as I try to see through the darkness; try to see Sophie. But it's no good. It's completely black without even a hint of light.

And then suddenly the darkness begins swirling like thick black smoke; it surrounds me, suffocating the atmosphere, and I'm gasping for air, gasping, gasping…

God, that light is bright. I'm forced to squint to prevent myself from being instantly blinded. It hurts as I slowly open one eye, then the other, but it's proving difficult to keep my eyelids up; they feel sticky and heavy. A yellow florescent strip light hangs directly above me and I'm surrounded by white. Is that a white ceiling?

I turn my head ever so gently to my right and it feels so heavy, like it might topple right off my neck. There are white glossy cupboards to my right lining a white wall and I can hear the faint tick-tock of an old-style clock.

I'm clearly lying down, but I've no idea why, or where I am for that matter. Pushing myself up gently until I'm resting on my forearms, I find it's a fight to keep my head upright. A wave of nausea washes over me. It's so strong that it nearly defeats me, but I close my eyes and swallow, taking deep breaths until it passes. The smell of antiseptic hits the back of my throat, nearly causing me to gag, and I realise instantly that I must be in a hospital.

Connor…the car chase…I remember going faster and faster. We needed to get somewhere…to the police station. That's right; we needed to get away from Connor and get to the police station. So what happened? And if I'm here then where's Sophie? Oh my God, Sophie!

I wiggle my toes, trying to get some sort of sensation back into my dead legs. They feel unresponsive and tingly, like heavy sponge. Leaning forward, I rub them until I can feel some life seeping back into my muscles. I need to get out of this bed, out of this room. I need to find Sophie. I need to know what happened. I need to know that she's safe.

I swing my disobedient legs around to one side so they're dangling off the edge of the bed, but the movement triggers a stabbing pain in the left side of my head that's excruciating and I screw my eyes up to try to block out the agony.

'Come on, you can do this. You can stand up and make it to the cupboards,' I will myself.

But my body defies me and I feel myself slumping over until my face is pressed firmly into the mattress.

'And where do you think you're going, young lady?' booms a stern voice that sounds somewhat familiar at the side of me.

I open my mouth to speak but my throat is too dry and only an unrecognisable squeak comes out.

'You need to lie back, please.'

I feel a strong grip taking hold of my arms, forcing me back into an upright position and then back down into a horizontal position on the bed.

'I'll get you a drink, and the doctor will want to see you. Please don't try to get up again. I'll only be a minute.'

I honestly don't think I could try to get up again even if I wanted to. It feels like an alien has taken over my whole body and it's drunk a whole bottle of tequila.

I hear the door open and close and then a grey-bearded man in a white coat appears above my head.

'Now then, Miss Storey. It's good to see you awake. You've had a very lucky escape. How are you feeling?'

He starts to twiddle with buttons on a machine at the side of me that I hadn't even noticed and for the first time I see that there's a tube coming from my hand connecting me to it.

A lucky escape?

He holds a pink plastic cup with a straw poking out of it near to my mouth and I suck at it gratefully. The liquid instantly soothes my cloggy throat.

'I feel like crap,' I mutter. 'What the hell has happened to me and where is everyone? Where's Sophie? Is Sophie alright?'

'You were in a car accident, Miss Storey, and you've had a trauma to your head. You've been out of things for a few days now.'

Oh God. And what about Connor? He was chasing us. Sophie hit him, He was like some crazed animal. Where is he now? Is Sophie safe? Is she in trouble for hitting Connor? I need to find Sophie.

'Your friend Sophie is absolutely fine, apart from a few scrapes and bruises. She hasn't left the hospital since you arrived.'

Oh thank God.

I reach up with my hand and touch the left side of my head. It seems to have doubled in size. It feels spongy and…argh!...really painful. Maybe that's where the alien is trying to escape from. No wonder I'm dizzy and wobbling all over like a drunken jelly.

'I'll give you something to ease the pain and then there are a few people in the waiting room who are anxious to see you too.' He presses random buttons 'I'll check a few more things and then I'll let them in to see you for a couple of minutes. But then you need to rest, alright?'

'Okay,' I mumble, not feeling like I can really argue with a doctor. 'How long have I been asleep?'

'Three days. But you're responding well to treatment. We'll keep an eye on you for a little while longer, to make sure the swelling in your head reduces nicely and there's no further damage underneath.'

'Right.' This is all a bit too much to take in and I'm feeling overwhelmed, and scared. It's pretty serious stuff.

'Everything looks like it should do at the moment, so I'll get your visitors.'

Then the nurse pops her head around the door.

'Can I get you a cup of tea or something?' she asks.

'A cup of tea would be lovely, please,' I whisper.

As they both leave the room I look more closely at the machine beside me. I slide up on my forearms again, careful not to sit up too far, to see a number of squiggly lines and numbers on a monitor. They mean nothing to me, but there seems to be a lot going on.

The silence in the room is suddenly broken by the sound of voices outside. I can hear Mum, but I thought she had flown back to New York? And Dad…

The door bursts open then and Mum strides in, closely followed by Dad and Margaret, with Joe, Simon and Sophie following closely behind.

Joe...it's so good to see him. My heart lurches. His dark brown eyes look haunted as he strides to the side of my bed and takes hold of my hand.

'Hey, how are you doing?' he brushes my knuckles with his lips and tears prick instantly at the corners of my eyes and I do my best to swallow them down.

'Hi, darling.' Mum leans over the bed and kisses me gently on the forehead like she did when I was poorly as a young child. Dad hovers next to her. 'How are you feeling?' Her voice is all sing-song like but I her eyes are all red and puffy. A tear escapes and trickles down her cheek and she quickly brushes it away.

'Mum, please don't cry. I'm fine, I promise' I sniff back my own tears but it's like a domino effect. Suddenly everyone is crying.

'I thought I'd lost you' I hear Joe's voice quietly and I squeeze his hand tightly. I'm too overcome with emotion to speak.

'I'm so sorry Emma.' Sophie manages between sobs. 'Thank god you're alright' she pulls me into a hug with Joe still gripping my hand, before she quickly releases me. 'I'm not hurting you am I?'

Before I can shake my head Dad kisses my cheek. 'You had us all worried there for a while.' His voice breaks.

Simon sits down carefully at the bottom of the bed looking forlorn and we're all in this weird bubble with everyone looking like they're exhausted and emotionally drained.

'Here's your tea.'

The atmosphere is diffused as the nurse reappears carrying a steaming mug, pushing through the bodies surrounding the bed. Joe's hand slips from mine as she helps me up to a seated position, squashing pillows behind me to keep me upright. I take the mug from her gratefully.

'Now, there are far too many people in this room.' The nurse looks around sternly. 'Miss Storey needs her rest, so I'm going to have to ask you to keep it to two visitors at a time, please. You have five minutes and then I need you all gone, okay?'

'We'll wait outside for a moment.' Margaret ushers Sophie, Joe and a protesting Simon out of the room, leaving Mum and Dad at my bedside. Before the door closes Joe stops and looks back and he holds my gaze for a second before he smiles at me and then he's gone. My heart feels so heavy and I want to call him back. I want him to hold me and to tell me everything's going to be okay.

Instead I take a deep breath and turn to Mum and Dad.

'What exactly happened?' I take in their tired faces and crumpled clothes. 'And what are you doing here, Mum? I thought you were in New York.'

Along with my raging headache an uneasy feeling has crept into the pit of my stomach.

'I was, but I got straight on the next flight here as soon as your dad called me to say…to say you'd been in an accident.'

'What happened, though?' I repeat. 'And where's Connor?'

Mum glances at Dad and he takes hold of my hand. 'None of that matters right now, Emmie. You need to concentrate on getting better, on keeping your strength up.'

'Dad's right. Focus on getting well. We thought, well, we thought…' Her voice crumbles as she strokes my hair.

'Hey, Mum.' I touch her hand with mine. 'I'm fine. 'I'm right here, okay?' I try to reassure her. 'Okay.' She leans down and kisses my forehead.

'Is Sophie really alright?' My voice is quiet.

'She has a few bumps and bruises, but other than that she's perfectly fine other than worrying about you.'

I take another mouthful of tea to prevent my emotions spilling over again as I try desperately to hold back the tears that are threatening to overflow.

'Try to rest, Emmie.' Dad squeezes my hand. 'There's plenty of time to discuss...um…everything when you're feeling better.'

'I'll pop by your house later so I can bring you some of your things tomorrow. Is there anything you specifically need?' Mum asks seeming to have regained a bit of her composure.

A new head perhaps?

I look down at my body, realising I hadn't even noticed that I'm only wearing what looks like a thin nightgown made from paper, which must be statutory hospital issue. How embarrassing! I hope it's not see-through. I pull the covers up a little higher just in case. 'Some clean pyjamas and my toiletries.'

'Of course.' She touches Dad's arm. 'We'll wait outside now and let the others in. Joe and Sophie have kept a bedside vigil since you arrived.'

'Thanks, Mum.' I don't really know what else to say at the moment. This all feels like some horrible dream.

'We'll be back in the morning.' She squeezes my hand.

'Get some sleep, Emmie,' Dad adds, looking a little tearful, which is unnerving in itself. I don't remember ever seeing my dad cry.

I take a deep breath as I watch them both leave the room.

Two seconds later Simon pushes through the door, closely followed by Sophie and Joe.

'Hey, hun. How are you feeling? You look like crap.'

'Simon!' Sophie whacks him on the arm, shooting him a disapproving glare, as I try not to laugh.

'Ouch!' he squeals as he approaches the side of my bed. 'Just kidding, Em. It's really good to see you awake.'

Joe's immediately at my side but his hands remain stuffed into his jeans pockets this time and I desperately want to feel his touch.

I swallow, realising that I hid this mountain of stuff with Sophie and Connor from Joe and it must have come tumbling down like an avalanche. I'm guessing he's wondering why I didn't tell him everything right from the start. What happened with Connor was before I met him so it shouldn't matter. But in my heart I know how I felt about myself following my one night stand, particularly once I realised who Connor was and if I could like myself less for that then there's every chance that Joe could like me less too.

'Hi.' He looks at me, but I can't read his expression. 'Are you feeling okay? Are you in any pain?'

'No. I was at first, but I think they must have pumped me full drugs as apart from feeling a bit dizzy if I move my head I can't feel anything else right now.'

'That's good'

I want to reach out to him, to let him know that I really did want to tell him, but I was scared. I didn't want him to look at me differently, for what I did with Connor to taint what I have with him. I hope Joe knows that; I hope he understands.

'Do you want me to bring you anything?' Sophie glances at Joe then back at me.

'Mum's getting me some stuff from home, thanks. But perhaps you can tell me exactly what I'm doing here, as no one else seems to want to put me in the picture.'

I see Sophie's face falter and Joe won't quite meet my gaze any more. Even Simon looks unusually uncomfortable.

'I think I'll leave you to it. I guess you've all got some things to discuss.' Simon leans down and kisses me on the cheek 'I'll check in on you again tomorrow, babe. Okay?'

'Sure, Simon. Thanks for being here.' I grab his hand.

He smiles at me before slipping quietly out of the room.

'I'm guessing I don't need to do the introductions between you two.' I look from Sophie to Joe.

'We've got to know each other quite well over the last three days.' Sophie fiddles with her hair.

I bite my lip nervously.

'How much do you remember?' Sophie asks cautiously.

'I remember being in the car with you, and headlights, really bright headlights.'

'It wasn't completely my fault,' Sophie starts. 'He hit us from the side with his car, which is how I lost control.'

'Connor?'

'Yes. He came alongside us on the wrong side of the road, remember? And then he swerved into us, hitting my car.'

'I remember spinning. It was dark and loud.'

'The car flipped on its roof,' Sophie whispers, wiping a silent tear from her cheek. 'I'm so sorry, Emma.'

'It wasn't your fault, like you said.'

'I'm sorry for everything. I should have believed you from the start, then none of this would have happened. You wouldn't be lying in hospital.'

'It's alright, Sophie. I understand. It was a difficult situation.'

I glance over at Joe, who has remained silent. By now he must know everything about what happened, all the sordid details of my one-night stand with Sophie's boyfriend. I should have been the one to tell him. I should have told him that I was going to confront Connor. I should have trusted him with the truth. As I look at it now I know Joe would have supported me but maybe he will feel different now he's heard it all second hand from Sophie.

I stare at him, my eyes pleading with him to understand and I will him to speak: Say something, Joe, anything! Not knowing what's going through his head right now is killing me.

'Connor didn't make it,' Sophie blurts out.

What? I spin my head around to face her and a skull-crushing pain shoots through the left side of my brain like I've been shot.

'He's...he's dead?'

A thousands thoughts are flipping through my head. I mean, I know I've wished Connor dead a number of times over the last few months, but I didn't mean it, not literally. I wanted him to leave us alone. But dead? No. No...

'They all told me not to tell you yet, the doctors, your mum, but I thought you should know the truth. I did the right thing, didn't I? I was right to tell you?'

I stare at her, dumbfounded.

'Emma...Emma?'

I can hear the words coming out of her mouth and I don't know whether it's the drugs that are numbing my mind and body or the simple shock of hearing what she's saying, but I can only sit there without a clue what to say in response. For once I have no jokey quip, no sarcastic comment, no answer at all. I'm completely numb.

The nurse bumbles back in and immediately starts checking the machine that I'm attached to. 'I'm afraid I'm going to have to ask you both to say your goodbyes. Visiting hours are over now and this young lady needs to rest.' She says politely at Sophie, then looks at Joe, who still hasn't uttered a word.

'But we're not finished talking!' Sophie protests.

'I'm sorry, but rules are rules. You can come back tomorrow from eleven a.m.'

'But –'

The nurse gives her a stern look.

'We'll come back tomorrow, won't we?' Sophie glances at Joe.

'Yes.' Joe turns to face me. 'We'll talk more tomorrow, Emma.'

And on that bombshell they're both swept out of the room by the nurse before I can attempt to say a word.

'We'll talk more tomorrow, Emma.' What does that mean? Is that good or bad?

I feel like I've traded Joe for Sophie. On the one hand, I've made amends with my best friend, but in doing so I may have inadvertently lost the one guy I've managed to find who isn't deranged or deluded. In fact, he's the nicest guy in the world, and for some unexplainable reason he seemed to be totally hung up on me too. What if he's the one I'm supposed to be with and now I've ruined it? What if he's The One?

What if he was The One?

With a soul-destroying feeling resting heavily in my heart, I buzz for the nurse to return.

She appears almost instantly.

'What's wrong, Miss Storey? What can I get you?'

'Um, my head is really starting to hurt,' I lie. 'Any chance you can give me some painkillers?'

She checks the notes at the bottom of my bed.

'I can give you a little boost, but that's all, I'm afraid.'

I nod gingerly, grateful of anything that can help to mask the emotional pain that I'm feeling and force me into oblivion.

'I wish I'd never met you. You changed everything for the worse'

Chapter Forty

I wake with an overwhelming feeling of grogginess and a heavy head. I feel hungover, but I didn't get the fun of downing shots of alcohol last night.

'Good morning, Emma.'

The nurse from yesterday is entering my room carrying a breakfast tray. Seriously do they have a spy camera in here so the minute you open your eyes that's their cue to pounce?

'I'm really not hungry,' I say dismissively as she places the tray on the table at the side of the bed.

'I don't remember asking you a question.' She looks at me knowingly. 'Doctor's orders. You need to eat or we'll have to carry on feeding you through the drip.'

'I'll try.' I scowl at her like a petulant teenager before looking down at the contents of the tray.

I wait until she leaves before downing the glass of orange juice like my life depends on it. I choke down a slice of dry toast and some warm liquid that I suspect was supposed to be tea, and then push the tray to one side. There's a magazine on the table that I didn't notice before. I stretch gingerly towards it and am relieved to find that the alien that was bouncing around my head yesterday is calm and presumably still sleeping. It's the latest edition of Cosmopolitan; must be a gift from Sophie. I flick aimlessly through the pages, looking for something to grab my attention as I pass the time.

'Hello, darling.'

Mum is exceptionally cheery as, a short while later, she pushes the door open and carries in a number of bags, closely followed by Dad. They both look better than they did yesterday. Still with an element of worry but less sleep deprived.

'I've got all of your things.' Mum plonks the bags down on the bottom of the bed. 'Well, at least I think so. If not, you can let me know what's missing and I can bring it in later.'

'Thanks, Mum. I'm sure I'll have everything I need. It's not like I'm going anywhere important over the next few days.'

'Of course.' Mum looks tearful again.

'And you don't have to come and see me at every visiting time you know. I'm fine, really.'

'Don't be silly.' Mum swishes her hand at me.

'Mum's right, Emma. We want to keep coming.' Dad fidgets uneasily. 'We want to make sure you're getting better.'

This whole situation – me in hospital and how I got here – is hard for us all, and Dad isn't as good as Mum at putting a brave face on things. His worry is clear in his whole demeanour, and I feel so guilty that I'm the cause of that. Guilt is a funny thing, I guess. I feel guilty about being here. I feel guilty about Connor. In fact, I feel horribly guilty about everything at the moment.

And what about Joe? Will he even come back to see me today?

'How are you feeling today? Any better?' Mum asks with a tinge of expectancy.

Physically I feel a little better – I think that extra shot of painkiller has momentarily sedated the alien trying to escape from the side of my head. But emotionally I feel like I've been run over by a steamroller and then reversed back over for good measure.

'My head doesn't hurt as much today.' I reach up instinctively and touch the bump, but it still feels spongy.

'I'll get us some drinks,' Dad offers. 'There's a coffee machine down the hall.' He gives my hand a little squeeze before he disappears into the corridor, and I realise that I've no idea what lies outside the confines of this white room.

'He finds it hard.' Mum swallows noisily as I turn to look at her. 'Your dad. He doesn't cope very well when you're ill; he never has done.'

'I'm sorry,' I mumble and a tear slips silently and unexpectedly down my cheek.

'For what, darling?' Mum sits down on the bed, leaning forward to wipe the tear away with her thumb. 'You have nothing to be sorry for.'

'But I...this whole mess. And Connor –'

'Hush, hush.' She strokes my hair. 'I don't want you worrying about all that. You were in a car accident, Emma, and it's pure damn luck that you and Sophie weren't killed.'

I sit in silence with my lips pressed together in a line, trying to force down the emotional tidal wave that's festering deep within me.

Dad returns a moment later carrying three polystyrene cups. 'Here we are.'

'Thanks.' I take one of the cups from him.

The conversation takes on a much lighter tone for the remainder of the visiting session, with Mum and Dad deliberately talking about anything and everything that has no importance whatsoever in a blatant attempt to avoid talking about anything and everything to do with the accident. By the time they're ready to leave I feel emotionally and physically drained again.

'Get some more sleep.' Mum kisses the top of my head. 'You look tired. I'm sorry, Dad and I have been talking too much, haven't we?'

'No, not at all. I'm glad to see you both. But please don't worry about me. The nurse says I'm doing much better,' I lie. 'And hopefully I'll be allowed home soon.'

'Hopefully,' Mum agrees.

'See you tomorrow, Emmie.' Dad winks. 'Make sure you rest.'

My eyes feel incredibly heavy and I think I fall asleep the minute they leave the room.

When I open my eyes again I see Sophie sitting at the end of the bed.

'Hey.' I clear my throat, which feels as dry as a desert again. 'What are you doing here?'

'It's afternoon visiting hours.'

'How long have I been asleep?' I push myself up to a half-seated position.

'A few hours.'

'I feel so tired.'

'The nurse says you'll be like this for at least the next few days. It's a mixture of shock and the drugs they're giving you, plus your body is trying to repair itself.'

I see.

'Can I get you a drink?' she offers.

'A tea would be nice, please. But if possible could you collar a nurse and beg her to make me a proper cup of tea? That stuff from the machine tastes like death in a cup.'

'I'll see what I can do,' she smiles. 'I'll be back in two minutes.'

Sophie gets up from the bed but pauses as she reaches the door, turning back to me.

'And Emma?'

'Yes?'

'There's someone here you need to meet.'

'To meet? Sophie I really don't feel up to –'

'I know, I know, but you really need to hear what she has to say.'

The persistence in Sophie's voice is a little unnerving, but she slips out of the door before I can protest any further.

Who the hell could I possibly need to meet right here and now under these circumstances? Has Sophie gone mad? Maybe she got a bump on the head after all.

A few moments later Sophie gingerly opens the door carrying two mugs of tea, and behind her I see a petite brunette. She looks tiny and perfectly made-up and is probably a similar age to us. As she hovers between the door and my bed she appears to be nervous and fiddles awkwardly with her hands.

'This is Dana,' Sophie says quietly, handing me a mug. 'Dana, this is Emma.'

I push myself up a little higher in the bed so I can at least meet her eyes, and I stare at the girl in front of me aimlessly, having never seen her before and with no idea of who she is or what she's doing here.

'Dana knew Connor too,' Sophie states flatly.

What?! My head instinctively snaps back to face Sophie, causing a violent wave of nausea as the alien is shaken awake.

'You need to hear her story.' Sophie has gone positively white as she looks between me and the random girl now standing at the foot of my hospital bed.

'O…kay.' I glance uneasily back towards Dana.

'Hi, Emma. I realise this must seem awfully strange,' she begins.

You're not kidding.

'I read about your accident in the local newspaper yesterday. His photograph was right there on the front page. They said witnesses had seen a car chase and that two girls were injured. It felt wrong. I needed to come, to see if he had done it again. If he had destroyed more lives or if it was just an accident.' She shakes her head sadly.

'I'm sorry, Dana.' I glance back at Sophie with an accusing look. Who is this girl and what is she doing here? 'You're not making much sense to me.'

'I understand,' she nods. 'Let me start at the beginning.'

I stay silent and wait for her to go on.

'I met Connor, or Rhys as I knew him, about three years ago.'

Rhys? Another alias? This doesn't sound like a good start.

'I was recently out of a relationship,' she continues. 'It was nothing too serious and it fizzled out. Anyway, I was out with a group of friends when I met him. We'd been drinking and I was quite merry when he sent a drink over to me from the bar.'

The hairs on the back of my neck instantly stand up on end and my skin prickles uncomfortably. This all sounds far too familiar.

'He came over, gave me a load of charm and flattery, and talked me into staying out with him for a further few drinks after my friends had decided to call it a night. To cut a long story short, I slept with him. We exchanged numbers but I never intended to call him; it was a one-night stand.'

I stare at Dana, transfixed, almost not wanting to hear any more of this story. Dread is churning in my stomach and I'm pretty sure it's going to get worse with every word she says.

'Two weeks later I met up with my friend, Helen, who introduced me to her new boyfriend, who was none other than Rhys the charmer.'

No, no, no, this can't be happening. I clutch the bedcover and pull it up tighter around me.

'It was a setup, Em; right from the start. He did the same thing to them,' Sophie interjects.

I stare blankly at Sophie and then Dana, trying to process exactly what's happening here. Through the blurry fog of concussion I feel an overwhelming sense of fear and an urge to throw up.

'He played us off against one another. Found out every little detail of our friendship and used what he could against us, to make us turn on each other.'

'You didn't tell your friend Helen…' I croak.

'That I'd slept with her boyfriend? Not at first. I hoped it would all go away, that Rhys would go away.'

I see Sophie look at the floor for a second before composing herself.

'How do you tell your best friend that?' Dana's voice is sad.

'It's an impossible situation,' I agree, swallowing hard. 'I can't believe he's pulled the exact same trick before. I knew he must have cheated on other girlfriends but to target two friends again – no. What happened to you and Helen? Did you work it out?'

Dana's expression falters for a second and she takes a deep breath before exhaling noisily. 'Helen took her own life shortly after the whole truth came out.'

My stomach flips a thousand times. I'm on the Big Dipper suspended upside down and all the blood is rushing to my head.

'She killed herself?' My voice is barely whisper.

'He destroyed her, us; everything.' Dana wipes a stray tear from her eye. 'Helen never got over that.'

An awkward silence fills the room. The only sound is my heart thudding loudly in my chest threatening to break through my ribcage.

'That's why I had to come. I needed to make sure that he didn't wreck another friendships; other lives. I knew if I told you all of this you could see that it wasn't your fault. He chose you as his victims, and that's what we all were: victims of his sick mind games.'

'This is unbelievable…' I put my head in my hands and close my eyes, taking deep breaths.

'Emma, Emma, are you okay?' Sophie gently touches my arm.

'I knew he must have cheated on girlfriends before. He was too confident to have only done this the one time but to have set up two friends like this before, and for your friend to have...'

'I know, I know.' Dana edges a little closer to the bed.

'How do you end up so emotionally sick that you do this again and again to people?

'May I?' Dana gestures to the bed.

'Yes'

She sits down softly on the edge.

'After Helen died I was really angry. Rhys – or as you now know him, Connor – had disappeared off the face of the earth. I needed to channel my anger, to distract myself from the horrible guilt and....' She coughs awkwardly. 'Anyway, I made it my mission to find out as much as I could about him, so I began searching the internet, trying to trace him and any family that might be able to shed some light on where he was. I wanted to confront him – you know, to get some answers.'

I know exactly how that feels.

'As it turns out, Rhys is his real name after all. I had a stroke of luck and found an address about a hundred miles north in a small village on the coast. So I drove there one day. I didn't know what I was hoping to find, but I felt compelled to see it, to talk to people, neighbours and so on, to see if I could find anything out about who he really was.'

She shakes her head. 'To cut a long story short, I found an old neighbour. Neither Rhys nor his dad had lived there for a while, but they remembered the family well. He was an only child. His mother was a bit of a local tart by all accounts. She cheated on his dad numerous times and then, out of nowhere, she just up and left. Rhys was only about five years old at the time.'

'She left her child?'

'Yeah, she left Rhys with his dad. Apparently his dad was known to be a drunk and aggressive man with a short temper. The neighbour reckoned she called social services nearly a dozen times after hearing a child's scream and cries, and on more than one occasion she saw the child covered in bruises. She reckons Rhys was about fifteen when she last saw him. His dad disappeared from the street a year or so after that.'

'That's horrible.'

I instantly think of my own parents and their separation. Would I be a different person today if they'd handled it completely differently? I don't remember bitterness and arguing; I guess they shielded me from anything like that. Either way, their love for me never felt like it was in question. I can't imagine how Rhys must have felt, abandoned by his own mother and then abused by his father – turned on by the two people who were supposed to look after him.

'It doesn't change what he did.' Sophie bites her lip. 'But I guess it gives us some understanding of why he was so emotionally damaged.'

'And why it would seem that he hated women and wanted us to suffer,' Dana adds.

'We were all collateral damage,' I whisper. My eyelids are heavy and drooping.

'I should go.' Dana stands up from the bed. 'You're obviously still exhausted and you need time to rest, to recover.'

'Thank you, Dana.' I close my eyes. 'Thank you for finding us and sharing your story. I'm so sorry things turned out so badly for you and your friend.'

'I hope you feel better soon, and that you and Sophie can get back on with your lives. I wish Helen and I could have another chance to do that.'

Her tone is solemn and my heart goes out to her. A single tear rolls down my cheek as exhaustion sucks me in and darkness welcomes me once more.

Chapter Forty-One

When I open my eyes again I feel much better. The nauseating pain in my head has eased and I feel like the annoying alien that has plagued me for the last two days has finally moved out. I blink a few times and the blurry edges start to disappear, and then I see him, Joe, sitting on the end of the bed, staring straight at me with a really strange look on his face. In fact, has he been crying?

'Joe, what's wrong? What's happened?' I try with some difficulty to drag myself up to a seated position.

'No, don't move.' He jumps up and is instantly at my side. 'Please lie still.'

'What do you mean? What's wrong?'

He grabs my hand, clutching it tightly to his chest. 'Apart from you being in a car crash, being rushed to hospital unconscious and then nearly losing you twice?!' I can hear the anxiety in his voice.

'Hey, hey, I'm sorry.' I reach out and touch his arm with my other hand. Nearly losing me twice?

'You don't need to be sorry.' He pulls me into a gentle hug and I smell the familiar scent of his aftershave and shower gel and it's incredibly comforting. 'I just want you to be okay,' he whispers into my hair.

'I am okay.' I squeeze him tightly, feeling his warm toned body pressed against mine. 'Everything's going to be alright, I promise.'

'I don't want to lose you,' he murmurs, gently stroking my cheek. 'When you blacked out the second time you really scared us.'

'The second time?'

'Emma, you've been unconscious for the last two days.'

Two days?

'What? No, I simply went to sleep for a little while. I was a bit overwhelmed or something – you know, from meeting Dana… hearing all that stuff…'

'I know. I spoke to Dana too. What happened to her and her friend was horrible. I think you went into shock. You blacked out literally the minute she left and we couldn't wake you; you wouldn't wake up.'

'It feels like a really bad dream. Everything that's happened over the last few months with Connor. I know in my head that it actually happened, but it's so crazy and a complete blur that I'm struggling to accept it. '

'You mean like the fact that you followed this guy twice and provoked him.'

Shit, I guess Sophie did tell Joe everything.

'I know I should have told you what was going on.' I hang my head, unable to meet his eye.

'You're damn right you should have. Anything could have happened to you – well, it did. That nutter tried to run you and Sophie off the road. It's a miracle that all three of you weren't killed that night.'

'I'm sorry.' I choke back tears.

'I wish you'd trusted me; trusted us.'

'I didn't want you to think less of me. If I'd told you why Sophie and I had fallen out, I'd also have had to tell you what had happened that night with Connor and...' I pause, feeling like the romantic bubble I momentarily found myself in as I woke up is ready to burst in front of my eyes.

'Emma, what you did before you met me is irrelevant; it's the past. I don't care what you did with Connor.'

'And what about the future?' I ask, regretting the words as soon the words they're out of my mouth. I've given him the perfect opportunity to walk away from me. I hold my breath as I stare longingly into his eyes, willing him to still love me.

'It's our future, Emma. You and me together.'

'I love you.' I gulp emotionally. 'And I promise I'll never keep anything from you again. I wish I'd never gone to the bar that night. I wish I'd never set eyes on Connor.'

'Forget about Connor. It's over.'

Joe kisses me on the lips and I fling my arms around him like my life depends on it, and in some ways I feel like it does. I nuzzle into his neck, secure, warm and safe here in the arms of the man I love, the man who loves me back. Joe's right: Connor can't hurt me or anyone else ever again. Everything's going to be alright.

It's finally over.

Epilogue

Six months later

'I can't believe that I'm in New York.' Joe squeezes me tightly and I snuggle into him.

'I know. I love this city. I guess I'm lucky that Mum lives here and I get to visit so often.'

'Speaking of your mum, she seems to quite like me.'

'Yeah, you appear to have charmed her and that's no mean feat.'

'Well, I am pretty adorable.'

'I know, I know.' I elbow him gently.

We stand for a moment, gazing out at the stars spread across the skyline. From the edge of the railings at the top of the Empire State Building, the view of New York City is quite literally breathtaking. A sea of colourful lights twinkle and glow in the night sky, making me feel like I'm in a scene from a movie; it's surreal, almost magical in fact. As I glance around I see the last of the other tourists heading through the doorway that leads back into the gift shop and the stairwell.

'I guess we'd better be making our way down too. As mesmerising as it is looking at this view, we don't want to be shut out here all night.'

'I think we're good for a few minutes yet.' Joe glances over my shoulder.

We're so high up you can barely hear a sound from the street below. There's an unusual calmness that comes with being so high that you feel like you're in the sky itself.

'You know, there were moments when you were lying in that hospital bed when I didn't think we'd ever be here. It was touch and go for a while.' Joe exhales.

'Hey, don't go there. I'm fine now and that's all that matters.' I kiss him and his lips meet mine in a warm, lingering response.

'I know that. But it really put things into perspective for me. It made me aware of how important you are to me, how much I love you.'

I swallow, feeling suddenly overcome with emotion. I don't want to think about what happened. I've tried to put all of that experience to the back of my mind. No good will come of wondering, what if I'd done this differently or that differently? I've had to try to accept that a lot of things were out of both mine and Sophie's control. Connor was sick in the head and we were victims of his warped mind.

'I love you, Joe,' I say, looking deep into his kind brown eyes.

'I know that too,' he smiles. 'I've had a lot of time to think things over and I don't want anything to come between us again. I want to spend the rest of my life with you, Emma. Taking care of you. Us taking care of each other.'

Oh…um…is this what I think it is? Is this really happening? My heart leaps into my throat as Joe reaches into his jacket pocket and produces a small black velvet box.

Holy shit. This is happening.

'Emma Storey…' He looks at me and I stand there, a quivering mess. 'Will you marry me?'

I gaze down at the ring. It's beautiful: a square diamond on a gold band. I couldn't have picked a better ring myself. It feels like something out of a fairy tale and for a split second I think that I might be dreaming. I pinch the skin on my wrist.

Ouch! No, I'm definitely not dreaming.

I glance up at Joe, kind, sweet, loving Joe, who's staring at me intently and I gaze back down at the ring, watching it glint in the moonlight. I know I heard the words he said but my brain is taking a few moments to process the fact that I've been proposed to under twinkling starlight right at top of the Empire State Building in the most amazing city in the world.

A vision of me dressed in a huge meringue pops into my head and I'm shocked that I like the idea. I want to be a meringue. I see Sophie smiling proudly, dressed in a slinky bridesmaid dress that's nowhere near pink, and Mum wearing the most inappropriately large hat that you could imagine; people are standing well back, giving her plenty of room for manoeuvring.

'I…I know it's a little quick.' Joe's expression falters and I realise that I haven't said anything yet. I've simply stared dumbly at the ring. 'But it feels….'

'It feels right.' I grab the hand that isn't holding the ring box and I squeeze it tightly.

Relief washes over Joe's face. 'Is that a yes? Are you saying yes?'

'Absolutely one hundred per cent yes!' I squeal.

'I do love you, Emma; like I've never loved anyone before.'

He takes the ring out of the box and I hold out a shaking hand. He slides the ring onto my finger, then cocks his head to one side and gives a thumbs-up.

I turn around to see the security guard giving me a little wave.

'I had to tip him so he'd let us stay up here after everyone else had gone,' Joe grins, and I think at that moment, if it's possible, I love him even more.

It's been one hell of a rollercoaster, and if someone had told me six months ago that right now I'd be standing on the top of the Empire State Building with an engagement ring on my finger then I'd have called them a liar to their face. But here I am, and that to me is living proof that when you feel like your world has turned upside down and nothing makes sense any more, somewhere, somehow it's all part of your destiny, so you can end up in the right place with the right guy.

I realise that this is it for me. I've found my happy ending. I've found the man who's going to promise to catch me if I fall.

And so we stand there for a few more moments, staring out at the bright lights of New York City under a blanket of stars. It's perfect, everything about this moment is perfect. And then Joe pulls me into his arms and sweeps me off my feet.

Interview with Sasha Lane

What inspires you to get out of bed each day?
I love to challenge myself daily – just doing a little bit of something, making progress, and I'll probably have thought of a really great book idea as I was falling to sleep so I'll need to rack my brain to try to remember it!

When you're not writing, how do you spend your time?
I work full time in the finance industry and am doing a Criminology Degree which is really interesting! I also do Yoga and Pilates to try to relax and I love spending time with my friends catching up over latte's and cupcakes.

Do you remember the first story you ever wrote?
When I was about thirteen my friend and I used to write stories on her computer (which was really old and basic back then!). We wrote about boys and being grown up. It was probably just overactive teenage imaginations but I was hooked on story telling from then on!

What is your writing process?
I spend a lot of time in my car driving for my job so my mind works overtime and I tend to get lots of ideas. When I get home I have to log on and just get them written before I forget them. I tend to write quickly all the stuff that's in my head and then go back and edit it. Most of the time I know how I want my story to end when I start writing it so it just then takes a few versions of the middle bit before I get all of the story ironed out.

Do you remember the first story you ever read, and the impact it had on you?
As a child I loved Roald Dahl and 'George's Marvellous Medicine' is the first book I remember reading. I think I just loved the fact that

I could escape into a different world and become totally consumed by it.

How do you approach cover design?
I want something that encapsulates the story and the reader I'm aiming it at. With images I just kind of 'know it when I see it' so I don't necessarily have a specific idea in my head before I start looking.

What are your five favorite books, and why?
Bridget Jones trilogy, by Helen Fielding – I love the fact that I can relate to Bridget. I think we've all had 'Bridget Jones' moments! and it's a funny, easy read.

The Runaway, by Martina Cole – This book made me laugh, cry, and shout out loud. I have read this a number of times and still get emotional reading it.

The Secret Dreamworld Of A Shopaholic, by Sophie Kinsella – The first of these books is the best in my opinion.

Danny The Champion of The World, by Roald Dahl – I've read this book as a child and an adult and I still enjoy it. Roald Dahl's imagination and story telling is timeless.

Retribution, by Jilliane P. Hoffman – I love the twists in this book and find the legal aspects of it very interesting. It's gripping!

What do you read for pleasure?
A mixture of Chick lit and Crime books, and of course, the collection of fashion/celebrity magazines that are strewn across my coffee table.

What is your e-reading device of choice?
I have an IPad so I can access iBooks and Amazon Kindle to give me plenty of choice.

Describe your desk
Clutter free and just a laptop (and coffee!) – I don't want any dis-

tractions when I'm writing. I need to get wholly into my book.

Where did you grow up, and how did this influence your writing?
I grew up in a small village outside a small town where people tend to grow up and stay there never daring to leave. I guess my writing came from always daydreaming about living somewhere exciting and doing something different. I think I didn't dare believe that people from where I came from could ever achieve anything as exciting as writing a book. I'm glad I proved myself wrong...

What's the story behind your latest book?
I wanted to write a Chick lit story with a bit of a darker side. I wanted to show the challenges of everyday women trying to balance jobs/careers, with family, friends and relationships. It's hard, and sometimes you have to laugh at yourself, which the main character, Emma, does, but I also wanted to show how important friendship is too at keeping us all sane! And we've all fallen for the wrong guy at some point in our lives...